GRACE *on the* ROCKS

GRACE
on the
ROCKS

ROSE PRENDEVILLE

First published by Eridani Press.

Cover illustration and design by Jessica Khoury

Names: Prendeville, Rose, author.

Title: Grace on the Rocks / Rose Prendeville.

Description: First edition. | Nashville, Tennessee : Eridani Press, 2025.

Identifiers: ISBN 978-1-955643-15-3 (trade paperback) | ISBN 978-1-955643-16-0 (ebook)

Subjects: LCSH: Hebrides (Scotland)—Fiction. | Barra Island (Scotland)—Fiction. | Man-woman relationships—Fiction. | Romance fiction. | BISAC: FICTION / Romance / General | FICTION / Romance / Enemies to Lovers | FICTION / Romance / LGBTQ+ / Bisexual | FICTION / Romance / Multicultural & Interracial | GSAFD: Love stories.

Classification: LCC PS3616.R452 | DDC 813/.6—dc23

LC record available upon request.

For Jessie

MacNeil Family Tree

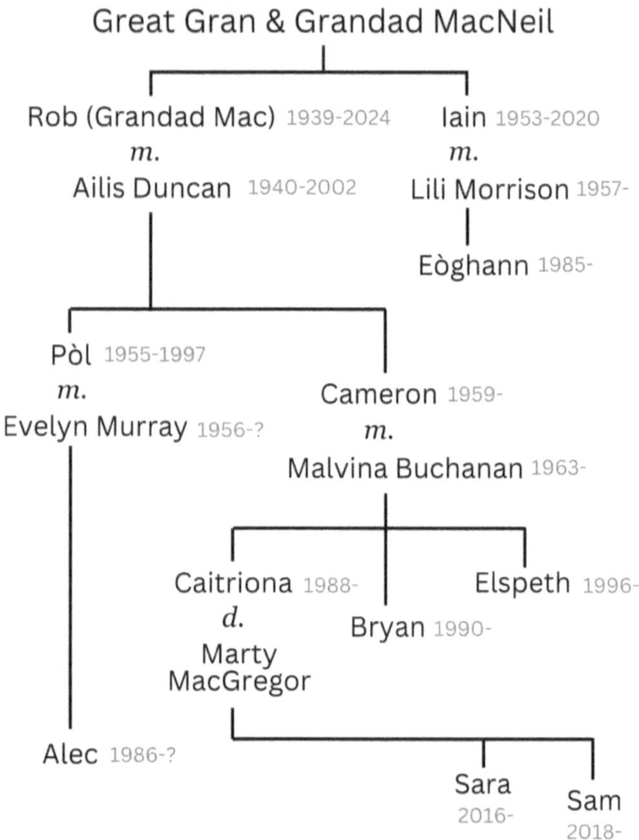

Guide to Gaelic Name Pronunciation

Teàrlach - CHAR-lugh (you can call him Charlie)
Eòghann - O-wen (Owen)
Eilidh - EE-lee
Dàibhidh - DAH-vee (David/Davy)

Buchanan Family Tree

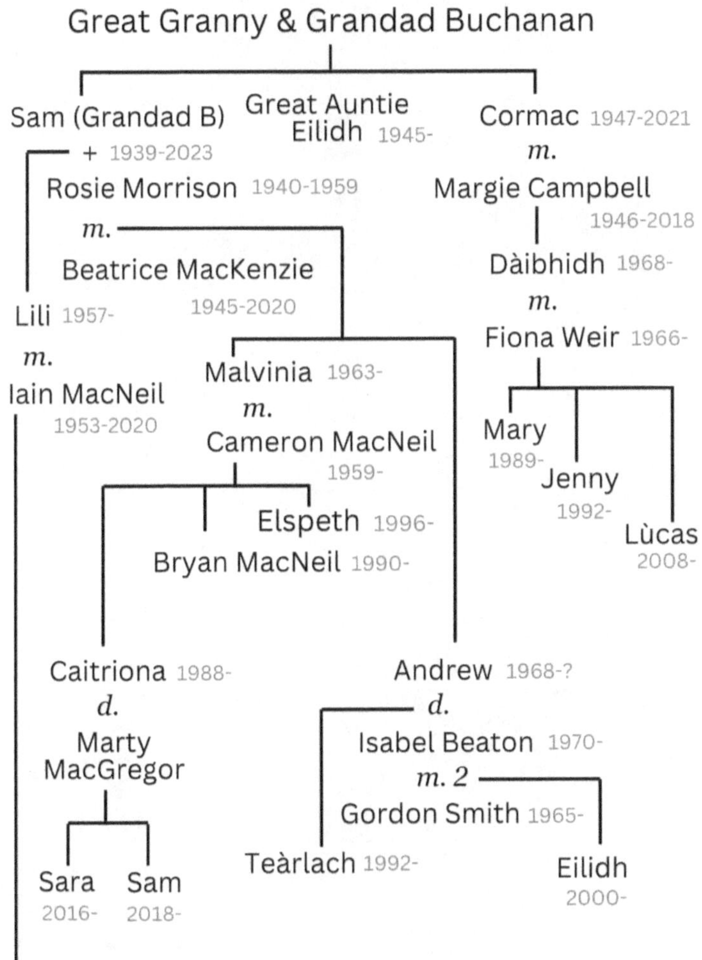

Chapter One

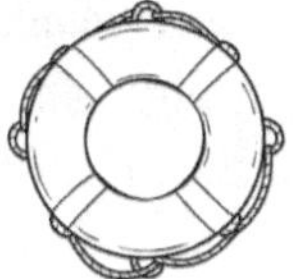

As someone who once took comfort in books, Grace had never realized staring at a whole wall of them could be so overwhelming. The spines were lined up taunting her like a class of skeptical eighth graders on the last day before spring break. She took a deep breath, trying to center herself in the first calm moment she'd had all day, and twisted the oval-shaped stone in her pocket. She ran her thumb over the ridges of variegated color, rubbing away the travel delays and looming deadline which had led her to this moment.

Books had always been Grace's solace—bookstores, her ultimate comfort zone—until now. She stood there, frozen in front of the YA section, after stumbling upon her own debut novel stacked six deep on the shelf, GRACIE RIOS emblazoned on the front in glittery gold letters advertising the most ridiculous imposter to ever live, a one-hit wonder for the ages. Once upon a time, it had been her dream to happen across a display of her own titles in a random airport bookstore halfway around the world. She would whip out a fountain pen and stealth sign them with glee like she was somebody. Now, the sight of her debut sitting there taking up space in between the likes of Alice

Oseman and Angie Thomas left Grace breaking out in a cold sweat.

Her phone buzzed for what felt like the tenth time in the past hour, and if her agent was trying this hard to connect, she probably shouldn't ignore it any longer.

"Hey, Maryanne," Grace answered, her voice high and a little shaky. "Sorry I missed your call…s—calls. I'm… at a writing retreat."

It was only half a lie. By tonight she'd be tucked up in her bed-and-breakfast on the Isle of Barra, ready for the writing frenzy to begin.

"A retreat? Good, Gracie, that's good. I was worried when you asked for another extension."

"Worried—?" Grace forced a laugh.

"They said no, by the way. I believe the exact quote was, 'Your readers are not Peter Pan. They won't be teens forever.' So. We deliver the draft in four weeks, or we return your advance."

Grace was going to throw up—actually throw up, right here in the middle of WHSmith like a travel-sick five-year-old.

"But hey, we don't have to worry about that, right? Because you've got this?"

"Of course I do…"

"Of course you do. Honestly, I'm a little bit insulted. I've literally never been asked to have an author return an advance. I can't believe they would even go there."

"Just dotting their i's and crossing their t's I guess," Grace whispered.

"Sure, sure. Hey, we've all got bills to pay. Even me. But it's not going to be an issue, right? 'Cause you're a rockstar!"

"I am…"

"And when you're a rockstar, I'm a rockstar."

Her voice was heavy with meaning. If Grace dropped the ball on this again, Maryanne would be forced to drop Grace.

"I'm nearly finished," Grace lied.

"That's my rockstar," Maryanne agreed. "Four weeks," she added one last reminder, before hanging up the call.

Grace stared at the rows and rows of books, their covers starting to swim at the edges of her vision. She wasn't close to *nearly finished*. Soon everyone would know her debut was a fluke and she, a complete fraud. Even Charlotte at Between the Covers would rescind her invitation for Grace to speak to the YA Book Club. How could she not?

Behind her someone cleared their throat.

She could feel them hovering impatiently, wanting to yell at her for taking too long, just like her agent. Just like the security guard who shouted at her to move along when she had paused to pick up the shiny flat stone she now twisted compulsively in her pocket.

How long had she been standing here, blocking the already cramped aisle with her suitcase and laptop bag?

The hoverer cleared their throat once more, and Grace shot a glance over her shoulder. Tall. White. Auburn. His strong bearded jaw and stormy green eyes were probably always set in that angry scowl.

"You're… in the way," he said in a slow, deep growl, as if she was the sum of all his exasperation in the entire world but he was too polite to say *move your overstuffed suitcase and your overstuffed American arse.* When Grace didn't answer, he added, "Maybe you can't decide 'cause you've outgrown this lot?" He nodded at the big sign that screamed YOUNG ADULT.

Was he calling her old? Shame and anger, two sides of the same coin, flamed up Grace's cheeks. Not even the delicious burr of his accent could soften the sting with her thirtieth birthday barreling closer every day.

"Are you the reading police? Books in this section happen to be quite layered," she sniffed, turning to face him and crossing her arms in defiance.

"Wasteful, innit?" he mumbled, rolling his eyes at the wall of words.

"I'm sorry?" Maybe she hadn't heard him correctly. Books? Were wasteful? "What kind of Neanderthal would actually say that out loud?"

His scowl deepened, like two birds retreating into the cliffs of his auburn brow, letting her know she, too, had voiced her inside thoughts.

The day had finally broken her—he had finally broken her.

From the moment she'd gotten out of bed, however long ago that was, after countless delays and missed connections, she and Wesley had both been dead on their feet when they arrived before a gate agent who informed the girls they wouldn't be allowed to check two small suitcases apiece on the chartered flight to their island getaway.

"Och, it's a tiny wee plane," the agent had said in a thick Glaswegian accent Grace could barely understand. "Picture the smallest plane you ever saw in your life, and then go smaller," she'd added, moving her hands closer and closer together to demonstrate.

Grace had nearly burst into tears.

"I knew booking the last two seats out of Glasgow was too good to be true," she had groused to Wes as they made their way out of the terminal and hastily repacked one bag each with only the essentials. "I'm sorry I conned you into this trip."

"Umm, this is my first vacation in three years. I'll go naked if that's what it takes," Wes had replied before they stored the extra two bags for an exorbitant rate that Grace would surely regret when her credit card bill arrived, and then raced back to security where she spilled the entire contents of her laptop bag all over the floor in her helter-skelter frenzy.

"Deep breath," Wes suggested.

"I just need to pop into that bookstore real quick," Grace had begged. "Grab some snacks." *Maybe cry for a sec.*

"Ooh, get me a trashy magazine, would you?" Wes had asked before hurrying back to their gate alone.

Honestly, was it any wonder that after holding it in all day when she would have preferred to scream, Grace had finally said the quiet part out loud?

Now the guy was staring at her like he couldn't quite believe she'd done it.

"Sorry, I didn't mean…" She finished her sentence with a shrug because what even were words? She *had* meant it. She just hadn't meant him to hear it.

"I only meant…" he tried.

"What?"

"It's… decadence, innit? Are all those really going to be taken home and read? And then what? It's terrible for the environment," he said. Then he snapped his mouth closed, pressing his lips together in a self-censoring sort of way.

"You're in an airport, bro," she snapped, cringing at how much she sounded like one of her students. "You think books are worse for the environment than the jet fuel about to carry your—" She was *going* to say *pretentious ass*, but she stopped when he raised one eyebrow, daring her to speak any louder. It was distracting, that raised eyebrow. Made her forget what she'd been about to call him. "I suppose you've carbon-offset your trip?" she asked instead.

His frown deepened. "You're right. I ought to have taken the ferry."

Grace was surprised by the admission. She, too, should have taken a ferry, but the flight delays meant she missed the last one, and now here they were. She allowed herself a tiny nod of vindication anyway.

"You are also in an airport," he said, stroking his ginger beard. "Guess that makes us even."

"I wouldn't say so," Grace argued, although from his accent he was obviously Scottish, so she had likely used far more jet fuel than he had today. "I personally would have preferred to ride a humpback whale, but I understand they have an aversion to passengers."

His mouth flattened again, like he didn't want to appreciate the joke but was fighting to make his face comply.

Grace shook her head to snap out of it.

"How many trees do you reckon were razed to write down all those words?" he asked, nodding at the bookshelves, his artfully mussy hair just a bit too short to move with the motion. He asked the question nonchalantly, like he was making casual conversation rather than being a complete ass. Would he say all this if he knew she was a writer?

"Is it these books specifically you have a problem with?" Grace spluttered. "You think just because something's beloved by teen girls it's somehow less valuable, is that it?"

"No…" he said, looking a bit perplexed.

"The books they adore are just as important as your"—she sized him up, his effortlessly casual waffle-knit henley, in a hunter green that he had to know made his eyes pop, tablet under his arm, sleeves pushed up just so: a too-cool-for-school tech bro if ever she'd seen one and he probably never read for pleasure a day in his life—"Six Sigma bullshit," she settled on.

He blinked and jerked his head back in surprise. *Good.*

"These readers write gorgeous letters to their favorite authors about how all *those words* changed their lives. Stories are what separate humans from animals! The ability to record our thoughts and history, to communicate."

"Any animal can communicate…" he snorted but trailed off.

"I mean…" *I guess?*

"The amount of information conveyed in dog feces alone is—"

"I'm sorry, are you comparing these works of art to actual shit?" she balked, and he blinked at her again, opening his mouth, and then closing it without spewing further fecal-related facts.

Grace smirked, pleased to have shut him down.

His eyes narrowed. "At least dogs communicate without the… hubris…"

"Hubris?"

"Ending another organism's life to record our… precious thoughts for future generations? Aye, hubris indeed."

The way he spat the word *precious* told her everything she needed to know about him and his thoughts on pretty well anything. "Well done, proving you're actually less evolved than the average Neanderthal."

"Aye, well, they didn't kill the caves to do it. Maybe they were more enlightened than us," he muttered.

And god, if that didn't hit home. Maybe they were. Maybe she could find one to finish her manuscript for the planned hundred-thousand-copy print run that made her want to throw up every time she thought about it.

When she kept standing there staring at him, he shook his head and reached past her towards a display of metal fidget spinners, his right sleeve pushed up to the elbow allowing her a glimpse of some kind of Celtic knotwork tattoo and leaving a cloud of sandalwood in his wake that almost made Grace heady. Not because he smelled good or anything, just because she was exhausted and overstimulated.

"Aren't you a little old for toys?" she croaked, determined to match him barb for barb despite her weakness for forearm tats and men's deodorant.

"A gift," he snapped, and for a half a second, she thought he was referring to her talent for the brutal retort. She was a writer after all.

"Well, I certainly wouldn't want to stand in the way of a gift," she replied, sliding one last look over the wall of literary honor, a wall she'd probably never see another book of hers added to. She dragged her luggage awkwardly away towards the more fitting wall of calories instead. Clearly a sweet or salty treat was the only thing standing between her and an epic hangry meltdown, given the ridiculous way she'd just been wound up by a total stranger.

His eyes seemed to burn the back of her neck as she snatched a bag of potato chips off the rack and went to find Wesley's gossip magazine. She chose one with a picture of Prince Harry on the cover and tossed it on the counter with her chips and a chocolate bar, just as Mr. Forearm Tattoo queued behind her.

When she handed over her credit card, the girl at the register bit her lip. "Machine's down," she said in rush that took Grace a moment to process. "D'you have any cash?"

Making a show of checking her wallet for paper money she knew she wouldn't find, Grace closed her eyes to fight back the tears and panic she'd been keeping at bay all morning. This was fine. Everything was fine. The entire trip was a mistake, of course, but it was too late now, and it would all be fine. Wes could live without her magazine and Grace could live without snacks.

Her stomach growled in protest.

Before she could gather the last shreds of her dignity, her new nemesis reached forward in another cloud of sandalwood, setting his fidget toy on the counter as if he already knew she didn't have the money and wanted to remind her she was in the way. First she'd taken up too much space, now she was taking up too much of his time, just like her life's work was taking up too many trees and by extension too much oxygen.

A tear dropped onto the magazine and she hated herself for it. Would they let her put it back now?

Then the tattooed forearm stretched around her once more, handing the cashier a twenty-pound note, his exposed skin at Grace's eye level, and honestly, pushing up his henley sleeves like that should be charged with criminal mischief, as should the tattoo itself, which she could now see was not only a Celtic knot, but one that resolved into a sort of bumble bee. And it was perfect, actually, because he was about as congenial as a hovering, stinging bee she wanted to swat away.

"Could you just wait a second," Grace begged miserably.

He tilted his head like he didn't quite understand and it should not have made him look cute when he was being so—

"My treat," he said, nodding to her, the cashier, and the purchases all in one magnanimous dip, while Grace shriveled to the size of a raisin and the cashier beamed at him and his stupid tattoo.

"Need a bag," the girl asked, looking from him to her to him again.

He lifted his eyebrows at Grace for confirmation.

"No," she whispered. It would cost an extra ten pence—*his* ten pence—and the cashier nodded her approval as she counted out his change.

"Lunch of champions," he commented as Grace gathered her junk food.

"And weary travelers," she said, turning to go. "Thank you," she added quickly, and meant it, regardless of whether he'd only done it to hurry things along.

She'd have to rush to her gate now, and the flight would be at least another hour. Who knew how long it would be until she sat down to a proper meal?

His only luggage seemed to be a duffel bag and that tablet, unless he had a gorgeous girlfriend waiting at his gate to fly off somewhere lush and exotic, filled with elegant people who didn't have deadlines. They were probably going someplace with sunshine and beaches like Barcelona or Mallorca. What did beautiful people do at the beach if not read?

Heat flooded her cheeks as she thought of *one* activity, because of course her brain couldn't just behave. Not that she wanted to engage in beach-side activities with Mr. How Many Trees—or anyone else for that matter.

"Nine hundred and thirty-five trees, by the way," she muttered, and he frowned at her again.

She'd been right about the perpetual scowl.

"For a print run of one hundred thousand books, if my math is right, it takes about nine hundred and thirty-five trees, assuming no recycled material in the paper."

She knew, because she had tried to use it as an excuse to reduce her print run. She couldn't bear the thought of all those books being remaindered when her readers realized she was a fraud. Instead, her publisher had pointed her to One Tree Planted and suggested she donate the money to plant nine hundred and thirty-five trees out of her generous advance, and then *please turn in the damn manuscript.*

After tossing this fact at him like a peace token, she turned heel and scurried away, relieved she'd never have to see his stupid chiseled jaw or his equally stupid forearm tattoo ever again.

"Jeez, you were gone forever," Wes said when Grace finally reached their gate. "I thought maybe you'd been detained by a hoard of Scottish wolfhounds or something."

"Is that a thing?"

"Come on, we're boarding," Wes urged, relieving Grace of her purchases so she could fish out her boarding pass. "Thanks for the magazine. What do I owe you?"

"On the house."

Wes snorted. "Put it on my tab at least. And let the birthday extravaganza begin!"

Grace rolled her eyes. "It's not a birthday party."

"Oh I know," Wes said with absolute seriousness Grace didn't believe for a second. "You don't celebrate birthdays." Then she handed Grace back her lunch, picked up her own luggage, and hurried towards the gate attendant.

"Final boarding call for flight 455 with service to Barra. Passengers Rios and Teal, your plane is ready to depart," the attendant said into a speaker while staring them down, knowing full well they were passengers Rios and Teal.

If Grace was already a shriveled raisin of shame, now she was on the verge of scattering into dust, but Wes laughed and began babbling her profuse apologies. "Sorry, sorry, sorry. This is our fifth flight in twenty-four hours. We don't know what day it is, let alone what time."

"No worries at all," the gate attendant said, all smiles and warmth for lovable Wesley. "Have a nice flight." To Grace she added icily, "You're only allowed one bag."

Grace looked down at her solitary suitcase in confusion.

"I see three bags," the gate agent said.

"My laptop can't go under the plane..." Grace said, but oh no... They were counting her purse too, of course, and there was no way it could fit inside her laptop bag.

"Oh, thanks for holding my purse, Gray!" Wes exclaimed, grabbing Grace's shoulder bag and shoving her own small clutch inside before turning sunnily back to the gate agent who pursed her lips once more at Grace's laptop, but scanned her boarding pass.

"Thank you," Grace mumbled to a stone-cold glare before schlepping down the jetway behind her friend.

The gate agent hadn't been exaggerating. The airplane was tiny, as though in another life it had been used for spraying crops. They had to go outside onto the actual tarmac and surrender their suitcases to a handler who loaded them into the storage bay before their eyes.

"I know they said it was small, but I didn't expect it to be this small," Grace whispered, ignoring the immature grin that spread across her friend's face and reaching for the worry stone in her pocket once more.

It had been a lucky find. Normally she wouldn't pick things up off the airport floor, but when her laptop bag had flown open as she collected it from the security conveyer, showering pens and sticky notes in every direction, the rainbow colors of the stone had been too beautiful not to scoop up along with the rest of her things, and a little soap and water in the ladies' room hadn't hurt it.

"It's like flying private. Like we're traveling with the President or something," Wes whispered.

"I think the President has a much bigger plane. With a board-room. And a bed." *Mmm, a bed...* Grace was desperate to take a hot bath and then stretch out under fresh clean sheets at the B&B and forget this entire day had ever happened. "Think there's a bathtub?"

"If I were President, I'd rather have a bathtub than a board-room. That would be amazing."

"Welcome aboard Barra One," the flight attendant, a black woman in her late twenties wearing a smart jacket and tie, teased, and Grace's face burned.

She hadn't meant it as an insult when she said the plane was small, merely a fact. By all accounts Air Force One was massive, but here, no more than twenty seats stared back at them, all but two already filled with irritated-looking passengers.

"Sit anywhere you like," the attendant quipped.

Wes buckled in and buried her nose in the gossip magazine, flipping quickly through the pages to see what was in store while Grace wrestled her laptop bag under the seat in front of her.

"Hey, Diego's in here. That why you picked this one?"

"What? No," Grace answered. She would never get used to her big brother being semi-famous. "What's it say?"

"Sandy Rios, blah blah blah… Rumors of a transfer—female Galaxy fans swoon in despair."

"He'll never leave LA. Princess Mathilda wouldn't allow it."

"Rumors of trouble in paradise—female Galaxy fans swoon in delight."

Grace snorted. "Don't get my hopes up."

"Does he have a black eye?" Wes asked, touching her nose to the paper for a closer look.

"Where?" Grace took the magazine and studied the glossy photo of her brother at a press conference sporting a pretty obvious shiner. He'd tried to cover it with makeup but done a poor job of it.

She skimmed the article. "It says, 'When asked if he'd come to blows with his teammates over rumors of a potential departure from LA, Rios laughed, gesturing to the light bruising above his right eye, and explained that he'd caught a flying elbow while practicing a set piece.' I swear to god that man needs to be bubble-wrapped."

"I don't think they want the Michelin Man in the central midfield." Wes laughed, taking the magazine back and flipping to the beginning.

"That's the last two," the attendant called to the cockpit.

"Hold for one more," the pilot shouted back, and Grace looked around wondering if planes this size allowed standing room like an overcrowded bus.

"Apologies for the wait," a growly burr murmured, and Grace's head snapped back to the front to see Mr. Bee Tattoo himself clapping the flight attendant on the shoulder and murmuring, "I'm with Buchanan," before locking eyes with Grace, rolling them ever so slightly, and then disappearing into the cockpit.

"Holy smokes, our copilot is hot," Wes whispered.

Grace's stomach fluttered in agreement. "You think?"

Wesley shrugged, squinting back down at her magazine. As usual she wasn't wearing her new glasses because she *hated everything about them*—her words.

"He sounded hot," Wes replied, and personally, Grace hated everything about the fact that she agreed.

"He wasn't wearing a pilot uniform," Grace murmured. In fact, he'd been wearing fairly indecent jeans with his hunter green henley.

"He's not. I am," the woman she'd mistaken for a flight attendant said, picking up a microphone handset. "Distinguished guests and rabble rousers, thank you for flying with us today. We'll have you on the Barra beach in just over an hour, where the local time is two p.m., and the local temperature is a brisk fourteen degrees. This aircraft is equipped with two over-wing exits, no lavatories, and no flight attendant, so please sit back, relax, and enjoy staying in your seats with seatbelts fastened."

After her announcement, the copilot also disappeared into the cockpit so at least Grace could burn with embarrassment in private. Wes opened her magazine again, holding it as close to her face as possible, while Grace sunk down lower in her seat and gripped the worry stone so tight she hoped it wouldn't snap during the bumpy ascent.

Chapter Two

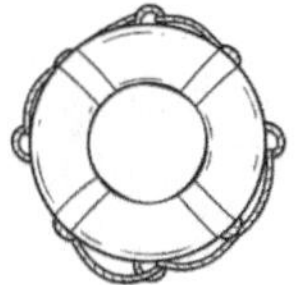

Squeezing himself sideways, Bryan plopped into the little fold-down jump seat behind the copilot, as his cousin, Captain Teàrlach Buchanan, began pre-flight procedures with barely a glance in his direction.

"Thanks for letting me ride up front."

Teàrlach shook his head. "A student pilot, Bry? Really? I swear, you could charm the scales off a snake."

Maybe that was true most of the time, but his people skills were certainly reverting to Barra-Bryan if his interaction with the Brown-Eyed Book Lover in the airport was any indication. "If I *were* going to train as a pilot, you'd be the only instructor I'd trust."

His cousin's lips quirked up. "You couldn't just buy a ticket like everyone else?"

"Didn't know I was coming until I came."

"Story of my life," the copilot agreed, taking her own seat, and Teàrlach burst out laughing.

Bryan stretched his legs as far as there was room without kicking the wheelchair stowed behind Teàrlach's seat. Then he buckled up and took out the new fidget spinner.

Hell of a time to lose his grandfather's worry stone. It had been right there in his pocket, just like always, but then security was a typical chaos of shouted orders to "Take out your liquids," "Empty your pockets," "Step forward—not that far forward," followed by "We're going to wand you," and "Is there anything in your bag that could hurt me?"

Somewhere in all that mess, the stone had vanished. Fitting, in a way, for the one piece of home he'd taken with him when he left, the rainbow-colored token of love and pride, to be free of Barra forever. An airport fidget spinner was a poor replacement, though.

He should have spent more time searching the floor around his security lane, but then he might have missed his opportunity to bicker with the American at WHSmith. What exactly had gotten into him? He didn't go around picking fights, especially not with brown-eyed strangers. There was just something about her... mostly something that got under his skin.

"Didn't buy a ticket because he didn't want a whole welcome committee, more like," Teàrlach told his copilot.

"I didn't know you'd be full up."

His cousin clucked his tongue. "It's the Bàgh a' Chiùil festival. You've been away too long."

"Bay-a-whatsits…?" the copilot asked.

"It's Gaelic. It means Bay of Music," Teàrlach explained.

Bryan groaned. So this wasn't just typical summer tourism. The island would be overrun with festivalgoers. God help him.

"How long's it been since you were here?" the copilot asked. She was young and pretty, tall and black, and most importantly not related to any of Bryan's island kin. He wondered if Teàrlach was dating her. She made him laugh, which was nice to hear.

"Seventeen years," his cousin answered for him, and the copilot turned to Bryan for confirmation.

"Half my life," he agreed with a nod.

She whistled. "Someone must have really pissed you off."

Teàrlach glanced back at him too and then answered for him once more. "Nah, he just ran out of girls to shag that he wasn't related to."

"Easy," Bryan growled, and this time the copilot roared with laughter, slapping her instrument panel in a way that made him nervous. He wanted to warn her to be careful, but he bit his tongue and fidgeted his spinner faster.

"There's always boys," she gasped.

"Ran out of them too," Teàrlach teased, and now the copilot was wheezing.

Bryan already regretted going home.

"Festival's gotten pretty popular the last few years," Teàrlach went on. "Sure you won't have any trouble finding a tourist to claim."

"No thanks."

His cousin was overexaggerating his conquests a bit. Tourist tail had almost always been too cliché for Bryan.

"Some of them out there are pretty," the copilot said, nodding towards the cabin. "Want me to put in a good word?"

Bryan scowled and shook his head as a tan face with dark brown eyes flooded his vision—the snarky woman from the airport shop again. Why her of all people? And now she was on his plane, heading to *his* island.

He hadn't meant to be an arse. In an anxious rush to make the flight, he'd tried to say, *Pardon,* but his larynx snagged on the *P* so his brain substituted the simplest path forward, instead: *You're in the way.* He even sounded like a prick to his own ears. No wonder she'd been insulted and turned into every primary school bookworm who'd ever looked down their bespectacled noses at him for struggling to read. In turn, he'd lashed out with schoolboy taunts, back and forth like a pair of hissing felines.

What was it about going home that turned him into such a child?

"You sure? I've been known to be a pretty good matchmaker," the copilot offered.

"Thanks, but no," he said. "I'm not here for that."

"What are you here for?" Teàrlach asked evenly, but there was a tension simmering below the surface.

They'd been constant companions as children, and then roommates on the mainland for a few years while Teàrlach attended flight school. When his younger cousin returned home like the prodigal son, Bryan continued to wander, leaving Glasgow to apprentice with the distilleries on Islay. One of the few people he'd kept in touch with during his exile, and sporadically at that, Teàrlach never overtly blamed him for leaving. But after so many years, maybe he, like the rest of the family, blamed Bryan for not coming back.

"I'm here to open a distillery," he answered after a too-long pause, and saying it out loud made his stomach swoop as though the plane were dropping altitude too quickly. Saying it made it real.

His cousin turned to check that he was serious, and Bryan resisted the urge to tell him to watch where he was flying.

"On Barra?"

"Why not?" Bryan demanded, a little too defensively. He took a breath. "It'll bring jobs. Tourism, maybe. There's an investor who liked Rionnagach well enough to give me the capital if I can demonstrate my commitment to net-zero carbon."

"Bry, that's amazing."

His stomach's altitude settled a little.

"He was lead designer for an Ardbeg expression that won a bunch of awards last year," Teàrlach bragged to the copilot, who nodded and made the mildly impressed sort of sounds people make when they're too polite to say they don't care. If Teàrlach noticed, he didn't show it. "Zero carbon too?" he went on. "They backed the right horse, there."

"Aye. Long as the islanders are open to it?" Bryan didn't mean to say it like a question, but when he was a young, idealistic lad of eleven, he didn't exactly endear himself to the townspeople with his passion for environmentalism. It was his greatest fear that the place he'd annoyed and then abandoned wouldn't have him back, hat in hand, jobs or no jobs.

Teàrlach shrugged. "Everyone loves a dram. Just maybe don't yell at them about their Sunday roast killing the polar bears this time."

Like he had with the woman in the bookshop.

Bryan shook his head in agreement. He'd only done it to needle her after she'd called him a Neanderthal. To place them on more equal footing.

"So you'll be staying then?"

Bryan liked to think he heard a hopeful note in his cousin's voice.

"Aye, well, I've got to impress the investor, buy land. It's kind of a lot." He took a deep breath. "Anyway, that's the idea."

"The family'll be glad," Teàrlach assured him.

The fidget toy was spinning so fast by now it could probably propel them the rest of the way home. "You think?"

"Aye. Where are you staying?"

"Grandad's." His gut roiled again. But no one ever said any of this would be easy. "Did you make it to the wake?"

"I did, aye," Teàrlach said, and of course he had. The whole island would have turned out: MacNeils and Buchanans alike, laughing and crying and sharing stories of old Grandad Mac, and only Bryan missing.

What kind of Neanderthal would miss his own grandfather's funeral? The words rattled his brain in layers of American snark. She hadn't said them, but she would have been right to.

He'd wanted to be there. Bought a suit and a plane ticket and everything. But then he had a panic attack about seeing everyone and being asked to make a speech, or worse, not being asked to.

In the end, he missed his flight. He'd spent the whole wake

sitting on the floor of the loo in a dank Glasgow hotel, raising a dram to the old man who practically raised him—practically raised them all—the four musketeers until one by one, three had left the island and Grandad Mac behind.

"And Alec?"

"Och. No one's heard from Alec in years, unless you have."

Bryan shook his head. It was just one more way he'd let the family down, losing touch with his older cousin years before. But he was back now. Maybe that could count for something. Maybe he could finally rediscover the peace Barra had once held for him, as Teàrlach had.

His heart swelled when the white sandy beach that would serve as a landing strip came into view, dredging up memories of running fast along the same beach with his three cousins, learning to make his new kite take wing, then doing the same years later with his little sister. Bryan had been half-afraid he'd feel nothing for the island, that after as many years away as home, the place he'd grown up would no longer welcome him. He swallowed down the lump in his throat, grateful to discover one fear, at least, was for naught.

"Beautiful as you remember?" Teàrlach asked softly.

"More," Bryan rasped.

"I never get tired of this sight," the copilot agreed, as Teàrlach put the plane gently on the ground, smooth as spreading butter.

As captain, it would have been customary for Teàrlach to wave the visitors off his plane, but he let his copilot handle the pleasantries while he reviewed his instruments and made notes in his flight log.

Bryan hung silently back in the cockpit for his own reasons until all the tourists had disembarked, and then a ramp was brought up for Teàrlach's wheelchair, and Bryan followed his cousin off the plane where an airport attendant was unloading luggage.

His older sister, Caitriona, was standing there waiting, her hair far grayer than he remembered. At the sight of him, her face drained of color, as if she'd seen a ghost.

Bryan cast an accusatory glare at Teàrlach. Had he radioed ahead to tell her?

His cousin shrugged and said, "Dude, you were with me the whole time."

"Cait? What are you doing here?" Bryan rasped.

She dropped some piece of cardboard she'd been holding and threw her arms around his neck. "I could ask you the same thing, ye wee devil." Stepping back, she held him at arm's length to study him before wiping her cheek on her jumper sleeve. "Let me look at you. Why didn't you tell anyone you were coming?"

"Element of… surprise?" he offered, and she slapped his arm, but not hard enough to hurt.

"How long are you here? You'll be staying with Ma and Da?"

"No, at—at Grandad's," he replied. Though he'd inherited the old stone house, it didn't feel right to call it his.

Cait's eyes widened and she bent to pick up the cardboard she'd dropped. "Grandad B's?" she asked coyly.

"Grandad Mac's. Why?"

"Do you mind? You're in the way," a familiar voice said, and there she was again, the brunette from the airport, stepping up to Bryan's elbow, suitcase in hand.

Her blonde, fae-like friend gasped, "Gray!"

Undeterred, the American Book Lover's brown eyes flashed at him for only a second before she turned a sunny smile on his sister that felt completely discordant with her irritating irritation.

He really must have pissed her off with his careless remarks. You'd think, as someone usually so meticulous with his words, someone who'd been forced to grow a skin thick enough for any insult to bounce off, he'd have been a little more considerate of a stranger in an airport shop. He'd have to file down those rough edges and polish up his manners before visiting Ma.

"You must be Caitriona," she greeted his sister, now ignoring him completely. "I'm Grace. This is Wesley."

Bryan actually read his sister's cardboard sign then, the name Graciela Rivera written out in thick, tidy marker.

Graciela, Bryan couldn't help mouthing. He liked the shape of it on his tongue.

"Welcome to Barradise," Cait quipped.

"Are you driving for Uber now?" Bryan asked his sister.

"Don't be ridiculous. We don't have Uber on the island. Teàrlach, you couldn't have warned me?" she shot at their cousin.

He threw up his hands. "Stowed away, didn't he? Nothing I could do."

"Mmm hmm. Still thick as thieves, the pair of you. The thing is, Ry—"

Bryan tried not to flinch at the old nickname. It stung like a paper cut under the nail, as though the *B* in his name was just too much trouble, as though she thought by saying it herself she would be forced to endure his stammer.

"—we weren't expecting you."

"And...?"

"And you can't stay at Grandad Mac's."

"Has the roof caved in?"

"Well, no. But I've let it as a B&B."

"S—I'm sorry, what?"

"It was just sitting there empty, and the hotels were turning folk away every day, so I bought some new linens and... it's done." She held up her hands in surrender, much as Teàrlach had.

Bryan stepped closer, putting his back between their argument and the crowd of tourists. "Undo it, Cait," he said softly.

"Well, I can't undo it, can I? They're here now."

He glared at his sister. All he wanted was to hide, alone, inside his grandfather's house and work on his proposal for the distillery, but now he'd have to play host to a couple of Americans unless he could palm them off on someone else.

Grandad's little house had two small bedrooms and one toilet. Would the American Invasion agree to share? Or would he be relegated to the lumpy old sofa, already six inches too short by the time he was sixteen?

Behind him, the one from the airport who called herself Grace was chatting to Teàrlach like they were old friends.

"If you'd told someone you were coming…" Cait began.

"You'd have what? Not rented out *my* house?"

"It's been vacant for months, Ryan Daniel MacNeil, with no word from you."

This time he couldn't hold back the shudder. His name was Bryan, damn it, and he'd never once asked anyone to drop the *B*, even when he couldn't pronounce it.

"Frankly, I never thought to see you again. We only knew you were alive thanks to Teàrlach here."

Sighing, Bryan raked a hand through his hair and turned away from his sister's accusatory glower to face his cousin and the two interloping Americans. The blonde was watching him closely.

"Double booked?" she asked.

"Apparently."

She scrunched her face sympathetically.

"How long are you here?"

"Four weeks," she replied.

Bryan tried to keep his own expression impassive, but Jules would be boots on the ground in just over three weeks, and they expected to see not only his finished proposal and the island as a whole but a completed proof of concept. How would he be ready in time with a matching set of American distractions?

"It's her birthday."

"It's not a birthday trip. I'm on a deadline," Grace corrected, clearly not as absorbed in her conversation as she seemed.

"I heard about your book," Teàrlach said. "Congratulations, I'm so proud of you, Gracie."

"You're a writer?" Bryan demanded.

Her gaze snapped to his, the scene in the airport suddenly so much more embarrassing. *Nine hundred thirty-five trees.* His neck burned at the memory while her eyes challenged him to insult her again.

Cait's gaze flicked from him to her guests. "Ready to go?" she asked, overly bright.

"We don't want to put you out," the blonde said.

"Nonsense. Welcome to Barra." Bryan punched the *B* with everything he had just to show his sister he could, before tossing his holdall into the back of her pickup and climbing in alongside the Americans' luggage for the drive down the road and along the coast to Castlebay and the house of Grandad Mac.

Chapter Three

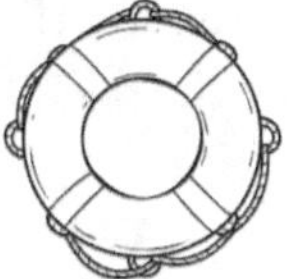

This whole trip was doomed from the start, and Grace knew it. She had known when her agent and editor conference-called her to demand an update on her manuscript the day after she won the trip, but she'd ignored her intuition. She had known it when Rebecca backed out at the last minute because her husband didn't want her to go, but Grace had pretended it was no big deal and invited Wes instead. There had been red flag after red flag, if one believed in signs from the universe. Grace had ignored them all, and now she was being punished.

She tried not to eavesdrop while Mr. Bee Tattoo hashed things out with their B&B host, but her mind was always doing too many things at once. It was a blessing and a curse. Even when she turned around and saw her brother's old bestie, Teàrlach Buchanan, of all people, some part of her brain was still listening to their hushed argument, panicking that she and Wes would be put straight back onto the plane.

Would the airport refund their bag storage fee if Teàrlach returned them to Glasgow tonight?

Had she known he was a pilot when they met at Diego's

wedding nine years ago? Was that why they'd sat in the back corner of the ballroom at some rich guy's mansion, sipping virgin mojitos and making snarky comments about the bridal party all night? As outsiders among the fashionable London set, they had certainly found each other to be kindred spirits, but what were the odds of running into him here?

"Don't worry about a thing, Miss Rivera," Caitriona was saying as she drove along the beautiful island road. "There's plenty of room."

"How many rooms, exactly?" Wesley asked cheerfully.

"Well. Just the two bedrooms. But Ryan's related to half the island. We'll sort it out."

"We don't want to inconvenience *Ryan*," Grace found herself saying.

The name didn't really suit him. Ryans should be charismatic and fun. Like Ryan Gosling. Except Mr. Bee wasn't exactly bringing the Kenergy.

"It's no inconvenience. And it would serve him right, showing up here unannounced after all this time. Are you here for the festival?"

Wes chuckled. "We absolutely love a good festival, don't we Gray?"

"I'm here to write a book."

"I see," Caitriona said with a tone that implied the very opposite. "What sort of book? One of those travel diaries?" she asked, knitting her brow like she was worried about what sort of mention her B&B might receive given this whole scheduling kerfuffle.

"A young adult novel."

"Like *The Hunger Games*?" the woman asked, brightening, and this time Wes snorted.

"Slightly less sociopolitical."

"Well, you've come to the right place for inspiration. Our wee island is very romantic and full of all sorts. Especially just now.

You'll have to be sure and attend some of the special events while you're here. Are you a writer too?" she asked Wes.

"No. I'm a frustrated interior designer on sabbatical from insurance at the moment."

"I see," Caitriona said again, sounding more confused than ever.

"I won this trip off the radio," Grace explained. "Six days and seven nights traveling around the whole of Scotland—"

"Seven nights? I have you down for—"

"Yes. I probably should have turned down the prize because my manuscript is massively overdue, but my friend convinced me to ask if I could stay in one place the whole time and work on my book. NPR agreed, and they saved so much money they extended our stay three extra weeks."

"You're a good friend," Caitriona told Wesley.

"It's true, I am. Not in this specific case, though. That was our friend Rebecca. She has the bad luck of being married to a raging narcissist. I'm simply the beneficiary of her bad luck."

"I see..."

"Does it seem like all our friends are with narcissists?" Grace murmured.

"Are you married, Caitriona?" Wes asked. "To a narcissist?"

"Wes!"

"What? As a writer, you must appreciate the value of field research."

"Americans have such a sense of humor," Caitriona said sounding like she'd never heard so much nonsense in her life. "Oh look, the seals have come out to welcome you." She pointed to an inlet with a rocky beach just off the road, where dozens of seals were sunning themselves lazily on the sand.

"How fun," Wes breathed, squinting vaguely in the right direction, still adamantly refusing to put on her glasses even for the sake of the seals. "Are they friendly?"

"Uh..."

"No petting wild animals," Grace warned her, glancing out the back window at Mr. Bee Tattoo, only to find him scowling out towards the seals himself. She'd clearly been right about his perma-scowl. Resting scowl-face. It suited him more than his name.

Soon they arrived at a cute little white-washed stone house on the edge of town. Mr. Bee Tattoo used those brawny forearms to lift the luggage out of the truck bed before Wesley and Grace had set foot on the pebbled driveway, more's the pity. Now he stared at the house with glistening eyes like a soldier come home from the war.

"I know it's not ideal," he murmured. "But you'll be comfortable here."

"It's fine," Grace said. "So it was your grandfather's?"

"Been in the family generations," Caitriona explained. "It's one of the oldest modern structures on the island. We're trying to get a plaque."

"He would hate a… plaque," her brother growled, spitting the word plaque with a mouthful of venom.

"Oldest *modern?*" Wes repeated and he nodded curtly.

"There's tumbledown church ruins that are older."

"Can I walk to them?"

He assessed her. Wesley was fair and blonde, tall and lean, with a hearty build. She was often mistaken for a lacrosse player, though she'd never played any sports to Grace's recollection, unless you counted the occasional round of frisbee golf in college.

"Aye, you could probably walk if you've a mind. But not today." He looked up at the cloudless blue sky. "It's going to rain."

"Back five minutes and he thinks he can predict the weather," Caitriona grumbled, rolling her eyes and unlocking the red front door. "Tell me, Ry, is it the rheumatism or your trick knee that gives it away?"

He glowered at her, gesturing Wes and Grace inside and

holding out his hand for the key, which his sister reluctantly handed over before following them in.

"There's live music on the beach every night during the festival, and a big ceilidh at the hall to finish it off," she told them, offering Grace a flyer. "You know what they say about all work and no play."

"Something like, it helps Jack pay his bills?" Grace quipped, handing the flyer off to Wesley, and Mr. Bee's lips twitched like he was actually fighting back a smile. The crooked expression made his green eyes sparkle in a rather arresting sort of way. *Good lord. Absolutely not, Gray.*

Caitriona led them through the little house, pointing out the single bathroom, awesome, and two small but tidy bedrooms.

"It's very cute," Wes whispered. "We can share a room."

"At least for one night. Maybe we'll get lucky and somewhere will have a cancellation tomorrow. But I don't want to bug you with my typing," Grace warned.

Smiling, Wesley shook her head. "I grew up in boarding school dorms. I think I can sleep through it."

"Really? Is that why you and your friends rearranged all the keys on that poor girl's keyboard?"

Wes snickered. "No, that was because she told Tommy Perkins that Melissa wet the bed. Besides, I won't be indoors much. I want to soak up every last sight I can."

Grace squeezed her hand and turned to their landlords, who were hovering in the living room like a pair of displaced ghosts. "Thanks for everything," she said. "Which room is yours, and which should we take?"

He visibly relaxed, though Caitriona began to splutter. "Don't be silly, he can—"

"That one gets more light. For writing," he said, nodding to the room on the left of the small bathroom. Grace nodded back, then she and Wes piled into the little room with their suitcases. It was fresh and bright, with cream-colored walls and an old braided rug on the stone floor. The bed looked old and simple, but the mattress was memory foam and covered with a cozy green-checked duvet. A sort of dressing table stood along one wall, drawers on either side, and a mirror with space to pull up a chair.

"We'll take it," she called over her shoulder. The only thing that would stop her from finishing this manuscript would be herself.

She laid her laptop bag on the makeshift desk and tucked her suitcase in a corner as Wes flopped onto the bed.

"Might get noisy," Mr. Bee warned. "I've a fair amount of work to do around here."

"What work?" his sister demanded. "We've taken care of everything—fresh paint, a new boiler."

"No one asked you to," he replied gruffly.

She huffed but seemed to bite back further retort. "Will you come and have a meal with the family? Ma's making lamb souvlaki and spanakopita." Her grimace suggested this was a terrifying culinary departure for their mother.

"Not tonight."

"When?"

"Later."

"Well just… be sure to look in on her. Only let me warn her first so she doesn't drop dead from the shock."

"Aye," he said, sounding utterly exhausted.

"You're welcome round for tea too, of course, though I imagine you'll be wanting to do your own thing," Cait added to Grace and Wesley. "You can walk to pretty well whatever you like. The Three Puffins is good if you want pie and karaoke. The Mustard Seed if you want something a bit more upscale."

"Pie sounds divine," Grace admitted, despite her insubstantial lunch.

Wes agreed, and then they all stood around awkwardly until

Caitriona realized they were waiting for her to leave. "Is there anything you need before I go?"

Grace shook her head.

"My number's on the fridge if you do."

"Thank you," Grace and Wesley chorused.

"It was nice meeting you both," Caitriona told them, reluctant to leave as though she thought her brother would toss them out and lock the door the moment her back was turned.

"Good night, Cait," he said.

With a sigh she plodded out the front, and they all three continued to stand awkwardly in the hallway staring at each other.

"We'll try to find somewhere else ASAP," Grace assured him.

He shrugged. "Stay as long as you like, Rivera," he said, and it shot a little thrill through her, whether he meant it or not.

"Are you sure we won't be in the way?"

"You'll definitely be in the way, but it's not your fault. I won't throw you out on your arse."

The awkward silence grew as Grace tried to think what else to say. She should apologize for the airport. "It's Rios, actually," she said instead. "Caitriona got the sign wrong. Rios Rivera. Or just Rios."

His cheeks burned beneath his beard. Grace had never really liked beards before, but the scruff suited him and his prickly demeanor.

"Want to go for a walk?" Wes asked brightly, to cut the tension, Grace suspected.

"All I want is a bath. Er, shower," she amended, glancing towards the bathroom. There was no tub. What kind of B&B didn't have a tub? She'd really been hoping for a long, hot soak to sort out her book problems. Honestly, it was a matter of public welfare. Sometimes a bubble bath was the only thing that kept her from getting stabby.

Wesley's shoulders sagged.

"Maybe we could walk to dinner?" Grace suggested. "Twenty minutes? Then we'll explore?"

"Deal, but I'm timing you," her friend said, glancing at a non-existent wristwatch.

So Wesley unpacked her one small suitcase like someone who was staying put for four whole weeks, while Grace scrounged up a clean pair of jeans and a hoodie. When she turned back around, Wes was checking the batteries on her favorite toy.

"You brought your vibrator on vacation?" Grace whisper-shouted.

"Hell yeah, I did. Vacation is for food and orgasms. If I was going to go without, I might as well have stayed home with Pierce." Wes held out the vibrator. "You can borrow him if you like. I call him Pablo, but he'll be anyone you want him to be."

Grace coughed on her own spit she inhaled so fast. "Thanks. I'm good," she exclaimed, rushing from the room and closing the door behind her, lest their landlord get embarrassed over Wesley's toy. Not that there was anything to be embarrassed about, she wasn't a prude. But he might be.

In the tiny bathroom, she spent a full five minutes staring dully at the faucet handle, trying to figure out how it worked.

She didn't want to ask for help. She shouldn't *need* to ask for help, for goodness' sake, it was a faucet. She'd earned two master's degrees and taught children life skills for a living, and he was a smug, self-righteous Scot with interesting forearms. If she asked for help, he'd probably lecture her on the evils of wasting water.

Ultimately, though, her desire to drown herself under a hot waterfall outweighed her pride, and she opened the door to find him seated on a barstool in the kitchen poring over his tablet.

"Can you?" she asked, losing her train of thought when he turned those green eyes on her. "The water. Your faucet is weird and confusing."

He stood and followed her back to the bathroom, glowering.

"It's not weird. Let me just..." As he attempted to squeeze past her in the tiny space, his arm brushed lightly across her breasts and she squished herself against the door of a linen closet, its knob jabbing into her ribs. Why hadn't she waited for him to go in first?

"Apologies," he murmured as the back of his neck flushed and he fiddled with the faucet. "It's a wee bit temperamental, is all," he said.

Grace wanted to retort, *Not unlike its owner,* but suddenly the lack of a window or any ventilation in the small room made her feel trapped. Her heart was racing and she couldn't breathe. Why would she cram into a bathroom with a strange man? Not for nothing, the bath was her sanctuary. There was no place for men in her sanctuary. She'd feel better if she just stepped out into the hallway, but a dizziness overtook her, turning the edges of her vision black.

Finally, he got it running, and Grace had no idea how he'd done it, so she'd better enjoy this shower because she couldn't bring herself to ask for help a second time.

Her host flicked the water off his hand and waved towards the faucet muttering something about how to adjust the heat. She blinked back the cloudiness and tried to focus on his words. Unable to maintain eye contact himself, he slid his gaze heavenward and pushed past her once more, shutting her inside the bathroom alone.

Grace gasped in a breath. Her skin was clammy. She wanted to lie down. What was wrong with her?

As a young college student, any boy with a mere hint of an accent—English, Irish, Australian... Cute or not, the accent alone would make her practically hyperventilate while her stomach did cartwheels and her face flushed ruby red. This wasn't that. She was definitely not doing cartwheels over his accent. It was a lot more like fight or flight.

Still damned inconvenient though. She had work to do. First thing tomorrow, they would have to figure out a plan B.

Chapter Four

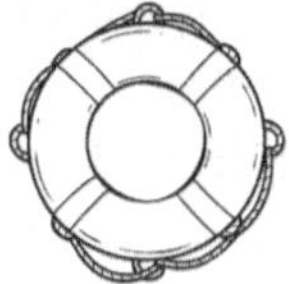

After helping his guest with the tricky faucet, Bryan returned to his barstool perch, unable to concentrate on the business plan before him. She'd been pale as a ghost, and he half feared she might keel over right there in the shower. She must be exhausted and more stressed than she let on about the living arrangements.

He couldn't blame her. Of course he'd never chuck them out with nowhere to go, but coming home, fixing the place up—it was a lot, even without the American Invasion. He ought to have climbed straight back aboard Teàrlach's plane the moment he saw Cait standing there with her chauffeur sign.

Should it make him feel a smidge better knowing his sister had gotten her guest's name wrong too? Of course not, but did it? Well. Bryan was only human, and it bound him to Grace in a strange sort of solidarity, whether she realized it or not.

Fate sure had a fickle sense of humor though. You accidentally insult one stranger in an airport, and suddenly you're saddled with them as a house guest for the better part of a month.

On second thought, maybe it wasn't a joke. Maybe Fate had his mother's sense of justice. The same way she used to tie his and Cait's wrists together with a bandana until they could stop fighting and work together, was Fate now shackling him to Grace until they could exist in the same space without sniping at each other?

They'd declared a truce, but how long would peace take when she instinctively knew just how to needle right under his windswept, freckled, clearly-not-so-thick-as-he-once-thought skin?

She had nice skin, he'd noticed. Figuratively no thicker than his own, given how easily he'd upset her, but her actual skin was flawless and dewy. *Danger, Will Robinson,* he reminded himself, taking a long drink of cool water to stop those kinds of thoughts in their tracks.

But then she scurried out of the loo wearing nothing but a towel and a messy pile of curly brown hair, and he couldn't clear out of his own house fast enough.

He snatched up his tablet and left to meet Teàrlach at the pub, still choking on the water he'd been drinking. The pub might be loud and chaotic, but he would have zero peace knowing Grace was getting dressed on the other side of his guest room door.

THE LITTLE BARRA LIBRARY WAS STILL OPEN FOR THE DAY WHEN Bryan walked past. What possessed him to step inside for maybe the second time in his life, he couldn't say, and he almost instantly regretted it.

"Ryan MacNeil. Heard you were back," the librarian, Jenny, another Buchanan cousin, said warmly.

He grimaced at her greeting. "News travels fast."

"Well, now that our mothers can text instead of having to ring up after tea, none of us stand a chance." She rolled her eyes ruefully. "How can I help?"

"Ehh... I was looking for a novel by..." he stopped to think. "Graciela Rios?"

"Gracie Rios? The young adult writer?" she asked, a little surprised, no doubt, hearing him ask for any book at all, let alone fiction for kids.

"You know her?"

"She won the Printz Award with her debut novel. I wouldn't be much of a librarian if I didn't," she replied.

"Then you have it?"

"Checked out. It pretty well stays checked out. But I tell you what," she said nodding at his tablet. "If you download the app and give me a tick, I'll buy a digital copy."

"Don't spend your budget on my account," Bryan said, looking around at the book-filled shelves.

"Nonsense. If you're back for good, you're my responsibility too," Jenny answered, tapping away on her keyboard. "And honestly, I should've bought a digital copy ages ago."

She handed him a library card, and he briefly wondered what name she'd registered him under.

"If the dyslexia still troubles you, it might be easier reading on the app, anyway. There's a special font."

Bryan stared at her. No one on knew about that, not his teachers or his parents. Not Grandad Mac. Or at least no one had ever mentioned it to him. Bryan hadn't been officially tested or diagnosed, though he figured it out after leaving the island.

"How did you...?"

She grimaced. "Sorry. Is it a secret?"

"No, no," he said. "The font will be grand."

She smiled sympathetically, and Bryan fidgeted with the stupid spinner in his pocket while he joined the library's Wi-Fi and waited for the app to download. Then he tucked the tablet into his jacket pocket and headed on to the pub.

THE THREE PUFFINS WAS MORE PACKED THAN BRYAN REMEMBERED for a random weeknight, but then it would be, thanks to the festival.

Bàgh a' Chiùil.

The Bay of Music festival wasn't a thing when he was young. It had been his father's brainchild sometime after he stopped representing Na h-Eileanan an Iar in Parliament, a way to lure more visitors to the Hebrides in general during pleasant summer weather, and to Barra in particular. According to Teàrlach it was a big hit, particularly with the American set. A real boon for the local economy. After all, who could resist the allure of Celtic music, ceilidh dancing, and a sun that hardly set?

It only galled Bryan because it was his father's brainchild.

Attempting to leave that particular chip at the door, he shouldered his way through the crowd to a table in the back corner and slid onto the bench opposite his cousin's wheelchair.

"Everyone settled?" Teàrlach asked, not trying very hard to disguise his amusement.

Bryan rolled his eyes. "You knew Cait was renting it out?"

"Afraid not, mate. I've been preoccupied with other things."

Relieved to hear his cousin wasn't keeping family secrets from him, Bryan felt a bit crap for being so self-centered. He was about to ask what was on Teàrlach's mind, but his cousin pivoted before he got the words out.

"Will you let them stay?" Teàrlach asked.

Bryan scoffed. "What else can I do? Throw them out in the rain with only the clothes they arrived in?"

His cousin snickered, but damn if the notion didn't conjure up a picture of Grace, damp from her shower and wrapped in only her towel—*his* towel, actually—as she hurried back to the guest room. She had a pattern of freckles on her left shoulder that looked like the Big Dipper, and he rather wished they could have used it in the Rionnagach whisky label design.

He tried to swallow, but his throat was tight and his trousers tighter. He shifted uncomfortably as a smirk spread across Teàrlach's face. Then his cousin slid a large faux leather glasses case across the table. "One of them left their specs on the plane."

"Neither of them mentioned it."

"Americans." His cousin laughed as he shook his head, but Bryan wasn't sure if he was actually laughing at the two women or at Bryan's predicament of having to play host to them when all he really wanted was to be left alone.

"Not exactly the homecoming I was hoping for."

"We did our best to take in the red carpet so you wouldn't trip over it."

A laugh bubbled up from somewhere long forgotten, and out of habit, Bryan fought to keep it contained. But Christ, he'd missed Teàrlach taking the piss.

"Anyone using this chair?" a voice asked, as another cousin emerged from the crowd. Eòghann—first in everything: first cousin, first hero, first person Bryan betrayed by running away from home.

Scrambling to his feet, Bryan stretched out an arm to his cousin, but then hesitated. Joining them for a pint might be a peace offering, a willingness to bury the past, but Eòghann might not be ready for more.

"Can't believe you're back, you rascal," Eòghann said, shoving that worry aside and yanking Bryan into a bear hug. "Can't believe you didn't tell me you were coming," he added, shoving Bryan playfully away before calling to a nearby server for three meatless pies with mushy peas and three stout ales.

Thank Christ some things hadn't changed. There might be a little grey scattered through his dirty-blond hair and beard, but from Eòghann's all-black attire like a lifetime spent in mourning, to his Commes des Garçons Kyoto cologne with its teakwood and patchouli notes, this was the same Eòghann Bryan had left behind, and he was overwhelmed that after so many years away, his cousin still remembered he was vegetarian.

When he turned back around after placing their order, Bryan could swear his eyes held a slight sheen. Guilt stabbed once more, not regret over the time away, but everything that came with it.

"So… back for a visit or a bit longer?" Eòghann asked, careful not to sound too hopeful, not to apply any pressure. Not, Bryan thought, to make him bolt like a wee Scottish hare, back to the mainland.

"I've got… plans. Here."

Eòghann smiled, genuinely pleased, and Bryan relaxed a little bit more.

"Well, what are they, lad?" he asked, looking between Bryan and Teàrlach. "Don't keep us in suspense."

"Long-term, whisky."

"Whisky?" Eòghann repeated, his grin growing broader, an intrigued smile, not a laughing-at-Bryan's-ridiculous-notions one.

"Aye. Completely green, zero carbon." He was nervous saying it, but Eòghann just nodded like it all sounded perfectly modern and reasonable, not a trace of hesitation over the memory of last time Bryan had tried to drag the island kicking and screaming into one of his eco-warrior schemes. At eleven, he'd believed he could save the world one side of beef or juice bottle at a time, but he hadn't had the words to make the rest of them believe.

"It tracks, right?" Teàrlach asked, and Eòghann nodded his agreement.

"What about the short-term?" Eòghann asked.

Bryan took a deep breath. He twisted the spinner in his pocket and forced the words out like ripping off a plaster. "Renovate the old cottage as a… proof of concept."

Both of his cousins' eyes went wide. "Off the grid and all?"

Bryan nodded, realizing for the first time how desperately he needed his family's approval of the plan.

Eòghann smiled slowly. "The old man would've loved it."

"You think?" he asked hopefully. It was true, Grandad Mac was the reason for his interest in sustainability. Well, Grandad and the Crocodile Hunter, but not having had the pleasure of meeting Steve Irwin, Bryan gave his grandad all the credit for encouraging him like no other.

A round of cheers erupted from the other side of the pub as karaoke started up, and suddenly, sitting with two of his best friends, surrounded by the sounds and smells of home, Bryan couldn't remember ever feeling more content.

He didn't deserve Eòghann. He truly didn't. Maybe coming home hadn't been such a terrible idea after all.

A kid up on stage crooned a plaintive pop ballad, the meatless pie was cooked to savory perfection, and despite his inconvenient guests, everything felt somehow right.

"Shall we take bets?" Eòghann asked Teàrlach, grinning at Bryan in a way that made him tune nervously back into the conversation.

"On how long before he beds her? Hardly seems sporting."

Bryan rolled his eyes. "How'd you know about my guests?"

Eòghann laughed. "That's right. There's two of them." He waggled his eyebrows lasciviously at Teàrlach, who snorted into his ale.

"You're both disgusting."

"One of them's more your type, Eògh," Teàrlach said. "The other one though…"

"Why'd you keep looking so delighted about it?" Bryan asked. "She's completely—"

"Careful," Teàrlach warned, flicking his eyes to the door where the two American interlopers had just stepped inside, the brunette looking somehow sexy and comfortable all at the same time as they scanned the place for an empty table. It did things to Bryan's stomach—unwanted things.

Eòghann turned to check them out and offered a low whistle. "Hardly sporting," he murmured.

"Arrogant," the word finally came to the tip of Bryan's tongue. "Rude. Shhharp-tongued."

Teàrlach tsked. "Och, he's considered her tongue. It's worse than we thought."

Suddenly, Bryan wished he had more food in front of him so he could enjoy the pleasure of throwing it at his cousins.

The two women squeezed onto one shared stool at the far end of the bar.

"Should we invite them over?" Eòghann asked, still staring.

"She's far too American," Bryan went on. "Also a little mean." They didn't need to know he liked her sharpness.

"One more word, sir, and I shall have to challenge you to a duel," Teàrlach teased in mock outrage. "You don't know who she is, do you?"

"What do you mean?" Eòghann asked, tearing his eyes from the bar to look at Teàrlach, who grinned like a Cheshire cat. "She the President's daughter or something?"

"Better. She's the sister of Diego Rios."

Bryan's mind went sort of blank, except for Grace's dark, flashing eyes. *It's Rios, actually. Rios Rivera. Or just Rios.*

"Our Diego?" He asked it louder than he meant to.

Teàrlach nodded gleefully. *I heard about your book. I'm so proud of you, Gracie.*

Rios. Rivera.

"You met at the wedding?" The one Bryan didn't have the bollocks to attend.

His cousin nodded again.

Christ. That was damned inconvenient. Bad enough to have an American staying with him, even worse to have trouble breathing around a tourist. He absolutely could not develop a schoolboy crush on his old friend's little sister.

"Are you sure?" he asked, searching her out in the crowd once more, knowing without a doubt Teàrlach was right.

Eòghann looked from one to the other. "Who's Diego Rios? Old boyfriend?"

Bryan rolled his eyes. "Old footballer," he muttered, feeling extra shitty for summing up a nearly fifteen-year friendship in two words.

Eòghann gave Teàrlach a look that said Bryan hadn't answered the question.

"The American who played for Celtic," Teàrlach explained. "And the only person with a crush on him was *my* little sister."

"Och, little Eilidh. Bless," Eòghann said with a sympathetic frown and a hand to his chest.

"He's back stateside now," Teàrlach added with a hint of melancholy.

Bryan shook his head like that would somehow clear it.

The footballer had known Teàrlach first, before he was recruited to Celtic, but during the Glasgow years, the three of them had morphed into a new set of musketeers. Now with five thousand miles and several time zones between them, they mostly followed each other on seldom-used socials and exchanged annual birthday texts. But Bryan still kept up with Diego's career, and he absolutely could not touch the man's little sister. Not that he wanted to.

He slapped the table to punctuate that thought and drained the rest of his beer.

"Keep going like that, we'll be sopping you off the karaoke stage," Eòghann teased.

"I do feel like having a go," he announced. It wasn't true, but before they'd started teasing him about Grace, who he was absolutely, one hundred percent not interested in, he'd felt almost cheerful. Maybe it was only the stout talking, but perhaps a song could recapture that feeling. "Reckon they've got any Donovan?"

"Hell, sing it acapella if they haven't," Eòghann egged him on while he could swear Teàrlach slid a little lower in his chair, trying to hide from the impending embarrassment.

Standing up, Bryan rolled his neck and the server handed him another stout. "Liquid courage, love," she said with a wink, and he grimaced at her as he headed to the karaoke stage on the other side of the bar.

Chapter Five

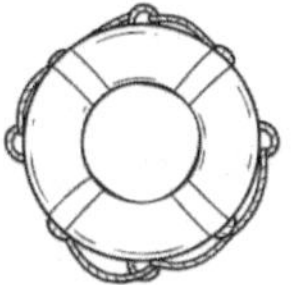

If she was being honest, Grace was mildly disappointed to realize that the *pies* on offer at the Three Puffins were various and sundry savory meat and veg pies, not giant portions of apple or rhubarb or whatever fruit pie was popular here. Fruit slice, Diego had called it.

Of course, it was silly to expect American pie in a Scottish pub, but Grace was jet-lagged and her brain filled in the blanks with what she was craving, not what made sense.

The meat pies on nearby plates smelled delicious, but she ordered fish and chips just to show her disdain for pie that wasn't sweet. Still, she and Wes sank onto their shared stool, back to back, and she couldn't help feeling somewhat content as her glass of sauvignon blanc warmed her tummy.

"Maybe it wasn't a complete mistake," she said over her shoulder to Wes.

"I'm so glad to hear it."

"You know what I mean."

"Only mistake I see is Rebecca bailing, and since that worked out very much in my favor, I could hardly call it a mistake. Sucks for her, though."

"She didn't bail. Her asshole husband threw a hissy fit until she backed out."

"Yeah, well, he was her *first* mistake."

"No argument," Grace agreed, and they clinked glasses.

The man at the next stool picked up his pint and tipped his flat cap to them before ambling away across the bar so Wes could claim his stool.

"Something-something about the kindness of strangers," she drawled in an exaggerated Southern accent before taking a long swig of her dark ale. It made her wince a little, but she licked her lips.

Across the bar, the karaoke crowd was getting raucous as a cute teenaged boy gave an earnest rendition of a Taylor Swift tune while all the young women in the bar swooned.

Maybe Grace should add a karaoke scene to her draft. Maybe that was the thing to save it, or at least jump start the nonexistent romance.

She sighed.

"Nope," Wes said, she of the killer hearing. "No fretting about your book. Not tonight."

Grace didn't bother to pretend she hadn't been thinking about it. "I don't know how to write it," she moaned.

"Luckily, you're marooned on a beautiful island with a gorgeous landlord."

"He's not gorgeous. He's a jerk with an overinflated sense of his own forearms." She took a gulp of her wine, trying to blot out the damn tattoo.

"What about his forearms?"

"You've seen them."

"Inspiration will strike." Wes rubbed Grace's back. "Promise. Just as soon as you tell me what he did to piss you off so bad. He seems sort of… nice, what with us hijacking his house and all."

"Nice?"

"Yeah, in a grouchy Harrison Ford kind of way. It's hot."

"You're deranged. That reminds me." Grace picked up her phone. "I was going to try to find a vacancy."

"Not! Tonight!" Wes gestured for the bartender to bring Grace another glass of wine. "We're all adults. We can share space for a few days without bursting into flames. You guys can even share a bed if you want."

"I don't want," Grace protested, mentally batting away the image of her bearded landlord with tousled bedhead. Bad enough she'd had to do the race of shame from the bathroom to the bedroom in nothing but her towel after Wesley's offer to share the vibrator had flustered her so much she left her change of clothes behind. Of course he'd been sitting right in the kitchen when she'd come out. She wasn't used to having to share space with anyone, let alone a man she'd known little more than five minutes. "Remember the part about him being a jerk?"

"I'm just saying."

"I came here to write," Grace reminded them both.

"Sure. But writers need a muse. You've said yourself you're stagnated, right?"

"I don't think that's exactly what I said," Grace protested, but Wes wasn't listening. "He doesn't like books." She frowned at her glass of wine so hard the bartender took it back to look inside. "Who doesn't like books?" she asked, and the bartender handed her drink back with a shrug.

"My point is, when did you last get laid? Maybe a no-strings island bang is exactly the inspiration you need—"

"What?" Grace spluttered, choking on her wine, and wishing her friend would crank the volume down a decibel or ten.

"Answer the question."

"I'm not going to answer the question."

"That, in itself, is an answer," Wes said, smirking like she'd won some sort of game.

"There's no *sex* in my book!" Grace whispered the word *sex* and glanced quickly at the bartender, who raised his eyebrows.

"So?"

"So how could it possibly be an inspiration for a book about *minors?*"

Wes snorted. "The fact you don't think minors are having sex tells me everything I need to know."

College. College was the answer to Wesley's annoyingly intrusive question. Grace had last slept with her college boyfriend about eight years ago, and then he went home to Jackson and she stayed behind in Knoxville, entering a long dry spell, which, honestly, she preferred.

Besides, she'd been very busy, first in grad school and then working the equivalent of two full-time jobs, as a school librarian and an author. An author who was about to be in breach of contract if she didn't deliver a second book by the end of this trip. A trip which wasn't a mistake, no matter how long they had to share their accommodations with a grumpy landlord and his bee tattoo.

"I wonder what his tattoo means," she mused aloud.

"Who's tattoo?"

This time Grace choked on a french fry. "My character."

"I thought your characters were all minors."

"It's just an exercise. Like, 'What kind of tree would you be?' Besides, he's an edgy artist and he's already designed the tattoo he's going to get the minute he turns eighteen." This was good. She'd have to remember to write it down later.

"So you've designed it, but you don't know what it means?"

"No," Grace answered, thinking quickly. "I just imagine it *would* mean something." Lying was exhausting.

Wes nodded. "Or he could be a dumb teenage boy and it doesn't mean anything except he likes pizza."

"Speaking from experience?" Grace teased, eyeing her friend, but Wesley's ink wasn't visible.

She grinned and shrugged. "I've never been a teenage boy," Wes replied coyly.

"The thing about YA is the characters are usually really deep and brilliant. They're the embodiment of every mature thing the readers wish or believe themselves to be."

Nodding once more, Wes whispered into her pint. "I bet your readers would be thrilled to have a hot holiday bang."

Grace sighed again and shook her head. When her editor had asked her to consider adding a romance to her sophomore book, she'd genuinely considered the idea before rejecting it completely. When her editor then explained how she could only offer a contract on Grace's option if she added the romance, she'd given in, complete and utter sellout in need of a more reliable car that she was.

And it wasn't because she'd grown up Catholic or because she was maybe a little bit of a prude, or any of the other things. It was because she didn't want to do a disservice to her young readers by conditioning them to an idealized fantasy about sex and happily ever afters. Now she was stuck, her draft was a year and a half overdue, and they were threatening to revoke her advance.

"I'm really tired. You ready to bounce?"

"I mean, I was hoping to sing a duet, but it's your trip I guess."

The Catholic guilt was strong with this one.

"It's *our* trip," Grace reminded her. "You want to make fools of ourselves, we'll make fools of ourselves."

Wes grinned and they crossed the pub to pick out a song and put their names down. The teen had finished his timid but perfectly pitched T Swift song to hoots and hollers from his rowdy friends, and the emcee shoed him off stage before glancing back at the list.

He pulled out a pair of reading glasses to check it again, much to the amusement of the crowd.

"Thought me eyes were playing tricks," he quipped, and they all chuckled. "Can it really be? Ryan MacNeil, the prodigal son, returns?"

Grace's head snapped up to see Mr. Bee himself making his way up to the stage, his permanent glower in place.

"B-B-B-Bryan!" someone shouted, and he gave them the finger before leaning over to whisper to the emcee, who looked equally annoyed as he changed over whichever song had already started to play.

"This one's for you, Mitchell Murray," he growled as the song switched to the opening beats of Pink's "Blow Me (One Last Kiss)."

Wes leaned in close. "Just me, or does this feel like an inside joke we're outside of?"

"Wait, is it Bryan or Ryan? Everyone's been saying Ryan, right?" Grace whispered, but Wes, merely shrugged, bopping her head in rhythm with the song.

Mr. Bee's forearms flexed as he gripped the mic in a possessive sort of way.

Was Grace jealous of a microphone right now? No, of course not, but his gravelly purr did something to her, like a swarm of bees rumbling deep in her belly. Suddenly she found herself shouting the lyrics alongside him because, after all, it truly had been the shittiest of days up until they landed on Barra's pristine white beach.

Eyes shining, Wes gleefully joined her for the refrain.

As she watched him sing, Grace had the oddest sensation that she was transfixed by his lips, physically unable to stop staring at them, at their shape and the way they moved. He had Bono lips— the only other man whose mouth she'd ever noticed, during an interview she'd seen in college. This time, she had the rather ridiculous urge to trace those lips, first with her finger, and then with her tongue.

What was wrong with her? Was jet lag causing her system to go haywire? She didn't lust after men, she wasn't here for that. She was here to write a book, damn it.

Vacation is for food and orgasms, Wes had said, and they were fresh out of food. Good thing for Grace this was work and not a vacation.

But it sure felt good to scream out her frustrations with Pink. By the end of the song, she and Wes were practically louder than he was and they'd gotten the whole crowd to join in.

When he finished, Mr. Bee glanced around the bar with a smug little smirk, and Grace hated how much she liked it. Boys who could sing had always been a weakness, even more than boys with accents. But he was a jerk, she reminded herself. He might have good taste in music and facial hair and dumb tattoos, but he hated books—her literal life's work. He thought he could just glower and flex his forearms and get his way. No, thank you, sir.

"That's us!" Wes shoved her towards the little stage.

"I didn't hear our names."

"He called us 'the American lassies who apparently cannae wait their turn,' so…" Wes rolled her eyes along with her *R*'s as she imitated the old emcee.

To reach the stage, they had to squeeze along a row of tables near the wall. Mr. Bee stepped between two chairs so they could pass, but Grace's shoulder grazed his upper arm, sending out a spark of heat as though she'd brushed against a hot oven.

"Sorry," she whispered up at him, catching another waft of smoky sandalwood. His green eyes, serious and scowling as usual, almost singed her. What happened to the smirk? Was he angry at them for drowning him out? For stealing his thunder?

As she took the stage, still burning from the way he'd looked at her, the pleasant buzz from her wine suddenly fled, but too late. The opening notes of "Bad Romance" were already skittering through the speakers.

She ran her hands down her waist, past the weight of the worry stone in her right pants pocket. "This is what you picked?" she asked Wesley, who smiled angelically.

"I'm going through things, remember?"

"You don't seem like it."

Wes shrugged.

Grace reached in her pocket to grasp the cool soothing stone and twist it in her anxious fingers. *Why not go for it?* the stone seemed to ask. She didn't know these people and would never see them again. Might as well sing her heart out.

Together, she and Wes gave the anthem everything they had, every last shred of energy and confidence and dignity, and when it was over, jet lag hit like a 747.

One sideways glance at Wesley and her friend nodded in agreement, so they shoved their way to the exit.

After the darkness of the bar, Grace was surprised by how bright it still was outside, and she stood blinking into the evening sun, the hands of her internal clock spinning helplessly out of control.

"I'll walk you," a familiar brogue rumbled as their landlord fell into step beside her.

"You don't have to," she protested.

"And let you accuse me of negligence when you wander into the ocean and drown?" he asked, raising that one cocky eyebrow.

"Well, we'd be dead, so…"

"Your song was very good," Wes cut in.

"Aye, you too, Ladies Gaga," he said, teasing, despite still sounding serious—and seriously put out.

"Really, we found our own way here just fine," Grace grumbled, but when Wesley elbowed her, she added, "I mean, in case you're not ready to go."

"I am," was all he replied.

"Then thanks," she acquiesced.

They walked in silence, far too close together, and there it was again, that whiff of fresh sandalwood. Or was it cedarwood? Or some other kind of manly wood—she choked.

"All right?" he asked, both he and Wes turning to her in concern.

"Fine! My spit went down wrong," she said, oh so smoothly, and when his brows lifted, she added, "Allergies. I don't think I'm used to it here. All the fresh air."

"Right," he nodded. "Where're you from? Tennessee is it?"

Had she told him that? She didn't think so. "How did you know that?"

"Cait said, didn't she?" he answered quickly, turning away from her and starting down the road again.

"I don't think so...?" God, was it her accent? Grace had often been told she didn't sound Southern. She *prided* herself on not sounding Southern. But, born and raised in Knoxville, maybe there really was no taking the Tennessee out of the girl.

A gentle rain began to patter as they strolled down the high street, and Mr. Bee handed her a small umbrella after casting them both an irritated look for not having brought their own.

"Do you want to crowd in?" Wes offered.

"Nah," he said, staring straight ahead with his mouth set in a line as the rain beaded up and rolled off his leather jacket.

They walked on in silence, though Grace kept getting the sense he was about to speak only to pull himself back. When they arrived at the tiny stone cottage, Wes went off to shower, leaving Grace and their host standing awkwardly in the kitchen once more.

"Night cap?" he finally grunted.

"Sure, why not?" she said, just to end the awkwardness.

"Let me guess. Gin and tonic?"

She lifted her chin defiantly. "And why is that your guess? Because it's boring?"

Putting his hands up in surrender he said, "Nothing dull about gin, Rios. It's versatile and... junipery..."

"And I strike you as... junipery?"

She didn't know why she was being so combative. Just, he put her on the defensive, and she didn't like being there.

He studied her, his jaw working back and forth like he had a lot to say but kept deciding not to say it. "What do you like then?"

"I don't really drink much."

"Afraid of the demon rum?"

"No, I just… don't know what I like besides white wine."

He tilted his head to study her after that pronouncement, as though he could see right through her to the words she didn't say, and it felt like flames were licking her arms and face until he turned away to open cabinet after cabinet, finding only dishes and a mismatched set of mugs and teacups.

He swore something Gaelic under his breath. "Just a tick," he rumbled, storming off to his bedroom and returning moments later with a bottle in hand. "Whisky all right?"

Grace shrugged. "Host's choice."

He snorted and took down a pair of juice glasses, pouring two fingers of amber liquid in each.

"Slàinte mhath, Rios," he said, lifting his glass and handing one to her, the name running through her like hot lava, so she took a large sip of the whisky to quench it, which merely made her insides match her outsides as it burned right down to her atoms.

He watched her swallow and waited for some kind of response.

"What do you think?" he finally asked with an anxious sort of scowl.

Honestly, Grace didn't *want* to like it, and he seemed to expect her to hate it, so why not give him that?

When she could breathe again, she said, "It's a joke, right?"

"What?"

"No one actually likes whisky. It's just a club to prove your manliness, like stout and black coffee? 'I'm a braw, manly man who eats fire and drinks Band-Aids!' It makes you feel like some kind of dragon warrior, right?"

"No," he said, still glaring at her, as though he was trying to decide whether to be offended. "I love it," he added, and for some reason she got the impression this time she was the bee and he'd felt her sting.

"Why?"

He looked away from her then, studied the glass of amber liquid in his hand. "Good whisky is extremely complex. It demands your attention."

"Are you sure you don't just tell yourself that because you're overly fond of feeling numb?"

"It heightens your senses, it doesn't numb them."

She snorted.

"Unless you overindulge," he admitted.

Grace turned towards the back door which opened out of the claustrophobic little cottage onto an ample covered porch with a view of the beach and the ocean beyond. "Will we get to see the Northern Lights here?" she wondered.

"Not likely, unless you extend your trip three or four months," he answered from close behind her, setting all the tiny hairs on her neck at attention.

He said it almost like it was an option, an offer, and Grace forced a laugh. "When I find somewhere with a vacancy, maybe I'll ask about long-term rental," she said.

Stepping past her, he led the way out on to the porch. It was still raining, just like he'd said it was going to.

"When *does* the sun set?" she asked, realizing her error.

He leaned against the porch rail facing her, his back to the gorgeous view. "This time of year? Doesn't really. You get a few hours of twilight around midnight. Cait's installed blackout curtains in the bedrooms though, no worries."

"That'll be handy," Grace said, taking another sip of the warming whisky to counterbalance the cool evening air, leaning her forearms on the porch railing beside him. "Maybe the extra sunlight will make me extra productive."

"Only twenty-four hours in a day. Why come here to write?" He sounded annoyed, or baffled maybe.

"I entered a contest with no expectation of actually winning. It was supposed to be a carrot to lure me to the end of the draft. Didn't work."

"Maybe you just don't want to write."

"Maybe you have a lot of opinions about someone you barely know!" she snapped, and he raised his eyebrows, posture stiffening.

He opened his mouth for a long, drawn-out minute before words finally came out. "...I only meant... after years of telling myself I couldn't come home—time wasn't right, I wasn't ready— I realized the inconvenient truth was I didn't *want* to come home. Maybe I'm not really an islander at my core. Not *of the island.*"

Was he suggesting she wasn't really a writer at her core?

That hurt. Like a truth-punch to the gut she'd been dancing around for weeks. "You want to be though, right? *Of* the island?"

He nodded.

Grace shrugged. "I want to *have* written."

"Why can't you finish?" he asked, turning the full force of his green eyes on her once more, and the air around them felt prickly with unintended innuendo. If only he knew.

He took a drink and she realized too late she was watching the way his Adam's apple bobbed as he swallowed. This was bad. *Get a grip, Gracie.*

"It's worse than that," she confessed. "I can barely get started."

The intense way he was watching her now made it impossible to breathe.

"Well," he said, his words always so deliberate. "May you find the words you're looking for." He lifted his glass in toast.

Were they still talking about her manuscript?

His gaze fell to her lips, and she drained the rest of her whisky to block them from view.

"What you won't find is a vacancy, not in the midst of the

festival. Unless you enjoy tent camping, might as well get used to… being in the way," he added with a quarter-moon smile before finishing his own dram and heading back inside, calling, "Good night, Rios," over his shoulder.

Grace sagged against the porch railing, her head starting to spin. For a moment, she thought he'd been about to kiss her, which was the absolute last thing she wanted or needed, no matter what Wesley thought. Grace Rios Rivera didn't go around kissing men. She didn't date them or sleep with them or even go out to dinner with them anymore, and she wasn't about to start getting distracted by them or their bee-tattooed forearms and Bono lips.

So why did she feel disappointed the evening had come to an end?

Chapter Six

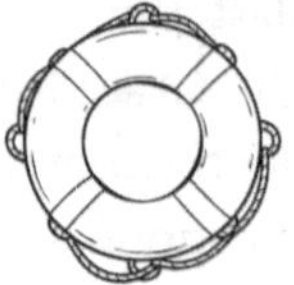

Somehow, returning to Barra had thrust Bryan right back into the same patterns of insomnia he'd left behind at seventeen, and the American Invasion was only partially responsible. Sure, he saw her dark brown eyes with flecks of shining ochre every time he closed his own, but he only closed them because everywhere else he looked, he saw his grandad.

This cottage had been his refuge as a boy—every time school became a bit too much or his father's disappointment weighed too heavily. Grandad Mac didn't care if words played hide-and-seek with Bryan's tongue or if his penmanship resembled the same scrambled chaos he saw upon each page of text. Grandad only cared that Bryan wasn't afraid of slow worms and that he could distinguish between the calls of a guillemot, a puffin, and a kittiwake.

The old man had nourished Bryan's curiosity when most everyone else gave up on him as stupid. He'd recognized Bryan's hunger to love and be loved by anyone who'd have him, and he'd always, always accepted Bryan just as he came. In return, Bryan had spent every possible second here in this drafty home, learning about the flora and fauna of the isle, picking up bits of spoken Ghàidhlig, and learning how to fix things around the place.

They'd been an almost feral pack of lost boys, Eòghann, Alec, Bryan, and Teàrlach, and Grandad Mac had encouraged them to leave, though he might have wished for them all to stay forever. In the end, only Eòghann had stayed, and Bryan constantly second-guessed how things might have turned out if he'd stayed too.

He loved the old house, but even after receiving word it was his, he didn't come right away. It stood as a stark reminder of his darkest days, a cave for him to hide in when the world was too big or too cruel.

And he still didn't understand why him.

He wasn't the oldest grandson. The cottage had belonged to Great Grandad MacNeil before Grandad Mac took it over, so it could just as easily have gone to Eòghann. Loyal Eòghann, who'd never left the island and never would, was Grandad's nephew and Bryan's double cousin. The family tree got complicated fast when uncle and nephew married a pair of half sisters.

Everyone on the island probably thought the house should have gone to Eòghann, though he'd already inherited Grandad B's place, and if not Eòghann, then Bryan's father or Cait should have been next in line. Instead, it was left to Bryan, just one more thing his father would probably hold against him until the end of time. And the neighbors, too. They saw Grandad Mac's as a slice of history, a history Bryan had trampled by leaving, one he had no right to reclaim now.

Despite his unworthiness, though, Bryan was grateful. He was excited. He only hoped Eòghann was right about the old man appreciating his plan.

He flopped away from the twilit windows, like a dolphin breeching the surf, and noticed a bouncing light filtering under his door accompanied by the soft creeping sounds of someone trying to move quietly through an unfamiliar environment.

He ought to ignore it. Ought to let them be.

Except what if they needed something?

He rolled his eyes. What would Grandad Mac think of his predicament?

The old man would probably find the whole situation hilarious.

Dragging himself out of bed, Bryan padded to the kitchen in his joggers without stopping to pull on a shirt. There, he found the American holding her phone as a flashlight while she rifled through a stack of papers on the counter.

"If you're a robber, you're terrible at it and there's nothing to nick," he said, making her jump.

She whirled on him with what looked like an apology on her lips until she took in his naked torso and not-quite-as-defined-as-they-once-were abs.

"I didn't take you for a light sleeper," she said, and out of habit he tossed her a lascivious grin.

"You've thought about me sssleeping?" he teased, immediately regretting his word choice because the accidental sibilance turned it extra creepy.

She shot him an ice-cold glare, making him cross his arms over his chest as he leaned against the wall.

"Hungry?" he asked.

"I was looking for the Wi-Fi password. I tried to guess, but RyanMacNeilLivesHere didn't work."

Bryan hated hearing her use that name, but he didn't want to get into it tonight. "Wi-Fi? At two in the morning?"

"It's only nine p.m. at home. What's your excuse?"

"A very large kitchen mouse," he said.

She pursed her lips. "Are you calling me fat?"

That was not what he'd meant at all. Why did everything get twisted about as the words traveled from his brain to his mouth? "Tall."

She leaned her head skeptically to the side, because at her height, no one had probably ever called her tall in her life.

"For a mouse," he explained.

She kept glaring, so he turned to the fridge, where Cait had left the password under a bumblebee magnet. He handed it over in a gesture of truce, trying not to notice the distracting way bits of her hair fell down from the messy pile at the top of her head, framing her face.

"Is it fast enough to stream?" she asked, waving her phone.

"Couldn't tell you. Wi-Fi hardly existed when I left home."

Her eyes crinkled. "God, that makes you sound ancient," she said in a tone which included herself in the ancient crowd.

"Makes me feel ancient," he agreed. "Hot FaceTime date?"

She rolled her eyes. "Soccer game. Sorry, *football*," she corrected dramatically. "It's a stupid superstition, but I don't like to miss a match."

Bryan nodded. "I get it." It was sweet, actually—little sister watching her brother's games from half a world away. It was also the perfect opening to tell her he knew Diego. He should tell her. He had to tell her.

He turned on the TV and navigated to download and log into the app she would need.

"Oh, I should probably—" she said, reaching for the remote, but he put in his details and the MLS games came up. She cocked her head in surprise.

"Galaxy?" he asked, turning on the pre-game.

"How did you—?"

"Rios? He's your brother, aye? Diego?"

She tilted her head again, blinking, clearly tired as her mind tried to catch up. "You remember him from Celtic? Or… did you know him? Through Teàrlach?"

Bryan nodded. *Through Teàrlach* was technically true. It didn't really do their friendship justice, but he hadn't really done their friendship justice, either, not for years now.

"Wait, were you at the wedding? You couldn't have been. I'd remember you."

Bryan's mouth went dry, though she didn't seem to realize she'd said she found him memorable. "No. Couldn't make it."

She nodded and turned back to the TV where they were starting an interview with her brother.

"I wish the bride hadn't been able to make it," she muttered.

An unexpected grin slid across his face before he could stop it, and she turned back to him in horror, like she was afraid he'd sell a soundbite to the press.

"I didn't say that out loud," she whispered.

"Didn't hear it," he replied, and they both turned back to the TV, where Bryan raised the volume a fraction so she could listen to the midfielder's voice.

She frowned. "Does he look tired to you?"

"He would be, wouldn't he?" Bryan said without thinking. Diego did look a bit worn out, and maybe he had dark circles under his eyes. *Bryan* was certainly tired, and he didn't run laps with twenty-year-olds for a living.

"What's that supposed to mean?" she demanded, instantly defensive once again.

He shrugged. "None of us is getting any younger, as you recently mentioned."

"He's barely thirty-three!"

"Which is about five years older than the average. Geriatric in footballer years." It was true, but why couldn't he stop needling her?

"He's the heart and soul of his team," she said fiercely, but with an edge of something like worry.

"Maybe he's just tired. Maybe an earthquake kept him up."

"Yeah. An earthquake called Mathilda Rivers." Grace glowered at the TV where the interview had ended and the national anthem was about to begin. It was time for Bryan to offer a proper truce by retreating to his room.

"He's tough. He'll be fine. If you need help with the Wi-Fi… give Caitriona a call," he said with a devilish tone, and she snorted.

The stifled laughter did funny things to his stomach—unwelcome things. She was his friend's sister. A tourist. She was not for him.

"Good night, Rios," he said to put some distance between them. "If you change your mind, I'm sure Cait left Mull Cheddar in the fridge," he added before making himself scarce.

Despite not sleeping, he was up and champing at the bit by an ungodly hour. He'd already drunk two cups of coffee before Wesley made an appearance, tousled and chipper, like a windswept mountain sprite.

"Hungry?" he asked, but she shook her head.

"Just eager to get out there and ramble."

"Ramble?" he asked, a little concerned she might get lost or end up somewhere she oughtn't go. "Anywhere in mind?"

Again she shook her head, though she didn't seem put off by his anxious questioning. "Everywhere," she said with a wistful tone. "I want to see it all."

"Ah." Bryan remembered the glasses case his cousin had given him the night before and fished it out of his jacket pocket. "Teàrlach found these. Are they either of yours?"

Her warm expression shuttered, but she reached for the leather case. "Thanks," she said without enthusiasm. "I was hoping I lost them."

Bryan quirked his head to the side, and she glanced at him sheepishly.

"Any tips for a nice ramble?"

"Good footwear and a warm jumper. If you come across a wee

s-snake, don't worry. They're harmless. Also endangered, so no tromping on them."

"Noted," she agreed. "What if I don't see it, and step on it by accident?"

"Run," he said with a grin.

"Who knew there were so many rules?"

He shrugged. "The snails are edible."

Wes grimaced.

"Really don't want to eat first?"

"A nice bowl of snails? No, thanks, I just want to get out there," she said, filling up her water bottle from the tap.

"Tablet for the road, then," he said, offering up a small bag of the sweet treat Cait had left, which Wes accepted before saluting and heading off down the beach.

Though it didn't come naturally, Bryan had intended to play the gracious host, to wait until a respectful hour before making so much as a single floorboard creak. But then his sister texted that Ma couldn't wait to see him for tea tonight. And his investor emailed to say they'd arrive in Glasgow on business in three weeks and would take the ferry out to see his island and his proof of concept, and just like that, he couldn't afford to wait another minute to get started.

It was over a dram of Rionnagach, discussing his and Jules' shared passion for whisky and their individual hopes for the future, when he first realized the house's potential. Today it was a dark, slightly chilly haven, but he could transform it into a beautiful symbol of growth and sustainability. Almost immediately, he'd begun making plans to return home.

Now, the leisurely vegetarian fry-up he'd planned was shoved aside for a bowl of cold muesli while he waited for Dàibhidh Buchanan's hardware store to open.

"Aye, your solar panels arrived last week," cousin Dàibhidh whispered. "But are you sure you want to put those things up for the whole island to see?"

"Aye," Bryan assured him. They weren't so bad looking.

"Only, your grandad's place has such a lovely thatch roof," Dàibhidh protested.

"Aye," Bryan agreed, although the thatch was only in front for looks. The back was pure shingle. He'd helped change it over seventeen years ago, side by side with Grandad Mac and Eòghann.

"Just, d'you mind not telling folk I ordered them for you?"

Bryan eyed his mother's cousin and shrugged, tossing the other odds and ends he needed onto the counter.

Dàibhidh rang up his purchases, glancing nervously around the store each time another old man came in for a browse and a chat. Finally he whispered, "Pull around back, and I'll have the lad load you up."

Nodding his thanks, Bryan took the bag of tools and fittings. He'd expected a little resistance from the town, but Dàibhidh's anxiety was killing his confidence.

"Lùcas!" Dàibhidh shouted out the back to a sullen boy Bryan had seen pretending not to sing his baleful Taylor Swift in the direction of another oblivious lad at karaoke the night before. "That lot in the back shed," Dàibhidh instructed. "Help your cousin load it up."

Lùcas shook the dark fringe out of his eyes and unfolded himself from a stool to amble off towards the shed.

"Eòghann says you're my Auntie Mal's son?" he asked, when Bryan finished backing his grandad's old truck up to the shed.

"Aye."

"So we're cousins."

"Sssecond cousins, I think, aye."

Together they hefted up the awkward boxes of solar panels one at a time and loaded them into the truck.

"Eòghann says you're renovating Old Mac's place?"

Eòghann had certainly shared a lot of information in the roughly ten hours since Bryan had seen him. "Does he?"

"Says maybe you'd give me a job."

Bryan lifted his chin to peer down at the lad, wondering whether Eòghann had really said any such thing.

"Is it true you left here when you were my age?"

"How old are you?"

"Seventeen."

Christ, but seventeen looked young these days. "Aye, it's true."

"Why'd you come back?" the boy asked in disbelief.

Bryan leaned on the tailgate crossing his arms. "Do you know anything about green renovation?" he asked.

"Like green paint?"

"Like environmental s-sustainability."

Lùcas shook his head.

"Why do you want to work for me?"

"Because you don't know me, and I don't know you."

Bryan laughed. He liked the kid.

"Eòghann'll vouch for me. Been helping him with odd jobs for years."

Eòghann would vouch for a Highland coo if it looked at him right. He literally only ever saw the good in anyone, like he was born with rose-colored retinas. "I'm sure he would," Bryan said, patting the kid's shoulder. "May not be able to pay you for a while."

"Can you give me a room once the renovating's over?"

A tiny pang hit Bryan's gut at the thought—more because it would mean trading one flatmate for another when he craved only solitude, certainly nothing to do with a desire for his current guests to remain. But he could use the help, especially if he was going to finish everything before Jules showed up on the afternoon ferry in three weeks.

"Deal," Bryan agreed. "Hop in. You can come today if your da doesn't mind."

Lùcas grinned at him and jumped into the passenger seat. "He can spare me."

As they drove back to the old stone house, Bryan explained his plans—knocking out the crumbling south wall to install triple-glazed casement windows, building a water reclamation system, and installing hydronic heating under the floors.

"So it's more than just the panels then? Da says they'll run you out of town for those alone."

Bryan took a deep breath. Counted to four. Let it out slowly.

He'd known in his gut the neighbors wouldn't like it. Gone seventeen years, but people don't change that much for the simple reason that people don't change.

"Really want the job?" he asked Lùcas grimly, but the boy tossed him a wicked grin.

"Wouldn't mind being run out of town, myself."

"Good." Bryan pulled the truck onto the beach behind the house and handed over his phone. "Find a YouTube video about installing this lot," he said, expecting the kid to scoff at his lack of preparation, but Lùcas just snatched up the phone and did as he was told.

"YouTube says it's not a job for the faint of heart," he reported back.

"Not my heart I'm worried about," Bryan mused. "You?"

Lùcas gazed thoughtfully at the gable and shrugged. "Not my roof."

Oh, to be seventeen and carefree. Bryan tossed him a pair of work gloves and leaned in close to watch the instructional video.

"Seems easy enough," the kid said when it finished, not a trace of sarcasm, and Bryan grinned at his young cousin's easy confidence.

Climbing the ladder onto Grandad Mac's roof a few minutes later brought back a flood of memories that Bryan should frankly have been prepared for, but they hit him all at once like the air from a jet turbine, so hard and fast he couldn't face them head on and still breathe. Instead he inspected the shingles.

They were newer, dimensional shingles in remarkably good condition. The roof he'd helped lay had been replaced sometime in the last few years. He'd been half-afraid he would need to do that before mounting the solar panels and beginning his green renovation.

"Eòghann says you're going to make whisky?" Lùcas asked, stepping off the ladder beside him, staring out at the beach and the ocean and the great wide world beyond.

"That's the dream."

"Why?" the lad asked, and he seemed to hang on to his breath, awaiting Bryan's answer. "I mean…"

"Good question. I guess cause… I like doing it."

Lùcas grinned and nodded, and they set to work, laying out the stanchions that would hold each solar panel in place atop its new home.

Chapter Seven

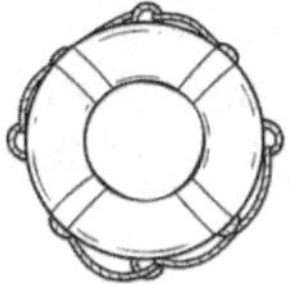

Because the sun never quite went down in Barra, Grace had no concept of time when she awoke to an almighty ruckus directly overhead, jumpstarting her heart like an unexpected third-period fire drill. Immediately nauseated, she ran a hand over her face and then Wesley's side of the bed. Cool. Knowing Wes, she'd been off to traipse the beaches and hills at some ungodly hour.

For a moment, Grace thought the clamor was a thunderstorm. Her whole life she'd been landlocked. Who knew what kind of storms sprang up in the middle of the ocean? But then the noise differentiated itself into metal hammering against metal and the whir of an electric screwdriver, a man-made not nature-made clangor.

Burrowing under the covers, she pressed a feather pillow to her ears to muffle the din. She was groggy, like she'd slept deeply and medicated, instead of just staying up ridiculously late to watch her brother play ball.

Only three years older, Diego had been her hero since she was a little girl, no less so when he moved to Florida all by himself as a young teen for the US Soccer residency program. She'd almost forgotten about the years he spent in Glasgow in his early twenties.

After three World Cups, it wasn't unusual to meet people who knew *of* him, but people who actually knew him? Well enough to call him *Diego* instead of the annoying press-sanitized, Mathilda-sanctioned *Sandy*? That was unexpected.

She'd recognized Teàrlach almost immediately. His hair hadn't been bleach-blond when she met him at the wedding, but his eyes were the same piercing blue, and there was something enticing about the delicate shape of his lips—a feature she now realized bore a striking resemblance to their host. Was it a Celtic thing?

Grace rubbed her face beneath the pillow, trying to clear the fog of jet lag and too little sleep. The way Mr. Bare-Chested Bee Tattoo had looked at her before turning on the game… Like he wanted to—she didn't know what.

How did he even have access to an American soccer stream? Surely he paid an arm and a leg for that. Was it to follow Diego's career?

And why on God's earth was he making so much noise at—if her phone could be believed—a quarter past eight? Like, thanks for the wakeup call because she was already hours behind schedule, but come on, Mr. Bee.

This morning, she didn't have the energy to do time-zone gymnastics before texting her brother.

> Charlie (sp?) Buchanan says hello
>
> Also your MacNeil buddy
>
> Was he always an absolute ass?

Diego texted back immediately.

> Teàrlach? Where the hell are you manita?

Now she did the math. Just past midnight LA time.

> Scotland. Why are you up?

> Shouldn't you be sleeping off that 3-0 victory?

> Were you hurt on the tackle? That pendejo should've been thrown off the pitch!

I'm fine. It always takes a while to come down from the adrenaline

> Hell of an assist, Man of the Match

Wait did you watch from Scotland?!

> Of course

Then why aren't YOU asleep?

> Loud hotel. And jet lag

Why not tell him she was staying at his friend's house and his friend was a terrible, noise-monster of a host? He'd either think it was hilarious, or be on the first flight out to kick some Scottish ass.

A surge of affection tightened her chest.

> I miss you

Come visit when you're back

She smiled.

> Or you could come home…

A bubble appeared indicating he was typing, then went away again. Finally, he sent another message.

We play in Nashville at the end of August

Meet me halfway?

Grace laughed. As if Nashville were anything close to halfway between Knoxville and LA.

Deal

So Scotland? And you just happened to run into the guys?

One of those crazy, random It's such a Small World you wouldn't believe it things, I guess

The earsplitting din grew louder, metal on metal. The world was maybe a little too small sometimes.

BRB, gotta kill a guy.

Grumpy Gracie :(

No killing. I can't afford international bail

Imagine the press!

My life flashed before my eyes

See you in Nashville

GRACE TOSSED HER PHONE ON THE DRESSING TABLE AND TIPTOED out into the kitchen to investigate the noise and wrangle up a cup of tea. Cait had left an assortment next to the kettle, along with something called tablet that looked a lot like fudge. It would make a nice little treat for writing a couple thousand words before lunch—if she was able to silence whatever the hell was going on outside with her headphones. Two thousand words wouldn't put much of dent in her manuscript, like three percent, but baby steps, right?

While she waited for her water to boil, Grace wandered around the small kitchen, which opened into the living room. She stood on tiptoe to peek through the patio door's small window at a disgustingly perfect view of the beach. It was a shame the whole room didn't share that view, but the stone and plaster walls closed it off like a cave against the elements. It wasn't the most aesthetically pleasing, but probably very snug in winter.

Maybe there was an outlet she could use on the porch to soak in some island air while she worked—once the hammering stopped, of course. If she couldn't write with a view like this, she might as well hang up her keyboard, because she wouldn't find a more perfect spot anywhere in the world. Stupid NPR, honoring her stupid request to turn the prize into her own stupid writing retreat. Better get to work.

With absolutely no enthusiasm to open her laptop and stare down the blinking cursor, Grace returned to the bedroom with a steaming mug of Scottish breakfast tea. Two thousand words should be easy. In undergrad, it might have taken an entire Saturday of pulling teeth, but she was a professional now. She'd drafted her first novel in stolen snatches between grad school classes and student teaching. Two thousand words shouldn't take more than a couple of hours.

Shouldn't.

She opened her laptop, freshly charged the night before they left Knoxville. It was dead, because of course it was. She'd intended to replace it with money from her advance, but a new-to-her six-year-old Subaru had taken priority.

After fishing out the plug adapter, she nibbled a piece of tablet as a consolation while waiting for the beast to boot up, and holy hell it was delicious—sweet, creamy, dangerous heaven in edible form! The whole piece was gone before the laptop agreed to cooperate.

As she waited, the rooftop pandemonium seemed to grow louder, ratcheting up Grace's anxiety until she couldn't take it anymore. She switched on her noise-cancelling headphones—thankfully *they* still had some charge—and the discordant chaos was instantly replaced by rhythmic, atmospheric tones. Now the only giveaway that Mr. Bee was attacking his roof was the thrumming in her bones.

Not that it mattered.

She stared at the blinking cursor, her mind as blank as the page, and all she could think about was the stern crease between his decidedly perturbed eyebrows, just begging to be smoothed. What did he have to look so cross about anyway? He lived in actual paradise, in a nice enough cottage, with an annoying sister close by who brought heavenly treats. Grace hadn't lived in the same state as her brother since she was thirteen years old.

But that had nothing to do with her book. It was time to focus.

BLINK. BLINK. BLINK.

Was the cursor blinking too fast? Almost flickering? Did that mean her computer was about to die for good? Or was she just fixating on the cursor to keep from fixating on another straight line, up and down, a chasm between deep-set green eyes?

Except her hero didn't have ginger hair or green eyes. He had black hair and grey eyes and sixteen-year-old Maya had been in love with him since sixth grade, only she didn't know it back then.

Grace rubbed in between her own brows. *Just start writing. The words will come.*

Eventually.

Right?

Her headphones beeped twice and shut off, letting the

muffled sound of screwdrivers and hammers infiltrate her peace once more.

Slamming her laptop shut, she threw her headphones on the bed and stormed out of the room, the cacophony growing louder as she crossed the kitchen. Grace yanked open the back door and strode out—right into a ladder, which sailed down onto the sandy grass with surprising elegance considering how inelegantly she'd knocked into it.

The noise stopped immediately as she stood under the porch roof, rubbing her forearm and shin. She'd have bruises later.

"Was that the ladder?" a young male brogue asked.

"Aye," her host answered on a long sigh. "I'll get it."

"Don't break anything, old timer."

"Careful I don't throw you off after it," he growled in reply.

And then he landed on his feet just in front of her, the disgustingly sculpted muscles in his back rippling in the sunshine. Like last night, he was shirtless. His pale, freckled skin was beginning to pink like someone not quite used to working out in the sunshine, skin that looked velvety soft to touch.

Seeming to sense her stare, he turned around and his eyes grew large, his mouth opening to form soundless words as she took in the dusting of auburn hair that glistened in the sun, trailing down his chest and disappearing into the waistband of his jeans.

"Lose your shirt?" Grace bellowed.

"What?" he asked, before looking down at himself as though he'd forgotten he was half-naked. Upon realizing it, he wiped his sweaty face on his forearm and placed both hands on his hips in a way that he must know was showing off his massive biceps as well as his abs.

"Don't *what* me. What the hell are you doing out here?" she demanded, locking her gaze on the bee tattoo rather than his sweaty face or naked chest or the tantalizing trail of hair.

"Working. Told you last night it may get loud."

Had he? Was that while he'd stood too close in the too-small bathroom, helping with his ridiculously complicated shower faucet? Or while he as much as admitted to paying for a Major League Soccer stream to keep tabs on her brother?

"But I have a deadline!" she protested.

He frowned at her and then shrugged. "Apologies. It can't be helped."

Grace stormed towards him, but he turned away from her and squatted down, filling out his jeans in an obscene sort of way.

"Did you kick over my ladder?" he demanded, lifting the object in question and placing it adjacent to the roofline once more.

"You don't understand," she moaned. "If I don't hit this deadline, I'm going to lose my book deal, my advance—my car. I'll probably never publish again."

His frown deepened, the vertical line between his eyebrows practically a chasm now, which Grace would never be able to climb out of. "When's it due?"

She sighed in relief. Finally, he was beginning to understand her predicament. "Four weeks." Laughable to think she could accomplish anything in such a short amount of time.

He shook his head. "I only have three."

"Three is good. Three what?"

"Weeks," called the teenager who'd sung Taylor Swift at the pub last night. He climbed down, jumping the last foot or so off the ladder.

"Lùcas, meet part one of the American Invasion. Rios, my cousin Lùcas."

"You were at karaoke?" the boy asked, shaking Grace's hand eagerly.

"Guilty. Sorry."

"Nah, you were grand." He turned back to his older cousin with a huge grin. "People weren't kidding, you do work fast."

Grace watched the color drain from her host's face as he

shook his head a fraction, but the boy had already turned back to her.

"Was it his accent? Or his winning personality?"

"If you value your life…" he threatened the boy.

"Oh, no, we didn't—" She shook her own head emphatically, but of course to an outsider it might look like she and Wes had picked the guy up at the bar and gone home with him. Could this get any more humiliating?

"Caitriona rented the house to Rios and her friend." When the boy's face clouded over, he quickly added, "You'll get your room the minute they leave."

Lùcas shot Grace a look like he now saw her as just as much of an interloper as his cousin did. "Best get back to those then," he said, nodding towards a pile of—

"It's going to take three weeks to put solar panels on your roof?"

Mr. Bee Tattoo shook his head. "This is only phase one."

"Phase one? You're going to renovate your entire house? In three weeks? While I'm on a deadline?"

"I didn't invite you here."

"You said there's nowhere else to go!"

"There isn't."

"You could always camp," the boy suggested.

Grace's breaths were coming short and shallow as she fought back tears for the second time in as many days. This was fine. It would be fine. She might lose some time this morning, but if she kept her headphones charged, surely it wouldn't matter if an entire house came down around her.

"I knew this was a mistake," she whispered to herself, pushing her hair back from her face with both hands and—oh god, she also hadn't put on a bra under the ridiculous LIBRARIANS DO IT IN THE STACKS t-shirt she'd slept in.

She crossed her arms over her chest and forced herself to

make eye contact, though he seemed determined to stare out at the ocean.

"Look," he finally said, and she did look, across the sparkling blue vista like he was doing, wishing she had her worry stone in hand. "My investor? Jules? They'll be here in three weeks to review my work. As a... proof of concept. Just give me three weeks and then I'll clear out. It'll be all yours."

It was a generous offer, but Grace was drowning. "That leaves me one week to write. I can't write a book in one week!"

"Can you write one in four?" he hissed.

Of course not, but she wasn't about to tell him so because it was hardly the point. "I came here to write."

"Then find an abandoned kirk or go to the library. Or back to s-s-s"—he stopped himself from what she was pretty sure was going to be *sodding*—"Tennessee." He closed his eyes, and when he opened them, there was pleading in their mossy depths. "I just need three weeks."

There was something about his desperation, something familiar and lonely that tugged at Grace. His throat was clogged with the same hopeless need she'd heard in her own when she begged NPR to alter her itinerary because maybe a change of scenery would help her get the job done.

The mix-up with her accommodation hadn't been Grace's fault, but it wasn't his either. Nor was her inability to meet her precious deadline extension.

"I suppose it's your house," she conceded uncharitably.

"It felt ungentlemanly to mention," he replied, tilting his head to frown at her, and damn it, he was almost cute doing some kind of stern-puppy impression. "If you're having trouble, maybe a..." he paused. "Maybe a vacation, a real one, is what you need."

Grace hated to agree with him, but banging her head against her computer certainly hadn't helped the words flow yet. "Would your work go faster if I help?" she asked.

His eyes widened in something like alarm, and he studied her skeptically, his gaze making her hot despite the brisk sea air. "You don't have to."

"Maybe I want to. I don't… vacation. I don't rest."

"Houston, I think we found the issue…"

She bristled. "I don't have an issue—"

"Except a looming deadline."

"Don't talk about my deadline!"

He raised his eyebrows at her ridiculous childishness.

"I don't have an issue except dead noise-cancelling headphones and this." She gestured to the roof, the beach, and him.

"You came halfway around the world for this. If you're going to be here, then be here."

Now it was Grace's turn to glower. "Do you want my help or not?"

He raised his hands in surrender. "Know which end of a hammer to hold?"

Grace rolled her eyes. "The shiny end? As I shove it up your—"

"Welcome to the crew," he said, cutting her off with a pacifying air as he took a step back from her.

"Should I leave you two alone?" the boy teased.

Grace had forgotten he was there. "No!" she and her host both thundered, and it fairly crackled in the air.

"Okey doke," the kid replied, turning his back on them to climb the ladder once more.

Chapter Eight

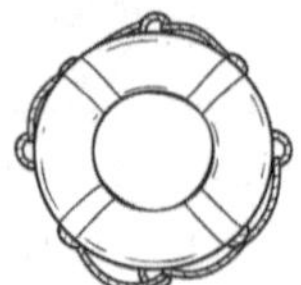

While the troublesome American went back inside, hopefully to change out of her thin-as-a-butterfly-wing cotton top, Bryan and Lùcas scurried back up the ladder. Not that it was her responsibility how his body reacted, but it would be a shame to drop a solar panel off the roof because he was distracted by the way her nipples pebbled beneath the almost-sheer material or to sever his own thumb because of the places his mind went when he read the saucy slogan.

"She seems fun," Lùcas said slowly.

Bryan grunted.

The moment he'd turned around and seen her there, with her very messy bun and that naughty t-shirt—over equally sinful pajama bottoms, he realized as she stalked away—he'd been overcome with an urge he'd not felt for man or woman in quite some time. And that was sort of… nice.

No distractions, he reminded himself. Never with tourists and especially not with his mate's little sister. Jesus. If he was one thing in this world, it was not a walking cliché.

Unfortunately, the tourist in question chose that exact

moment to pull herself off the ladder and onto the roof, mercifully clad in jeans and flannel, but damn. Those jeans didn't help cool his libido like he'd hoped, not even a little. He packed the newly surfaced urges away, deep in a bunker surrounded by sharks and barbed wire, and took a calming breath.

She glanced hesitantly at him, and then over the side to the ground below. Her little not-quite-apologetic half smile sent Bryan's belly into instant somersaults, and he batted those down too, asking, "Heights an issue?"

"No," she snapped, immediately on the defensive, but then she softened the tiniest bit. "I don't know. This is the first time I've been on a roof."

"Lucky me." He meant to say it as a joke, but it came out a growl, which was good because he didn't need her to realize he actually did feel a bit lucky—Christ knew why. Relief, perhaps? At her offer of help? Why had she done it?

And why couldn't she allow herself to just lie around on the beach like a normal person? Some part of him wouldn't mind exploring that with her.

"Lucky both of us," she sassed, and he handed her a spare pair of work gloves. "What should I do?"

"Can you hold the flashing down while Lùc screws these in?" he asked, holding up the bolts for the stanchion posts.

Grace nodded, and Bryan directed her further along the roof to where she should kneel. They didn't technically need her help for this, but extra hands were better than idle fury, in theory.

"A little to the left," he told her. When she mirrored him, scooting the flashing to her right, he said, "Your other left," and she gave him a very annoyed eye roll that for some reason looked more cute than angry, as she moved the piece far too far to her left.

Bryan knelt opposite her, their faces close enough now he could discern the peach notes in her shampoo and count her eyelashes, spread out like a fan against her cheeks. He placed his gloved hands on either side of hers, unable to avoid cupping them as he guided the piece to where it needed to be. Despite their gloves, he could swear he felt a tremor when he touched her.

Lùc's shadow fell across them and Bryan scrambled back, sheepishly stepping out of the way to allow his cousin to finish the job.

"Hold real still, just like that. Perfect," Lùcas crooned with a gentleness that surprised Bryan coming from the typically sullen teenager. Youngest of three, he was a late-in-life surprise for Bryan's Uncle Dàibhidh and Auntie Fiona, whose second daughter, Jenny, was nearly out of school herself before wee Lùcas was born. Apparently, there was more to the lad than mere eagerness to escape the island or sing plaintive pop ballads like someone who'd had his heart broken every damn day of his young life.

Grace smiled at his encouragement and continued to hold the flashing just like he told her to.

Once the bolt was drilled into place, she moved on to the next stanchion they'd set out before the ladder had fallen.

"Don't work too hard," she teased Bryan, taking note of his loitering. Lùcas snorted.

"I'm s-s-supervising," Bryan bit out, and she laughed at him, her lips pursed together, trying to keep from smiling at his hissing stammer.

When he looked away, she nudged him. "Come on, supervising?"

Was she really going to give him a hard time about it?

"Isn't that the oldest joke in the book? How many middle managers does it take to screw in a light bulb? As many as it takes to hire someone they can supervise doing the actual work."

He huffed out a begrudging half laugh. Maybe she'd been making fun of his words rather than his speech. Maybe she really didn't notice his troublesome S's. If she was laughing at him for being an uptight micromanager, well... he could live with that.

"I'm not middle management," he said as arrogantly as he possibly could. "I own this operation."

She rolled her eyes again and shook her head before turning back to the work.

Once the stanchions were all securely mounted, Bryan switched places with Grace, allowing her to supervise as he and Lùcas heaved the panels into place. They weren't heavy, just awkward as all hell to maneuver while on your knees on a roof.

On your knees. An unfortunate turn of thought while looking up at her with the sun lighting her from behind.

"A touch to the left," Grace told them, so they scooted the panel to Bryan's left. "Your *other* left," Grace corrected, just as he'd done to her earlier. Except his other left would be his right. So was she messing with him as payback?

"You mean *your* left, then?" Bryan growled.

She blinked for a second and then laughed rather sheepishly. "That's why I was an English major—so I could have an editor to catch things like that. Perhaps I meant *stage* left?"

"Did you always want to be an author?" he asked, gesturing for Lùcas to shift right.

"You're an author?" the kid perked up. "Are you rich and famous, then?"

Grace coughed. "Hardly. I'm a school librarian by day," she told the boy, and then to Bryan she added, "Yes, always. Did you always want to be a..." she trailed off, no doubt unsure what to say.

"No," Bryan answered.

"What kind of books do you write?" Lùcas asked.

"Young adult fiction," she answered, staring daggers at Bryan while speaking to his cousin. "Although I'm getting a bit old for the genre myself," she added.

A familiar rush of blood washed up the back of his neck and over his face, but he supposed he deserved it, so he didn't take the bait.

"Not like kids can write them," Lùcas told her with more generosity than Bryan had shown in the bookshop.

"I suppose that's true."

"I was banned from the library five years ago," he said, matter-of-factly like it happened to people all the time.

"What on earth for? Did you want to burn all the books like Ryan here?"

"I didn't s—how would that help?" Bryan jumped in, unable to resist this time. "Once the trees are chopped, it's just wasteful. Fire would only release more CO_2!"

"You're a book burner?" Lùcas asked him in horror.

"I'm not," he repeated, catching the flicker of a smirk on Grace's face. She liked giving him a hard time. Well, two could play that. "I'd rather not... print them at all."

Now both of them turned a combined glare almost powerful enough to knock him backwards over the ledge like the force of a couple of Care Bears.

"But they're art," Lùcas gasped.

Bryan groaned. "I've no objection to the art of them. Go on, why'd your own sister kick you out of the library? Does your da know about this?"

Now it was his cousin's turn to flush and look away, a tiny smirk playing guiltily at his lips. "I kept illustrating in the margins."

"Graffiti you mean?" Bryan looked over to gauge Grace's reaction, as both a writer *and* a librarian. She was quirking her mouth to the side to suppress a mischievous smile of her own.

"Okay, the author side of me is intrigued, but"—she glanced at Bryan—"the librarian side of me wants to give you a choice between lifetime detention and murder. How often were your drawings obscene?"

Lùcas looked deeply offended for about a second before another coy smile creeped in. "Only sometimes."

"Definitely murder," she said to Bryan.

"It's funny!" Lùcas protested.

"I get it! I agree." She shook her head. "Up until a ban-happy parent sees it and the next thing you know, they've found every single sketch you've made across every book and demanded those books be withdrawn from the collection. They're not even objecting to the books this time, just one silly drawing, but it's not like we have the funds to replace them all. It drips gasoline on an already smoldering fire, and suddenly everything's up in flames."

The kid stared at her.

"Sorry," she said, blinking self-consciously. "Occupational hazard."

"They really do that?"

"They don't here?"

"Not often," Bryan told her.

"Sorry," she said again.

Lùcas had the decency to look horrified, and Grace shook her head again. "Sorry," she said for the third time. "I didn't mean to go off on a soapbox at you. I think it's cool, I just…"

"Occupational hazard," Bryan repeated and she nodded. More like the kid accidentally activated a librarian sleeper cell.

"I didn't know," Lùcas said.

"You should do it for authors on social media. Bet they'd pay you."

The kid scoffed.

"No seriously. *I'd* pay you."

Lùcas turned beet red then, and it was kind of her to say that when she'd never seen his illustrations.

"I mean, not the obscene ones."

"Maybe I could start with some that were pulled from your library. Use the money to donate new copies."

Her face softened. "I meant I'd pay you to do it for *my* book. What an amazing way to engage with the text and get people talking about it! I'll be your first client, if you want."

"Is that what's causing your writer's block? Not enough kids read your first one? Didn't it win an award or... whatever?" Bryan asked, and her gaze flickered to him, all sorts of electric, before she pulled a curtain across her expression to shut him out.

"I don't have writer's block. And no. More like too many people read it. And then it won an award or whatever."

"So, what's the issue?"

"I told you, no issue."

"You came all the way here to write."

Grace deflated. "Yeah, I did do that... I don't know. Maybe I'm too old to write YA, like you said."

Not exactly what he said, but she was clearly never going to let him live it down.

"Maybe that's why I'm having creative differences with my editor."

"They want you to add in zombies, or something?" Lùcas asked.

"I wish. I could pull in some incredible Dia de los Muertos subplots if that were the case. No, it's worse, actually. She wants me to add a big dumb romance."

"What pish," Bryan grumbled without meaning to, and her eyes snapped to his.

"You don't believe in romance?"

"I don't believe in forcing it where it doesn't fit," he replied, and then bit his lip to keep from smirking at the unintentional innuendo.

"My editor thinks I need to make it fit," Grace said, without a trace of humor.

"Will they fire you if you don't?" Lùcas asked.

She stared at nothing for a good long while. "They're threatening to—"

She was interrupted by a strangled sort of yelp as something collided with their ladder for a second time that morning."

Chapter Nine

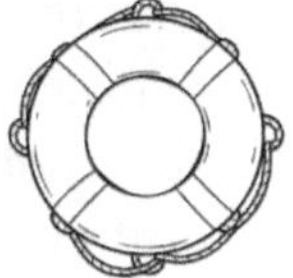

Rushing to the edge of the roof, probably faster than she ought to, Grace peered over the side, definitely faster than she ought to. It wasn't exactly the Sunsphere, but it was still a roof, and it made her head swim worse than watching Diego from the highest box at the World Cup.

Mr. Bee Tattoo grabbed her arm just below the shoulder to keep her from falling, not that she was in real danger of it. He seemed almost surprised to discover she, too, had muscles there. His thumb ran down her bicep in an involuntary, almost exploratory sort of way, and she didn't know whether to be turned on or take offense, so she did the next best thing—rolled her eyes at him—before leaning over the edge again while he kept holding on. She could get used to being held like that and—*Oh my god, now was* not *the time.*

Poor Wes lay in a heap, all tangled up with the ladder, and Grace's heart damn near pounded out of her chest as she yanked her arm free. Had she dragged one of her best friends halfway around the world only to kill her off in a freak accident? Was there a hospital on this island? And would they honor her health insurance?

"Wes," she called, swallowing her panic and searching frantically for the best way down.

The reply was a muffled, "Fuck's sake."

"She's fine," Grace breathed. Mr. Bee gave her shoulder a tiny squeeze and rubbed his neck sheepishly.

The boy, Lùcas, had already dropped to the ground and was pulling the ladder off Wesley. He tipped it back up against the roof next to Grace, and her host made an *after-you* gesture, squatting to hold it steady while Grace scrambled down to her friend.

"Are you okay?" she asked, offering a second hand alongside Lùcas to pull Wes to her feet. "Where does it hurt?"

"My upper dignity and my lower pride," she muttered.

Face flaming red against her pale blonde hair, Wes rubbed her hands down her torso, dusting off the sand.

"And I've gone and torn the priest's sweater," she moaned, noting a hole in the cozy, dark grey cable knit.

"The priest?" Lùcas asked.

"Total Father What-a-Waste… Did I say that out loud?"

Grace nodded, trying to keep her face solemn, although it wasn't as if Wes could have blushed any darker.

"Well, it's true, he's very sweet. And also quite handsome," she whispered. "I ran into him, not quite so literally, at the newer old church. When he saw me shivering, he insisted, even though I'm the idiot who left my jacket behind. Sorry about your ladder."

"No harm," Lùcas assured her. "Rios knocked it over first."

Grace stuck her tongue out at him and he grinned.

"I suppose I should've been wearing my glasses," Wes sighed.

"It's really all right, long as you are," their host assured her.

Wes nodded and reached in her pocket, withdrawing the frames she hated so much. They were completely smashed, one arm bent at an odd angle, the other lens cracked.

"Oh no," Grace breathed, but Wes simply pursed her lips like it was the glasses' fault for misbehaving.

"There's a shop in Castlebay can order you new ones," Lùcas suggested.

"Wanna bet?" Wesley sighed.

"Special prescription," Grace explained.

"Oh well. I didn't want to wear them anyway. But it will make mending this a lot harder," she lamented, peering closely at the hole in her sleeve. "I can't give it back to Father Eòghann like this!"

"Father—?" Lùcas began, but his cousin elbowed him, and he shut his mouth.

"Do you want me to try?" Grace offered, counting on Wes to decline.

"No offense, but your knitting is abominable."

Mr. Bee coughed, trying to cover one of those bursting sort of laughs that just pop out whether you mean them to or not, and Grace glared at him.

"Who could possibly take offense to that?" she muttered.

Wes pattered her arm sympathetically, as though she hadn't been the one to say it. "I'll see you later. Maybe I'll have located my pride by then."

Once the door closed behind her, Lùcas asked, "Eòghann's no priest. Is he?"

His cousin shrugged. "Dresses a little like one."

"S'pose so," Lùcas said, frowning. "Guess she really did need those specs."

"It's called Stargardt disease," Grace blurted out before she stopped to think whether Wesley might not want her private medical history shared with these veritable strangers, no matter how Scottish and charming they might be when they wanted to. "Her vision loss was slow at first but, lately..." she explained to their curious stares. "She says the glasses don't really help much. Please don't say anything to her," she backpedaled. "It's not a secret, but... she doesn't..."

"We'll keep it to ourselves," Mr. Bee agreed, looking sharply at Lùcas, who nodded.

"She doesn't… like to be treated as if she needs help."

Both of them nodded again, and Grace had the distinct impression that her host understood—possibly better than she did herself. The realization made her chest feel a little too tight and a bit fluttery. She cleared her throat and squinted past him at the roof. "So, where were we?"

"I think we were about to make dinner."

"Dinner, huh?" Grace asked, looking up at the midday sun. "So, haggis and, what? Irn-Bru?"

His eyes flashed, but that was the only indication her needling annoyed him. "Hell yeah, Irn-Bru. Couple of those and you won't remember what writer's block is." One side of his mouth quirked up along with an eyebrow, a smug challenge.

Grace glowered at him. "I don't remember now. Because I don't have writer's block."

Lùcas's eyes flicked back and forth between them.

"Then why aren't you writing?" her gracious host fired back.

"Because you were pounding on the roof like you thought it was some kind of oversized bodhrán."

He blinked and then tried to suppress a grin, as though he thought he'd won. "Bodhráns are Irish," he said with a patronizing shake of his head.

"All the more reason you shouldn't be banging one," she retorted, immediately regretting the use of the word *banging* though he didn't seem to notice.

Except then he said, "When I bang, it won't be a bodhrán," punching his *B*'s for emphasis.

Grace's mouth fell open, but she couldn't think of a single reply, like even her tongue had friggin' writer's block.

Great, now she was thinking about tongues *and* banging.

"Should I leave?" Lùcas asked.

"No," they both snapped once again, glaring at each other, and just what was Grace's problem? She used to be *Go-With-the-Flow Grace*. Also *Grumpy Gracie*, sure, sometimes it simply couldn't be helped, but she didn't pick fights with strangers, least of all men. She wanted everyone to coexist. Peace, love, and the Loch Ness Monster.

But he was very good at pushing her buttons. Maybe it was because his stupid auburn hair had just the right amount of wave without being curly. Or his seemingly effortless exactly-the-right-length beard, which was probably quite a lot of effort, actually. Or those distracting forearms.

Maybe it was because within two minutes, he seemed to understand her friend better than she did. Or his not-so-subtle insinuation that her entire life's work was ridiculous, a crime against trees. Or maybe it was because after being so vocally rude in the airport he was still scowling and quietly irritated by seemingly everything about her, as she continued to be *in his way*.

But mostly it was the forearms.

"What does your tattoo mean?" she demanded.

Her question forced him to break their staring contest first. Point to Rios.

"What?" he asked, staring down at his own obnoxious forearm like he'd only just realized the ink was there. "Nothing," he barked, pushing past her and into the kitchen.

Careful to keep his back to her, he scanned the contents of the refrigerator before opening and closing the pantry door.

"There's only eggs and oats," he grumbled. "What exactly did Cait expect you to live on?"

"Frozen curry, apparently," Lùcas said, peering into the freezer.

"God, have those been in there since Grandad…?"

Grace caught a glassiness in Mr. Bee's eye before he turned to stare back out at the ocean.

A lump formed in her own throat. She suspected she'd lost her abuela years before he lost his grandad, and while the ragged edges had been filed down by time, the grief still sometimes overwhelmed her.

His shoulders sagged like the roof was caving in and he was keeping it up by sheer force of will, instead of just adding a new power source to the top of it.

She cleared her throat. "My favorite saag comes from the microwave," she said, joining Lùcas at the freezer, giving their host a minute.

"Americans," Mr. Bee scoffed quietly, and she stuck out her tongue behind his back, making Lùc's nose scrunch up in silent snicker.

"Are you going to the ceilidh next week?" the boy asked, wandering over to a flyer Cait had left behind with a wistful expression on his face.

"I really need to write," Grace answered automatically. Though a ceilidh sounded sort of fun, but then again, not if *he* was going to be there, surrounded by a posse of thin, glossy admirers. Grace could only imagine that one well-timed glower from him would have ladies' panties falling at their feet like he was some kind of Scottish Mr. Darcy. *No, thank you.*

"We're going," Wesley contradicted her, stepping into the kitchen in a wave of fresh lilac and recovered pride.

"But—"

"We're going," Wes cut off her protest. "I already told Mal."

"Who?"

"My mother..." their host said, turning to face them, grimace freshly cemented in place.

"She said hello, by the way," Wes told him. To his cousin she added, "We'll be there, and I expect you to save me a dance."

Lùcas beamed at her, and Grace felt her deadline slipping away.

Chapter Ten

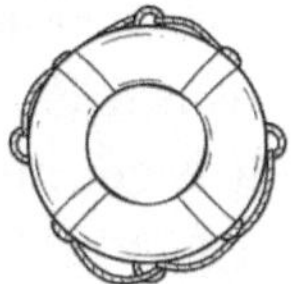

Bryan expected Grace to revisit her manuscript after eating the tiny ready meal, but instead she clambered back out on the roof with him and Lùc. Her tenacity reminded him of her brother, clawing his way into the starting defensive midfield position with The Bhoys of Celtic FC when he was barely nineteen years old. Diego made himself invaluable to his first professional club before being traded to the EPL for big money.

That same doggedness must have driven Grace to sell her debut novel in her twenties, earning her one of the most prestigious literary awards in youth literature, according to Google. Now she was procrastinating from finishing her second book by wasting time here with him. Why?

And worse, was he doing the exact same thing?

After Rionnagach was such a success, Ardbeg had offered Bryan another expression of his own, but instead of graciously accepting the bird in hand, here he was eco-renovating an entire house so that *someday* he might distill his next whisky under his very own label. Was he actually just delaying the inevitable because he was afraid to fail?

He scowled at Lùcas as they hefted the next solar panel up the ladder, as though the lad were the one suggesting Bryan was procrastinating.

He wasn't. This was the right next step. He couldn't make whisky for someone else forever. Grandad had understood. Hell, the master distiller at Ardbeg had understood, so why was Bryan still having phantom arguments in his head?

This renovation was a means to an end. In a way, he supposed it was one for Grace too, if it got him out of her hair as he'd promised. And so they worked on.

Though curious eyes tickled the back of his neck, he ignored the neighbors who gathered on the beach to gawk as they mounted the solar panels one after another atop his grandfather's roof. The same villagers had raised a ruckus when Grandad decided to replace the back with modern shingles, leaving only the street-facing side with its historical and beautiful, but difficult to maintain, thatch. Now they were clutching their pearls over the eyesore of his solar panels. Would they forgive Bryan as readily as they had his grandad?

He could see their point. All those years ago, Bryan had felt both ways about it. Thatch wasn't only aesthetically pleasing, it was far more eco-friendly than most of the shingles on the market at the time. But thatch also needed a great deal of maintenance, especially on the ocean-facing side of the house. Bryan hadn't planned on being there to help repair or replace it, and a man in his seventies shouldn't have been up and down the ladder at all hours, so he'd embraced the shingle plan. For years he'd been disappointed in himself for compromising his principles in exchange for his freedom, but if he hadn't, the roof would never be able to support solar panels now.

"What the hell is this monstrosity?" his sister yelled up at him. "And don't tell me you've put your guests to work too, Ry!"

He grimaced. Somehow, he'd almost expunged the awful nickname from memory during his years away, and hearing it now was tantamount to rubbing his own skin off with sandpaper.

"I can see the one-star reviews already," she went on.

Beside him, Grace snickered.

"Folk hand over good money to do hard things on vacation," he called down, wiping his forehead on his arm.

"Digging wells for the less fortunate or hiking to the top of Everest, you mean?"

It was exactly what he meant, so he stayed quiet.

"Have you spared a thought for what the town will say?"

He'd thought of little else. "As it doesn't affect them, they can say what they like," he snarled.

"All this to save you, what? A fiver a year on your power bill?"

"Not about that," he grit out, before yawning to force his clenched jaw to release. "If you tried, you might find them attractively futuristic."

"Attractively futuristic? What am I, a Flintstone meeting the Jetsons?" she shouted.

Grace froze, no longer fiddling with the screwdriver she'd been holding, likely reminded of her insult in the airport just as Bryan was. *What kind of Neanderthal...*

Did she regret it? Should it matter to him if she did?

"What do you want, Cait?" he demanded.

"Brought cullen skink for the girls."

"Mmm," Lùcas murmured.

"No one eats that, Cait."

"I would eat some," Lùcas whispered, but he shut right up when Bryan shot him a look.

"Guests expect it, actually."

"According to the one-star reviews?" He rolled his eyes, leaning more and more into the role of bratty little bother with each moment she stayed, invading his space and his peace of mind.

"When are you coming round? Ma set a place for you last night."

"I told you I was tired."

"Not too tired to sing at the pub, apparently."

Christ, he missed the city. Even on Islay, everyone might know his business, but he kept himself to himself and they left him alone.

"I had things to discuss with Eòghann."

"What sort of things? You've already got wee Lùcas up there. Don't tell me you've dragged Eòghann into this scheme as well?"

"It's not a—"

"Father Murphy needs him down at the church. You can't just waltz back into town and expect everyone to drop everything and run amok with you."

"I didn't ask for Eòghann's help. I didn't ask *anyone* to help," he added under his breath, cognizant of the side-eye from both Lùcas and Grace.

"Tonight then? She's trying her hand at vindaloo."

Bryan sighed and set down his spanner. He didn't want to have this conversation shouted from the roof, least of all with Grace and her enormous brown eyes looking on, likely thinking what a terrible brother and son he was. If Diego asked her to come round to tea, she'd probably go in a heartbeat.

"I'm busy tonight, Cait."

"Tomorrow then? Auntie Eilidh's been asking after you."

Had she? When he was young, his Buchanan auntie had seemed to have a general aversion to small, noisy children, not to mention Bryan's own aversion to sitting quietly indoors. But they shared a love of rugby stats and following the Glasgow Warriors. The salty old woman taught him some of his first swear words in the stands of the Barra rugby pitch.

"I'll come when I can," he told Cait. Couldn't let her think she could guilt him into visiting simply by invoking the family matriarch, or he'd never know another moment's peace.

"The sooner you do, the sooner I'll let you alone."

"Doubt it," he muttered, and Grace snorted, though she was steadfastly pretending not to listen.

"I'll just leave this inside then," Cait called.

"Grand."

The door banged shut behind her, and a moment later slammed again to announce her return.

"Grace, I left you a schedule of all the events for the festival. There's bands day and night, a comedian or two. There's a theatre troupe in town as well."

"Thanks, I'll let Wes know," she replied.

"You picked a fine time to turn up, Ry. This is our biggest Bàgh a' Chiùil yet. Even you have to appreciate what it's doing for the local economy."

"All thanks to the great Cameron MacNeil, no doubt," he growled.

"Aye," Cait laughed. "More or less."

She remained awkwardly looking up for a few minutes longer, but when Bryan didn't engage, she wrapped her cardigan tight against the brisk breeze and headed off again.

He glanced over at Grace, daring her to comment on what a shite he was being. Almost as though she could feel his eyes on her, she finally looked up at him and smiled sympathetically. "Family, huh?" she said with a shrug. "They must have really missed you," she added, and it sounded like a rebuke.

"They know how phones work," he retorted.

Her eyes narrowed. "I mean, what's not to miss? Wit, charm, sunny disposition. I can't imagine how they got by the last— what's it been? Five? Ten years?"

He scowled at her. "How long are you here for again?" Four weeks was starting to feel interminable.

"Not long enough to be missed."

He narrowed his eyes at her, and she looked away, like maybe she'd said it because it was the truth rather than to be mean.

"You ought to take your friend out tonight. She'll want to hear the music."

"My *friend* has a name. And she's fiercely independent. If she wants to hear music, she will. I don't go out."

"You and *Wes* went out last night. Looked like you even enjoyed yourselves."

"I went under great duress and as a favor to her."

Bryan snorted. "Forced to endure an evening of wine and good food alongside my caterwauling. Absolute torture."

"The ultimate sacrifice," she agreed.

"The music tonight'll be authentic. Far more agreeable."

She shook her head. "I've wasted my whole day. I can't waste my night too."

Her assessment stung a bit if he was being honest. *Wasted.* Of course she had, wasn't he thinking as much himself? He couldn't fathom why she'd joined him on his grandad's roof to begin with. He nodded, offering her a wry smile. "You might be the only person in the world as actively disinterested in my father's festival as I am."

Lùc snickered. "But you both came here to be mad about it."

"True," Bryan agreed with is cousin. "Why'd you enter that radio contest if you hate Scotland so much?"

"I don't hate Scotland."

"You're determined to avoid experiencing anything but bad karaoke in an average pub."

"Oi!" Lùcas jumped in, insulted by either the slight against his singing or against the Three Puffins.

"I have a deadline," she protested.

"Then why aren't you home finishing your novel? You couldn't defer the trip until you were ready to actually be here?"

"Why do you care?"

Why did he?

He didn't. Except he did.

"Why are you hiding up here with me?"

Grace opened and closed her mouth in a way that made Bryan hear schoolyard taunts of *Codfish* and *Tangle-Tongue*, and he studied his dirty hands instead of her.

"Good question," she finally said, and promptly climbed down off the roof, slamming the door as she went inside.

"Is it a contest? Are you trying to out crabbit each other?" Lùcas asked.

Bryan hung his head. "I don't know. The woman just gets under my skin."

The boy nodded. "I went to school with a guy like that."

"Aye? What did you do about it?"

Now it was Lùc's turn to hang his head. "Got super mad wae it and boked on his shoes at the end of term do. He's off to St. Andrews in the fall, so at least I won't have to see him around much longer."

"Might not go away forever," Bryan said, because Lùcas looked so sad about it. "Why don't you head home? Come round tomorrow. We'll mount the rest of the damn things."

"The old-timers are going to hate it even more than Cait did."

"Reckon they'd prefer it if we could paint them up with MacNeil tartan?"

That made his cousin laugh out loud. "Aye probably so."

"Would ruin them of course. Then they really would be nothing more than an eyesore."

"Give it a few years," Lùcas replied. "There'll be all kinds of skins, just like you can get for your mobile."

He probably wasn't wrong, but Bryan didn't have to like it. He tossed his gloves at his cousin as the kid disappeared off the roof still laughing.

Chapter Eleven

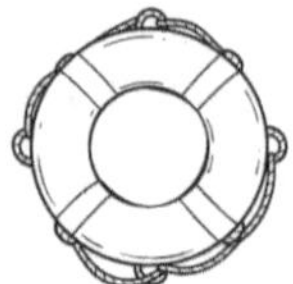

Despite being snarky with her host about it, Grace had intended to let herself be dragged out to whatever beach-side stage Wesley wanted and to dance barefoot until long past when the sun should have set in a normal, less magical land.

But while Wes was painting her nails, Grace had sat down at her keyboard and a different kind of magic took flight. Words began to flow for the first time in almost a year. If in the morning they'd been a trickle, this evening they were a veritable Fall Creek Falls, pouring out so quickly she almost didn't have time to worry about whether they were the *right* words or not. They were words, and even Grace could see the value in getting them down on paper.

Thus engrossed, she nearly jumped out of her skin when a bowl of mouthwatering fish stew was placed at her elbow.

Wearing her skinniest jeans and knee-high boots, Wes offered a sunny smile. "It's happening!"

"Give me ten minutes to change," Grace told her, running a hand through her messy hair and shoving her chair back from the dressing table.

Wesley shook her head, pressing Grace firmly back into her chair. "I don't want to interrupt. This is good."

Grace glanced back at the ancient laptop. "It probably isn't. It's probably flaming hot garbage."

Wes shrugged. "Gotta be shit on the page before you mine it for truffles, isn't that what you always say?"

"Is it?" Grace teased.

"You know it is. So keep churning out that shit, babe."

"You really don't mind going out alone?"

"Gray, I am an only child. I broke up with my boyfriend so I could finally go places alone again. And because he was bad in bed, but partially the other thing. I'll be fine."

Grace studied her. Wes was one of those wonderfully underrated friends. How many others would have been content to tag along on this last-minute trip and then spend so much time on their own? She was a true, loyal… horny friend. "You're going to look for your mysterious sweater guy, aren't you?" she asked.

Her wonderful friend's cheeks turned pink as Wes spluttered a false denial. "I don't know what you're talking about. He's a priest, Gray. A *priest.*"

"You're not Catholic."

Putting her hand to her chest as though incensed, Wes said, "Excuse me, I respect the cloth!"

"Yeah, but he—"

Wes put up her finger, demanding silence. "I can't help it that he smells amazing. Eat something before you get a migraine." Then she grabbed her denim jacket off the bed and headed out.

After devouring the delicious soup, Grace wrote until she couldn't see straight. Both the good and bad thing about this northerly island was how the sun never quite seemed to set. It was easy to lose all sense of time. Before she knew it, Mr. Bee would probably be hammering away again.

What had possessed her to offer to help? He was stuffy and

arrogant, and she didn't know the first thing about renovating a cardboard box, let alone a historical stone cottage.

But he hadn't thrown her and Wesley out of his place when he'd had every right to. And he'd been Diego's friend, back when her big brother was a lonely rookie four thousand miles from his family and too busy being the big football hero to admit a shred of homesickness.

Worst of all, despite how much the guy irritated her, being near him seemed to spark her utterly dormant creativity in a way long walks and classical music and yoga had failed to do. Poking him just to get a reaction was an extra little treat. She liked watching him struggle to remain unbothered until finally he clapped back with a snappy retort—it was fun, right up until she pushed him too far and his retort landed in her own backyard. It was silly to get mad, but at this point, angry writing was better than no writing at all. Sparring with him somehow made her faster, sharper, all the things both said and unsaid spewing out onto the page.

At this rate, if she just kept rubbing him the wrong way, she might finish the whole damn book early.

Not that there was a *right* way to rub him. Bees were delicate and sting-y after all. *Head in the game, Gracie!*

WHEN SHE FINALLY STOPPED FOR THE NIGHT, GRACE REALIZED TWO things: First, she was beyond ravenous, like so hungry if she didn't eat something right this second she might pass out, and secondly, Wes had already returned from the evening's festivities and gone to bed, all while Grace was in the zone. She closed her laptop softly and tiptoed out to the kitchen in search of more soup.

What she found was a freshly stocked refrigerator, with

shelves of bread and cheese, fresh fruit and hummus, as well as a pantry bursting with earthy-crunchy snacks and staples. She turned back to stare into the refrigerator's glow, wondering for a moment whether she'd been writing merely for hours or actually for days, when a gruff whisper said, "I recommend the cheese straws."

Grace hoped it was somehow dark enough he didn't see her jump, but light enough he caught the dirty glare she cast over her shoulder.

"For a midnight nibble," he clarified. "Hands down the winner, good any time of the day, and especially for fueling late-night activities."

Unable to stop herself, Grace smirked at the word *activities.*

He looked away. "Work-related activities."

"Doesn't sound very appetizing," she said, letting him off the hook and leaning down to search the lower fridge shelves for the mysterious cheese straws.

"Neither does haggis," he reasoned, rousing himself from his living room chair and coming up behind her in a way that made her spine tingle.

"Exactly," she agreed, a little breathless.

He turned to the pantry, and she couldn't help noticing the outline of his toned behind hugged by soft joggers. When he turned back around, she shifted her gaze up in time to see the box he was handing over.

"Have you ever tried haggis?" he asked.

"Definitely not."

"Exactly," he agreed with a smug smile.

Grace snatched the box of what looked like long, thin cookies, with a strong resemblance to bread sticks from the pizza chain of her childhood. She focused on tearing the box open, instead of looking at his dumb beard or his smug lips or his stupid arms as he crossed them over his chest.

"I suppose you eat haggis every meal?"

"I don't have a death wish, Rios. I'm vegetarian." He set down a tablet on the island and flipped the folio cover closed.

"What are you reading?" she asked, to change the subject as she bit into the savory, annoyingly delicious cheese straw. Good lord, where had these been her whole life? She took another before finishing the first.

"Ssspreadsheets," he whispered, drawing out the *S*'s like he was making fun of his own boring ass.

"Gross. But better you than me."

He snorted, scrubbing a hand over his eyes like he was exhausted.

"Is it going to be super expensive? Your late-night work-related activity?"

He nodded. "I try not to focus too much on the expense."

"Because you're turning the house into a distillery?"

"No, the house is just a demonstration of what I can do. I mean, it needs doing anyway, which is… convenient."

"I don't get it."

"My investor's very keen to see how it could work: a carbon net-zero distillery. I'm adapting the house to demonstrate a little of what it would take."

"Like a diorama?" Grace asked, remembering a fourth-grade science project about the solar system.

He nodded enthusiastically. "Like, how energy from the panels would run everything, how the water would be collected and filtered, how the flavor could be achieved without peat, all of it. There's things we do 'cause it's how they've always been done, but finding a new way forward is an art as much as a science."

His face lit up and came to life as he talked about his plans and, for maybe the first time since they'd met, he didn't look angry or annoyed. It took years off him. Grace had kind of assumed starting a distillery was just some youthful dream to have unlimited booze at his disposal, garnering the adulation of all the other drunken hooligans. She'd figured the eco thing was just a gimmick, his grandfather's house a convenience. But this whole endeavor lit a fire inside him the way writing used to do for her not so long ago.

"Jules already likes my whisky. When the house is done, they'll know they can trust me to operate green. If they like what they see, hopefully they'll recognize the value in locating it here and give me the capital to get to work."

God, but Grace was a sucker for a man with a plan and the passion to make it happen. It did things to her chest and her belly, things she'd rather not dwell on. It was all so terribly inconvenient.

"Do your neighbors understand all this?" she asked, nodding out towards the beach where more than one local had stopped to gawk that day, hurling insults loud enough to be heard each time the trio had set their hammers down. It had to be wearing on him. "Ryan…"

He shook his head, scowling more deeply than ever.

"Have you told them though? With those exact words like you just told me?"

He opened and closed his mouth a few times as though testing out whatever hurtful things he planned to say when he told her to butt out. For some reason, she liked this careful side of him, as if he were a writer himself, revising before he spoke words onto the page.

More people should be that careful with their words instead of letting them fly the moment they entered their heads like both of them had done in the airport. He clearly regretted the whole exchange and was trying to avoid any further first-draft mistakes in conversation.

"They don't give me a chance," he finally explained, rather than telling her to mind her own beeswax.

And wasn't that a familiar problem? There was nothing worse

than being held to account for someone else's mistakes, stumbling more with each unfair accusation to find the words or the fortitude to defend yourself.

Grace supposed it was the same reason she became a writer. As a kid, she'd always had the right words at the wrong time. As a writer, she could give her characters the speeches her teenage self had been unable to say, the courage she'd been lacking.

Could she do the same for him now?

"They will listen," she said, with more conviction than she felt. "You'll make them." Where was this coming from? How could she even know? "Or you won't, and they'll either get over it or run you out of town."

He looked like he might actually cry.

"I'm kidding. People hate change, but they'll get over it."

"It'll create jobs."

"Yeah?"

"Not many: one, two percent." He shrugged. "That's ten new jobs wouldn't be here otherwise. Not to mention, hopefully, increased tourism. Islay's got the peated whiskies. Lewis has the stones. Give folk a reason to come down here aside from Bàgh a' Chiùil," he spat, rolling his eyes.

"One percent, huh?"

"Give or take."

"That's like three million jobs back home. You're bigger than… Microsoft."

His brow furrowed like maybe that was too much pressure.

"If it doesn't work out, you could always get a job as the spokesperson for these cheesy things," she said, shoving another one indelicately into her mouth.

"Good, right?"

"Oh my god. When I have to buy new pants, I'm sending you the bill."

He barked out a laugh, covering his mouth too late, and they both glanced towards the bedroom, hoping they hadn't woken Wesley.

She shouldn't have said that about her pants, as though she weren't wearing any. Didn't they call underwear *pants* here? A sweaty feeling ran over Grace, but when she looked back at him, his gaze was on the counter as he reached for a cheese straw himself, as though she hadn't just mentioned pants like it was nothing.

Was it nothing? Was she just being ridiculous?

He looked younger with his eyes downcast and the shadowy summer light playing across his cheekbones, the residual smile of his unexpected laugh still gracing those fine lips. A smile looked good on them.

The effect was ruined the moment he bit into one of the cheese straws and moaned lasciviously.

"You're disgusting," she said. "I hope they push your distillery into the sea."

He laughed again, but then his face grew taut. "They might."

"Why do it, then?"

He frowned, and for a moment she worried she'd hit a little too close to home with the brusque question.

"What, follow my dream?" he asked in a sarcastic tone.

"Why do it here?" she elaborated. "When you're already fighting an uphill battle? You have a Sisyphus complex or something?"

Why was she asking? It was none of her business what he did or didn't do with his house and his ambition and his time. She was only here for a few weeks, and then she'd be back home straightening Percy Jackson books on the school library shelves and reminding rebellious adolescents to spit out their gum. But since her novel felt a lot like rolling a boulder uphill too, she found herself desperate to know his answer.

He eyed her for a minute, like he might just tell her to fuck off back to bed, and she wasn't sure she'd blame him. But then he slumped against the counter.

"I regret the manner of my leaving," he finally said with a half shrug. "Our cousin Alec went off to uni. And Teàrlach was sent to Glasgow for treatment. Me, I just pissed off in a huff like a toddler having a tantrum and left Eòghann here all on his own. He didn't deserve that."

Her heart did something funny at his admission, too chock full of too many feelings. She'd been the one left behind when Diego went away. Did he ever feel guilty for following his dreams and leaving her to fend for herself in Catholic school?

"He could've gone too, if he wanted," she pointed out, offering her companion the same forgiveness she held space for in her heart.

"No. He couldn't," was all he replied. "Alec… never came back." He shrugged, frowning. "I didn't want to be like him anymore."

"What was your tantrum about?"

He smiled ruefully and shook his head. "What wasn't it?" He stretched then, a thin line of hairy tummy peaking between his t-shirt and the waistband of his joggers, which set off a warmth in Grace's own belly that she tried to ignore. "You're off the hook tomorrow," he said, and she ought to have felt relieved instead of set aside. "It's getting crowded up there. Mounting the rest is really a two-person job, and Lùc needs something to keep him out of trouble."

Why did it please her so inordinately that he said two-person and not two-man? If he'd said *man*, she'd have snapped at him that she was as capable as any man, and then she'd have been stuck spending her day doing more manual labor instead of the job she came here to finish.

"It's late," he muttered, shoving off from his leaning perch. "Wouldn't want to drop one of those panels on a council member."

Grace snorted. "As a renter, I better not be held accountable if you do."

"Och, I'll tell them it was all your idea so they let me off."

She scowled at him, but he winked at her, and god damn that should be illegal.

"Night, Rios," he murmured, and wandered back to his room, leaving her in a bit of a tangled tizzy.

Chapter Twelve

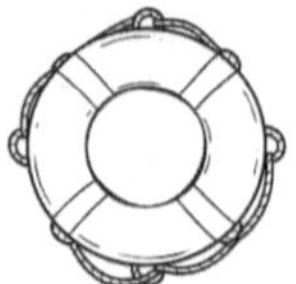

Sweat dripped down Bryan's neck and beaded along his hairline, but it felt good to be working under the bright Barra sun. He'd gone soft in his ten years on Islay, spending more hours indoors with the master distiller than working either his muscles or his hands.

Being up here on the same roof he helped shingle right before he left the only home he'd ever known, the last days he spent with his grandfather—it brought everything full circle in an emotional way he hadn't anticipated. Probably didn't help that he wasn't sleeping.

He'd left his tablet in the kitchen deliberately so he wouldn't stay up all night reading, but he couldn't stop thinking about an awkward fourteen-year-old girl who had lost her abuela and was worried no one would attend her quinceañera. How much of Gracie Rios was hidden within the pages of her book?

Reading it felt like spying, in a way, like nosing through his older sister's diary. Which was ridiculous. The book was published—it had won an award for Christ's sake. Loads of people had read it before him. That was sort of the point.

But still. It felt too personal.

He should've spent the whole night locked in his room pouring over his business plan instead of hovering like a creep in the living room, just in case she emerged from what Wesley called her *authorial fever*. But what if she needed something? He wanted her to know about the grocery shop he'd done, about the cheese straws and other snacks, to know it was him and not Cait who'd seen to it. Why exactly did he care?

He didn't. Of course he didn't. He was just on the verge of drowning in worry and doubt, and he knew her own skittish nature would make her sharp and blunt at the same time. Every encounter seemed to send Grace straight into self-preservation mode, and her cutting wit with just a dash of meanness could pull him out of himself. He craved it, Christ help him.

He wanted to fight with her.

Or, perhaps more accurately, he wanted her to have a go at him, to take him down a peg or two. He deserved it for leaving Eòghann and his grandad, Ma and Teàrlach and his little sister, El —and Cait, who'd married, had kids, and divorced all without a little brother to lean on. He honestly deserved every insult any of them could hurl, but Grace was a stranger. It didn't sting as much when she gave him what for.

Things had started off well enough trading innocent barbs over cheese straws, but then for some reason he told her about his plans and Alec, and she'd gone all soft—and how was that any help? He needed her to voice the insecurities in his head, to make him defend himself, not to be on his side.

"Your dear old granda'll be spinning in his grave, he will," Ellis Stewart, a third cousin on the Buchanan side, hollered up at Bryan, perfectly willing to put him in his place if Grace wouldn't.

"If he could do that, then he'd be a zombie, and he wouldn't give a toss about this house because zombies don't have brains!" Lùcas yelled down at the old man.

"You watch your mouth, young Lùcas, or your father will hear about it from me. You'd do well to mind the company you keep."

Lùc shook his head at the old man and turned back to his work.

"You should've stayed gone and let the tourists have it if you're hell-bent on destroying the old place," Bryan's other neighbor, Nellie Combe, agreed, with a shrill yip from her little black terrier for punctuation.

"Just going to let them take the piss?" Lùcas asked with a sigh.

"What's the difference? I argue my grandad had an eco-warrior's heart, and they'll retort that his heart was for the island first and for the home his own grandad constructed after that."

"You could just growl and look scary."

Bryan rolled his eyes, involuntarily grumbling deep in his throat.

"Exactly like that," Lùcas agreed.

"Shut yer yap and lift," Bryan told him, picking up one end of the solar panel and backing up the ladder when his cousin took up the other end.

"It really doesn't bother you?" Lùcas asked, his face contorted with frustration.

"Does it you? Thought you were the antihero."

The boy attempted to shrug, bobbling his end of the panel, and Bryan's heart leaped into his throat, but Lùc recovered and neither of them dropped it.

"Don't. Ever. Do that. Again."

"Sorry."

"Don't be sorry, be better," he snapped, his father's words tripping off his tongue before he could stop them. "Shite." He winced. "I apologize, Lùc. Maybe it does get to me a little."

"Don't be sorry, be better," Lùcas parroted back with a grin. "Why do they care so much what you do, if it's not hurting them?" he asked quietly.

Bryan thought back to his conversation with Grace the night before, to warm brown eyes and honesty in the kitchen.

He hadn't expected to be welcomed home with open arms,

but he supposed maybe he'd hurt the whole community, leaving the MacNeils to fret over yet another faraway son, leaving his mother to worry, his little sister to grow up without a brother. Leaving his father to bury his grandfather, then inheriting the old house despite not being there to say goodbye.

The thing was, before he left, Bryan didn't think the island particularly wanted him or would miss him in the slightest when he was gone. As a whole, they'd rejected what little he had to offer. In turn, he'd rejected all of them too, never looking back at the neighbor whose yard work would be left undone without Bryan there to trim the hedges or water the plants, never pausing to consider the recycling project he'd started in primary school and maintained through graduation or the younger cousins he wasn't around to lead on adventures as Alec and Eòghann had done for him.

The MacNeils and Buchanans were knit into the fabric of the community like the weaving of tartan or Eòghann's old, worn sweater. The family might forgive, but the town apparently wouldn't be so quick to forget. They probably wouldn't rally behind anything he did now he was home.

"That's the price for leaving I guess."

"Nah," Lùcas disagreed. "It's the price for coming back," and if that wasn't the most astute thing Bryan had ever heard, he didn't know what was.

They fell into a companionable silence after that, working quickly and efficiently to mount the remaining panels. He'd be lying if he said he wasn't a little disappointed Grace stayed inside writing all morning instead of coming out to complain about the noise or threaten to shove a hammer up his arse.

"What's next?" Lùcas asked when they finished up in the early afternoon without having stopped for a break.

"Next I watch a lot of instructional videos about connecting the wiring and transferring the electrical," Bryan replied.

His cousin's eyes went wide.

"Joking. I apprenticed with a guy in Glasgow before Islay. Come back next week with a s-sledgehammer."

"Aye?" the boy asked, breaking into a grin.

"Looks good," a voice said, and they both turned to find Wesley Teal standing behind them, squinting up at the roof a safe distance from the ladder, tall and willowy and perpetually windswept.

"You think?" Lùcas asked hopefully, and she laughed.

"I don't know. I imagine so."

She was still wearing Eòghann's jumper with the hole in the sleeve.

"My Great Auntie Eilidh could likely mend that," Bryan told her. Hell, for all he knew, she'd been the one who knit it for Eòghann in the first place. He'd received a similar cream-colored jumper in the mail his first Christmas in Glasgow.

"I'll take you to her house," Lùcas offered. "It's not far. See you next week then, cuz?"

"Don't be late, or I'll dock your wage."

"You're not paying me," the lad shouted back, leading Wesley off to Great Auntie Eilidh's without a backward glance.

AFTER A QUICK SHOWER, BRYAN EMERGED FEELING ALMOST HUMAN, only to find his humanity alive and well and stirring itself to attention at the sight of Grace leaning against the kitchen counter wearing leggings and a t-shirt with LIBRARIANS HAVE TIGHTER BUNS emblazoned on the back. He froze in the doorway, and she must have sensed him watching her, because she practically jumped back a step with a guilty expression on her face.

On the counter before her lay his open tablet. His humanity instantly shrank to nothing, as his heart rate sped up like it might explode.

"You left it open," she said, clearing a rasp from her throat.

"Did I?" Since he hadn't taken it to bed with him, he'd continued reading her novel this morning with his coffee and porridge. Then he'd gone to pour coffee in a travel mug for Wesley's ramble, and Lùcas had tapped on the back door, and he'd been itching to read more ever since.

He rubbed the back of his neck sheepishly. Could he explain it away? Turn it into some kind of joke?

"Why?" she asked, looking genuinely perplexed. "You don't even like me. You hate books."

She said the last part as though a person disliking books was far less fathomable than a person disliking her, and it made him sort of want to beat the living daylights out of whomever had made her feel that way—including himself.

"You won a… Printz," he said weakly.

"Do you even know what a Printz is?"

"Googled it."

"So you're just, what, Ryan? Reading my novel—which is for young adults, by the way—so you can justify hating it on a more personal level?"

"Rios…"

She lifted her chin. "Go on then. Tell me everything that's wrong and immature about it."

"You're wrong and immature about it," he blurted in frustration.

"What?"

What?

He shook his head. "Rios… I'm reading it 'cause I wanted to know…"

"Know…?"

He gestured at her. He wanted to know her. "What moves kids to write letters," he tried again. She looked completely confused. He wasn't making any sense. "I think it's… bloody brilliant," he admitted, hating the way he stumbled over his words.

She took another step back, away from him, waiting for the *but*, because he'd really done a number on her with his careless words in the airport.

"What happened to *books are terrible for the environment?* What happened to *YA is for adults who don't want to grow up?*"

Christ, he'd been an arrogant douche, but he didn't think he'd said that. "I didn't—"

"You insinuated it."

"It's an ebook," he answered feebly. "No trees were harmed in the making."

She just kept staring at him with this look of betrayal, like she couldn't quite decide whether to stab him or cry.

He sighed. "You ought to know by now I'm full of... shite. I mean, I do care about the environment, obviously, but... I was stressed."

"So was I."

"I was in fight or flight, and... I chose fight. I didn't know you were a damn author when I lashed out with the first words to enter my mind."

Say you're sorry, he told himself, and for some reason he could hear it in his mother's voice from his childhood. *Say you're sorry*, except those *S*'s never had come easily.

"Does it help?" she asked, throwing him off balance once more. "The dyslexic font?"

Bryan felt the color drain from his face, right down into his stomach, her words like a record scratch across his brain.

She must have noticed because she scrambled to explain. "I've thought about asking for a line in my contract requiring a dyslexic font print edition, but I wasn't sure how much it really helped."

He swallowed. He started to say, *Sometimes*, and then he started to say, *A bit*, but he settled for, "Aye."

No one knew about his dyslexia, except apparently his cousin the librarian, Lùc's sister Jenny. Growing up, most of his family and teachers had assumed he was slow at best, lazy at worst. It wasn't until an acting coach on the mainland casually mentioned the connection between dyslexia and stammering that he had any kind of name for his condition, and what good was validation when it came a lifetime too late?

"Aye," he repeated, his throat thick and tight. "It helps."

She nodded, but the awkwardness had fully settled over them, like a cat, unwilling to be shifted. And somehow it felt up to Bryan to shift it.

"It's lovely, by the way. You're insanely talented—"

"Insane, maybe."

"Talented. I'm no great reader—obviously—never was. Maybe if I'd had this as a kid, I would've been."

She swallowed, her eyes going a little bit soft, and he needed them to stay hard and wary because the softness did funny things to his chest.

"If only I could do it a second time," she muttered.

"'Course you can."

She sighed and shook her head.

"What, 'cause of the romance?" Pointing to the tablet he said, "You've ten different kinds of love in this novel, you know that right?"

"Not romantic love. It was never supposed to be about that. Sixteen-year-olds don't know anything about love, it's all toxic Romeo and Juliet bullshit."

"It's real to them." Every single one of his heartbreaks had felt like the first and last at the time.

"It's real until it's not," she said. "I'm almost thirty years old. I've never been in love, not for real. But I'm going to shove that down some poor kid's throat? With their too-big hearts and their too-raw feelings?"

Were they still talking about books?

Eòghann and Teàrlach liked to tease that Bryan had left a string of heartbreak in his wake, having slept with everyone his age he wasn't related to, male and female alike, but the truth was more complicated. There had only been one boy on Barra he'd ever kissed, a tourist at that. The rest were unrequited.

Bisexuality—one more word he couldn't utter because it started with a *B*—hadn't made his already rocky relationship with his father any easier, and he'd had to travel to the mainland to really explore it, but it wasn't why he'd left. No, his too-big feelings had all been tied up in paternal disappointment over his academic mediocrity and the words he couldn't say.

Bryan's head was spinning a little, and the moment felt heavy with meaning, too heavy for him to stay quiet like he wanted while a crocodile did death rolls in his chest.

"Then use it," he blurted out like a shotgun as he pushed away from the counter.

"What?"

Bryan turned his back on her to make speaking easier. Slicing a loaf of bread to keep his hands busy, he imagined the knife cutting away tethers that tightened his throat and tangled his tongue. "You don't believe in love, and it's holding you back. From finishing your manuscript," he clarified. "Use it, instead of letting it control you."

"You're not making sense," Grace said.

They were the four worst words in the English language, the ones he most hated to hear.

He should've stayed quiet. When he lived on Barra as a child, he'd learned to stay quiet, but somewhere over the years, with his elocution lessons and his extra work on film sets, with his bartending and dram-fueled karaoke, holding his tongue had become a little less necessary. Could he relearn how? Did he want to?

"I don't know if I can pull it off," she whispered.

Oh.

"You absolutely can. Just like Maya and her perfect quinceañera."

She laughed a little sadly, and he turned to hand her a piece of brown bread and butter.

"Was it based on yours?"

She stared at the slice of bread for a minute, almost debating her answer with herself.

"I didn't have one," she finally said, looking up to meet his gaze with her glassy eyes as she reached for the bread, her fingers skimming the sensitive skin of his wrist. "I got into some trouble, and my papa was pretty angry. He didn't mean it, but he shouted that we should cancel it, and I was eager to avoid everyone. So I agreed. My mom, you know, she's white. She didn't get it, didn't try to talk me out of it. She assumed I'd have a big sweet-sixteen party instead. So that was that."

"Wait, you really cancelled it?" Bryan asked without thinking.

Her brow creased.

Shite. He studied the floor. "Diego. He came to the flat in an absolute fury. We'd been out drinking the night before to celebrate his World Cup call-up when he realized the dates. He told the gaffer he'd be late to camp, and they said if it was so urgent he go home, then he could stay there. They'd take an alternate to South Africa. He was wrecked over having to tell you. When he heard you cancelled it…"

"He thought it was because of him?"

Those glassy eyes grew glassier. *Christ.* "I don't know what he thought. I just always assumed you uninvited him."

"Fuck," she said. Then, "Sorry."

Bryan shrugged.

"I need to call him."

"Don't—"

"I have to."

"Please don't. It's six a.m."

"Fuck," she said again, and this time she didn't apologize. "It had nothing to do with him."

"It was a long time ago. I'm sure he knows that now."

She shook her head.

"Do you want a drink?" he offered, because she looked like she could use one, but she shook her head.

"It's early. Not six a.m., but early. For me."

"A walk then? Just down the coast? I'll point out all the things I hated leaving behind, things I came back for."

She smiled at him then, a sad, watery sort of smile that felt like the sun peeking out after a storm to make a rainbow. Christ, she was going to be trouble.

"Views will be worth it, even though you hate me."

"I do, it's true." She nodded in solemn agreement. "But I suppose I can put up with you for a nice walk and a good view."

And for the first time, Bryan didn't mind being hated.

Chapter Thirteen

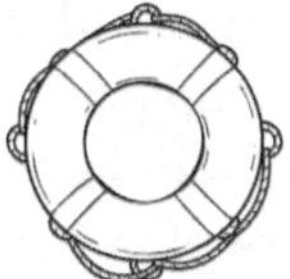

Grace once read an article about how honeybees were obsessive perfectionists at the micro level but not the macro level, and as she walked down the beach with her own Mr. Bee, she wondered if the same was true of him. He was certainly very hard on himself, focused on all the steps to achieve his goals, but a little sloppy sometimes in the execution. He seemed genuinely upset over his sharp words at the airport, and if she was being honest, she'd behaved just as thoughtlessly, and it ate at her. She knew a thing or two about being a perfectionist.

Now he was doing his best to rein it in, ignoring the angry glares from his neighbors and shaking off the bitter criticisms, until they reached a long stretch of quiet wilderness where he and Grace could pretend they were pirate castaways, alone and safe from the big wide world.

"It's disgustingly beautiful here," she sighed.

"Do you hate disgustingly beautiful places?" he asked.

"Absolutely. Almost as much as I hate disgustingly beautiful whisky distillers."

She peeked up at him to see his head kind of jerk to the side as he realized she was complimenting him, and she had to fight to smother a giggle that threatened to erupt.

It was unforgivably charming. How very rude.

As they walked, he pointed out the optimal tide pools for sighting crabs and the perfect spot to watch purple sandpipers forage mussels. Grace wasn't fussed about seeing crabs, and she wouldn't know a purple sandpiper if it pooped on her favorite sweater, but she liked the way his eyes lit up and his words flowed more freely when he talked about them.

"Alec and Eòghann taught me, and later, Teàrlach, to a fly a kite right along here," he confided. "And then I taught Elspeth."

"Is this the best beach in all of Barra for kite flying?"

"The very one."

Grace could well imagine them all as children, running wild and free, trying to coax a homemade kite to stay aloft in the brisk Hebridean breeze, their cheeks ruddy with chill and exercise—the same way Diego's face would redden as he sprinted back and forth across the soccer field.

"I can't believe he thought I cancelled my whole party because he couldn't be there. He was training for the actual World Cup, for god's sake. How self-centered does he think I am?"

"I don't reckon he'd think you'd do it now."

"He probably doesn't think I'd invite him now. Tell me the truth, Ryan," she said, stopping him and grabbing his hand impulsively. He closed his eyes for a second like he wished she hadn't touched him, so she dropped his hand but not the subject. "Did it ruin the World Cup for him?"

He shook his head. "He had a grand time. Except for the losing part."

She chuckled. That pretty much summed up how the whole family had felt.

"Any regrets? About cancelling it?"

Grace didn't have to think, though she wasn't sure why she answered at all. "The dress."

He grinned. "Really?"

"It's weird, I know. I was never much of a pretty dress kind of girl. Comfort over fashion, right?"

"Exactly how I feel about pretty dresses."

She elbowed him in the ribs and he darted sideways, letting her catch his hand again before he got away and sliding his fingers between hers.

For a second, she couldn't breathe. What had they been talking about?

"Were you Sssporty Spice?" Mr. Bee teased.

Right. The dress. "Not in the slightest. I tried to be. Up until D moved to Florida, all I wanted was to keep up with him and the boys. But I wasn't fast, and I wasn't coordinated. My soccer coaches probably assumed I was adopted. I think being bad at sports is what made me resent everything girly. Except for some reason that dress."

He looked at her with a faraway gaze, like he was picturing it based on the description in her book. She'd never told anyone those bits of her novel were true. It was unsettling to realize how much of her he'd figured out.

Pulling her hand out of his, Grace sat down on a nearby rock and took off her shoes. She rolled up her leggings, allowing her toes to burrow into the soft white sand, grounding her. She was here, in Scotland, all grown up. She wasn't fifteen years old navigating high school politics ahead of her quinceañera.

"I knew exactly what I wanted my dress to look like from the time I was eleven years old. I drew pictures of it obsessively, the same dress, over and over. Kids are weird."

"Do you still have them? Your drawings?"

She shook her head. "Part of me wishes I'd put one in the book, but I burned them all when I turned sixteen."

He frowned, probably fretting over the carbon emissions of

burning so many sheets of paper. "It was the inspiration for Maya's dress? In your novel?"

"Absolutely. I figured one of us ought to get to wear it, even if she was only fictional."

That look came over his face again, the one that made her want to hold his hand and never let go.

"I hate you never got to wear it."

Grace shrugged. "It was a lifetime ago. Literally half my life. I'm fine, I'm over it." She wasn't, but fake it 'til you make it, right?

He frowned again, which was more like it. Frowning was safe. "You're not though, are you?"

"I want to be."

He nodded like he understood and offered a hand to help her to her feet. When she took his palm once more, it was warm and strong, and she let go quickly. *This* was never going to happen.

"I caught my first newt behind that rock," he said, shoving both hands in his pockets and nodding towards the boulder she'd just been sitting on, which looked very much like any other on the beach.

"What, that exact rock?"

"Obviously."

"What did you do with it when you caught it?"

A mischievous grin spread across his face.

"Tell me."

"And lose any progress I've made? Not a chance."

"Progress?" she asked, teasing him by pronouncing it with a long-*O* sound as he did.

"Making you hate me less," he said, striding off down the beach, hands still in his pockets, but relaxed and devil-may-care.

"You couldn't possibly make me hate you less, so you might as well spill," she called, running across the sand to catch up.

That earned her a sideways quarter smile.

"First, I wrestled it to the ground like I was the Crocodile Hunter and it was the most massive croc to ever live."

"Of course you did. And then?"

"Then I left it in Caitriona's bed."

"You didn't!"

He nodded sheepishly. " 'Course I did."

She shoved him a little. "You monstrous little brat," she said, shaking her head.

"To be fair, she more than deserved it."

All Grace could do was shake her head some more.

"I made it up to her," he protested.

"A croc in her bed? How could you possibly?"

"I collected enough shells out here to make a necklace. And a wind chime. And to absolutely cover a mermaid castle."

"A mermaid castle?" Grace asked, delighted by the whimsy.

He nodded emphatically. "I ferreted out the finest cardboard on the island. Not flimsy cereal cartons, mind, the good ones for mailing all sorts."

"Of course."

"I taped them all together and covered the outside in sand and shells. 'Twas a right proper castle. Her Ariel doll lived there for years until the day wee Elspeth buried her at sea."

"She threw her in the ocean?"

"Toilet."

Grace burst out laughing. "Okay maybe I'm glad I only had an older brother."

Strolling along the beach with Bryan did wonders to clear Grace's head. She managed to hammer out two thousand words that afternoon before Wes came looking for her.

"I know, I know, you're behind schedule. But you do have to eat sometime," Wes whined. "And if you say, 'I'll eat when I'm dead,' I'll…"

"What?" Grace teased.

"I don't know. Kill you, probably."

"Well then spare the government an extradition order, because I'm actually… not behind for once. Let's eat."

Wesley's face brightened and then she gave Grace a sultry look. "I knew this island was going to be good for you."

Chapter Fourteen

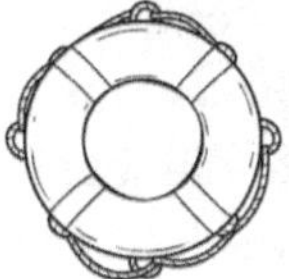

It took Bryan two more days to talk himself into tea with his family. He avoided it for a while by diving deep into solar manuals and wiring. Once the system was online and storing all the glorious summer sunshine, he disappeared down the beach to his favorite secluded hideaway, far from resentful neighbors, but also a safe distance from brown eyes and the witty retorts of American librarians who recognized dyslexia but didn't judge.

Judgment, he was used to. It was her empathy he didn't know how to handle.

Finally, though, Sunday afternoon arrived, and he couldn't hermit any longer. Like a prisoner bound for the gallows, he plodded with heavy, sand-covered boots back to the house. He showered and trimmed his beard, even ironed his best shirt: a paisley number that looked smart with charcoal corduroys. He selected an unopened bottle of Ardbeg Rionnagach and walked the long way through town to reach his parents' house, trying to relax his shoulders from their preemptive hunch.

It was only a family meal. He'd sat at the same table biting his tongue thousands of times.

Auntie Eilidh would throw barbs at random to keep them on their toes, and everyone else would be polite for the sake of the grandchildren. Maybe Eòghann would be there making wry faces at him across the table like old times. He could do this.

As he dragged himself up the ramp he and his grandad had built for Teàrlach all those years ago, Bryan reached reflexively in his pocket for the worry stone, but of course, the pocket was empty. He hadn't even picked up the airport fidget spinner, more's the pity. He could do this, but he'd be doing it alone.

He rang the bell, and two children he knew from photographs raced to the door with a sheep dog he didn't recognize at all.

"You're late," the girl, Sara, complained.

"Your ma said four o'clock sharp," Bryan told her. She just shrugged.

"You're 'posed to say, 'Fifteen years late,'" her little brother, Sam, told her.

Christ. They'd indoctrinated the children to hate him.

"Good one," he replied. "Your grandad teach you that?"

Sam, grinned and nodded.

"Gran said he wasn't allowed to say it himself," Sara volunteered.

"Your delivery was flawless," Bryan told Sam.

"Have you brought us a present?" Sara asked.

"No," he admitted, after double-checking his pockets to make sure he didn't have any sweeties hidden away. "Should I have?"

They both nodded angelically, with big green eyes that matched Cait's.

"I'll try to do better next time," he promised, and they stood aside to let him in.

"The prodigal son returns," his younger sister said from the hallway, where she leaned against the wall watching him meet his niece and nephew for the first time.

"El," he whispered, relieved to see a friendly face, and she opened her arms for him to sink into.

Elspeth was six years younger and had visited him a few times in Glasgow and a few more on Islay over the years, despite his abandoning her the moment he reached his majority. It was El who texted him pictures of the kids, because Ma never quite got the hang of smart phones and Cait said if he wanted to see them, he could join Facebook or come home. It was El who had let him know when Grandad was in a bad way.

She took his free hand and led him into the living room, where his father stood by the fireplace, the same tall, imposing figure Bryan remembered, and yet somehow smaller too.

"Is that my nephew?" Aunt Eilidh called from her corner rocking chair, one of the matched set Bryan's grandad had made just for her.

"It's me, Auntie," he said, turning to face her. He was stunned to find his blonde house guest kneeling at her side watching Eilidh mend Eòghann's jumper.

Wes waved at him awkwardly. So then was Grace here somewhere too?

"I hardly recognize you," Eilidh said.

"The whiskers?" he asked, running a hand over his face, which suddenly felt like teenage scruff instead of the distinguished look he'd been cultivating.

"No, the wrinkles, ha!" his aunt exclaimed, turning to wink at Wesley who looked completely bemused and unsure how to react.

"Those are all new, on account of my house guests," he teased for Wesley's benefit.

"How very dare!" Wes said, sitting up in mock outrage.

"He's always been the cheekiest of the lot," Aunt Eilidh confided to Wes. "About time you turned up. The girls in my sewing circle have been threatening to go down to Ladbrokes and bet their pensions on whether you'd come to see me before I'm in the ground."

His stomach twisted. Had they said the same about Grandad Mac? He should've come back sooner. He hadn't known how.

"I didn't realize you were ill, Auntie," he tried to tease.

"I'm strong as an ox, but we're all dying from the moment we're born, so they say."

"Well, I'm here now. Who won the odds?"

"I did," she said, smiling up at him, and when he bent to kiss her cheek, she patted his and murmured, "The whiskers suit you."

Bryan's heart flooded with warmth for the old lady. Maybe he could do this after all. "What do you think of the Warriors this season?"

"Absolute rubbish, the lot of them. But they'll win the league, you mark my word."

"They might, at that."

Bolstered, he straightened and offered a hand to his father who remained stoic by the fireplace. The great Cameron MacNeil.

His father accepted his hand, and just as Bryan let his guard relax a little, Cameron pointed to his beard and said, "Still pretending to be your grandfather, I see."

Bryan bit the inside of his cheek.

"He loved his little mini-me. He was probably with you on the day, instead of us, wherever you were."

"I was—"

"It's fine."

Biting down harder, Bryan refused to be sucked into an argument. He deserved the rebuke, and anyway, his tongue was tied in knots. He'd worn a beard for as long as he could grow one, not to cosplay as his grandad but as a mask to hide behind. If it made him look like his grandad, well, that was genetics, wasn't it?

Elspeth pressed a bottle of Belhaven's Best into Bryan's free hand, reminding him of the whisky. Robotically he offered the Rionnagach to his father, who accepted it with a quick nod and set it aside.

"Is that my wean?" his mother called, stepping out of the kitchen and wiping her hands on her apron, and Christ, but she looked tinier and older than he remembered, despite El's pictures.

"You came," Cait said from over her mother's shoulder, as Ma pulled him into a hug.

"Told you I would," he mumbled, as Grace peeked out from behind Cait mouthing *sorry*, but he was folded in his mother's arms and anyway, he'd pretty well gotten over the shock of having dinner with Grace and Wesley the minute his dad started in on him.

"I hope you're hungry," his mother said. "I've finally perfected the beef Wellington."

Bryan's jaw clenched, and he caught Elspeth's nervous glance. They'd forgotten he was vegetarian, had been since the age of eight, and they all just… forgot. Or didn't care.

The children were called to wash up, and Aunt Eilidh was heaved from her chair, and everyone gathered around the too-small dining table which had been overflowing with family for as long as he'd been alive. Muscle memory took Bryan to the spot between his mother and Cait, where Sam was pulling out the chair.

"I sit here," his nephew informed him, so Bryan squeezed in on the other side, between his aunt and little sister, across from Grace, in an uncomfortable folding chair because he was neither family nor company.

He picked up his napkin as one by one the others bowed their heads.

Oh hell.

Bryan closed his eyes, and his father began a safe enough prayer of thanks for the food and for Sara getting over her recent cold and for their guests all the way from Tennessee. But he couldn't just leave well enough alone. No, not Cameron MacNeil.

"Thank you also for loved ones near and far, especially the

return of our beloved son, brother, nephew, and uncle. Guide Ryan's"—Bryan flinched—"endeavors, wherever they may take him. Grant him the wisdom, humility, and strength to finish what he's begun."

Bryan's face burned. He couldn't say whether it was his father's confidence he would fail or the smell of the beef turning his stomach. His fingers found his pocket, before they remembered he'd lost the worry stone, so they worried the side of his corduroys instead, as he breathed through his mouth.

"What's this I hear about you tearing down Robbie's house?" Great Aunt Eilidh asked, passing Bryan the potatoes as soon as his father shut up.

"Not tearing it down, Auntie," he mumbled, glancing at Grace and then quickly away. Bad enough he had to be here at all, but with her and Wes to bear witness… he might take back the bottle of Rionnagach and down the whole thing in one sitting.

"That's what I heard from Nellie Combe down at the shops."

"You know Nellie Combe's a mean old telltale," Elspeth interceded.

"What is your plan, then?" Cameron asked, fixing Bryan with his steady gaze. "Assuming you have one."

"Renovation," was all he could manage. He focused on scooping up potatoes and root veg.

"Pass the gravy to your uncle," his mother whispered to Sara, who handed him the dish which he immediately passed off to his aunt.

"Renovation, my eye," Caitriona grumbled. "The cottage is in perfect condition. Tell me, is there a thing lacking?" she added, turning to Wesley and Grace, trying to pull them into the squabble.

"Cait," his mother begged.

"Is there?"

"Solar power?" Wes suggested timidly.

"A tub?" Grace asked, eyes wide like a deer in headlights.

Cait's jaw dropped. "Has he put you to work again? Can you all believe he put the guests to work? I found this one on the roof just a few days ago. I hope your insurance covers falls, Ry."

"Pass your uncle a Wellington," his mother begged Sam.

"I'm fine, really," Bryan said, and she looked at his half-empty plate in surprise.

Elspeth glanced between them, then quickly away, and his mother's face turned stricken. "Never say you're still vegetarian?" she whispered.

"It's all right, Ma. The veg is grand."

"You said it was a phase," she said accusingly to Cameron. "Is that why you look so tired?"

"No."

"You know, your hero the Crocodile Hunter ate meat. I looked it up once," his father crowed.

"Okay," Bryan replied.

"You could've said something, Ry. Do you want me to make you some omelet?" Cait offered with a sheepish look for having forgotten.

"No, really, the tatties are fine," he said. The last thing he wanted was to drag this meal out any longer.

"Pass him a Wellington, Sam," his father said. "He can eat the mushroom."

Sam's face instantly fell into a look of disgust, the same as Bryan felt at the thought of scraping out the layer of beef-soaked veg.

"He'll eat the mushroom," his mother whispered in shock.

"Omelet's no trouble," Cait said, pushing her chair back with such force that it obviously *was* trouble.

"Cait!" he snapped, freezing her in place. "I don't want omelet."

"Can I have omelet?" Sam asked brightly.

"No," Cait replied sharply, dropping back to her chair. "Granny spent all day cooking this feast and you'll eat every bite."

"Don't like mushroom," the boy grumbled.

"This crust is so flaky," Grace jumped in before Cait could start really yelling at her son. "How do you get it so crisp?" she asked.

"That'll be the egg brushed on the outside of the pastry," his mother answered, relieved by the change of topic.

"Oh, of course," Grace said. "I always forget the egg."

"It has egg on it?" Sara whined.

"It's so delicious," Wes raved. "Is it a local cow?"

"So, are you back for good then?" Cameron demanded, ending further discussion of animal products.

"That's the idea," Bryan said, though right now he'd prefer the floor to open up and swallow him forever.

Cameron nodded. "Dàibhidh down at the hardware store's hiring. I imagine you'll need a job."

Bryan didn't answer. He couldn't think of a single response that wouldn't sound like a stammering ten-year-old.

"I don't think the hardware store's right for him," Aunt Eilidh volunteered.

"Well, he's got to do something. Selling Da's house won't bring in much, and with no degree and no trade to fall back on he'll have to take what he can get."

"I've a trade," Bryan muttered.

"You're selling the house?" Elspeth asked.

"No."

"I'll buy it from you," Cait said. "Right now, before you wreck it any further. How much do you want?"

"It's not for s-sale."

"If Grandad wanted you to have it, he'd have given it to you," Elspeth told Cait. "But I do hate the idea of selling it."

"I'm not," Bryan insisted. How could he explain what the old house had meant to him over the years? It was the place he ran to after every argument from the age of six to sixteen. Then Teàrlach had returned from Glasgow with his wheelchair, and

Bryan made himself stop running away—up until he ran away for good.

"Do you know football, Uncle Ry?" Sam asked. "We need a new athletics teacher."

"I'd prefer one who taught us tumbling," Sara griped.

"Football sounds more up Uncle Eòghann's alley," Bryan said, although he'd picked up quite a bit from Diego.

"Eòghann's got a job," his father said.

"Really, Cameron," Ma begged.

"It's not a judgment, it's a fact."

"For Christ's sake, I'm going to open a distillery," Bryan exclaimed, and everyone fell silent.

Then Grace jumped up, and suddenly everyone was staring at her instead of Bryan.

"I just remembered. I left a candle burning! I'm so sorry, thank you so much for a… lovely dinner. But I could never forgive myself if my stupid candle burned down your ancestral cottage."

She gave Wes a look, and the blonde eyed her barely touched Wellington, then picked the whole thing up in her hand. "I better go with her. She's the clumsiest person when she's in a hurry. Be a shame to knock the candle over trying to blow it out," she finished pathetically.

"Maybe we'll see you at the Shakespeare later," Grace told Elspeth.

"I want to go to the Shakespeare!" Sara exclaimed.

"You wouldn't like it," Cait told her daughter through gritted teeth as the American Invasion scurried out of Bryan's childhood home. That was one way of putting him out of his misery, he supposed.

Everyone sat in stunned silence for a moment, and then Sam picked up his Wellington in his hands and prepared to take a big bite like it was a sandwich.

"Absolutely not," Cait told him.

"She did it!"

"She's American," his sister snarled.

Sam wasn't the least bit mollified, but he slapped his food down and picked up the fork.

"So, a distillery," Elspeth said brightly.

"We have a distillery," Cameron replied, setting down his silverware.

"Islay has nine," Bryan said.

"Islay's ten times the size of Barra, so by your logic, we're all set."

"Are you going to put the distillery in Grandad's house?" Elspeth asked.

"The council would never approve it," Cameron scoffed.

"Wasn't gonna."

"Where, then?" Cait demanded.

"S-somewhere else."

"So this whole idea is more aspirational than anything." Cameron nodded like he'd suspected it all along.

This was a mistake. Bryan had known from the moment he accepted the invitation. Whoever said you can't go home again wasn't kidding. He clenched his jaw tight and pushed the potatoes around on his plate.

"It's good to have dreams," his mother said softly.

"Not at thirty-five," his father argued.

"I dreamed all my teeth fell out," Sara volunteered.

"I assume family will get to drink for free?" Auntie Eilidh asked.

"He's lying," Cait said.

"Why d'you assume he's lying? He's been working at Ardbeg for years," Elspeth jumped to his defense.

"Not about the whisky. About the house. Why would he buy other land for his whisky experiment when Grandad's place is right there, his for the taking?" she demanded, glaring daggers across the table at him. "Who would do that? He doesn't have that kind of capital even after selling the house. It doesn't make sense."

"I-I-I—" Bryan stammered.

"Capital!" his father scoffed. "That's a good point. How are you going to pay for this so-called distillery?"

"I—"

"Do you have any idea how much it will cost?"

"Let him speak, Cam," his mother insisted.

"I have a p-p-p— I know what I'm doing!" Bryan thundered.

Sara immediately burst into tears.

"Jesus, Ry, there's no need to yell," Caitriona scolded.

Bryan tried to relax his jaw and turned away from his sister. He took a deep breath, and then another, picturing his grandfather's worry stone between his fingers.

"Ma, thank you for tea. Auntie Eilidh, I'll give you all the free whisky you can drink."

With that, he stood up to leave.

"I made chocolate cake," his ma said helplessly.

"Give mine to S-S-Sara."

His niece looked up at him, tears instantly gone. He winked at her and stormed out of the house.

What an almighty unmitigated disaster.

Chapter Fifteen

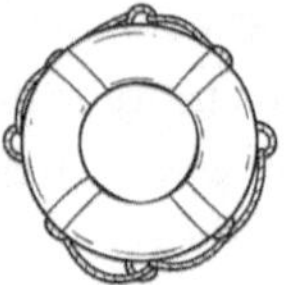

Of course, Grace had not left a candle burning, because who takes a random candle on vacation? She just couldn't stand to sit there another minute while Ryan died a thousand deaths.

"I don't get it," Wes said for about the hundredth time. "They're all so… nice. His dad seemed totally charming until he showed up."

"I don't know." Grace picked at a loose thread in the blanket they'd spread on the beach to watch *A Midsummer Night's Dream.* "There was an undercurrent the whole time." She didn't know them, but they'd all seemed on edge—his mother and Cait flitting around trying a bit too hard, his father putting on a mask every time he was pulled into conversation, Elspeth watchful and wary.

"An undercurrent? I guess," Wes said. "Hope they worked it out once we left."

Grace nodded. Hope their host hadn't high-tailed it back to the mainland. "No one can make you small quite like your family."

He'd reminded her of a lonely freshman, sitting miserably in his little folding chair, too low for the big dining room table. He looked young and vulnerable as he poked at the potatoes instead of reminding his mother he was vegetarian while everyone hammered him about the house.

Stubborn to the last, he kept glancing at her with a fierceness in his eyes, angry that she and Wes had encroached on the private family moment, daring her to join the public shaming.

"Gray, are you fretting about your Stoic Scot? Or your book?" Wes asked during intermission.

"My book obviously," Grace answered too quickly, and Wes raised an eyebrow. "You know how I get!"

"You're right," Wes conceded. "It's my fault for expecting a different outcome. But do you think Shakespeare worried this much?" she asked, gesturing at the oceanside stage.

"Probably?"

Wes shook her head. "He was too busy drinking and fornicating to worry this much. Maybe you should try it."

"You're right—about the worrying. I'm not sure you're right about Shakespeare."

"Agree to disagree. But?"

"But it's not that easy." *When I stop worrying about my new book problems, I start worrying about the landlord reading my old book and calling it brilliant, and what's that supposed to mean?*

Had anyone else ever called her words brilliant except maybe the Printz committee?

"It's not that easy," she said again. "I won an award…"

"Hell yeah, you did," Wes agreed.

"And I'm still not sure my parents take this 'book thing' "—she used air quotes—"seriously."

Wes blinked at her. "Ah… so dinner was a little triggering?"

Grace looked away. "I'm sorry I'm ruining your vacation," she said, nudging Wesley's shoulder.

"Hey, I'm the one who let old Auntie Eilidh con us into that fiasco back there."

"Maybe she thought if we were there, they'd all behave."

"I don't think that lady's behaved a day in her life," Wes snickered. "I want to be her when I grow up."

"Why *did* she invite us then?"

"Because I'm a delightful conversationalist."

Grace snorted. "You're a delightful something, all right."

"She probably wanted to study you like a specimen in a museum—you know, the rare and migrating writer who leaves her natural habitat only to bury herself in a stone cavern in a foreign land when she's on a deadline."

"Rude."

"You know what might help?"

"Help who?" Grace asked, already guessing where the conversation was headed.

"We could figure out plans for your birthday," Wes replied, catching her off guard.

Inwardly, Grace groaned. "You coming on this trip was all the gift I need."

"Great. Gift sorted. Where do you want to eat and how do you feel about those party cracker things they do over here?"

"Those are for Christmas."

"Fine. Shortbread or cranachan for dessert?"

"I don't know what cranachan is."

"Forget it. I have a better idea for dessert anyway."

"Oh?"

"You need to get laid."

Grace groaned and threw her jacket at her friend, who balled it up for a pillow and reclined back on the blanket.

"I'm just saying. Birthday bang could solve all your book problems."

"Again, I remind you, I write YA."

"Not everything's about research. It might help clear your head. Among other things."

"I hate you."

"I know. I'm the worst. How dare I care about your physical

needs more than you do," Wes agreed as Demetrius entered the stage pursued by Helena.

It wasn't Wesley's fault. She was a girl who loved love and didn't know all the gory details of Grace's hang-ups. She only knew it had been a long dry spell. And considering Wes had broken up with her last boyfriend when he proposed because he was—in her words—incapable of finding a clitoris with a flashlight, she couldn't possibly understand that Grace had less than zero desire to get laid.

All around them, the audience laughed at the antics onstage as characters pranced around their woodsy bacchanal hell-bent on doing just that. Why was midsummer's eponymous play also one of the horniest? It was starting to feel worse than high school.

And there it was, her book's theme: Maya, surrounded by sex-obsessed teenagers, while she tried to sort out love and lust and what to do about the boy next door.

Grace itched to take out her phone and jot down the idea before she forgot it, but the problem with the Hebrides in summer was that this play was being performed in broad daylight, and it would be the height of rudeness. If only she'd brought a little notebook, she could pretend to be a theater critic or something.

Instead, she reached in her pocket, her fingers closing around the colorful worry stone. She turned it and turned it, tracing the letters on its soft, cool surface, spelling out her notes to commit them to muscle memory. She would write it all down, quick and dirty, as soon as they got home.

Or, back to the house, rather. *His* home.

Damn it. Now she was thinking about him again.

She kept on twisting the stone, pretending to pay the slightest attention to Shakespeare.

"Want to stop at the pub?" Wes asked as they neared the house an hour later. She was probably starving despite having taken her beef Wellington with her and devouring it before the second act.

"I'm sorry, but I—"

"Have to write. I knew better than to ask."

"Please don't ever stop asking," Grace begged, putting her key in the front door. "Seriously, don't."

It was one of the things she loved most about her friend, that she hadn't given up trying to force Grace to have fun.

Wes grinned at her, then jumped at the sound of an earsplitting crash.

They looked at each other with eyes the size of frisbees, then dashed inside to find their host had set up a pair of support posts jacked clear to the ceiling and was now attacking the back stone wall with a sledgehammer.

"Oh shit," Wes said. "I guess dinner didn't get better."

"Ryan?" Grace asked cautiously between hits. "Is everything okay?"

"My name"—WHAM—"is not"—WHAM—"Ryan." WHAM! WHAM! WHAM!

Shit. She'd never asked, since literally everyone called him Ryan except the heckler at karaoke.

WHAM.

"Do you think you could—"

WHAM.

"Stop hitting the wall?"

He stopped himself mid-swing and turned, swaying off balance. "Were you trying to write? I didn't think you were home."

His face was red, but he was eerily calm, despite the sledgehammer and cracking stone.

"Do you want to talk about it?" Grace asked.

"Nothing to talk about. This was next on the list."

She glanced at her watch. It was nine p.m., despite the bright light outside.

"Lùcas is going to be really bummed you started without him," Wes interjected.

Grace put a gentle hand on his arm, so he let the hammer slide to the floor.

"Everyone calls you Ryan…"

He flinched, and this time Grace didn't see annoyance, she saw pain.

"Everyone except that guy at karaoke. He called you—"

"B-B-B-Bryan," he imitated, his face set like stone.

"I thought you had some kind of crazy alter ego as a DJ."

"No. I had a…" His throat contracted, and his mouth tightened into a grimace. He took a breath. "I have a s-stammer."

In that moment he looked like such an ashamed little boy with a pasted-on beard, and every punched *B* and *P* came flooding back to Grace.

"Well, if Grace loses her hearing, we can be the perfect trio," Wes piped up. "Hear no evil, see no evil…"

"So they all call you Ryan because—"

"Had trouble with my *B*'s."

"That's so fucked up," Wes said, and when they both turned to her, she added, "I'm going to go pee," and made herself scarce.

Grace had a weird urge to reach out and hug the man before her. She stuck her hand in her pocket to twirl the worry stone instead. "Why didn't you tell me I was calling you by the wrong name all week?"

He took a deep breath and huffed it back out. "Much the same reason you didn't tell Caitriona you go by Rios and we didn't tell Wes my cousin Eòghann isn't a priest."

Her heart squeezed a little bit. She was putting together more and more of a picture about why he left and why he stayed away so long. Casting around for the right thing to say, she finally landed on, "Family can be the worst, can't they?"

He huffed again, half laughing. "Aye, well, me too."

She laughed. "Oh definitely. You're at the top of my worst list. Before Putin. Before Sister Mary Agnes, even."

"Christ. There truly is no hope for me then."

They were silent for a moment, taking up a little too much of each other's space. Where was Wes? Grace twisted the worry stone.

"I take it dinner didn't improve?"

"I wish you hadn't witnessed that."

Grace wanted to say she was sorry he had to experience it, and especially sorry there were witnesses. "Is it just the reno?" she asked.

He shook his head. "It's everything. Going away but not to uni. Keeping away for years on end. Missing Grandad's wake, when they think *I* was his favorite."

He frowned, fighting off tears, it looked like.

"Well… fuck 'em," she said, because it was all she could think of.

He burst out laughing. Then he sighed. "I didn't intend to tell them about the distillery, not until I know Jules is all in. Didn't want to have to face them if I fail."

"Then I guess you can't fail, Bryan," Grace said, and that name sounded right. It fit Mr. Bee in a way *Ryan* never had.

He nodded and shook his head at the same time, still scowling.

"You want to go to the pub, Bryan? I was going to write, but I don't have to."

"No. I had an idea in mind for the two of you—before every-thing went to hell," he added, eyeing the wall. "Give me ten minutes to clean up?"

He was covered in plaster dust, and when Grace raised her eyebrows, he looked around sheepishly. "Maybe twenty."

WHILE BRYAN SHOWERED, GRACE TOOK A MOMENT TO JOT DOWN her ideas from the intermission.

Bryan.

God, how embarrassing. She'd been calling him by an insulting childhood nickname for over a week now. She thought about telling him he could taunt her with *Gordita Gracie* as her penance, but she couldn't quite bring herself to do it.

"Everything okay with our Stoic Scot?" Wes finally asked.

"Why are families so adept at making the good things bad?"

"Maybe I'm not the best person to answer that."

"Oh my god, I'm so sorry," Grace said.

Now her friend's eyes narrowed. "Why?"

"Well. Because. You…"

"I am mature enough to realize that having a shit dad might sometimes be worse than losing an okay one. I only meant, you know, I was six when my dad deployed, eight and a half when he died, my mom hasn't been super present, but she hasn't ruined anything. Just, you guys are my family. So please don't ruin anything."

Grace grabbed her friend and hugged her tight, squeezing into the hug every ounce of the *ditto* that would sound trite if she said it out loud.

There was a knock at the door, and Bryan called, "Y'all ready?" affecting a terrible Southern accent.

"That ruined it," Grace said.

"Definitely," Wes laughed before hollering back, "Hell yeah, we're ready," in a far more Southern accent than Grace considered strictly necessary.

"You don't have any idea what he's planning," Grace hissed.

"I'd be up for anything with that man. And so should you."

Grace rolled her eyes and stomped past her friend to the door.

"So, what's the big surprise, Bryan?" she asked, aware that using his correct name as often as possible was just making it weird instead of making up for the past.

In the kitchen, a rock playlist droned softly from a Bluetooth speaker, and Bryan stood on the opposite side of the counter like a bartender with his cuffs turned up just enough for the bee tattoo to peek out. What magic in his shower had transformed him from an angry bear into this suave host?

"Welcome." He gestured them to the two stools he had pulled up to the bar, and a charcuterie board he'd prepared over to the side. "Ssstill or sparkling?" he asked, holding up a fancy bottle of water in each hand.

"Sparkling, please," Wes trilled. "I'm all about those bubbles."

"Wise lady." Bryan set down the bottle and two tumblers.

"Thanks, Bryan," Grace said, unable to stop overusing his name. She needed to say something rude quick to put them back on equal footing.

His eyes flicked to hers. "You're welcome, Rios," he said before she could think of anything, and it made her tummy do a little somersault.

"Aren't you joining us?" Wes asked, digging into the mouth-watering slices of meat and cheese and briny olives. "I mean, not this part, obviously," she added, mouth full as she pointed to the meat.

"No, this is all for you. Fill up, and then I have a s-special treat."

"This isn't the treat?" Grace asked.

"This is an ordinary treat, not a special one."

"Oh! We like special treats, don't we Gray?"

"We sure do, Wes."

"Thank you, Bryan," Wes teased.

"Thank you, Bryan," Grace echoed, and she could see the tops of his cheeks redden above his beard.

Once they put a good dent in the charcuterie, he produced two plaid bandanas folded up like blindfolds. Wesley's eyebrows shot up as she darted a look back and forth between Grace and their host, her filthy mind going places Grace didn't want to imagine.

"Go on," Bryan prompted when neither of them moved.

"Mr. MacNeil, just what are you proposing?" Wes asked saucily as she reached for a blue and green blindfold, and if he'd proposed a threesome, Grace was pretty sure Wes would say yes on the spot.

Vacation is for food and orgasms. And they'd already eaten food. Her pulse sped up, preparing to take flight.

Bryan looked down at the bandanas as though surprised by their hesitation. "Taste test," he said, like the obtuse male specimen that he was.

"It's not haggis, is it?" Wes asked, wrinkling her nose.

"Different kinds of cheese straws?" Grace asked, daring to be hopeful.

"Neither," he beamed. "It's whisky."

Wes and Grace exchanged uncertain glances.

"I'm game," Wes said. "But why the blindfolds? We don't know anything about Scotch anyway."

"The color can alter your… perception of the flavor," he said, offering the other bandana to Grace. "And it's more fun."

She didn't really want to taste more whisky. Wasn't it all the same? But she had an inkling of what he was trying to do for Wes, and it was unbearably kind. He was making it damned hard for her to dislike him.

So she took the plaid and tied it around her eyes.

"If you prefer not to s-s-swallow"—Grace's face burned beneath her bandana. Was she the only one hearing innuendo in every other word? Bryan went on without missing a beat—"I'll forgive you for using this mug," he said, putting Grace's hand on a ceramic handle, and she felt a tiny bit better, if rattled by the slight frisson running up her arm to her flushed cheeks.

She listened carefully as he uncorked a bottle and poured two splashes before placing one gently in her hands, tickling her palm ever so slightly as he pulled away. The glass wasn't a straight-sided tumbler, but rounder and tapered, and her tingling hand almost knocked it over.

"The Glencairn glass," he rumbled softly in that deep Scottish burr, as he covered her hand to help steady it, "is designed to let you give the dram a nice whirl, opening the nose. What do you smell?"

Grace leaned down to give it a sniff. At first, she was hit by the strong scent of alcohol, but then she realized there was a whole rich tapestry behind it.

"Barbecue smoke?" Wes asked.

"Aye, that'll be the peat."

"And something sweet. Sort of a peppery chocolate. Do you smell that, Gray?"

"I smell Band-Aids in the ocean," Grace said, feeling like she was letting them both down.

"Well done," Bryan laughed. "Now taste it. Hold it on your tongue and roll it for a moment."

When Grace swallowed, it burned all the way down, allowing her to trace its path to her stomach by the warmth it left behind.

"Bacon," Wes gasped. "Sweet, smoky bacon!"

"It really does taste like a campfire," Grace agreed, trying not to cough. "But also… cinnamon?"

"Yes! Cinnamon vanilla toffee," Wes agreed.

"Is it a little bit fruity? Is there fruit in whisky?" Grace asked.

"Or like… olive brine?" Wesley suggested. "What is this? It's like a symphony on my tongue."

"It's not what I expected, for sure," Grace agreed.

"Very good. Is this really your first time?" Bryan asked, and

Grace burned at the innuendo, intentional or not. "'Tis called Ardbeg Rionnagach, from the Isle of Islay, renowned for its sssmoky, peated drams."

"I've never tasted anything like it," Wes said with wonder.

Grace thought maybe she had, the other night when she and Bryan had shared a drink on the back patio, but if so, she hadn't fully appreciated it, and she didn't want to embarrass herself by asking in case it was a different whisky entirely. Across the bar, she could almost feel him puffing up with pride, and she thought maybe she understood a little better why he wanted to open a distillery.

"If you like, here's some chocolate to bring out different notes," he said, handing Grace a quarter-sized foil-wrapped candy. "And your water's just there."

"Wow, just wow," Wes said. "Oh, that's good chocolate too."

"Toast for a cleanser," he offered.

"There's more?" Wes asked like an awe-struck little kid at Christmas.

"Oh, aye, a whole tour. We're leaving the Islands and on to the Highlands next."

He poured again, and this time there was no smoke. It was sweeter, fruitier, creamier.

"Reminds me of Kentucky bourbon," Wes said. "But I like this more."

"Glengoyne 10," Bryan told them. "A few drops of water can change the flavor, too."

"Mary mixed her whisky with water in *Downton Abbey*," Grace murmured.

"That's 'cause Michelle Dockery likes hers that way," he said.

"Wait, what?" Grace asked.

"I was an extra a few times, it's not important. May I add a drop of water to yours?" he asked, brushing her fingers as he came near with the water.

"Sure," she managed, hiding her breathlessness in the tulip-shaped glass until he moved away. "Now I taste almonds," she observed.

"Oh, me too," Wes agreed.

"You're quite good at this game," Bryan told them, and Grace thought she could bask in the glow of his praise forever, no matter if he was a braggy-Mac-*I-met-Lady-Mary-when-I-was-an-extra*-braggerson.

"Ready for the next?" he asked.

"Yes, please," Wes said enthusiastically.

"How many are there?" Grace asked, trying not to feel alarmed by the warmth spreading through her belly and out her limbs. It was only a few sips of each, and they were taking their time, but she didn't trust her own decision making after hard liquor.

"Thought we'd do five, one for each region."

"Perfect," Wes agreed.

Grace could actually feel her own smile freeze in place as panic welled up inside her. "Are you trying to get us drunk, MacNeil?"

"Use the mug if you like," he said evenly.

"Don't you dare spit out good booze, Gray," Wes chided. "We're on vacation!"

Beneath her blindfold, Grace rolled her eyes, but if he wanted to get her drunk, he wouldn't have given her the mug. She took a breath and tried to relax.

"Don't roll your eyes at me, either," Wes added.

"How did you—"

"I could hear them!"

Bryan chuckled, and Grace shoved a bite of bread in her mouth to keep from saying something rude. Why was it the best bread she'd ever eaten?

"What's next?" Wes asked.

"Macallan 12," he said, unstoppering the bottle with a satisfying pop.

"What does the number mean?" Wes asked.

"Years aged. This is a Speyside, from the Spey River in the northeast. Might remind you of a Christmas pudding."

Grace was hyperaware as he leaned forward to splash the Speyside in her glass, a wave of his own fresh sandalwood scent washing over her and leaving her heady. When his shadow backed away without taking his sandalwood with him, she inhaled deeply into her glass to settle her nerves. The dram did sort of smell like Christmas.

"Fruity," Wes observed.

"Aye. You might catch a hint of ginger, as well."

Grace tasted it, letting the spicy flavor roll around her tongue and burn its way down her throat. Either she was adjusting to the liquor, or this one was very smooth.

"I like it," Wes declared. "If that's meant to remind me of Christmas pudding, I'll have to try one."

"Aye? The winner, is it?"

"Oh, I don't know. I should probably go back and sample them all again."

Bryan didn't reply, just pushed the bread and chocolates closer to them.

"You're smiling," Wes told him. "I can hear it in your breath, but I'm not kidding. I only ever mixed Jack with Coke to get drunk at parties, aside from my grandma's mint juleps."

"Ah, the infamous mint julep," Bryan replied, and now Grace could hear his amused smile too.

"Have you ever tried one?" Wesley asked.

"Afraid not."

"It's gross," Grace said, and then felt them both turn towards her. "What? Steeplechase was like the highlight of my mom's whole year."

"She has an unsophisticated palate," Wes told Bryan.

"Clearly," he agreed.

"I... don't hate these!"

Bryan barked out a laugh that warmed her almost as much as the whisky. She liked the way his laughs seemed to burst out of him like he was so unaccustomed to it they even caught him by surprise. She also liked being at least partially responsible for it. Laughter looked—and sounded—good on him.

"Maybe that will be my distillery's tagline. *Finnbar. You won't hate it.*"

"It's not the worst slogan," Grace said, a little sheepish. She didn't hate it. In fact, she was enjoying herself more than she ought to be.

"Not the worst is exactly what I was going for. And for the record, these are far above to any bourbon. No offense."

Wes snorted, but Grace found herself grinning for no reason.

"What is it you like so much about whisky?" she asked, emboldened by the alcohol and the blindfold. Somehow, despite making her feel more vulnerable, she also found it easier to talk to him.

His clothes rustled, and Grace could picture him shrugging his shoulders practically up to his ears.

"Where else can you find a whole industry known worldwide by a common name unless it comes from one country? There's whisky, and then there's Scotch."

Grace tried to think of another example, but cheddar wasn't quite the same.

"A million different ways to make it, and all of them ours. Every drop is infused with history and culture, tradition and innovation, perseverance and love. Maybe a little Celtic alchemy."

"Wow," Wes said. "And Finnbar?"

"Patron saint of the island."

Grace nodded. Bryan's passionate homage to his country's national drink made her throat feel thick, and she took a long gulp of fizzy water.

"Ready for more?" he asked.

Whisky she could take or leave, but hearing him wax poetic in his low, growly burr? More of that, please. All day, every day.

He poured a lowland next. "You mentioned bourbon. This Auchentoshan American Oak was aged in bourbon casks."

"That's where the sweetness comes from?" Wes asked. "I swear I taste coconut cream."

Grace was starting to think maybe they all just tasted the same, or maybe like whatever you were hungry for, but she enjoyed listening to the game enough to play along.

"Coconut, definitely," she agreed.

They moved on to the final selection, a ten-year-old Campbeltown called Springbank, which Bryan said was a mix of a little of everything: bourbon casks and sherry casks, and light peat for a sweet, smoky finish.

It was pretty good, and not just because she was tipsy.

"Ohhh, I like this one," Wes gushed. "You saved the best for last."

"Aye? A winner after all?"

"One hundred percent."

"What about you?" he asked, handing Grace some more chocolate, brushing his fingers against hers once more in a way that made the heat in her stomach spread out like fireworks through her whole body.

"This one was nice. But I think the first was my favorite. Which is yours?"

"Mine?" he rasped, in a tone that sounded surprised.

Grace pushed the blindfold up and blinked at him in the sudden brightness.

"Surely one of them's your favorite?"

"Ah," he said, relaxing a little.

After being deprived of her vision for the past little while, everything about him just seemed so much more—more vibrant, more scruffy, more handsome, more hungry.

"Impossible to choose," he said.

"Was it your favorite from each region?" Wes asked, still blindfolded and sniffing each empty glass again in turn.

"Aye."

"What's your favorite region?" she asked.

"Islay. But I may be… biased."

Grace noticed his throat working hard to produce the word with barely a hitch.

"Biased?" Wes asked.

Bryan nodded, though she was still blindfolded and he was staring at Grace. "I worked under a master distiller there the last ten years. The Rionnagach was mine."

"Shut up!" Now Wes ripped off her blindfold as both she and Grace stared at him, dumbfounded, and his cheeks turned scarlet as heat swept down his throat and up to the tips of his ears.

"Yours?" Grace repeated. "Like you made it?"

He nodded shyly.

"Let me taste it again," Wes demanded, and he poured her another tiny dram.

She closed her eyes and savored it. "I was wrong," she finally said. "The Campbeltown was exceptional, but this campfire shit is where it's at. Final answer."

Bryan rolled his eyes at her a little, but he was obviously bursting with pride.

"You saved the best for first," Grace agreed. "I don't know how you even begin to create something like this."

His blush deepened, and he studied the floor. "You create whole worlds," he mumbled. "This is just ssscience."

Chapter Sixteen

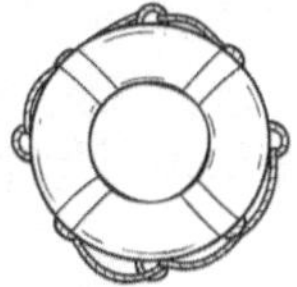

She was gazing at Bryan in a way that made his chest feel tight and his eyes sort of sweaty, while his tongue tied itself in knots and clogged his throat. He nudged the charcuterie board closer to his guests so they could soak up some of the whisky.

"This pancetta is really amazing," Wes said, oblivious to the electricity swirling around the kitchen. "I respect your choices, but you're missing out."

"I'll let Eòghann know you approve."

Her head shot up at the mention of his cousin, but then she looked back down, suddenly entirely focused on the cheddar. "Eòghann picked it out?"

"I rely on him to choose all my meats"—he grimaced at the innuendo hanging in the air—"when the occasion calls for it."

"That's nice of him," she mumbled, her cheeks turning pink. Had she figured out his cousin wasn't a priest yet?

"Really nice," Grace agreed, eyeing her friend in a way that suggested she had not.

"That's Eòghann. Kindness to a fault. Unlike me."

"Agreed. You're not nice at all," Grace said. "This whole thing"

—she gestured at the empty whisky glasses and half-eaten food tray—"incredibly rude."

"So rude," Wes agreed. "How am I supposed to go back to drinking beer and appletinis now?"

"A thousand apologies," Bryan said, though he wasn't the least bit sorry.

"Seriously." She offered him a shy smile. "Thanks for the sensory overload."

"I'll give you one to take home," he promised, and she clapped her hands giddily.

"You going to stay up and write?" she asked Grace, unfolding herself from her stool and stretching languidly.

"Depends. You going to bed?"

"I'm going to get *in* bed."

The two shared a look laden with meaning that Bryan couldn't unpack.

"I'm probably too tipsy to write, but I'll stay up awhile."

"I was going to make a fire," Bryan told Grace. "You're welcome to join me if you won't be too cold."

The Americans continued to stare at each other.

"A campfire sounds perfect," Grace finally said.

"Grand," Bryan said, a little too loudly for a man trying to play it cool.

"Grand," Grace replied.

"Grand," Wes agreed.

Grief was a cunning devil, sneaking up to slap you sideways when you least expected it. The most mundane tasks could knock you down flat if you weren't careful. Laying a fire in his grandad's old sand pit brought another wave of memories flooding back, and all Bryan could do was kneel there and breathe through it, holding onto the kindling for dear life and hoping Grace didn't notice before he escaped the undertow.

He should've been here. Should have come home sooner. All those nights pouring out plans over FaceTime, but he could have told Grandad Mac in person while sharing a dram around the fire. He could have made sure the old man was warm, breathed in his tobacco scent, and basked in the musical tones of laughter that a phone could never quite reproduce.

"I still can't get over how light it is this late," Grace said, crashing into his melancholy, throwing a life preserver of distraction around his chest.

Bryan cleared his throat and added some biochar to make the wood smoke. "Aye. Reckon it must be unsettling if you're not accustomed. Have you had trouble sleeping?"

"No more than usual. You were right, the curtains are good."

He nodded, dragging a pair of chairs from the patio to the pit.

"Should we roast marshmallows?" she asked as he reached for a box of matches.

Bryan shook his head. "I ought to have warned you. I'm testing an eco-friendly alternative to peat. It'll be a touch smoky."

Grace shrugged, so he lit the fire.

It smoked all right, almost immediately, and the smell was godawful. Like ten thousand dirty athletic socks and old wet dog and food-turned-science-experiment in the back of the fridge.

"Is that how it's supposed to—"

"No."

He dumped a bucket of sand over the whole thing, extinguishing the flame, but the rancid smoke still hung heavy in the air.

"Come on," he grumbled, grabbing the hand not being used to cover her face and practically dragging her back to the porch.

"The chairs?"

"Leave them," he coughed.

Fortunately, the porch was downwind tonight, and the smoke

didn't quite reach it. He collapsed onto the loveseat, pulling her down beside him, coughing and rubbing his burning eyes. Whisky without smoke was like sweets without sugar. If he couldn't find a sustainable biochar that didn't smell like absolute arse, he'd be done before he got started.

"What was that?"

"An effective experiment demonstrating I've not yet found a replacement for peat."

She giggled, and it was like all the sharp, tiny bubbles in her sparkling water were forcing their way to the surface.

"Funny, is it?" Had he stammered without realizing? Mixed up his words? He tried to play them back in his head, but her laugh was too distracting. He couldn't recall precisely what he'd said.

"I love how you spin it. Not a corpse flower–scented mistake, just testing a hypothesis to rule out a potential solution."

Flames licked up the back of his neck. She probably didn't mean anything by it, but calling it *spin* made him think of his father.

"That's how experiments work. 'Course I'd rather it didn't reek," he said archly. "Hopefully the next won't."

She sobered. "Suppose I could use that excuse?"

He bristled again at the word *excuse* but focused on the purplish evening sky. "How d'you mean?"

"I haven't failed to write my book. I've just written a million words that aren't the right ones. Not that I've written anything close to a million words."

Bryan frowned. Was that what he sounded like to his family?

"You could've brought out your laptop," he snapped, not meaning to sound so testy.

"Is there an outlet?" she asked, squirming around on the seat so her arse brushed against his thigh, sending tremors of heat straight to his groin.

He crossed his legs and cleared his throat. "No."

"Then there's no point. It needs charging."

"Ah."

She studied him a moment, and he knew his face was scrunched up in a resting bastard face, but he couldn't seem to relax it.

"Thank you," she said, almost uncertainly. "For what you did tonight."

And that did it. Those words were all it took to finally ease the knot in his brow and loosen the one in his throat. "My... pleasure."

"Was it true? About the color altering your perception of the flavor?"

" 'Course. What do you imagine a dark whisky tastes like?"

"Strong and smoky?"

"And a light one?"

"Smooth and fruity."

"Exactly. Total bollocks. The color comes from the aging cask. It's often enhanced for aesthetics."

She scoffed.

"You think I'm lying?"

"I don't. It sounds like something a company would do."

"Folk want an eye-catching dram as well as a tasty one."

She watched him for a moment, a little too intently, and his scalp prickled.

"Was it your grandfather who taught you to love it?"

"Not really. But he was damn chuffed when I took the apprenticeship. He crowed about it to everyone he met and made sure I knew it too. Quit drinking Laphroaig in favor of Ardbeg from that day on." He smiled to think of those phone calls, Grandad Mac so eager to hear every detail about the still and all.

"I'm sorry you lost him," she said. "I lost my abuela not long after Diego left home." Her voice was thick and low with the weight of her own sadness, and it shouldn't have done funny things to his belly, but it did.

"To play for Celtic, you mean?"

She shook her head. "He went to Florida first. A sort of soccer academy there. They did take him to Scotland for some kind of camp, though. That's how Celtic knew about him when he went to UNC."

"That's when he met Teàrlach."

Her eyes went wide. "Before Celtic?"

"Aye. Hurt his wrist, I think? Met Teàrlach in hospital."

She shook her head. "What are the odds?"

"You missed him. When he left home?" If it was that long ago, Diego would've been a teenager, and Grace just a kid, maybe no older than Elspeth had been when he left Barra.

"Every second of every day. It's crazy to think how close we used to be."

"Used to?" His heart clenched.

"If I told him how much I missed him, he might have given up the game and come home. It was easier to just… stop talking. By the time I came over for his wedding, he was a stranger."

"Ah. I'm familiar."

She looked at him curiously. For someone who spoke as little as possible, around her, he sure couldn't seem to shut up.

"Didn't talk to Eòghann for years. Reckon I was afraid he'd ask me to come home before I was ready."

"Would he have?"

He thought about it for a long moment and shook his head. "I don't think he would."

"Did you never ask him to visit you?"

"Nah. Eòghann's *of* the island. He'll never leave. He…" But it wasn't really his story to tell, was it? To his eternal shame, Bryan had only been an extra standing on the sidelines. "All the rest of us left, and Eòghann was trapped here, holding the family together with two hands. Alone. Just like you after Diego and your abuela left."

"She didn't leave, she died."

"Amounts to the same thing though, doesn't it?"

"A gaping hole," she agreed.

"Is that why you write friendship so well? On account of you're lonely?"

She studied him intently, like she was trying to see through his words, searching for a hidden insult among them. If anyone could find fault with his clumsy speech, it would be her.

"No," she finally answered. "I center friendship in my stories because I stopped being alone."

"You're not alone now," he whispered, and he meant it as a question, to probe deeper, to learn about the people close to her, like Wes, who followed her halfway around the world as a cheerleader on her quest. But it tripped off his tongue like a statement full of prophecy and laden with meaning he hadn't intended.

Her brow furrowed and he wanted to kiss it smooth, to show her his words were right and true, she wasn't alone. He was here, he understood—a maddening turn of events.

"I'm not?" she asked, and it completely undid him.

"Not if you don't want to be," he whispered, leaning closer. "Can I kiss you?"

She pulled away. "Why?"

He choked back an anguished laugh. *Why?* " 'Cause I—'cause I can't think about anything else."

What a stupid answer. He should've said how pretty she was, or how she made him feel like his bones were nothing but custard, how her novel had filled up the cracks in his heart and soldered it back together stronger than it was before.

But magically, they must have been the right words after all, because she rocked forward, smoky whisky still lingering on her breath—his whisky—as she tentatively kissed him.

It was all dry, cracked lips and erratic breathing, like she was as hungry and unprepared for him as he was for her.

She scraped her nails lightly through the hair at the base of his skull, sending wave after wave of shivers down his back, and he cupped both of her cheeks to keep his hands the right side of appropriate. When she finally broke the kiss to catch her breath, he pressed his forehead to hers.

"You're b-beautiful," he whispered.

"I'm sure you say that to all the ladies."

"Ladies, gents, I'm not fussy," he teased, immediately regretting being glib, but she laughed nervously, and he pressed his lips to her throat to absorb the vibrations of her mirth.

She stopped laughing then, breathing in sharply, right in his ear, a little whimper that made every hair on his body stand on end.

They snogged on his grandfather's loveseat for what felt like hours as the sun dipped to almost the horizon on its journey through nautical twilight, never quite setting, as though they had all the time in the world, without looming deadlines or rampant expectations.

The whole while, Bryan kept his hands where she could see them, though he desperately wanted to run them the length and breadth of her gorgeous body, cover every inch of silky skin, slip up beneath her sweater before dipping down into her waistband, but he knew better than to rush.

She was an inexpert kisser, although an enthusiastic one, clashing tongues with him like a fencing match, give, then take, changing it up, keeping him guessing. She kissed with her entire personality, and it was the most intoxicating thing he'd ever experienced. He couldn't get enough.

When she ran a hand over his chest, it made his breath judder to a halt, and when she kept going down the rock-hard length of him aching against his joggers, he thought he might never breathe again.

Then she froze.

Perhaps copping a feel had been an accident.

He opened his eyes.

Hers were wide, a trapped doe, as a flush spread hot across her cheeks like so much spilled bourbon.

"Sorry," she gasped.

"It's f-f— It's… No worries," he replied, leaning in to take her mind off it with more kisses, but she turned her head and pulled back.

"I'm on my period," she whispered.

"All right," he said, confused. "I wasn't trying to—"

"Of course not," she interrupted him.

He scanned her eyes, searching for the minefield beneath the surface. What was the right thing to say? It had sounded like a brush off. Did she actually mean she wanted him but was merely offering a warning? Or was this some kind of fact-sharing game? Every possible reaction seemed like the wrong one.

"I mean, if you're keen—" he offered.

"No! Don't be ridiculous."

He tried not to let irritation at her repeated interruptions bloom and spread across his face. It was an old wound, one she wasn't responsible for.

"I'm not, I wouldn't," she said.

"Fine. Only if you did, it's no harm. 'Cause I—"

"I said no."

"Right." He slid to the edge of the loveseat, staring straight ahead instead of facing her. "That you did."

"I should go to bed." With that pronouncement she scrambled off the bench careful not to brush against him again. "Lots to do tomorrow."

"Aye," he agreed, bewildered by the change in her.

"Good night, MacNeil," she said, returning to their earlier formality.

"Night, Rios," he managed to return, but she didn't let him get the words out before slipping through the door.

And it wasn't a good night, not for Bryan, as he tossed and turned, unsure what had happened, what she thought of him, what she wanted from him. Morning and a chance for a fresh start on that stone wall couldn't come soon enough.

Chapter Seventeen

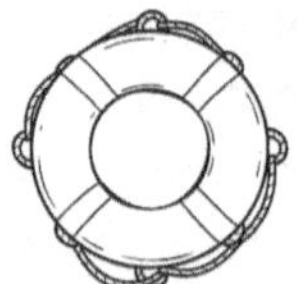

After a night of tossing and turning that *only* Wes could have slept through, Grace sprang out of bed the moment the clock turned from 6:59 to 7:00.

Last night's kiss had been…

Well…

Thinking about it made her skin feel tight and itchy, like he was poison ivy and she was now rashy from head to toe.

The kiss itself had been nothing short of magical. That was the problem. Because then Grace had accidentally groped the life out of him, and of course he interpreted it as an invitation—how could he fucking not?

I'm on my period.

God.

First of all, mighty presumptuous to assume the kiss was leading anywhere, because was it? But then again, he was a man and they were both adults, so wasn't it, whether she'd felt him up or not? Wasn't it *always*? What date had ever kissed her just for kissing's sake? Or done it half so well?

God.

But *I'm on my period?*

Dios mio, her abuela's voice sounded in her head. *What were you thinking, mija?*

She wasn't thinking at all. It was the first excuse to pop into her head as she grasped for a way to exit one situation before it led to a whole other situation. Because if he *had* gotten any ideas thanks to her wandering hand, she was too close to the edge of a bad decision to turn him down, despite knowing she'd end up regretting it.

So she used the only excuse that ever worked.

Because the kissing had been *good*—his heat and the smoky, spicy taste of him, and his hand on the small of her back, and him being *nice*—and of course she had to stop it right there before they took it further. Because further never ended well.

Not for Grace.

So she told him she was on her period and scurried away to the bedroom like a freaked-out freshman at the junior-senior prom.

She had ten thousand words to catch up on writing today, but *I'm on my period* were the only four rattling around in her brain, over and over on a humiliating endless loop.

No wonder she couldn't write.

She sat staring at her dark computer, trying to order her thoughts and plan her chapters for the day, and definitely not hiding as he pottered softly around the house. Eventually he'd get to work, and she could sneak out of this room unseen.

When the force of his sledgehammer attacking stone shook the walls, and floor, and ceiling, and practically rattled Grace down to her bones, it was finally enough to rouse Wes, who rolled over and pulled the pillow against her face.

He let loose another swing and she moaned a little. "Your Stoic Scot is really pissed at that wall, huh?" she asked in the froggy, morning voice of someone who'd slept deeply and peacefully for nine hours the night before. "Why are you already up? Are you writing? Did you go to bed? Or come to bed?"

"I'll go tell him to knock it off," Grace said, slipping out the door, but as soon as she was in the hall with no bra and burning cheeks, she realized she'd do no such thing.

The muscles in his shoulders rippled as he took another swing.

Grace abruptly detoured for the bathroom to catch her breath.

The sight of the tiny, ugly shower reminded her how desperately she missed her bathtub back home. It was the one redeeming feature of her apartment.

Next time she picked a B&B, she'd ensure there was a nice big tub. Not that she'd chosen this one.

She closed her eyes and leaned back against the door, softly knocking her head against it. The sight of a pair of brawny biceps in cut-off sleeves should not unsettle her so easily.

When she opened her eyes again, she took in the tiny room anew. Could she hide in here forever? Was there an outlet for her computer? She could sit on the toilet with her laptop on the counter… Her gaze landed on a basket placed strategically by the sink. That hadn't been there last night.

It was a plain wicker basket, but it held—*oh god*. It held everything: a variety pack of sanitary pads, a similar assortment of tampons, a hot water bottle with a soft, fuzzy cover. There were abdominal heat patches, a bottle of ibuprofen and another of paracetamol, not to mention a bunch of Cadbury chocolate bars.

Her heart flip-flopped at the gesture even as she willed the floor to crack open and bury her alive. Maybe Caitriona had left it somewhere, and Wes set it out?

On second thought, it was probably for the best there was no tub, or she might be forced to drown herself to end the tidal wave of embarrassment now battering against her. Lucky for Grace, humiliation didn't leave visible bruising.

She slid down the door to sit on the floor as, out in the living room, Bryan took another whack at the wall, and this time she couldn't decide if she was shaking or the bathroom was.

Who really was Bryan MacNeil? Was this care package an overreaction to his disgust at the idea of her being on her period? He'd hidden it well last night, but what man wasn't completely grossed out at the very thought, let alone willing to set foot in the women's health aisle?

She tried to picture Diego buying products for Mathilda, but he'd already left home by the time Grace experienced her first, so the image was as incongruous as her own father would have been. He'd had to ask their neighbor to take Grace to the drugstore because her mom was working a double shift.

There was a knock at the door.

"Sorry, Gray, you going to be long? I have to pee so bad it's about to shoot out my ears," Wes called.

Grace scrambled to her feet and opened the door.

"You okay?" Wes asked, looking her over in concern.

"Fantastic," Grace lied.

Wes eyed her skeptically but got distracted by the big honking menstruation basket. "Ohhh, this is so nice! Perfect timing too. Were you all done? If you want to shower, I promise I'll be quick."

"It's fine. Take your time," Grace said, backing out of the lavatory.

"Okay, but hey, we still need to talk about your birthday."

"I really don't think we do."

"Come on," Wes begged. "Anything you want, I'll make it happen. Go to the mainland and see a show? I'll buy tickets. Fly to London and repatriate the stolen shit from their museums? Say the word. Find some stones and travel through time? I'll call a guy."

"You know me, I don't do birthdays."

"Gray."

"I'm on a deadline," she said, taking another step back. "All I want is to finish my book in peace! If I manage that, we can do whatever you want."

"I don't accept that. You have the rest of your life for deadlines. You only turn thirty once."

"It's just a day."

"Besides your twenty-first, when's the last time you had a party?"

"I don't know. Thirteen or fourteen. I didn't have a party for my twenty-first," Grace protested. What a weird thing to say. Wes of all people should remember the only party that summer was the one celebrating random holidays, partying for the sake of partying.

Wes pressed her lips into a straight line.

"Panda-monium? That was to celebrate Ya Li's twins… and International Chicken Wing Day and World UFO Day…" Grace reminded her.

Scrunching up her nose, Wes said, "No disrespect to the pandas, but that's what we told you it was for."

Grace opened her mouth, but she didn't know what to say. Her friends had thrown her such a surprise party that she was still surprised nine years later? She was so anti-birthday they had to trick her into celebrating? Had they been laughing at her ever since?

"I honestly thought you knew and were just playing along," Wes said.

Grace looked up at her friend's sweet, perplexed face. "Didn't you need to pee?" she asked.

"I've basically gone numb," Wes admitted. "Please don't be mad about this. Don't turn it into a whole thing."

Grace shut the door on Wesley and turned around, right into the sweaty chest of the hammer-wielding Scotsman. She squeaked and scurried back to her room before he could say a word or flex his biceps.

But at least now there was plenty of awkward fodder to fuel

the next chapter of her book. Except unlike Grace, Maya always had the perfect pithy comeback right on the tip of her tongue.

"Bryan says he hopes he didn't wake you," Wes told her when she returned fifteen minutes later, toweling her wet hair.

"He didn't." Grace slapped her laptop shut. "He woke you."

"Strangely didn't seem as concerned about that," Wes replied. "Though I made it abundantly clear he owes me. But since I owe him for last night, we're even."

Grace snorted. She envied Wesley's easy banter with men in general and this one in particular. She pictured his biceps again, not wanting to think too hard about what her friend might demand as payback.

"You really don't want to do anything to celebrate your big day?" Wes begged.

Grace turned sideways in the chair to face her friend. "Creative Ice Cream Flavors Day?"

Wesley grimaced. "Sometime in July. It was all very convenient."

"And Piña Colada Day?"

"They were all real, Gray, just begging to be collected into one big theme for a party."

"A theme for a *birthday* party."

Wes shrugged. "You wouldn't have come otherwise. Are you seriously mad we threw you a party a decade ago?"

"No. I'm not mad about that. Because that would be insane."

Unable to sit still any longer, Grace strode into the living room, where Bryan and his cousin were surveying the almost completely destroyed wall.

"You guys mind if I have a go?" she asked, nodding to the sledgehammer.

"It's heavy," Bryan warned as she hefted it over her shoulder and swung with all her might.

The wall exploded in a shower of dust. The two Scotsmen had made so much progress that Grace's weak hit really did some damage, and she stood back, breathing heavily.

"Jesus," Bryan whispered. To Wes he added, "Is she mad at you or me?"

Grace didn't hear Wesley's answer.

"That felt good," she said, rearing back for another go. So Bryan pointed out where to hit it, and this time the rest of the wall crumbled before her eyes, much to her disappointment because, left unchecked, she felt like she could mow down the whole damn house.

Lùcas stared at her with impressed surprise, as Bryan relieved her of the sledgehammer.

"What?" she asked, wiping her sweaty forehead on her arm.

Lùcas turned his shock on his cousin who shrugged and said, "Americans."

When the dust settled, they were met with half a dozen angry glares from down the beach, where neighbors had gathered to watch the destruction.

"What the blazes are you thinking, Ryan MacNeil?" an old man hollered. "Just you wait 'til your daddy hears what you've done."

"Aye, old Rob'll be spinning in his grave again, sure enough," a woman agreed. "Curse the day you ever came back here. You ought to be ashamed."

"Tearing down an island institution," another shouted, shaking his head. "No respect for anyone or anything."

"And leading young Lùcas astray, as well. Does your mother know you're here, Lùcas Buchanan?"

Bryan stood fairly tongue-tied, and Lùcas glowered red-faced at the floor. Grace felt awful for them both. Usually they were full of teasing bravado and bluster, but the town reduced the two of them to a pair of kicked puppies with tails between their legs.

Not that she was any stranger to holding her tongue in the face of unfair accusations, but she was a woman, raised to mind her manners and her mouth. She was surprised to see the guys reacting this way. She wanted to live vicariously while Bryan and Lùcas set them all straight. Barring that, she wanted to rage at the self-righteous islanders herself.

Instead, Bryan set his jaw and turned his back, loading the debris into a wheelbarrow.

So Grace left them to it and returned to her room, where Wes was getting ready to go out for the day.

"A piñata," Grace told her friend before she could talk herself out of it.

"A piñata?"

"For my birthday."

"Ohhh," Wes practically squealed. "I can do that. What shape? Filled with candy or tiny bottles of booze? Or... condoms?" she added as an afterthought, because she was Wes.

"I don't care. I just want something it's socially acceptable to beat the crap out of with a really big stick."

Wesley's eyebrows shot up in surprised delight.

"I knocked down a wall," Grace explained.

"You sure did."

"And it felt fucking amazing."

A huge grin spread across Wesley's face. "I'll get you a million piñatas," she promised.

Chapter Eighteen

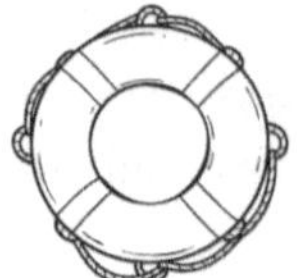

Of course there had been an audience when the wall fell, like the Barra beach was East-Fucking-Berlin. Except judging by their reactions, that would make the townspeople communist sympathizers.

Bryan hadn't been totally surprised to see the crowd gathered out back, not with the noise of his demolition probably echoing across the whole island. But he was a bit shocked by the power with which Grace had wielded the hammer.

It would have turned him on, if not for the fear she was picturing his face on the living room wall as she absolutely crushed it. He had almost said something trite like, *Remind me not to get on your bad side,* just to goad her into admitting he already was, but then the neighbors started in on him and Lùc, and Graciela-Fucking-Rios turned around and stalked back to her room, slamming the door hard enough to snap the hinges.

Lùcas also looked like he wanted to mutiny.

"That went well, I think," Bryan quipped for something to say.

"You realize if they run us off the island, I'm going to have to stay with you," Lùc said darkly. "Haven't got any skills besides defacing public property."

"Was it you graffitied the back of your da's shed?"

His cousin's glower was answer enough.

"Come on." Bryan clapped him on the shoulder. "Help me hang these tarps. We'll check in with your da about the windows and then I'll treat you to a pint.

"It's half nine!"

"A fry-up, then. Move your arse."

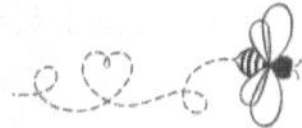

THEY TOOK THEIR TIME FIXING THE TARPS IN PLACE. WHETHER IT was because Lùcas preferred a pint to breakfast or because he didn't want to ask his father about the windows, Bryan wasn't sure. Grace didn't emerge from her room the entire time, not even to yell at them to quiet down. On the one hand, a fellow couldn't really complain about not being shouted at. On the other hand, it gave Bryan far too much time to overthink everything.

Had it been the kissing she objected to? He'd asked permission first, and she'd seemed keen, seemed to enjoy herself right up until she suddenly didn't.

Was it when he sucked on her bottom lip that sent her running? Before or after he buried his face in the valley where her shoulder ended and her neck began? Kissing her there was an excuse to discern the components of her shampoo like he would a fine whisky, losing himself completely in notes of jasmine and peach and something else entirely, something pure Grace.

In a moment straight from an adolescent daydream, she ran her hand roughly down his crotch and his mind went fairly blank. By the time he caught up again, she was apparently menstruating and he had been relegated to the doghouse.

At six a.m. on the dot, he'd driven straight to the market on the other side of the island, only hesitating when he realized it was his own mother flipping the sign from CLOSED to OPEN. Then he'd screwed up his courage and gone inside anyway.

"Darling," she had whispered when the door closed behind him, and then he was burying his face in *her* hair, like an overgrown child, as she folded him up in her arms.

"I'm s-sorry, Ma," he whispered.

She smoothed the fringe from his forehead and then took his face in both hands, tears shining in her eyes.

"How could I forget a thing like that? Not eating meat was always so important to you."

"Doesn't matter."

"Of course it matters."

He shook his head, and she rubbed his bearded cheek.

"I didn't mean you look thin. You look good, my handsome lad. Just a wee bit tired," she added, searching his eyes for the truth. "You never did sleep enough."

"Working a lot," he said, squeezing her hand and looking around the old shop. "As are you, apparently."

She shook her head. "When Nellie Coombe wanted to cut back to one day a week, someone had to pitch in. Especially during the festival. And, like your Grandad Mac always said, 'If you're going to be here, be here.' "

The same words Bryan had said to Grace. Maybe he needed to take his own advice. "Are the tourists running you ragged, Ma?"

"Och, I enjoy it. What about your tourists?" she asked, raising one cautious eyebrow.

"Ah, that, aye. Well. They may have come unprepared."

She nodded wisely. "We're all out of slickers, I'm afraid."

"No, not that. Ah, lady troubles," he said, dredging up the term she and Cait had used when he was a boy.

"That I can help you with!"

After purchasing every single item she'd recommended and a few she hadn't, he'd felt a little silly leaving it in the loo like some sort of apology bouquet, but he'd hoped it would erase last night's awkward tension.

Based on Grace's demeanor this morning, however, it may have only made things worse. Hopefully his second peace offering—a quiet, empty house—would be met with more enthusiasm.

By the time he and Lùcas had confirmed with Uncle Dàibhidh that his order of casement windows was delayed at least a week, the lunch crowd at the Three Puffins was picking up, and they were barely able to snag a two-top in the corner.

"Half eleven late enough for a pint?" Bryan asked, but his cousin's only reply was a sullen shrug.

He was still agitated after the neighbors' open hostility and a stilted conversation with his da at the hardware store. Bryan well remembered those angsty days before he fled the island and stopped speaking to his own demanding father all together.

"You didn't think to check on the windows before starting in on that wall?" Lùc groused.

"Aye, I thought about it."

Lùcas gave him a look as if to say, *And yet...?*

"Needed a good airing out anyway," Bryan teased, trying to chivy away his cousin's bad mood. "So, what do the kids do for fun around here these days?"

"Make questionable decisions about karaoke songs, mostly," Lùcas replied with another shrug.

"That's always a good time."

"Is it?"

Now it was Bryan's turn to shrug. Since his stammer plagued him less while singing, karaoke had been just about the only safe group activity when he was a teen.

"What were you, the karaoke king?"

Bryan shook his head. "I dunno, maybe I was."

"Is that why all the girls liked you?"

A server popped up just then with their pints and pies, saving

Bryan from having to answer that the girls probably felt sorry for him.

Their server was the same age as Lùcas, who was actively not looking at him.

"All right, Lùc?" the other boy asked.

"Yeah, you?"

"Yeah, all right," the kid said, then nodded at Bryan and left them to their food, as Lùc finally looked up to track him all the way back across the bar.

"He's cute," Bryan said, taking a stab in the dark.

His cousin's gaze flicked to him, instantly guarded. "Don't be a perv, you're like forty."

Bryan rolled his eyes and took a long drink of his ale.

"Is it true you like guys?" Lùcas asked hesitantly.

"Sometimes."

"Is it easier liking girls?"

"Sometimes."

Lùc chewed on that for a minute before turning the tables. "Is the American one of those times?"

Bryan shot him a death stare. "Don't be a perv, you're practically in nappies," he growled, and his cousin laughed, dark cloud finally chased away for the time being, as he dug into his pie.

Chapter Nineteen

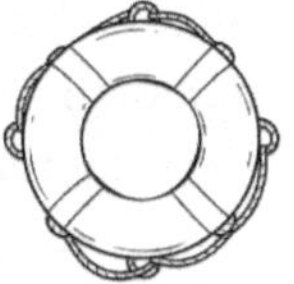

When Grace committed to a new endeavor, it was always with her whole chest. She was nothing if not the A+ overachieving daughter of two over-achieving parents, so avoiding Bryan, with a *B*, for the next week was easy. All she had to do was adjust her schedule to stay up writing all night and then sleep through his pandemonium with liberal use of ear plugs, melatonin, and utter exhaustion.

She essentially reverted to her natural Tennessee biorhythms, writing until she was too tired to see straight and then crawling into bed and passing out. It made for some interesting dreams.

Because Catholic guilt was real even for a reformed Catholic who hadn't been to church since her parents divorced, she apologized almost constantly for abandoning Wesley to her own devices, though she knew her friend would forgive her simply because Wes was Wes. As she continued to remind Grace, rambling the island alone suited the Wesley Teal aesthetic and was, in her words, "a small price to pay in exchange for getting the whole double bed to myself while you work yourself to the bone. Instead of boning."

Wes would always be Wes. Just like this trip was always meant to be a sabbatical for her and a work-a-thon for Grace.

And slowly, oh-so-painfully-slowly, but surely, the novel began to take shape. It was a truly terrible first draft because she allowed it to be. At least words were on the page.

When the house was deathly quiet, Grace would creep out to raid the pantry or use the toilet and examine the guys' progress. It had taken no time at all for them to frame out a new south-facing facade, and in contrast to the cavernous stone they'd knocked down, Bryan had designed a whole wall of windows, which would open out to the porch and the gorgeous ocean vista beyond. Everything was still tarped to keep out the elements, but there was evidence of a future built-in window seat that gave Grace's tummy a little twist of delight.

They had laid out heating coils along the stone floor and were beginning to cover them with more modern stone tiles, a sort of classic call-back to the original floors, but installed to efficiently warm the cold little cottage. Even with the floor unfinished and the wall still torn up, Grace could see how cozy it was going to be. The lighting alone would be a massive improvement over the previous space.

Bryan's vision had opened the room significantly, allowing it to breathe as it was always meant to. The previous wall had been a sacrilege, blocking such a gorgeous view with dull, white-washed stone. Once the windows were installed, she was sure it would still be protected from the harshest gale, but brighter, even on the darkest winter day.

For now, twilight poured through the tarps like blue and brown stained glass, and Grace couldn't help taking the risk of bumping into him and his forearm tattoo—she tucked herself into the in-progress window seat, right up next to the drafty tarps, and began typing away on her phone instead of her outlet-dependent laptop.

After all, wasn't it every girl's dream to write in a window seat by the sea? How could she not?

That was exactly how Bryan found her when he padded out to the kitchen, nothing but a pair of joggers slung low on his hips. He froze when he saw her, and she froze too, as though by not moving he wouldn't notice her there, never mind he already had.

"The vampiress emerges," he murmured.

"Sorry. Did I wake you?"

He shook his head. "We didn't work as hard today. Not hard enough to tire me out." He lifted the kettle to offer her a cup, and she nodded, though she'd already drunk enough to flood the ocean.

"You've done an incredible job," she told him, her stomach doing annoying things when he allowed his back to straighten and a tiny smile of pride to tug his lips.

"Thanks. And you?"

"Oh, I didn't do much," she said, simultaneously proud of her help with the roof and the wall destruction, but also ashamed that she hadn't done more like their bargain had stipulated.

"I… meant your… writing?"

"Oh." Her cheeks burned. "Me too. I didn't do much. Just a few thousand words."

"How many do you lack?"

"Maybe twenty? Another week and I should have the ending. If I can figure out how it ends."

His eyes widened. "You don't already know?"

"I know *what* happens. Broadly. I just don't quite know how we get there. Yet."

"If only you could take a holiday…"

Grace leaned back against the wall beam. "I know. I should be enjoying my time here. I *am* enjoying it. I've never seen a more beautiful place."

Bryan turned back to prepare the mugs of tea. She liked the

way he made a ritual of it: measuring out loose tea into little beehive-patterned metal steepers, adding a dash of milk and honey to each cup.

When he handed the mug over, his fingers brushed against the inside of her palm. Was it his touch that singed her, or the tea?

"Careful," he growled. Then, "You should come out tomorrow. It's the midsummer ceilidh everyone's been on about. To mark the end of all this festival nonsense."

"Sounds…" Honestly it sounded liked like a big noisy, sweaty, chaos party. Not that she had much experience with parties. "Loud," she finally settled on.

"Oh aye. Quite the stramash, if tales of years past are any indication."

"Yikes." *Stramash* sounded a bit scary, if she was being honest, except for the way it slid silkily off his tongue.

And now she was thinking about his tongue again, and how somewhere along the lines, his beard had gone from reminding her of a dangerous, spiky stinger to instead the soft, fuzzy butt of a bumble bee.

"Torture," he agreed. "Please come."

And why did she like *those* words from the Stoic Scot's lips quite so much?

"With an invitation like that, who could refuse?" she asked, a little breathless.

"Everyone should experience a ceilidh once in their life."

"I don't know how to dance," she protested, peering into her tea and taking tiny sips to keep from scalding her tongue. "And I didn't bring a dress."

"Come as you are, as long as you come."

And there were those words again, he was practically begging. *OMG Gracie, settle down.*

"What's in it for you?" she couldn't help asking. After kissing and then disappearing on him, she couldn't imagine he thought of her as very good company.

He studied her intently for a moment before looking away. "Wesley and Eòghann obviously fancy each other. But she won't let herself enjoy it if she imagines you're miserable at home."

"You think?" Grace asked, but she knew he was right. When he didn't answer, she said, "I'll consider it," but she already knew she was going to concede.

He nodded pensively, then stared into his own tea.

Grace wanted to ask why it mattered if she came or not.

She wanted to ask if he was sorry he kissed her, or if he even still thought about it like she did? She wanted to ask about the renovation, too. Where were the windows? What was next after the floor? Was he angry she'd stopped helping him, or actually relieved?

And had he read any more of her book? Did he like the ending?

When the emptiness filled up with her unasked questions, he said, "I'll let you get back to it," and lifted his tea in mock salute.

"Sorry," she replied out of habit—for being in his space when he might wish to be alone, for not being a more interesting conversationalist if he didn't, for everything that happened after last week's kiss.

"You apologize too much," he observed, frowning.

"Sorry," she muttered automatically.

His scowl deepened, that deep chasm between his eyebrows popping out like a demanding cursor.

"I mean… suck it, MacNeil," she corrected herself, and the man almost choked on his tea.

"Quite," he agreed through fits of coughing before scurrying away.

When Grace awoke the next day, the first thing Wes asked was whether she'd deign to drag herself away from the computer long enough to attend the ceilidh.

"I know you're not here for vacation, but even high school kids go to formal dances, so in a way this would be hands-on research. Or hands-off, if you insist. I'd say we could sneak around and spike the punch, but this is Scotland. It'll already be spiked."

"That sounds like a gross generalization," Grace laughed. Because despite Wesley's very cogent argument and puppy-dog eyes, it was Bryan's grumpy golden-retriever face that had already convinced her to take the evening off.

Running into him the night before hadn't been as awkward as she'd feared. Maybe they had both silently agreed to move on from the kissing and everything else, sweeping it under his new radiant flooring, never to be spoken of again. Grace couldn't decide how to feel about that.

"Don't make me go by myself," Wes begged. "I have no problem doing just about anything on my own—Orgasms? A given! Movies? More popcorn for me. Dinner out? Literally what Wesley Wednesdays were invented for. But please for the love of… whatever. Do not make me go to this dance alone."

"Fine, I'll come. But only because I'm the world's greatest friend."

"I mean, I wouldn't go that far. Rebecca made up with her terrible husband *just* so I could take her place on this trip."

"Ugh, Marshall," Grace agreed.

"Forget Marshall, we have outfits to plan," Wes said, throwing open the closet and selecting a twirly, brown-plaid, A-line skirt.

"That's… my skirt," Grace said. "That wasn't even in the bag I left in Glasgow. Why do you have my skirt?"

"Semper paratus," Wes said with a shrug, as though vague non-Church Latin was any kind of answer, but at least Grace had something to wear.

Chapter Twenty

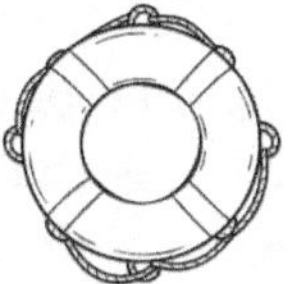

Bryan absolutely, without a doubt, one hundred thousand percent did not want to attend the ceilidh with his family and hoards of neighbors bent out of shape over the renovation.

But his grandfather's words, *If you're going to be here, then be here*, burned in his ears. Being here meant being a part of things like the end-of-festival ceilidh. Maybe if he wanted the town's support, it was time to stop keeping them at arm's length. Maybe the same could be said for Grace, and so he had begged her to come with him. It was a rash decision, but it had been late, and he was tired and thrown off guard by seeing her sitting in the window seat, a last-minute addition she'd inspired in his floor plan.

Miracle of miracles, she'd agreed, so now he had to go. But old habits die hard.

Resenting the town for seeing him as a child who couldn't talk—his father's stammering mini-me who disappointed them all by eschewing politics—and for refusing to see him as a grown-up when perhaps he refused to act like one, it was all second nature. He'd carried that chip on his shoulder so long he'd forgotten it was there, might actually miss it if he ever managed to dislodge it somehow. But you can't just blow into town and build an industry if the town doesn't want you. He needed their support. More than that, he wanted it. Now was the time to show them the man he'd grown into, occasional stress-induced stammer and all.

Thank Christ Grace had agreed to come.

Polite hospitality for the sake of the Americans might not shield Bryan from the worst they could dish out, but if nothing else, having Grace at his side might help him keep his Barra-Bryan temper in check.

He took the old MacNeil kilt from the back of his closet. Like the closet, it smelled of Grandad: of tobacco smoke and oiled leather and sycamore resin. Tears clogged his throat as he breathed it all in and then closed it all back behind the door.

Had it been a truly terrible mistake, coming home and changing everything? Knocking down that wall like it would somehow set him free? Would Grandad have wanted the house enshrined in history, unchanged for evermore as the neighbors seemed to think?

Don't ever let them make you doubt yourself, lad, his grandfather's voice came to him once more, as though through a portal to the past, staticky, like they were talking down the phone line. *You know what you're about.*

He'd said those words when the town had laughed at Bryan's big ideas for recycling, reducing carbon footprints, and saving the bees. He'd used the same words again when Bryan confessed he might like boys as well as girls. Saving the world and saving himself, Grandad took it all in stride. The same advice applied because it was all just part of living.

So Bryan did as he'd done the day he left the island. He squashed his doubts down deep and got himself dressed, everything else be damned.

He looked like a complete tosser in his white button-down

shirt, charcoal waistcoat, and matching skinny tie, with the blue and green kilt and flashes on his knee-high socks. He'd debated the flashes when he found them in his grandad's drawer. Were they too much?

It was all too much.

Turning up the sleeves to expose his tattoo felt more natural. He ripped off the tie so his collar could hang open leaving his throat unconstricted, and he kicked off the stodgy dress shoes, pulling on his favorite tall boots instead. Not exactly traditional, but they made him feel more himself. He left the flashes on as a concession to Grandad.

When he emerged from his room, the Americans were stepping out of theirs as well, and for a moment they all stood in the hallway gawping at each other.

It was definitely too much.

He shifted nervously, resisting the urge to dart back inside and change into jeans and a leather jacket. His hand clenched reflexively, seeking the familiar old worry stone. When would it accept the thing was gone just like his grandfather, nothing left but echoes and memories?

"Wow," Wesley said, breaking the awkward staring contest. "You clean up nice."

Bryan's face heated, but he cleared his throat. "You too. And you," he added, darting a shuttered glance towards Grace. She was resplendent, actually, in a soft cream sweater and silky tartan skirt that hugged all the right curves in all the right ways. Suddenly his collar felt too tight again.

"This old thing?" Wes asked, indicating her own lightweight summer dress, a pale-yellow sleeveless number with stitched poppies sprinkled liberally along the hem. She looked cute, but she was going to freeze unless she planned to steal another jumper off Eòghann. "I was hoping you might have a bit of plaid lying around I could use as a wrap," she admitted, as though reading his mind.

"Eòghann will know someone who does," he said, pretending not to notice Wesley's blush before he sent his cousin a text.

THE HALL WAS A CRUSH OF FLUSHED STRANGERS DRUNK ON THEIR last night of vacation and islanders who'd known Bryan since infancy. When the three of them stepped inside, the very air seemed to thicken around them, clogging his throat so he could hardly breathe, let alone speak.

He powered forward with Wesley on one arm and Grace on the other, telling himself heads kept turning their way because the ladies looked so incredible and not because of him, the prodigal son walking among them once more. His pulse sped up anyway, and sweat began to slick his back and palms. He should have left the damn waistcoat at home.

"You almost look respectable with these two on your arm," Teàrlach said, approaching with a broad grin. "I hope you don't plan to keep them all to yourself."

"Teàrlach!" Grace exclaimed, dropping Bryan's arm and gripping his cousin's hand instead. "It's so nice to see you again."

"Likewise," Teàrlach agreed, smiling up at her, and Bryan remembered with a pang how they shared a history at the wedding he'd avoided like a coward. "I fly at daybreak, so if you want to spend another evening teetotaling in the corner being snarky about the drunks, say the word," he told her with a wink, eliciting a laugh that made Bryan's stomach do stupid things. "Eòghann's looking for you," Teàrlach added to Wesley.

"I meant to bring back his sweater, but I forgot," she confessed, overly loud to compensate for the fiddle and pipe band and perhaps for the obvious lie. Even Auntie Eilidh had to know Eòghann would never see his jumper again.

Bryan scanned the room for his older cousin and spotted him on the other side, his gaze already fixed on Wes.

"Hiding in the corner might be wise." Grace's voice dragged him back to the conversation at hand. "These people look like they know what they're doing."

"No harder than line dancing. Isn't that a requirement where y'all come from?" Bryan drawled, and she glanced up at him sharply, her eyes full of both amusement and challenge.

"A rare joke from the Stoic Scot," she teased.

"Christ, is that my new nickname?" he asked. "I assure you, I was quite s-serious," he added, eyes still locked on hers, hoping his falter on the *S* sounded intentional. If she noticed it, she didn't let on.

"You requested a wrap," Eòghann said, extending a length of gold and red Buchanan plaid to Wesley.

It was a perfect match for her dress, and Bryan smirked at his cousin.

"Thank you," she whispered, reaching reverently towards the soft, vibrant fabric. There was no way Eòghann was getting that back either. It, like his jumper, would be flying coach back to Tennessee one day all too soon.

"Allow me," Eòghann murmured, unfurling the yard of plaid and draping it around Wesley's shoulders, inhaling the scent of her pinned-up hair as he did.

Uh oh. His cousin had it bad, and Bryan knew the feeling. What was wrong with the pair of them? They knew better than to get mixed up with tourists.

And yet, the two looked perfect together, Eòghann in his dusty ancient hunting tartan and black turtleneck, and Wesley matching in resplendent crimson and gold. Bryan tried to catch his cousin's attention to offer a smug smile, but Eòghann only had eyes for her.

"Care to dance?" he murmured, whisking Wes away before she could decline, not that she would have.

And then there were three.

Bryan watched them leave, envious of how easily his cousin moved in the world. At a ceilidh, Bryan stood out more for not dancing than he would've if he'd just grabbed Grace's hand and led her into the fray.

Picking up the conversation where they'd left off, Grace said, "My brother wanted the Electric Slide at his wedding, but his English wife wouldn't hear of it."

"And how is the lovely Mathilda?" Teàrlach asked with a certain edge to his tone.

Grace looked away from Bryan and turned back to his younger cousin. "Lovely as ever," she said, matching his tone, and he grimaced.

"Had I known D wished for line dancing, I'd have insisted we got one started. I'd have tied up the DJ and risked the bride's eternal wrath."

Grace grinned. "I wouldn't have dared back then."

"Shall we make up for it now?" Teàrlach asked. "I'll talk you through the steps, easy as landing an Otter."

Grace looked to Bryan, for what—permission?

"Have fun," he said, so she nodded her agreement and followed his cousin out to the dance floor, leaving Bryan the most alone he'd ever been inside a crowded room.

Teàrlach was more comfortable and graceful in his wheelchair than Bryan had ever felt lumbering about in his too-tight skin. Most likely a more patient teacher, too. Grace was in good hands.

Not wishing to stare too obviously at her as she laughed and tripped along to Teàrlach's instructions, Bryan forced himself to look around the community center. Lùcas was over by the drinks table, so Bryan made a beeline.

"You look very dapper," Elspeth said timidly, intercepting him along the way.

"You too, El. About the other night—"

"I should have reminded them you're vegetarian." She shrugged. "You know how they can get when they're excited about a project."

Bryan cocked his head in agreement. He did know, and maybe he got that way himself.

Elspeth nudged his shoulder with hers and took a pint of amber lager from the table, turning her back to lean alongside Lùcas. It was a good vantage point to watch the swirling dancers unobtrusively.

"Looking forward to having your house back to yourself, now the festival's over?" she asked.

Was he? He'd kind of gotten used to late-night chats over football and whisky, and anyway, he'd promised the room to young Lùc once the Americans cleared out.

There were more years between Bryan and El than his gap with Cait, which almost made their relationship easier somehow. She smiled sympathetically, seeming to understand his ambivalence.

The back of Bryan's neck tingled as he selected a dark beer and turned to lean against the table beside his sister. When he did, he came face to face with Old Man Ellis, the neighbor who had spent the better part of a week glowering and shouting at him from the beach as he worked on his house.

"You've a lot of nerve wearing MacNeil plaid, young man."

Bryan sagged and took a sip of his beer. If by nerve the elderly busybody meant anxiety, then he was bang on.

"Once a MacNeil, always a MacNeil," Bryan said with more confidence than he felt because *fake it 'til you make it*, as Grace would say. Then he found himself searching for her in the crowd as though she were a beacon who could guide him safely away from rocky shoals.

When his cousin had asked her to dance, she hadn't batted an eye at the fact he used a chair, and if Bryan hadn't been falling for her already, seeing her now, laughing and flushed, would have sealed the deal.

"If your grandfather was alive, he'd disown you for what you've done to his house. Isn't that right, Nell?" Ellis called over his shoulder to a table full of pensioners who all nodded their heads in sober agreement.

"My grandfather was an environmentalist," Bryan said. "I think he'd appreciate every choice I've made."

"Set your son straight, Cam," Ellis all but hollered, shooting an arm out to stop Bryan's father as he tried to pass by.

"What's he done now?"

"The house!" Ellis exclaimed. "We've got a petition for an injunction to stop it."

"There's nothing to s-s—there's nothing to stop," Bryan stammered.

"It's an abomination! Panels on the roof, knocking down walls, leading our youth astray," Ellis added, with a nod towards young Lùcas, who cast Bryan an apologetic shrug and slunk away with Elspeth at his heels.

"Knocking down—what's this?" Bryan's father demanded.

"Walls, Cameron, whole entire walls! Your great grandaddy dug up those stones with his bare hands, and now they've been reduced to rubble."

"They're in the garden—"

"There'll be nothing left of that house once the lad's finished, you mark my words," Ellis went on.

"Whole walls, Ryan?" Bryan flinched. "You said you were fixing things up a bit. Making them more green."

Was it Bryan's imagination or did his father actually sneer at the word *green*?

"I-I-I—" he struggled, and a wave of nausea washed over him as the crowd of angry neighbors grew larger and the pipes and drums and fiddles all faded into a foggy buzz.

"What does knocking down walls have to do with distilling whisky?" his father demanded.

"You'd do better to keep renting it to tourists."

Oh good, Cait had entered the chat.

"It's an experiment," Bryan blurted out, closing his eyes immediately, anticipating the backlash at his poor choice of words.

"An experiment!" someone exclaimed. "On the oldest house on the island?"

"Knocking out walls is an experiment, Ryan? What's next, lighting the place on fire?" Nellie Combe demanded.

"Experiment on the mainland, why don't you?"

Christ, he couldn't breathe. Every effort made his lungs feel tighter and his head lighter. He opened and closed his palm, stopping short of twisting his kilt in anxious, empty fingers.

"Not exp-exp-experiment," he said. "A p-p-proof of c-c-c—proof of conce-concept."

If a fault line could crack open and swallow him into the ocean right about now, that would be perfect. He hadn't stammered this badly since he was a kid, not after his theater classes in Glasgow.

Bryan scanned the dance floor, again but he'd lost track of Teàrlach and Grace. He couldn't find her anywhere.

"What's that, Ry? We can't understand you when you stammer," fucking Mitchell Murray from karaoke shouted, and suddenly Bryan was ten years old again, fighting on the playground.

"Proof. Of. Concept," he gritted out.

"Proof of concept, he says," Ellis hollered. "What's that supposed to mean, Ryan MacNeil? D'you plan to knock down my wall next? Tear up every old house on Barra?"

Old Nellie Coombe gasped. "I won't stand for it! You stay well away from my house, do you hear me, Ryan MacNeil? I won't stand for it!"

"Aye, no, none of us will," Ellis agreed.

"I d-d— It's n-nothing to d-do with you," Bryan argued.

"Calm down, Ry, take a breath," Cait said, in a way that he supposed was meant to be soothing, but Bryan jerked as though she'd slapped him, his breaths growing more and more shallow.

"Just spit it out, Ryan," his father murmured in that disappointed way he had whenever Bryan couldn't speak.

"Still as much of a tangle-tongue as he ever was," fucking Mitchell Murray whisper-shouted for all to hear, making a face and grabbing his throat like he was choking.

Bryan could be wrong, but he was pretty sure this was actual hell, payback for all his many sins, and he would much prefer to simply blink right out of existence instead.

As a kid, he'd had a few exit strategies from this exact scenario, none of which were appropriate for a man of thirty-five. One was to let his fists fly, literally fighting to be heard. Another was to burst into tears, never a difficult feat when they burned so close to the surface of his frustration. The third option was to throw up on the closest tormenter's shoes. Another few minutes, and he could probably pull that one off.

He never should have dared try to come back to this place.

"What's the matter with you people?" a familiar American voice demanded, all brash and ballsy and brave, and his chest loosened enough to allow in a tiny whoosh of air. "You should be ashamed of yourselves."

Suddenly she was beside him, Grace Rios Rivera, giving his friends and family a dressing down that made them take a collective step back, and he sort of loved her and hated her for it at the same time.

"First of all, his name is *Bryan*," she said, the very words he'd wanted to scream for nigh on thirty years. "*Bryan*," she said again, emphasizing the diabolical *B*. "He can say it, and so can you."

He dragged his gaze up from the floor to peek at Cait, whose own face was turning a dark shade of crimson.

"And secondly, if it's any of your business what *Bryan* does with *Bryan's* property, then you should be thanking him."

Christ, he loved the sound of his name in her light American drawl, craved hearing it in a desperate sort of way.

"Thanking him?" Mitchell Murray scoffed.

"I know *I* didn't stutter," she said, deadly serious. "Yes, thanking him. Bryan's updates are making that drafty old cave cozy and inviting. They're making it modern and sustainable. They'll cut his energy costs, and if you still want to rent it out to guests, they'll be lining up to stay there because it's going to be gorgeous. Maybe if you ask him nicely, he'll show you how to do the same thing in your own homes."

"That's what we're afraid of!" Ellis shouted. "That house is a hundred years old. So is mine, nearly, and it's fine the way it is. I don't need him to prove to me that his new ways are better."

"Good thing he's not doing it for you then," Grace went on, and for some reason Bryan found himself rapt, as though it wasn't his story she was telling, but someone else's entirely, someone who should be admired for a job well done. "Bryan has big plans," she told them, and there was that name again—his name—slipping so easily off her tongue. "Are you people so self-absorbed you don't know where he's been? What he's made of himself?"

"Something about whisky," his father muttered.

"He's a master distiller!"

"Not quite yet," he demurred softly.

"He's a whisky genius with an Ardbeg expression all his own," she went on. "And he brought his brilliance and training back home to you, god knows why, to build a sustainable distillery right here. He'll bring jobs—good jobs—and publicity, and tourism, and revenue.

"He could have done it anywhere, but he chose to bring it here to you people like a freaking gift. And all you seem to give him in return is grief. If he's made any mistake at all, it was hoping you short-sighted, narrow-minded, ungrateful *jerks* would give him the chance to succeed.

"And if I ever hear you use that expression again," she said to fucking Mitchell Murray, who'd called him tangle-tongue, "I swear to god, I will cut yours out and shove it up your ass until you choke," she said, and Mitchell turned white as a ghost before going bright red.

She finally stopped talking to take a breath, and Bryan noticed Teàrlach nodding encouragement—at himself or at Grace, he wasn't certain, but it made his heart swell.

With shame-faced murmurs, the crowd dispersed until there was no one left but his father and sisters, and his cousins flanking him like sentries on either side, as the fiddle music came roaring back into his ears. He might have to pull up stakes and leave forever after that humiliation, but it had been something to witness.

"I'm sorry, Ry—Bry," Caitriona said, catching herself. "I had no idea you hated it."

His father just looked at him long and hard, assessing, passing judgment, and Bryan assumed he fell short of the mark when Cameron took a beer from the table and moved off into the mingling crowd without a word.

Chapter Twenty-One

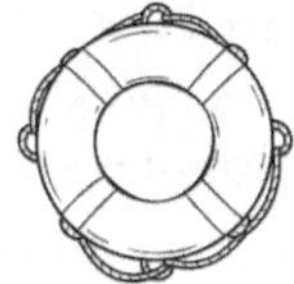

Dancing with Teàrlach was the most fun Grace had had in years. His enthusiasm was contagious, and he was an excellent teacher. And in a way, his chair had made it possible for her to feel okay not being perfect. They couldn't do every step exactly like the people around them, so it didn't matter that she hadn't mastered any of the steps at all. It was just joyous, messy fun, like dancing ought to be. For a moment, she'd forgotten about the stress of her second book and the merry-go-round of emotions she was having over Bryan. She'd been able to relax and give herself over to the movement and music, to the thrill of being surrounded by laughter and Scottish accents and people loving life.

And then the music had changed, and the air along with it, and angry voices infiltrated her happy bubble.

When a tickle ran down her spine, she'd looked up, searching the room for Bryan, only to find him surrounded by an angry crowd of family and neighbors, his cheeks stained scarlet, his eyes downcast.

She must have faltered, because Teàrlach turned his gaze to follow hers.

"Perhaps sit this one out," he murmured.

"Yes, I could use a drink," she had agreed before they made their way over to Bryan and his audience, which appeared to have tormented him into a stammer as he tried to explain his plans for the distillery.

Grace hadn't meant to step in, only it seemed like he was drowning—desperately in need of a minute to catch his breath—and A+ Grace had always been good at stepping in whether she was needed or not. Besides, she'd been the one to encourage him to explain his plans.

When that asshole started with the schoolyard slurs that probably still haunted his worst days, she physically couldn't stay quiet any longer. The teacher in her had pulled out a lecture, and once Grace started yelling at them, she'd been unable to stop.

He had stood stock still the entire time she was speaking, an all-to-familiar stance, as though he were the one in trouble, and a tiny voice in her head kept telling her to stop, but it turned out she had quite a lot to say. When she was finally finished, she looked each of them in the eye until she was confident of their shame. Bryan might drive her up a wall when he wasn't setting her nerve endings on fire, but he was also passionate and achingly kind, and he didn't deserve any of the bullshit they were hurling his way.

It made for an awkward walk back to his house, though, as the silence stretched between them. Just like after a long day of writing, Grace felt spent, like she'd used up all her words, but she also knew something more needed to be said because he hadn't asked for her help, and like the family dinner, he probably wished she hadn't been there at all.

"I'm sorry," she finally blurted out. "If that was out of line. It *was* out of line. Really, I'm just… sorry."

He was silent a moment longer. "What did we say about apologizing?"

"I know, but seriously. It feels like maybe that was the worst thing I could have done right then. I just can't stand the way they've been attacking you. But I know you don't need me to speak for you or over you."

"It didn't feel like that's what you were doing."

"Oh."

"It felt like you were on my ssside. And in my head. In my mouth, even." He grimaced. "Not like that."

"Oh. Yikes," she teased.

"Tell me about it," he agreed. "And thank you. For s-saying what I couldn't," he added in a small voice that kind of broke her heart a little.

"You could have," she assured him, and he snorted.

"Clearly."

She resisted the urge to repeat the empty-sounding platitudes running through her head. "You have. You've said all of that to me. More or less."

"I didn't have a conflict with Diego's wedding," he told her suddenly.

"No?" she asked, confused. Had he been there after all? Had collage-aged Gracie been mean to him? Oh god, had she unknowingly teased him about his stutter?

"He asked me to be his b-best man. It was always meant to be Teàrlach, but Mathilda wasn't happy with the optics. Afraid his chair would ruin the aesthetic or pull focus or s-something."

Grace shook her head. That sounded just like Mathilda. "And Diego didn't drop her right then? I don't get it, man. I don't blame you for standing up for Teàrlach, though."

"Aye, well. Much as I wish it were, Teàrlach wasn't the only reason. I couldn't face having to make a s-s-speech."

Suddenly Grace understood a lot more about her brother and the tensions surrounding his special day. He'd seemed distracted, annoyed with Mathilda, a little bit sad. Grace had always thought he'd been having second thoughts. "God, I hate her."

"My cowardice wasn't Mathilda's fault."

"Please. You never would have been in that situation if she wasn't such a conniving narcissist."

"That bad?"

"The only good things to ever come out of that woman were my niece and nephew."

Bryan laughed out loud, which after tonight, felt like a win.

"Seriously. You know she's the reason he goes by Sandy in the press? She even anglicized our last name for herself and the kids. Rivers…" Grace rolled her eyes. "She thinks she's so clever."

"Can't help who you love?" Bryan suggested.

"Maybe. Also can't help who secretly stops taking birth control…"

"Ah."

Way to make it awkward again, Gracie. "Anyway. We can just agree that one was all her fault. Do you know she wanted me to go on a diet before the wedding? For the photos? First time in my life I gained weight on purpose."

That surprised another laugh out of Bryan, and it was such an adrenaline rush to pull one out of the Stoic Scot.

"Thanks for coming tonight. Even if it was another unmitigated disaster," he said, his voice a warm rumble that reached deep into Grace's belly like a long sip of whisky.

"Up until the yelling, it was a real nice party," she quipped, and he grinned at her sideways, and god, how was that bearded smile so devastating? He was her brother's friend! She wasn't supposed to have a thing for him. Diego would never allow it—not that he had any say, but still.

"Fancy another fire? I've got a new biochar. I don't think it will reek like the wrong end of a donkey this time."

Now it was Grace's turn to burst out laughing. "Well then I'm definitely in."

He grinned at her.

"There's your new slogan. *You won't hate it, and it's better than the wrong end of a donkey.* Does that mean there's a *right* end?"

He laughed.

"Got any marshmallows?" she asked.

"Don't think I do. You really want to roast them?"

"Hell yes, I want to roast them! And then nestle them between graham crackers and chocolate."

"And you ingest this concoction?"

"Proudly," Grace said with a laugh. "Have you really never heard of s'mores?"

"Do I look like a Boy Scout?"

She took in his kilt and turned up cuffs. "Maybe a Scottish one. I can't believe you never heard of s'mores."

"Of course I've heard of them," he protested a little grumpily, and that, too, did things to her belly.

But, his pantry was one for three, so Grace had to settle for splitting a Cadbury. Luckily, however, the new biochar did have a nice, lightly smoky scent, and Bryan poured her a dram of his special reserved Rionnagach.

A deep contentment settled over her, as they sat in companionable silence on the loveseat, looking out across the ocean.

"Thank you for dancing with Teàrlach," he said after a while, even though she could tell from his face that *thank you* wasn't quite what he meant. "When you live in the town where you grew up, around all the folk you grew up with, they don't always see you the way you see yourself," he tried to explain. "Your entire history can haunt you."

And perhaps he was talking about his own relationship with the island, not just Teàrlach's.

In a way, Grace could relate. "It can be lonely when no one really sees you," she said.

"Aye," he agreed. "The fear is you'll be even more ashamed and lonely once they do see you." As if realizing what he'd said, how desperately sad it sounded, he added, "The trouble with growing up on a tiny island with your whole family is not learning how to ingratiate yourself to folk who don't have to love you no matter what."

He said it with a laugh, but she could hear the loneliness underneath.

Grace tried to think of something encouraging to say, but like a first draft, she was lost for words. "You seem to be doing okay," she finally murmured.

Bryan walked out to stoke the fire, more from a restless energy than being cold as far as she could tell. But when he retook his seat, he was very close, his body heat warming her far more than the fire as his words rattled in her head.

The fear is you'll be even more ashamed and alone once they do.

"If you're embarrassed about earlier, you needn't be," she said, nudging his shoulder.

"I completely melted down tonight."

"People from your childhood have a way of making you feel like a child," she told him. "I don't associate with literally *anyone* from my pre-college days. I decline reunions and retirement parties and wedding invitations. Like, a part of me still expects someone to walk up and whisper *Gordita Gracie* in my ear."

"You must think I'm ridiculous for coming home," he said softly.

She shook her head. "I hope I made it pretty clear I think they're the ridiculous ones."

He rolled his head sideways to look at her, and he was so close she could count the freckles sprinkled across his nose. She expected him to say something sarcastic, but he just stared into her eyes until her breath hitched.

"Thank you for tonight," he whispered.

Then their lips crashed together. Grace couldn't have said if she leaned in or he did, more like they were two magnets unable to resist each other's pull.

And god, it was hot. She had always loved kissing, it was only what came after that ruined everything. If they could draw the line at kissing forever, she'd be just fine.

She batted those thoughts away, losing herself in the scent of his cologne mixed with the smoky fire and tinged with salty sea air. She focused on his hands, one cupping her face, the other around her shoulders, as he nibbled her lips and tangled his tongue against hers.

This was the only reference to tangle-tongue she would ever allow.

The muscles of his biceps rippled beneath her hands as he ran his own up and down her arms, her back, her thighs, pulling her into his lap.

She felt a heat growing at her core, a heat that made her want but also made her panic, yanking her out of the moment.

When she pulled back, so did he. Panting for breath, he pressed his forehead to hers.

"All right?"

Yes. No. She wanted him, and she wanted to get far away from him.

When she didn't answer, he leaned back further, studying her, and ran a thumb down her cheek.

God, she wanted to grab him by the vest and drag him to her bedroom and make him make good on every desire she read in the heat of those eyes.

"All right?" he whispered again.

"I'm on my period!" she protested, scrambling off his lap, and his brow creased.

"All this time? Is that… healthy?"

"Rude," she huffed, leaning away from him and crossing her arms as she did the math.

He looked so sad and confused and after everything he'd been through tonight, how could she be anything but honest with him?

"I wasn't. Before. But I am now. I think." When he scowled at her she explained, "It's a defense mechanism."

His whole hairline shifted backwards as his face broke out in saucy relief. "What, like a lizard sheds its tail?"

"Are you serious?"

"Are you?"

He figured out pretty fast she was and sobered.

"Defense against what, Grace? There's lots of other ways—"

Grace put her hand on his chest to stop him. She was pretty sure her face could not be a darker shade of red if she'd eaten a hundred Atomic Fireballs in a row. "I get that you can bang anyone and everyone," she said, and the mischievous gleam was instantly replaced by a troubled one. "I'm like, the complete opposite of that," she tried to explain. But how do you explain that you want nothing to do with something everyone else seems to be obsessed with?

He gave her one curt nod, clearly pissed off, and shifted away from her, a whoosh of cold air replacing his body heat.

"It's not you, okay? It's me," she tried again, but her words sounded sharp and trite even though she meant them sincerely. It *was* her. She was the problem.

He glared at her.

"I really have to go," she muttered and scurried into the house, straight to her bedroom where she could spend the night alone, hating herself, wishing she were more like him, more like Wesley, who was probably having causal island sex with a handsome Scot who was definitely not a priest right this very minute.

But that wasn't Grace. It had never been Grace. And she knew it never would be.

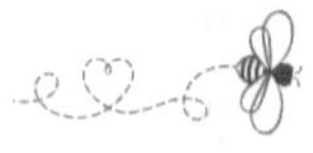

SAFE INSIDE HER BEDROOM, SHE LEANED BACK AGAINST THE DOOR.

She wasn't going to cry—not because she'd wrecked the kissing and definitely not because he was angry at her for pushing him away. Better he be angry now than later. Somehow a guy being pissed at you when you still had your clothes on didn't sting quite as much.

And honestly, what *right* did he have to be mad?

Did he think she was leading him on when she succumbed to his kisses? Was he out there right now calling her a cocktease? Because fuck that. At least she hadn't accidentally groped him this time. Was it her fault he looked irresistible in a kilt? Was she supposed to resist him anyway if she had no intention of putting out?

Sister Mary Agnes would say yes.

Sister Mary Agnes would say she should have resisted every temptation so he wouldn't get the wrong idea, and maybe she should have, but damn. Did that mean the only reason he begged her to go to the ceilidh at all was so he could get in her pants later? Was she not allowed to have any fun ever because of the strings that might be attached?

She racked her memory, trying to decide who had leaned in first. If it was her, then it was her fault for leading him on, and if it was him, then it was her fault for not running away sooner, according to Sister Mary Agnes.

Grace had never liked Sister Mary Agnes.

"You're spiraling," she told herself. "This is not helpful."

But knowing it didn't make it any easier to stop.

So what if he had expectations? She had consented to kissing and nothing else. His hurt feelings were not her responsibility. Right?

She could barely look him in the eye when she stopped him, her hand on his chest like she hadn't just been contemplating ripping his whole shirt off, as she confessed to lying about her period before. Then, when she tried to explain how she wasn't like everyone else, and he got so quiet, she had allowed herself one quick glance, hoping for a sign he understood. Only she didn't see empathy and understanding. He didn't look angry yet either, no—in that split second when his expression changed from mischievous to completely closed off, what she saw looked more like a flicker of pain, and she had put it there on his beautiful face.

He had tried to hide it immediately, but she knew.

He was disappointed by her change of heart, and honestly, maybe it was unfair, but she was disappointed in him for feeling that way.

Of course, the rejection must have stung his ego, especially tonight on the heels of being spurned by his neighbors and family. But this wasn't about him. It was never about them.

God, what terrible timing.

What an absolute mess.

Why couldn't she be brave enough, find better words to explain? Would it have made any difference if she had?

She'd known from the start it was a mistake to have any level of involvement with this guy. She had known, and she'd done it anyway, and the worst part of it was she didn't just like him. She'd allowed him to become a friend—a real one—someone to keep in touch with for years to come, but now it was Justin Everett all over again.

Even the flash of pain in his eyes reminded her of the look Justin gave her in ninth grade when she had told him she was sorry the other boys were picking on him but she couldn't possibly send him a naked photo of herself. She had expected understanding that time, too, even an apology for asking. Instead, her refusal had been the lever that started the unraveling of an almost ten-year friendship.

Justin was her first best friend. He was her first partner in crime, first crush, first heartbreak.

In the end, though, when she wouldn't do what he wanted, none of the rest of it mattered. But that look of pain and disappointment in his eyes, like he was the one who'd been hurt while she was trying to pretend away the betrayal—that look still haunted her, and it mirrored what she saw on Bryan's face tonight, and quite honestly, fuck both of them to the moon.

Chapter Twenty-Two

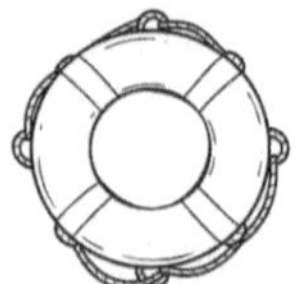

The fire smoldered down to embers, but still Bryan sat, watching as the sparks died out one by one. At least the biochar had worked, so the night wasn't a complete failure. It gave off an appealing scent, though of course the true test would be in the barley flavors it evoked, but he was definitely on the right track.

Too bad he couldn't seem to enjoy it.

I get that you can bang anyone and everyone. I'm like, the complete opposite of that.

The pressure of her hand was still imprinted on his chest, cutting off his words. Pushing him away. Stopping the retort that it had, in fact, been quite a long time since he'd banged anyone at all.

He took a deep slug of Rionnagach to burn her touch and her words away, but they were still there as sure as he still had skin. Maybe if he got to the bottom of the bottle, he would figure out why things kept going sideways just when they started to feel the most right.

His cousins liked to take the piss, but had he really given the impression he was some kind of skanky island Lothario? On an endless loop, he replayed every interaction of the last two weeks. He had flirted a little. There'd been some innuendo. In the midst of flirting, he'd made a glib joke about being bisexual, as he often did, a gentle way of coming out early to avoid a future big serious conversation.

Was the flirting so wrong when she waltzed around his house wearing those librarian shirts? NAUGHTY LIBRARIANS HAVE NO SHELF CONTROL? Come on.

And for the record, she hadn't seemed to mind the flirting, so what just happened?

Sure, he was more of a serial dater than long-term relationship material, but he was hardly a player. He just called it early when it became clear things wouldn't work. Why drag out the inevitable?

After another long slow sip of whisky, he was willing to admit this might be one of those times.

And yet…

Like a moth to a flame, he was drawn to the fire inside her that would knock down whole walls and tell off whole communities for not giving him the credit she thought he deserved.

You don't need me to speak for you or over you…

Tonight, it had seemed like it was them against the world. She truly had his back out there—until it was just the two of them. Then she jumped to conclusions and put words in his mouth like marbles.

The last little bits of his firewood hissed and went out, but he didn't want to go inside, so he pulled up the football on his phone. The Wi-Fi signal was terrible this far from the house. LA wasn't even playing, and the Portland and Seattle players kept stopping and starting like a game of freeze tag, but Bryan couldn't bring himself to go inside.

"Mind if I join you?" Wesley asked, dropping onto the chair next to his. "Something smells really good."

The whisky made him slow to respond, but seeing as she

hadn't waited for an answer, he supposed it didn't really matter. He waved one hand in magnanimous welcome and glanced sideways at her. Either it was his imagination or her lips were red and kiss-swollen. As predicted, she still wore his cousin's plaid.

"I'll bring down another chair when Gray gets back," she said, so obviously fishing she almost looked embarrassed.

"She won't be back. It's all yours."

Wes studied him for a second, and Christ but he didn't want to talk about it. Not with her. With his luck, she'd give him all the gory details of a hot and heavy night with his cousin.

"Are you watching... American soccer?" she finally asked, mercifully changing the subject.

"Aye," he said, handing her the bottle of Rionnagach.

She lifted it in thanks and took a swig.

Once the burn subsided, she nodded to his phone and asked, "Don't they expatriate you for things like that?"

He exhaled a pretend laugh.

"Well, if they do run you out of here, you can always come to Tennessee. We can't get enough of whisky there. They'd be all over you."

He nodded once. Appealing as that offer sounded, he already knew Grace would be the only reason he'd ever go to Tennessee.

"For what it's worth," Wes offered, "I admire what you're doing."

She was sweet, but Bryan scoffed. What was there to admire? Pissing off the entire island? Tearing down a piece of history?

"No, really. It's like Gray with her writing or Diego with soccer. Even when you have the passion and the talent, it can still be scary as fuck to go for it, but you're out here putting one foot in front of the other towards your goal. It's commendable. Most people can't be bothered."

"I take it you have a passion and talent for something other than..." Bryan trailed off, realizing he had no idea what Wes did for a living.

"Oh, I absolutely have a talent for insurance billing."

"And passion?"

"Like no other," she answered sarcastically. "It's so important, you know? Keeping the wheels of Big Insurance chugging along." After a moment, though, she sighed heavily. "My dream was to be an interior designer. Especially set design."

Bryan sobered. "Was?"

She shook her head. "I gave up on it. Gave up on myself." She pointed to her eyes. "I went through some shit, and at the time I didn't see the value in doing something I loved for a little while if I might not be able to do it forever."

"It's not too late, is it?" Bryan asked. After all, she was young still, and he'd read enough about her condition to know she should retain some amount of vision even if it was mostly peripheral.

Wes turned to him like she was prepared to argue, but then she smiled. "No. You're living proof it's not too late."

"It's true. I'm ancient. If I can do it…"

She laughed and shook her head. "I only meant this trip has made me reassess some things."

Bryan raised his glass to that, and she raised the bottle in salute.

"How do you say *cheers* here?"

"Slàinte."

"Slàinte," she replied, and they each took another drink. "I love how much daylight there is," Wes murmured, looking out to sea.

"Aye?"

"I have a tendency to always feel like I'm running out of time, so I rush and rush constantly."

"That's fair."

"But here… it's almost like there's an abundance of time. I feel like I can finally slow down and take a breath."

"Don't visit in winter, then," he said.

"Are the winters hard?" she asked.

Bryan shrugged. "Can be. Every season has its own trials as well as magic."

"Well, the changes to your house will go a long way to making winter more tolerable."

"Is that your professional opinion?"

"From an insurance perspective, the increased warmth and sunlight inside the house will elevate serotonin…"

He burst out laughing, surprising himself, and Wes smiled.

"It may be hard for untrained eyes to see in its present state, but your vision is clear. I agree with every word Gray said tonight, by the way. You've an eye for aesthetic and you're bringing it to life."

Maybe it was a sign of too much whisky or simply the reminder of Grace, but his throat felt thick as he nodded his thanks and raised his glass to her once again.

"Can I ask you something?" She nodded, so he took a breath and pressed on. "Have you and Rios heard… I dunno… rumors about me?" he asked.

Wes grew very serious. "Oh. Yeah, I mean I thought you knew. Everyone's saying you're in league with the Big Bad Wolf to blow down their houses and force them to live off the grid."

Bryan huffed. "Aside from that."

"I mean that's pretty much the hottest goss on the island. I guess I did hear this one rumor that you're pretty great at karaoke, but since I don't pay any attention to rumors"—she leaned forward, setting the bottle of whisky on the ground at his feet—"I think I'm going to have to see that again for myself."

"What, right now?"

"The pub's still open. I just walked by."

"I'm quite hammered."

"Me too, fella. Best kind of karaoke." She jumped to her feet. "Know any John Prine?"

"Of course I know John Prine," Bryan growled, rolling his eyes at her. "I wasn't raised on a desert island."

Wes giggled and took his hands, pulling him up. "Come on, Stoic Scot. Let's get you out of those feelings."

And because just about anything sounded better than stewing in his thoughts, Bryan let Wesley drag him off to the Three Puffins and put their names down for karaoke.

Half an hour later, after they'd sung both "Falling in Love Again" and "In Spite of Ourselves" to the amusement of the stragglers still hanging around until close, Bryan's morale had actually improved. Maybe it was the spirits, maybe the silliness or just the singing, but he felt a little better.

Wes tilted her head at him and asked, "So what rumors were you really fretting about?"

"Something along the lines of me being a whore."

She laughed, choking on the beer she'd been nursing. "No, that's new. Are you?"

"Not really."

"Did something happen with Grace?"

"Not really," he said again.

Wes nodded slowly like she understood, and Bryan felt a bit shit for kissing and telling.

"You know in *White Christmas*, when Vera-Ellen tells Danny Kaye that Rosemary Clooney is 'a real slow mover'? And Danny Kaye says, 'She's in there with the champ'?"

"No…"

Welsey's jaw dropped like she was shocked he'd never seen the old movie. "Some people's kids! Are you sure you didn't grow up on a desert island?"

"Raised by puffins," he laughed.

"Must have been! Listen, Bryan," she said, taking his face in her hands. "Are you listening to me?"

He took a deep breath. "I'm listening."

"Good." She let go of his face and drew her own breath.

"Grace is one of my best friends in the entire world. Maybe *the* best, but despite my bad influence, she's kind of a little bit of a prude. It's not her fault, and we love her for it, but it is a fact. She has trouble talking—even writing—about this stuff. Do you understand what I'm telling you?"

Bryan nodded, because he supposed he did. Real depth with Grace would take time, time he didn't have, which is why you don't get attached to tourists.

"No one thinks you're a whore. Not even Gray."

He nodded again. True or not, he appreciated hearing it.

"She might think I'm one. I don't know. I'm afraid to ask, honestly."

He laughed at that.

"You have a good smile, Stoic Scot. You should let it out more."

Chapter Twenty-Three

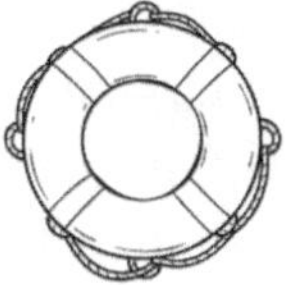

Somehow, despite tossing and turning in a broken, angry fluster for what seemed like hours, Grace was asleep before Wes ever came to bed, and she woke with a start to find her friend already dressed and tying her shoes the next morning.

"You're up early," Grace said.

"I'm always up early. I want to see the castle. Thought maybe we could pack a lunch and borrow a kayak."

"Kayak?" Grace moaned. She was not a kayak kind of girl—not really an open water kind of girl, to be perfectly honest. She had cramps and despite thinking she was all cried out last night, she just wanted to lie in bed today, curled up with the fuzzy hot water bottle, watching *Sense and Sensibility* on her phone.

"What do they call it then? A dinghy?" Wes asked, acting oblivious to Grace's current mood.

"It looks really far away."

"Thus my desire for a closer look," she replied, slapping an orange University of Tennessee ball cap on her head.

Grace moaned again. "Aren't you exhausted? You were out so late."

"I mean, I tried my best."

"Finally hook up with your handsome Scot?"

"Grace, he's a priest!" Wes exclaimed, but her scandalized air seemed mostly put on for the only actual Catholic in the room.

"Wes," Grace began, because someone was going to have to tell her she'd gotten it all wrong about Bryan's cousin.

"I know," Wes interrupted her. "He's only human. But he smells so good. We did, in fact, share a kiss, and he was surprisingly excellent at it—like, sinfully good, like—how? Like, frankly he has no business kissing like that, but obviously he wasn't born a priest, you know? But I guess he's been one for long enough, because then his eyes went all wide and he ran away like a traumatized woodland creature."

"I know the feeling," Grace told her, guilt prickling down her back for doing the exact same thing to Bryan. Again.

"I stayed out as long as I could to give you every opportunity with *your* Stoic Scot, so imagine my surprise to find him despondent, drinking whisky alone, watching *American* soccer."

Oh god, had Grace missed a game? She never missed a game. "Did they win?"

"I have no idea."

"Did he say anything?" she asked, hating herself for asking.

"Who, Diego? I don't know if he was playing."

"Bryan. Did Bryan say anything?"

"I'm not fluent in moody man grunt, but I'm pretty sure he offered me a drink which I accepted, and we sat in wounded silence, sang some karaoke, and then he asked if I thought he was a slut."

A twinge of envy and a whole heaping of regret slid down Grace's throat and settled heavy in her gut. Had she gotten it all wrong last night?

She thought his pride was wounded because she wasn't willing to sleep with him. Was it actually over her dumb comment about not being like him? She hadn't meant anything by it! He was normal, like everyone else. *She* was the problem. That's what she was trying to say. A slut? Come on. Wasn't that some point of pride for most guys anyway?

He was probably just upset she found a reason to leave.

Right?

"Don't look at me like that. I handed you an empty house on a platter with a man whose face said he wanted to worship you for days without stopping. What the hell happened?"

"The same thing that always happens," Grace hissed, getting up to hide in the bathroom and feeling a little bit proud and a little bit disgusted with herself for not letting either door slam behind her. Blinking back the bright bathroom light, for a second she looked around in confusion. Like the living room, the floor was a mess and walls were tarped off. Was he trying to tear the whole house down around her while she slept?

When she emerged, there was Wes drinking tea in the kitchen with Bryan, whose perma-scowl was even deeper than it had been last night.

Grace eyed him and he eyed her, and Wes's head jerked up from her phone like the icy tension was palpable.

"I hope you told her it was a terrible idea," he growled, and her stomach sank to hear him admit it out loud. Of course getting together would never work, but damn, Mr. Bee.

"I really didn't peg you for a spoil sport, Bryan MacNeil," Wes grumbled. "What's the point of having a castle if tourists can't go and visit it?"

Oh. Right. The castle.

"You're not familiar with the currents, nor the tides. The water is unforgiving, even in the bay." He spoke to Wesley, but he never took his eyes off Grace.

"Then you and your cousin should come with us," Wes pressed him, determined to be perky to the last.

This time he didn't answer, though he continued his staring contest with Grace, like he was asking for permission.

"They're busy," she told her friend. "Look at the state of things," she added because it was starting to seem like there was more destruction than renovation happening, and she felt partially responsible, like her rejection of Bryan had turned him into a tempest.

He nodded grimly, but the encounter at the ceilidh last night had clearly taken the wind out of his sails. He didn't look fired up to work—he looked like he could lie down and sleep for days.

"Lùc will be here at nine. We've got to get the windows in before the gale blows through."

"Maybe Eòghann could go with us," Grace suggested, since he was the cousin Wes had been referring to. She was willing to go toe-to-toe with her friend in the matchmaker department. Wesley deserved to have nice things even if Grace didn't.

"He won't," Bryan growled.

"Why not let him speak for himself?" she demanded. Was this the end of everything then? She rejected him a second time and now he couldn't even be cordial for Wesley's sake?

It made her want to goad him more than ever before.

"He's *of* the island, you said. He should know all about the water."

"Aye, he'll know to keep well clear of it ahead of a storm."

Grace huffed. "What storm? There's not a cloud in the sky."

"Walk over to the bay. From the ferry dock you'll get a fine view. Or call Elspeth. She'll drive you to the docks."

"There's a ferry to the castle?" Grace asked.

"Not today," he said, and left it at that.

"Of course not."

"Go for a nice walk. There'll be folk around with b-binoculars." He didn't seem to like the look Grace and Wesley shared, but he glanced at his watch. "P—Will you promise me you won't hire a… boat?" he demanded.

They exchanged another look.

"Rios," he growled, and what was it about her surname when

uttered with that angry Scottish burr? It kindled a fire in her belly against her will. "Rios?" This time he was begging.

"Fine!" she snapped. "We'll go for a walk."

AS THEY STROLLED DOWN THE BEACH UNDER A CLOUDLESS cerulean sky, Grace grew more and more angry, as well as disappointed on Wesley's behalf. She'd felt badly about possibly hurting Bryan's feelings, but his anger just pissed her off. What right did he have to be so angry? They had kissed, that's all, and if he expected more—well, life was full of disappointment!

"Eòghann did say he had some work to do around the church. Maybe tomorrow they'll go with us," Wes suggested glumly.

"I don't want to go with *him* anyway," Grace snapped, and they both knew she meant Mr. Bee.

"Well… I suppose we only promised we wouldn't *hire* a boat," Wes said, mischief glinting in her eyes. "Auntie Eilidh offered to lend us one."

"Did she? That's interesting," Grace agreed, though she doubted Bryan would see it that way, but what right did he really have to tell them what to do anyway?

And it wasn't as though she'd said the words, *I promise not to get in a boat today.* She had said they'd go for a walk, and they did.

They walked right down the beach to Auntie Eilidh's house and asked to borrow her inflatable dinghy.

It was a beautiful day. It wasn't going to rain. He was just trying to ruin her fun because she ruined his last night when she ran off to her bedroom.

"Don't venture too far out," the old lady warned them. "Skies can turn on a dime," she added with a laugh before offering cheese and pickle sandwiches and two bottles of Irn-Bru, which they accepted gratefully, before heading down to the water dragging the little boat between them.

"We'll stay close to the shore," Wes said, unconvincingly. "If the tides drift us over to the castle, what can we do?"

"Use the motor?" Grace muttered.

"It's the perfect day for an adventure," Wes replied sunnily, and they shoved the dinghy into the water. "Nothing like a little excitement to help your writing process."

Wesley's determination to enjoy herself proved contagious, despite Grace's bad mood. How could she focus on her annoyance with Bryan while enjoying the endless sunshine and the brisk morning air? It was a good reminder to get up from her keyboard and look around now and then.

"Bryan probably didn't know we meant to take a boat with a motor," Wes said, getting that mischievous glint in her eye once again. "He probably thought we were going to try and row ourselves out to the castle." She scoffed. "Paddles are for chumps!"

Grinning, Grace tugged the cord to start the engine. They could be there and back before anyone was the wiser. At the second yank it fired right up, and they headed out towards the middle of the bay.

After half an hour, though, the castle was still very far away, much further than it had seemed. They had made it about half-way, and now they didn't seem to be getting any closer. The engine sputtered hard against the current, and a few clouds had blown in, beginning to obscure the azure sky.

"We probably should have launched from the ferry dock where Bryan mentioned the view," she called over the little coughing motor.

"Probably," Wes yelled. "I guess we can let him gloat about it while we pick out a new place to stay."

Grace's stomach dropped. "What do you mean?"

"The festival's over. Rooms will be opening up. You two

clearly hate each other too much to get over it and get it on, so I figured…"

"Oh."

"Do you not want to?" Wes asked.

No. Grace was finally writing again. Bryan had become a part of the background noise, even something of a muse. Like not shaving a playoff beard or changing your lucky socks, you don't mess with a streak.

"Oh my god, then why don't you two just bone already?" Wes demanded, and Grace cringed at the crude description of doing exactly what she'd been trying not to fantasize about for days.

"It's not like that," she argued feebly. "I'm not like you."

"So you think I'm a slut too?" Wes demanded, a lot more pissed off than Grace would've expected—despite Bryan's similar reaction after she said basically the exact same thing to him.

"I never said you're a slut."

"You definitely implied it."

"I'm really not trying to insult you here."

"It kind of sounded like you were, though."

"It's a statement of fact. I'm not judging. I just can't have no strings, no emotions—I can't even *with* strings and emotions!"

"Just so we're clear, though, this thing with Bryan would definitely be a case of the former, no emotions at all whatsoever?" Wes shouted sarcastically.

"There's not," Grace protested.

"Excuse me, I was in the room this morning. I literally needed a shower to wash off all the pheromones you two were spewing at each other."

"That is absolutely not true. He's still furious with me for turning him down last night, and honestly, I'm still pretty pissed at him."

"Since when do the two have to be mutually exclusive? Given the slightest encouragement, that man would have climbed you like a fireman's pole."

"I don't think they climb—"

"You know what I mean, Gray. If you don't want to bang him, what possible excuse do you have to stay? It's his house. He's making an ever-loving racket. You are a thousand percent in his way, and you both have deadlines."

"But I'm also finally writing. It's a delicate process. I don't want to rock the boat—"

Speaking of rocking the boat, the tide or waves or what-have-you seemed to be rocking theirs quite a lot as the sky grew dark and the air charged and chilly.

Then a foghorn blared, and Grace looked over her shoulder to see a much larger vessel bearing down on them. "Oh shit."

"What is it?" Wesley squinted.

"A ferry."

"I thought there wasn't one."

"Heading to the mainland, I guess."

"What should we do?"

"I would say paddle like hell but…"

"Paddles are for chumps," Wes whimpered.

Grace tried to turn the little boat out of the ferry's path and choke more speed from the already weary motor as the sea battered and tossed them and the ferry horn blared once more.

"Not how I pictured my own death," Wes muttered.

Grace was still trying to think of a snappy retort when a wave from the ferry's wake smacked the side of their dinghy and she went overboard.

Chapter Twenty-Four

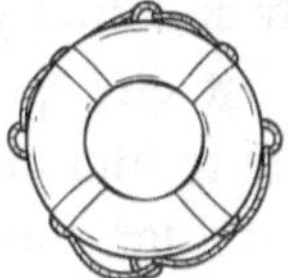

Throughout the morning as Bryan and Lùcas raced to install the new living room windows, he kept one eye on the darkening sky and an ear out for the Americans' disgruntled return. They would at least be mollified that he was right about the storm. Maybe he could take them to the castle tomorrow.

The wind picked up and he cast a wary eye out towards the water. They'd been gone a long time. Too long, unless they had found something else to do besides stare at the old pile of stones.

Could be they were just staying out to enjoy fresh air before the storm chased them indoors. Deep in his bones, though, he had a sense of foreboding he couldn't shake, the kind that haunts you for hours after you wake up from a bad dream.

Perhaps it was only the urgency of getting the house water-tight before the weather broke, or the pall of yesterday's run-in with his neighbors hanging over him, but his stomach churned like the roughening surf as he and Lùcas spread caulk around a frame and set the next window in place.

A single raindrop landed on his arm, and he clocked the sky

again. Good timing that it had waited until the end of the festival —and until they'd gotten the drywall up.

"How soon do you reckon I can move in?" Lùc asked, out of nowhere. At Bryan's confused frown he added, "Wes asked for recommendations on places to stay, so I thought…"

Bryan had rather hoped they'd all moved on from such notions. Had he completely and utterly misread the situation? If he could misread that, what else had he gotten wrong? Was Grace, in fact, not attracted to him in the slightest? Kissed him back because she felt sorry for him? Kissed him, and then regretted it because she hated him? Or his face? Or his beard?

"Umm… Can I still? After they leave?" Lùc asked, hesitantly.

"'Course," Bryan told him, then suddenly asked, "What do you think of the beard? Keep it or shave it?"

His cousin looked up, head tilted like a pup. "It's a nice beard," Lùc said, scratching his own baby-faced chin.

Bryan just shook his head and got back to work.

"Can I have a job in the distillery when it's done?" the boy asked.

"Do you want a job in a distillery?"

Lùc shrugged, and Bryan sat back on his haunches, wiping his sweaty forehead on his shoulder.

"When do you leave school?"

"Already did."

Bryan nodded for Lùcas to help him pick up the next window and heft it into place. "Going to uni?" he asked.

When Lùc didn't respond, he glanced up at and his cousin shrugged again. "What would *I* study at uni?"

"What *would* you?" Bryan turned the question back on him.

"Art, I suppose," Lùcas said, shaking his head.

It surprised Bryan a little, but maybe it shouldn't have, coming from someone who couldn't resist illuminating the margins of library books. "Great opportunity to get off the island for a while, if you think you'd like to explore," Bryan suggested.

Lùcas shook his head again, slapping caulk on the next frame. "If my da has his way, I'll work at the shop and never leave until they put me in the ground."

"And if you had your way?" Bryan asked.

Again he shrugged.

"It'll take a while to get the distillery up and running," Bryan explained. "But if you're here and still want a job, it's yours."

That seemed to please the lad, whose shoulders relaxed a bit as they continued to work in silence until Bryan had an idea.

"One thing I'll need sooner rather than later—a logo and a label. You wouldn't have any interest in helping me design them, would you?"

His cousin's face lit up like Bryan had switched on a megawatt light. "Truly?"

"If you're keen."

"I'll start drafting ideas tonight!"

Oh, to be seventeen and have the energy to do anything after a day of hard labor.

They picked up the next window just as thunder cracked overhead, and together they slid into a faster pace. There was only one left to mount when Eòghann burst through the back door, wild-eyed and breathless.

"Are they here?" he demanded, and Bryan's stomach sank.

"What d'you mean?" Bryan asked, though he had the worst kind of feeling he already knew.

"Gavin down at the ferry called, said two idiots in a dinghy were out in the middle of the ferry lane. Captain said he didn't see them until he was right up on top of them. Gavin said by the sound of it, 'twas Eilidh's boat. She hasn't been out in years, so I thought—"

"Aye," Bryan said grimly, as a paralyzing chill ran through his bones.

"They wouldn't have taken it out? Not in this weather. Tell me I'm wrong."

Bryan opened and closed his mouth, but no words came out.

"They went for a walk, you said," Lùcas offered.

"I b-b-begged them."

Eòghann's face went another shade of white.

"Eilidh's little motor?" Bryan asked.

His cousin nodded, stricken.

He was going to be sick. He had to get to them.

It thundered again, and Bryan looked up at the gaping hole that was the last window.

"I can finish on my own," Lùcas assured him.

Bryan stared at him dumbly, trying to think what to do, until another crash of thunder made him jump.

"Go!" Lùc yelled, and Bryan raced inside with Eòghann on his heels.

THE YOUNG GUARD AT THE FERRY OFFICE DIDN'T WANT TO LEND him a speedboat or the fuel to take her out.

"It's me or the Coast Guard. Your choice," Bryan growled, furious the ferry office hadn't already called in Search and Rescue.

None too eager to rally the troops over a pair of errant tourists who may or may not actually be missing, the kid relented and handed over a key and three life jackets. Minutes later, Bryan was flying towards the castle, peering through the fog for signs of life. This couldn't be happening. Not to Eòghann, not again, and not to Bryan, either.

Suddenly his hurt feelings over last night's words seemed so stupid. Why hadn't he told her to wait a day? Why not promise to put aside everything he'd planned to do tomorrow and just take them? What was a few hours in the grand scheme of his renovation? It would have been a small price, but now…

Christ.

The water was choppy as he sped across the surf. The ferry guard had pointed out approximately where they'd been spotted, but Bryan was no expert, and out here it all looked the same, just a whole lot of darkness and wind and spray. His lungs ached, and not just from the cold. He couldn't lose her, couldn't lose either of them, not like this.

Seeing no sign of Aunt Eilidh's dinghy or anything else in any direction, he turned the speedboat towards the castle. He'd just have to start at Kisimul, and if he didn't find them there, radio Eòghann to call for backup and then work his way back to Eilidh's place, and back and forth again if he had to.

The storm finally broke before he reached the island, amping up the sour churn in his stomach. They absolutely could not drown, not on his watch. How could he ever face Diego? Or Eòghann? Or anyone else?

Up ahead there was a flash of orange, out of place in the colorless gloom, and he cut the engine, searching for that flash again as the surf crashed nearly over the side of his boat.

Had he imagined it?

He wiped his face on one damp sleeve before staring back out at the water, and there it was again, the bright orange hat Wes had donned that morning, glowing like a beacon. But though he squinted through the driving rain, searching until his eyes began to cross, there was nothing to be found, not the boat, not the American Invasion, nothing.

Scenario after scenario flooded his mind, each more dreadful than the last, as the rain soaked through his thin t-shirt. He shivered, but he didn't regret not stopping to grab a hat or slicker.

Then he saw something—dark, curly hair floating near the surface—Grace!

Bryan leaned way out of the boat, but he couldn't quite reach.

A bolt of lightning lit up the sky and the water, and he yanked his arm back when he realized it wasn't Grace at all, just a bunch of kelp churned up to the surface, all tangled in something that on closer inspection appeared to be the remnants of Eilidh's dinghy. The motor was trying to drag it all down through the kelp, but strips of PVC still floated at the surface.

He dry-heaved but nothing came up, and he forced himself to slide back down in the boat to catch his breath and get his bearings.

"Call the Coast Guard," he yelled down the radio. "The dinghy's sunk."

Then he turned the engine back on and slammed the boat forward at speed, praying they had washed up on shore. The sky was so dark now he could hardly make out the beach around Kisimul Castle until he ran up on some rocks, the hull of his boat groaning in protest. He cut the engine and vaulted into the water with his shoes still on, dragging the boat as best he could further up onto the tiny beach.

"Rios?" he shouted. "Wes?"

He scanned left and right along the outer edge of the castle. Christ, what a nightmare, but if they had any sense, and the physical ability to do so, they'd have tried to find a way inside. The grounds would be locked of course, and the tide was creeping ever closer.

With a first aid kit slung over one shoulder, Bryan made his way around the tiny island towards the back side of the castle where the building itself might provide at least a little shelter from the driving rain. "Rios! Wesley!" he shouted again, and then suddenly Wes jumped out of the mist, throwing her arms around him.

"You were right," she yelled. "I'll eat all the vegetarian crow on the planet, you were right."

"Are you okay?" he shouted, holding her at arm's length to assess her bedraggled state.

She was bleeding from a scrape on her cheek, and there were bits of bracken tangled in her hair, but she nodded that she was all right, biting her lip and holding back tears. "I never swam so hard in my life."

"Grace?" he asked her, hardly daring to breathe.

"Twisted her ankle on the rocks. She's around the corner," Wes yelled, pointing in the direction he'd been headed.

"Wait here," Bryan shouted, pointing at the boat, "and radio Eòghann to call off the Coast Guard."

She nodded, and Bryan was pretty sure now she was crying.

He found Grace huddled against the castle's outer wall, trying and failing to use it for shelter from the rain. His heart leapt at the sight of her, whole and hale, but the adrenaline was quickly converting his fear to fury. Her eyes seemed to light when she saw him, too, and then she dissolved into tears.

Without pausing to think, Bryan cupped her face, proving to himself she was real. He pressed her up against the old crumbling stone and kissed her fiercely.

She kissed him back, her breath sweet like Irn-Bru, and for a moment, all of his anger and anxiety were forgotten, replaced by her jasmine and peach scent and the warmth of her tongue battling his, as the tightness in his chest finally loosened for the first time in over an hour.

When he stepped back to take a breath, she looked up at him with such vulnerability in her eyes, just for a flicker, before they turned hard, preparing for a fight, and just like that, his anger came roaring back too.

"You p-promised," he shouted.

"You had no right to make me," she argued, and Bryan looked around at their predicament in disbelief that she could still be so stubborn.

"I didn't make you. You're an adult," he countered. "Even if you don't act like one."

"What's that supposed to mean?"

"I told you it was too dangerous, but you just do whatever you want, is that it? Typical American."

"How dare you! I was trying to do something nice for my friend. She wanted to *see* it. Do you get that? What it means to her?"

"You know I do. But she won't be able to see anything at all if you get her killed!"

"It was a beautiful sunny day!" she hissed.

"And I told you it wasn't going to s-s-stay that way! Did you not hear me?"

"Oh, I heard you."

"Did you not—did you not believe me?"

"No, I didn't believe you," she replied, and it stung right down to his core.

He tried to make his throat work, but for a moment he just strangled on air. "Why?" he finally croaked.

"You were acting like a controlling jerk. You couldn't be bothered to ask Eòghann to go with us? We'd have been here and back in plenty of time."

Bryan gestured at the island and the storm raging around them. "Eòghann would have told you exactly what I did. Would you have listened to him? Are his words so much more p-p-persuasive than mine?" God damn his stammer, popping up as if to illustrate the point.

"He wouldn't have tried to stop us, because he has a thing for Wes!"

"Not enough of a thing!" Running his hands through his wet hair, Bryan wanted to scream in frustration. Was she trying to say *he* didn't care enough about her to go with them, when clearly he cared enough to warn her off *and then to come out in the storm after her*? "Eòghann would never have agreed to this. I can't get my head around why *you* agreed to this! You were just hell-bent on doing the opposite of what I wanted from the moment I said no."

Her eyes flashed dangerously telling him he'd hit a nerve.

"If I'd insisted you go, then would you have—"

"I don't need to be told what to do by an illiterate oaf who thinks he can read the sky!"

Bryan swallowed.

"Sorry," she said immediately, her eyes filling with unshed tears. "I didn't mean that."

"'Course you did." He tried to smile but was pretty sure it came off as a sneer. "You wanted to be cruel and cutting, and you knew exactly how to hit your mark. You can't take it back just 'cause you regret it." She might not mean the words, but she'd meant to say them. She was lashing out like an animal that was hurting somewhere he couldn't see, and he didn't understand why.

Grace studied the ground. They were both soaked to the skin, and the rain ran down her cheeks like so many tears, and he kind of wanted to cry himself. Before last night, he'd thought she heard him in a way most people never did.

"Why are you here?" she demanded, but what was the point of admitting he cared for her now? She probably wouldn't hear that either.

"Why are you?" he asked, and her teary face turned belligerent again. "You're not leaving yet. You've loads more time for Wes to see the castle. Why did it have to be today, when I asked you... when you p-p—when you promised not to? Why, Rios?" he pressed.

"Because I was angry at you!" she exploded. "Because I was *furious* that you were pissed at me for not wanting to sleep with you last night!"

Bryan took a step back, his head spinning. She thought he was upset they didn't hook up?

"You don't get to be mad about that, you do not get to be mad at me," she yelled, her eyes brimming with tears once more. "So why are you here?" she asked again.

Bryan opened his mouth, but no words would come, and he closed it again.

She was staring at him, waiting, and she deserved an answer.

"Couldn't lose you," he finally managed, shrugging one shoulder. "Cait would never let me live down the reviews if a guest died on my watch," he added, to lessen the impact.

Her face crumpled as she looked up at him, and he got the sense she was about to say more mean words, just to keep him at arm's length. So he tilted his face down to swallow them before they had a voice, and she stretched to meet him, despite not putting weight on one foot. He put his arms around her and under her to lift her so she wouldn't hurt her twisted ankle, and they kissed as deeply and fiercely as ever before.

They kissed until Bryan couldn't feel his lips any longer. He pressed all of his fear and worry into that kiss, and she kissed him right back, hungrily, grabbing his sodden t-shirt in her fists like she wanted to punch him, her tongue fighting his like the unkind words he knew she wanted to hurl. Another defense mechanism to try and protect her soft underbelly.

Then a cough behind them pulled him back to his senses and he slowly lowered her to her feet.

"Eòghann says if we're not back in ten minutes, he's calling the Coast Guard anyway," Wes reported.

"Can you walk?" Bryan asked, unable to look Grace in the eye.

"Yes."

"Then let's go." He took her hand, but she stumbled gingerly forward on the twisted ankle, a soft cry escaping her swollen lips.

So he scooped her up and carried her out to the beach, dropping her heavily into the boat and taking a little cruel delight in her murmured, "Ouch," when her bottom hit the bench.

Wesley handed Grace a life jacket, and Bryan helped her step into the boat before he shoved it back off the beach and sloshed out to jump aboard.

His frustration provided a sharp focus for navigating through what remained of the storm, but he hardly drew breath until he handed the keys off to the kid in the ferry office.

Eòghann was leaning against his pickup, the wildness in his eyes relaxing only the tiniest bit as Wes helped Grace squeeze onto the bench behind the driver's seat. Bryan was shivering and relieved for his cousin to do the driving, though Eòghann's knuckles were white the whole way to Grandad's house, his glance darting furtively between Wes in the rearview and Bryan beside him.

Bryan hated that his cousin had been dragged into this mess. Except if it weren't for Eòghann, he might not have… he couldn't even think it. He only hoped it wasn't too triggering.

"Warm up," he suggested, gesturing vaguely to the shower when they were safely back inside his grandad's house. As he stalked into his room to change into dry clothes, he heard Grace whisper, "My kingdom for a bathtub," and he tried not to let it sting. He never invited them here. This was *his* kingdom, and they the invaders. Maybe it was time they moved on, after all.

Chapter Twenty-Five

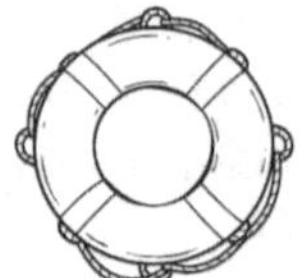

Grace watched, fatigued and disappointed, as Wesley packed up her things. "You don't have to go," she murmured meekly, wanting to toss the open suitcase off the bed, scatter her friend's clothes, and trap her there so Grace wouldn't be left alone.

Wes paused to give her a withering look and then resumed packing.

"Why are you mad?" she asked tentatively, leaving the quiet part unsaid. *It was your idea.*

Wes sighed. "I'm not. I'm embarrassed. Deeply, shamefully, appallingly embarrassed. Bryan warned us not to go, we did the stupid, classic American tourist thing anyway, and he had to *rescue* us, Gray. Leaving is the least I can do." She took Grace's hands in hers. "Thank you for supporting me in nearly dying. I let my need for adventure get out of hand sometimes. Now I need to be a grown-up."

A grown-up. That stung. "But we didn't. Die."

"No. And I'm really glad to know I can swim like that in a crisis. But we could've drowned, and he took a huge risk coming after us."

"Yeah." He was upset at her, but he still did that.

"This was always supposed to be temporary, anyway. Just until the festival ended. It's over. We're in his way. I don't get why you want to stay. I mean I'm not *blind*, I do understand. But… I don't want to be in the way anymore. You know how I feel about… I'm not some damsel who needs to be rescued. Only this time, I was."

And what could Grace say, except some traitorous part of her *liked* being in his way, for all she ran from him. She was transfixed by the renovation unfolding around her. She wanted to be invited to help with it again, deadline or no, and she was desperate to see the final product.

She craved more late-night soccer and more kissing. She'd also hurt him today, deeply. She couldn't just walk away now.

Wes sighed and shook her head, but she was smiling. "Stay as long as you need to. If he comes to his senses and throws you out, give me a call."

A car door slammed, and Wesley zipped her suitcase closed.

"Father Eòghann's going to drive me. Don't want to keep him waiting."

"Wes, he's not—"

"Oh gosh, no. I've booked a room at the Beach Road Inn. Double beds, in case you change your mind. Let's get dinner tomorrow. We still have to make birthday plans."

Then Wes hefted her bag to the floor before Grace could argue, leaving her to deal with the mess they'd made alone.

For the rest of the day, Grace stayed locked in her room as Bryan and Lùcas made all kinds of racket. It sounded like the house was being torn down around her, but she didn't dare emerge to find out. She couldn't face him after the fighting and the kissing and her absolute inability to admit he was right. He was always right, predicting the weather as easily as he predicted her instinct to say something she'd regret just to win a fight. And then he'd kissed her to shut her up, saving her from doing so a second time in one day.

Well, he could keep his manipulative kisses. They were tainted now. She'd almost rather be a bitch and live with the consequences than have him kiss her and not mean it.

The more she dwelled on it, the more she still wanted to let the hurtful words fly, but she didn't need more to regret, so she stayed put and let her fingers do the shouting, writing angry words instead of saying them. Her characters' worst selves were on display, yelling all the hurtful things they had wanted to sling at each other and all the painful truths they'd needed to share since the moment they first met in chapter one.

She wrote and wrote and wrote, still fighting with Bryan in her head and on the page until, exhausted, she crept out to watch her brother's game against their crosstown rivals.

The living room wall was finished except for sanding and painting, and the windows were gorgeous, opening out to the stormy sea. The cushioned seat was just as perfect and cozy as she'd imagined, with a brand-new electrical outlet for charging wayward electronics, and the space beneath the bench housed a long, low bookcase. It was exactly the kind of room she would write for herself. And there, on the couch, in his low-slung sweatpants and bare feet, Bryan watched her instead of the pre-game he'd already turned on.

She froze, staring at him. Suddenly, with the walls up, the room felt too closed in despite its new windows, and her chest constricted.

"I can leave if you prefer," he rumbled. An olive branch she couldn't possibly ignore.

"No. I'd like the company."

"There's beef stew if you're hungry. You need a warm, hearty meal on a day like today."

Her stomach rumbled before her mouth could lie, and he smirked a little, hearing it all the way across the room.

"I thought you were vegetarian," she asked before she could shush herself.

He shrugged, but then seemed to change his mind. "Split it and added the beef to half towards the end."

God, he was perplexing. Why would he do that for her? He'd even left it warming on the stove, knowing—or perhaps hoping?—she'd eventually emerge for Diego's game.

She filled a bowl and joined him in the living room, collapsing onto the opposite corner of the couch and tucking her feet under her. When she took her first bite, she made an indecent noise, and then blushed hard. He seemed like he was going to pretend not to notice, but then he said, "It's Eòghann's recipe. I'll tell him you approve."

Whether he meant it to or not, mentioning Eòghann drew a shutter of awkwardness down between them, and they both pretended to be fully absorbed by the game.

Diego looked exhausted. Was he getting enough rest? He started every match, because when he wasn't on the field, the team couldn't seem to find their momentum.

Bryan cleared his throat.

Grace kept her eyes glued to the game.

He cleared it again, not like he was trying to get her attention. More like he was uncomfortable. "You asked, the other night, if I'm ashamed of the s-stammer," he finally said.

Now she tore her eyes from the TV and met the full heat of his penetrating gaze. "You shouldn't be. That was all I was trying to say."

He looked away then, back to the game, where Diego sent a chip pass to a striker who blasted it off the crossbar.

"When I was about three, we were at the p— at the local pool.

Eòghann was eight. He was running, as kids do. Tripped and fell in, hit his head…"

Suddenly Grace lost her appetite and lowered what was left of her stew.

"No one noticed but me. I tried to sc— to sc— I tried to call for help. Couldn't get the words out. The lifeguard thought I was just overexcited. I had to s-stomp and jump and p-point until finally they noticed him."

"God, Bryan. That wasn't your fault."

"My cousin almost drowned that day, 'cause the one person who could help him couldn't fucking get the words out. *That* is my sh-shame."

Grace's heart ached—for the little boy he had been and the burdened man he'd become.

"He's terrified of the water now," he added softly. "It's why he's never left the island. Why he never visited me."

"Why you couldn't ask him to go with me and Wes. Aside from it being a terrible idea in general."

He nodded.

"I'm sorry for not listening."

"How can you listen to what I don't s-s-say?" he whispered, beating himself up to let her off the hook, though neither of them deserved it.

Someone on TV scored, but they weren't paying attention anymore. The air in the room felt electric.

Bryan was hurting, under some kind of guilt about their escapade to the castle. Maybe he still thought she hadn't listened because he hadn't warned her loudly enough or clearly enough, rather than just because she was stubborn and angry and thought she knew better.

She had done that to him, hurt him in the worst possible way.

Disappointed yelling from the crowd on TV seemed to underscore her fuck up.

She couldn't let the same trauma happen again, here and now.

Grace had to say not just *something* but the *right* thing. "I can't have an orgasm," she blurted out. Not exactly the apology she was going for.

"Fuck, do you not have a clitoris?" he asked, so taken aback by her announcement he didn't seem to register the random shift in conversation. "Christ, that was inappropriate. Apologies," he added, turning three shades of red to match her own blush.

So they were going to do this. A shame for a shame.

She took a breath, the beef stew curdling in her belly, threatening to come back up. After setting the bowl down on the coffee table and pushing it as far away as possible so she wouldn't have to smell it, she took another steadying breath. "I have all my parts," she said, focusing on the game where Diego's keeper batted away a header off a corner kick. "They just don't work right."

That proclamation was met with uncomfortable silence.

"My doctor says it's all part of being a woman, but I don't know," she added quietly. "Sex—" she tried to say, and it came out an inaudible whisper, so she said it again, and this time it came out overly loud. "Sex—" My god, how old was she? "It's very painful. I don't get wet. And I don't orgasm."

"Your doctor is bullshit," he said emphatically. "What kind of lube do you use?"

"What? It doesn't—sorry, I just…"

"No, no, I apologize, it's none of my business but…"

"It's—it's not the lube. It's me. There's something… off. I'm not normal down there."

"Fuck normal."

She shook her head. This wasn't the reaction she expected, she didn't need his outrage or his sympathy. She was sharing in the interest of fairness. To heal the rift she kept tearing between them. "I just… thought you should know. A shame for a shame."

"It's not… What, never? Or never with… penetration, you mean?"

"What? No. Never. What?"

"Not with oral? I mean that's the reason people like it, right? Less invasive."

"Umm. No… no."

"Not even, you know, with yourself?"

"Oh my god, can we not?" Why was he so curious? Just talking about it made her feel overly warm, the blackness encroaching like she was about to faint. She'd expected him to acknowledge it and never speak of it again, at the worst to be appalled or consider himself to have made a lucky escape, but not this… empathetic curiosity?

With no one to pass to, Diego made a breakaway run down the pitch and a Hail Mary shot on goal that slipped cheekily over the keeper's outstretched fingers. Grace and Bryan went as wild as the crowd, jumping from their seats and cheering. She held up her hand for a high five, but Bryan picked her up and swung her around, and god, he smelled good.

"That's why the old man's still team captain," Bryan murmured. "He makes things happen."

Grace nodded her agreement, tears in her eyes for her big brother. D was a midfielder, a damn good one, but she could count on one hand the number of goals he'd scored for LA.

She texted her mom in Florida and her dad in Mexico, and Diego, so he'd see it the minute he stepped off the pitch. For a second, she even considered texting Mathilda, too, just to keep from having to face Bryan and resume their conversation, but she couldn't quite bring herself to do it.

"There's nothing wrong with you, Rios," he whispered after a long moment.

"I'm pretty sure there is."

She could see his face change out of the corner of her eye, and she didn't want his sympathy. She just needed him to understand why she kept running away so she wouldn't be responsible for making him feel badly about himself. She'd had enough of men who blamed her sex drive when the relationship inevitably fell apart, or who blamed her for being too picky or for masturbating too much—*as if*. What was the point, when she was incapable of getting off? She'd had enough of men blaming her, but she couldn't stand the thought of him blaming himself.

"When was your first time?" he asked softly, and Grace inhaled sudden and sharp. Hadn't they shared enough for one night?

Her phone lit up with a text from her friend Andy, an explosion of emojis indicating he was watching Diego's game too.

"Apologies. Too personal?" Bryan asked.

Abso-fucking-lutely right, but she decided to answer him anyway. "It was almost in high school. After prom. I wasn't really keen, but he was, until he realized I was… on my period. He ran screaming into the night like we'd reenacted a scene from *Carrie*. So, I got a reprieve until my freshman year of college," she said. "I didn't particularly want to then, either, but I really liked him, and I thought if I didn't, he'd leave. Joke was on me. Boys don't like it if you cry too much. He dumped me anyway."

Bryan made a sound in his throat, something like a growl. "Sounds like your partners couldn't handle the evidence of their own ineptitude," he grumbled, and it did funny things to her stomach, complicated things she'd rather it didn't do.

He was too confident, too self-satisfied. He saw her as a challenge to fix, and when he couldn't, he would blame her too, for not wanting to be fixed, not trying hard enough. Just like always. It was why she hadn't dated for almost eight years.

"Maybe," she answered softly, as the game went to halftime. "Or maybe it was nothing to do with them. I'm not some puzzle for you to solve like your biochar or your next renovation project. I'm not."

"Renovation," he breathed. "What could I possibly renovate about you?"

It was maybe the sweetest thing anyone had ever said, but

though he didn't physically move, she could feel him withdraw at her sad smile, backing off, giving her the space she was trying to tell him she needed.

"I'm sorry," she said. "I'm tired, not great company. I should go."

"What did we say about apologizing? Stay and finish watching your brother win this match," he said, his voice smooth but formal, as he got to his feet. "Good night, Rios."

But LA didn't win. Diego was injured in the second half, and though he limped off the pitch on his own, it was hours before Grace could shake her anxiety over witnessing the tackle. Despite the red card to the other player, the team seemed as shaken as she did and ended up going down three to one, unable to recover. Maybe she was bad luck all around.

Chapter Twenty-Six

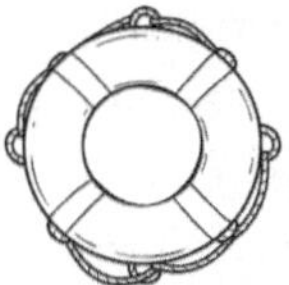

Sleep was for the weak, right? Anyway, Bryan kept telling himself so as he lay awake hour upon hour.

He'd made a terrible misstep with Grace, one he might not be able to walk back.

Tossing and turning, hard as stone, he couldn't stop imagining various experiments they could perform, all the ways they could try to help her orgasm—though he knew she'd castrate him on the spot for daring to think it.

'Cause she was absolutely right. She wasn't his problem to solve.

It just seemed such a very great shame for her to go through life without ever coming if she wanted to, and Christ, he wanted to try. She might not get there, but they'd have a good time.

Finally, her bedroom door opened and the loo door closed, and he waited to see if she'd react to the state of it. When she returned to her own room without comment and shut herself inside with her laptop, he rose and dressed and set to work.

He and Lùc had already done most of the prep: tearing out a linen closet to make more space at the entrance and ripping up the old lino flooring to get at the pipes and lay additional heating coils. Then came the tricky part, where they'd cut a hole, all the way through the outer stone wall, and inserted steel beams to add in a window. Shockingly, the neighbors hadn't flayed him alive for it immediately, but the added light was really going to open up the tiny room.

Now it was time for the most difficult part yet: rerouting pipes. Bryan was no plumber, but he'd learned a bit operating the still at Ardbeg, and a bit more chasing leaks around his Islay flat. Hopefully it would be enough.

By the time Lùcas arrived, Bryan had torn out the remaining shower tiles and split the incoming water pipes. He'd also rerouted the drains to carry greywater outside to the site of his future reclamation garden. His cousin's eyes bugged out at the spiderweb of piping, and Bryan didn't blame him. He wasn't completely confident he wouldn't flood the whole house the minute he turned the water back on.

"Was your da able to order it?" Bryan asked.

"Didn't have to. For some reason he had one in stock. He'll bring it tomorrow."

Bryan blinked at that. "We can go get it."

Lùcas shrugged. "Said he'd deliver it. I think he wants to help. Or at least get an eyeful," he amended.

"Best get ready for him, then," Bryan said, with a choked laugh.

They affixed new hexagonal tiles in shades of honeyed cream down the walls and along the floor, working in companionable silence to convert the tiny, tired old bathroom into a fresh, more open, more beautiful space. Instinctively, Lùcas seemed to know better than to bring up what happened yesterday, and before long they were finished, except for the part that would cover the piping.

"Now what?" Lùc asked.

"It'll be an arse ache to have to tear it out if we needed to access the pipes again," Bryan worried.

His cousin nodded. The argument made perfect sense. The part Bryan wasn't saying out loud was his fear they'd have to do just that, and sooner rather than later, thanks to his plumbing skills.

"You could just hide it?" the boy suggested—the artist was a visionary, it seemed. "But actually, I meant now what do we do if anyone needs to pish?"

Bryan's stomach sank. Of course the tile would take hours to cure before anyone could walk on it. He could go in the backyard if he had to but… "She'll have to go next door," he grumbled. She would probably join Wesley in a hotel by teatime.

He taped a note to the door suggesting the library, the pub, or the neighbor's if Grace needed the facilities, and they went outside to build a low sort of cabinet which could be set over the new piping for easy access. Bonus, it could also double as a tiny bench or stool. Then Lùcas helped him set up the rows of planters which would triple filter the bath water before cycling it back inside to flush the toilet.

With that done, there was nothing to do but wait, so Bryan made them sandwiches and they sat out on the porch watching the last of the storm clouds blow away. Lùcas showed him some ideas he'd had for whisky labels and distillery logos, some of them incorporating the bee from Bryan's own tattoo.

"These are incredible, Lùc, really."

His cousin didn't stop beaming the rest of the afternoon.

followed her lead. After Lùcas left, he took out his tablet and spent the better part of the evening spinning his wheels trying to compose a speech.

After the scene at the ceilidh, he was more than a little

worried the town would tar and feather him alongside his investor, who was coming here in the hope of meeting villagers as excited about the project as they were. If Bryan was going to win Jules over, he would need to win his neighbors over, too.

It was nauseating to contemplate, but he knew it was true. He needed to open the house to the whole island, perhaps share his business plan and explain how he'd preserve what each of them cherished most about Barra, just as his father's Bàgh a' Chiùil festival had done.

To that end, he was planning a reception where he would try to speak from the heart, to say all the things Grace had been able to put into words which he had not. If only he were as good at it as she was.

The next afternoon, once Bryan had finished installing the new shower glass, he was hanging shelves, recovered and refinished from the old linen closet, when Lùcas arrived with his father and the pièce de résistance: a beautiful, gleaming slipper bath. Lùcas had measured well. It would fit perfectly under the new window between the shower and the opposite wall.

A wave of pleasure settled low in Bryan's belly.

Uncle Dàibhidh had indeed come for an eyeful as Lùc had predicted, but he looked around in seeming awe of what his son and nephew had accomplished. He patted Lùc's shoulder, nodding, and the boy flushed with delight.

Once the tub was settled into place, Uncle Dàibhidh clapped Bryan on the back too and said, "Sure and your grandad wouldn't have turned up his nose at a soak in this masterpiece."

A knot in Bryan's chest loosened as his throat grew tight. "Do you mind having a look at the pipes?" Bryan rasped, swallowing his nerves.

His uncle was only too delighted to offer an opinion, and aside from tightening a few fittings, he pronounced everything in perfect order, the water ready to be turned back on. Bryan allowed him to do the honors, and thankfully nothing flooded except his pride.

THE DAY WORE ON, AND BRYAN GREW MORE AND MORE RESTLESS over Grace's complete absence. He hadn't seen her emerge for food or water—indeed he'd be convinced she'd slipped out without saying goodbye except he could hear the rapid clacking of her keyboard. He knew better than to interrupt, so he tried again to work on his speech, but he simply couldn't focus.

It wasn't healthy for her to stay locked up in there so long.

Of course, he was eager to show her the new tub, and it was long past time to switch the power over to run off the fully charged solar battery. Jules would arrive in a matter of days, and if anything went wrong with the cutover, Bryan would need time to keep his head and get on with fixing it before they arrived. For some reason he didn't want to face that moment of truth alone.

After a bit of pacing and wringing his hands, he tapped on her door. When she didn't answer, he peeked inside.

How far gone was he that wearing a t-shirt emblazoned with MIND IF I CHECK YOU OUT?, purple leggings, and a bun so messy a bird could nest in it, she was the most appealing person he'd ever seen, hunched over her laptop with a pen between her teeth?

He swallowed. "Rios?"

"One sec."

"Sorry to bother—"

"You're not," she interrupted.

"I need to cut over to the solar power."

"Awesome," she replied, about as interested as if he'd told her he'd seen a seagull outside.

"Okay then…"

He wanted her to ask what all the noise next door had been

about, but the headphones charging at her elbow had probably blocked most of it.

"Congrats," she murmured in a way that sounded more dismissive than congratulatory.

He lingered in the doorway. Was she listening to him at all, or responding without hearing? In his imagination, she would have joined him as he switched over to the battery and then shared a celebratory dram, maybe even a hug, but those were purely selfish desires when clearly she was in the zone.

"I'll just do it now then."

"Sounds good," she said, not looking up from her typing.

"The lights will go out. The Wi-Fi too."

"Uh huh."

It was his fault, of course, for interrupting her when she was working. Her deadline was looming for this book, another award winner, no doubt. Of course this wasn't the most important part of her day. Maybe she still hoped he'd make good on their deal— cut the power over and then just fade away, leaving the house to her. Why else would she have put up with him so long? But there was still the cistern to install, completing his water reclamation circle, along with a few other odds and ends.

With something awfully like regret, he closed her door and headed to the fuse box inside his bedroom closet. It took only a moment to shut down power to the house and route everything over to the new solar battery. The lights were back on in a few minutes. So far so good.

And then Grace howled, "Are you fucking kidding me?" and his stomach sank.

When he peeked in her room, she was slumped over the laptop with her head in her hands.

"What is it?" he asked cautiously.

"You!" she rounded on him. "What did you do?"

"I—"

"Did you accidentally blow a fuse or something?"

"I—"

"I've lost everything!"

"What?"

She gestured at her laptop, hands splayed like she wanted to strangle something. "Days' worth of work! The entire last third is just…" She made a *poof* gesture.

Bryan blinked, not quite understanding. "But… but it's a laptop."

"A laptop that needs power! No power, no save. The Wi-Fi connection's been janky, and apparently that little surge wiped out three days of autosave. Or maybe autosave is broken too, I don't know. This thing is such a piece of shit."

She hadn't pressed save for three days?

"I warned you I was about to—"

"What? When?"

"Just a minute ago. You said 'awesome.' You said 'congratulations.'"

She stared at the ceiling as though thinking back over the last few minutes and then she moaned.

"Don't laptops run on b-battery? Isn't that the whole allure of a laptop?"

"Don't laptop shame me! It's old. It doesn't hold a charge anymore."

"I'm sorry, Rios," he said, feeling proud of himself for not adding *why would you write so much without making a backup?*

She hung her head. "I'm sure my editor will be glad to hear it."

Her sigh was so deep it broke his heart a little. He knew she hadn't been listening, not really. She'd been deep in her *authorial fever*, but he'd gone ahead and pulled the plug anyway.

"What can I do?"

She shook her head.

"You should take a break," he said, keeping his voice even. "Let me show you—"

"I don't have time to take a break. Have you heard anything I said? I just lost so many words!"

"Just for a minute," he persuaded.

If she saw the tub, he knew she'd calm down. Then she could take a long hot bath and relax and either find the missing backup or remember the missing words.

"Please?" he coaxed.

Scrubbing a hand across her glistening eyes, she relented to being led next door to the loo, and when her gaze landed on the tub her face softened for half a second.

"Do you want to try it out?" he whispered, his voice husky with excitement.

Just like that, her face drained of color and she shrank away from him, her expression shuttered. "Are you serious right now?"

Oh. Maybe this had been another miscalculation. "Yes…?"

"A bath?" She was nodding her head like some kind of bobble toy, fighting off tears. "And then what?"

"And then…" he faltered. His mouth opened and closed like a codfish, trying to find his own lost words. "Whatever?" he finally managed.

"You think you're the first man who tried to seduce me with a bubble bath, Bryan MacNeil?" Now she shook her head repeatedly. "Maybe the first who went so far as remodeling a whole bathroom, but whatever you seem to think, you're not going to fix me."

"That's not—"

"You're all the same. I don't have time for this."

"Rios, there was no—"

"Right," she interrupted again, squeezing past him, pressing herself into the wall so she wouldn't so much as brush against him as she rushed out of the bog that no longer looked as bright or beautiful or inviting as he'd thought. Now it just seemed old and tired and try-hard.

"This wasn't a ruse to get you into b-bed," he said, following her out of the loo.

"Of course not. It never is, right? *There's other ways?* Come on."

"I didn't know what you wanted from me that night. I don't now! This isn't—I just thought you could relax—"

"I don't need to relax. I actually work better under pressure, but thanks." She was breathing too fast, blinking back tears. "I know none of this is your fault, okay? I shouldn't have stayed here. Wes was right, it was silly—no, really." She stopped his protests before they could leave his lips. "You're just doing what you need to do, I get it. Your deadline is sooner than mine, and as I've told literally everyone on this island, this is your place. I'm the one in the way. I'm the problem, again—Wes tried to tell me that. *You* tried to tell me that. And honestly, if I would have just listened, we wouldn't be here right now."

"You d-don't need to g-go," he said, cursing himself for choking on his words now, when he needed them most. "You're n-n— You're not in the way. I lo— I'm in lo—"

"Thanks, Bryan, truly. But I should go. I think we both know that."

She was throwing clothes into her suitcase now, and he was powerless to stop her. He couldn't get a word in. Why wasn't she hearing him? "S-s-stop." He intercepted one of her t-shirts, but she refused to look at him.

"Let's not try to force something where it doesn't belong. I was always going to leave. This is vacation. It's not real life."

She threw the stupid laptop into a satchel and turned back to her suitcase.

"Rios—"

"It's no big deal," she said.

But there were tears in her eyes and he didn't understand what was happening. Sure, he hadn't originally included a bathtub in his remodel, and yes, maybe he'd bought it for her, but only because he knew how much she'd like it. Did she really think he was trying to lure her into bed?

"It clearly is a huge deal, and not just about your novel."

"Just?" she repeated, but the outrage she was reaching for had burned itself out. Her face and throat twitched and contracted like she was trying desperately to hold back the tears he could see filling her chestnut-colored eyes.

"Please talk to me. I can't fix it if I don't understand."

Grace slumped onto the bed beside her suitcase, holding the dress she'd worn to the ceilidh, and Bryan took a hesitant seat on the other end.

"Did I misinterpret your desire for a bath?"

"I love a bath." She shook her head. "I'm sorry. I... panic. Sometimes. Especially in bathrooms. With men."

Bryan wanted to hold her. He wanted to understand, but he sat very still, squeezing the wrinkles out of the t-shirt still clenched in his fist.

"It isn't you," she started over. "I know you would never..." She took a shaky breath. "It was a knee-jerk overreaction. The bathroom is beautiful. The tub looks amazing."

An overreaction to what? he wanted to ask, but he knew first-hand it was best to stay quiet when someone was having trouble speaking their truth.

"I'm tired is all."

She hazarded a look at him and must have seen plainly from his face he wasn't buying it, because she closed her eyes to start again.

"When I was fourteen, almost fifteen, my best friend was this boy, Justin Everett. We grew up together—our brothers played soccer together until Diego left home."

A sick feeling settled in Bryan's stomach, but he kept his eyes on her face.

"Justin got picked on a lot at school. He was kind of small. He liked math a little too much, played the clarinet. Anyway, he started hounding me for one of my bras or my underwear… then, for a naked picture… so he could earn some cred with the other guys."

Bryan sighed, and it accidentally came out as a low growl. He already hated Justin Everett.

"I kept telling him no. So one day, I was showering after gym and somehow he snuck into the girls' locker room with a digital camera. He got his picture."

She bit her lip, and a tear finally trickled down her cheek.

"Every boy in school had seen it by the end of the day. Sister Mary Agnes gave me a three-day suspension, because clearly I had done something to encourage his behavior, or at least not enough to discourage it."

"You were fourteen, for Christ's sake," Bryan growled, ready to tear both Justin and Sister Mary Agnes limb from limb.

"Almost fifteen," she said again, and that's when he realized. Her quinceañera. This was the reason she'd cancelled.

"I'm so—"

"Don't say you're sorry."

Bryan frowned. "If you want me to kill them, I will. Even the nun."

She laughed, and then her face clouded once more, and she shook her head. "You've done an incredible job with the house, MacNeil," she said, tossing the dress in her suitcase and zipping it closed with such a sense of finality. "Your investor's going to fall in love with it as much as I have. The whole town will, the minute you let them in. If you need help writing your speech or anything, let me know. Otherwise, I'll see you around."

"You don't have to," he said, reaching for her hand.

She cupped his face, running her thumb tenderly over his cheek, and he almost melted into the touch. "I think I do. Going home was always going to hurt. Maybe it's time. I'll be here for the big reveal."

And like the breath of fresh air that had blown onto the island with her, she left in the same unexpected way she'd come, and he stood there and let her go, still clutching her t-shirt like a lifeline.

Bryan watched through the bedroom window as she hurried down the walk, where a group of neighbors had gathered in front of his garden holding signs that said Not On Our Beach and Elderly Citizens for Elderly Homes and No Change Means No, and when the hell had they started picketing him?

They parted to let Grace pass as though expecting her to yell at them, and she looked like she wanted to, but she shook her head and kept going, so Bryan yanked the curtains closed and climbed into bed to lick his wounds alone.

Chapter Twenty-Seven

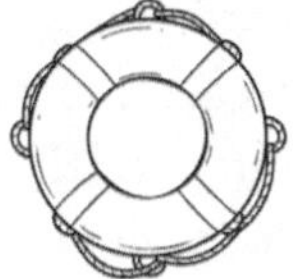

Wes rubbed Grace's back as she cried snotty tears into a lumpy hotel pillow.

"Explain it to me again."

"I lost everything."

"Everything meaning…?"

"Three days' worth of everything," Grace amended feeling maybe a little melodramatic.

"Ah, back to the book. It's a crushing blow, Gray, but you wrote it once. You can write it again."

"You clearly don't understand," Grace grumbled, although Wes understood better than she'd like.

"I don't understand the part where he renovated an entire bathroom in his own house so that you, who will be leaving in a week, could take a bubble bath and you—"

Grace groaned. "I think maybe I overreacted."

"Do you think so?" Wes asked, and only she could manage to sound sincere when they both knew she was being sarcastic.

"I told him I can't orgasm," Grace admitted in a tiny voice. "I thought he was taking it as a challenge, and I had this visceral sort of… panic attack."

Wes brushed Grace's hair out of her face. "You mean you can't reach the O with P in V?" she asked sympathetically.

God, this was humiliating. There was a reason Grace had never told anyone, including her closest friends. "I mean at all."

"At all with a man?" Wes repeated, her voice so gentle you almost couldn't hear the confusion.

Why was this such a hard thing for people to grasp? They must think she was a total freak. "I mean at all," she said again.

"Well, no wonder your relationships crash and burn, Gray. How can you tell them what you like if you don't have a clue yourself?" she asked, reducing more than a decade of frustration to something so simple it stunned Grace into silence.

It made her mad, but it also made a sort of sense, which was doubly infuriating.

"Is it a purity-culture-in-your-head thing because you're not married? Or more of a physical vaginismus-type thing?"

"I don't… know what that means," Grace admitted.

"What does your OB-GYN say?"

Grace hid her face in the pillow. "That it's normal for woman to find sex painful."

"Then your OB-GYN is a dick. Come on," Wes said, unfolding from her perch on the edge of the bed and pulling Grace by the hand.

"Come where," Grace moaned into her pillow.

"We're going out."

Grace groaned louder in protest, but she washed her face and put on shoes.

When she had run away that afternoon, she'd texted Wes who showed up in the back of the sole island cab minutes later, a cab driven by Bryan's sister Elspeth, of all people. To her credit, El offered Grace a sympathetic shrug but didn't say a word. Grace had burst into tears the moment she sat down in the car, and she pretty much hadn't stopped since.

"Pick up the pace, the whole town shuts down at five," Wes urged.

"Pubs don't," Grace argued.

Wes didn't respond. Instead of stopping at the pub, she led the way to a general store with a bell that jingled jauntily as she threw open the door, and Grace kind of wanted to rip the bell down and throw it into the sea. How dare it jingle at her when she was miserable.

"Hi, Mal," Wes called, and Bryan's mother came scurrying out of the back to tend the register. God in Heaven, was nowhere safe from the damned MacNeils?

"Nice to see you again, Wes! And you Grace," Malvinia MacNeil added, her smile flickering for a second as she took in Grace's tearstained face and scraggly hair.

Wes made straight for Aisle 2: Personal Care. She flitted past the shelves of toothpaste and deodorant, hovering in the section chock full of condoms, snagging a few bottles before Grace could read the labels, and then she sidled back to the register.

"Mal," she said in a low, conspiratorial stage whisper. "Have you by any chance got a vibrator for sale?"

If Grace could have spontaneously combusted on the spot, she would have done so. A vibrator, for god's sake?

"Only one brand, I'm afraid, dear," Mrs. MacNeil answered cheerfully, "but it's the highest-rated one in Scotland."

"I'm sure it's perfect," Wes agreed.

"I keep them in back, so the kids won't try to steal them and the Karens won't clutch their pearls. Just a tick," she said, scurrying off to the back again.

Grace tried to speak, but her voice cracked immediately like an adolescent child. "You really just did that?"

"Somebody had to."

"I'm pretty sure that's not true."

"Trust me."

"Wes, I don't think—"

"Shut up," Wes said. "My treat. Happy birthday. If you hate it, give it back to me."

Grimacing at the idea, Grace couldn't decide which was worse—her best friend buying her a sex toy, or her giving it back in disgrace.

"I know they always say the best way to get over a man is to get under one, but in my opinion, the best way is to take care of things yourself."

Grace literally wanted to die.

How high was the heat turned on in this store? She needed to sit down. Her ears were buzzing, and—*oh no*. She felt like she was going to faint, and this time she wasn't overreacting. She swayed a little and put her hand on the counter to steady herself.

"When's the last time you ate?" Wes asked, and she sounded far away.

"Don't remember." Grace tried to catch her breath, but her lungs didn't want to cooperate. The edges of her vision were starting to get black, like the storm clouds rolling in off the bay.

"That man didn't feed you?" Wes muttered. "He seriously had *one* job." She dragged Grace around the counter and pushed her onto a stool. "Drink." A bottle of cold blue sports drink materialized out of nowhere, along with a bag of salty crisps.

The next few minutes were a hazy blur as Wes paid for their purchases and Bryan's mother fretted over Grace, bundling both of them into Elspeth's car for the short trip back to the hotel. In the front seats, mother and daughter kept exchanging meaningful looks, so Grace rested her head on her friend's shoulder and shut her eyes.

"Gray," Wes began, rubbing her arm tenderly just like Grace's mother used to do when she was ill. "I know the book's important, I know you have a deadline, but you have to take better care of yourself. You can't expect to keep going on hopes and dreams alone."

"I know."

"Do you?" When Grace didn't answer, Wes took her hand and asked, "How much of it did you actually lose?"

"It doesn't matter. It was mostly garbage."

"Maybe he did you a favor, then."

"It wasn't his fault," Grace admitted.

"Does he know that?"

Grace started to cry again. She was pretty sure she'd told him in her haste to get out of there, but whether he believed it was a whole other thing.

Back at the inn, Wes tucked her into bed with a promise to wake her at eight for dinner. Then she took herself off to who knew where.

The room was too quiet without Bryan's incessant hammering, and too empty without his essence, but eventually Grace drifted off to restless dreams.

When she awoke, she rolled over, right onto the brown paper sack from the general store. Inside, she found no less than three different bottles of lube—*good lord, Wesley*—and a rather scary looking vibrator. How was it supposed to work?

She opened the box to examine it more closely. It seemed aggressively large, but it already had some charge in the battery which was… thoughtful.

Glancing at the time, she noted Wes wouldn't be back for more than an hour. She almost put it all away rather than risk the inevitable disappointment, but curiosity got the best of her.

The first attempt was terrible: painful, uninspired. Grace couldn't help crying all over again. Even Scotland's highest-rated sex toy was too much for her. She wanted to throw it across the room, but she didn't have the energy. Instead, she just laid there and cried.

Probably, she was trying too hard. Overthinking almost certainly made it impossible to relax in the slightest. It was way too much pressure. Why was she doing this? She didn't want to do this.

She put it all away and vowed to make Wes take it home with her.

But then her mind drifted back to Bryan, to that soft beard and those biceps, and his bee-tattooed forearm. He never had explained what it meant. She would remember to ask in the middle of kissing, and then his tongue would do something clever and her mind would go pleasantly blank.

Contemplating his kisses made her sad, but her body didn't know to feel sad, so she was flushed all over too, and there was no point trying again, but at the same time… she hadn't been accused of being stubborn her whole life to quit now.

By the time Wes returned with takeaways from the pub, Grace was flushed and somewhat satisfied. It hadn't exactly been life changing, but at least she finally understood the rising tension followed by a brief euphoric rush when, once again, her mind went too blank and still to overanalyze things.

And maybe she wasn't quite so broken after all.

Wes took one look at her and said, "Fucking finally. Now what are we going to do about your Stoic Scot?"

That killed the glow a little bit, if Grace was being honest. "He's not *my* Scot."

Wes gave her an *oh please* look. "Pretty sure he was yours the moment you climbed up on that roof with him."

"What's the point of starting something when we're just going to leave in a few days?"

"Practice?" Wes asked. "The very best kind of no-strings-attached, remember-it-fondly practice?"

How Grace wished she could be a no-strings-attached kind of girl. Anyway, one afternoon with a new toy was not going to suddenly cure everything.

"It wouldn't be fair to him," she told Wesley.

"Maybe not. Or maybe he should be the judge of what's fair to him. Besides, I don't know if you've heard, but there's this amazing new invention called the telephone. It even works over Wi-Fi now!"

"I came here to finish my book," Grace muttered. "I have a few days left to actually do it, and then we go home."

But she didn't write that night. She and Wesley watched a movie, and then Wes went out to a party on the beach, and Grace tried out the bottle that said not for use with toys. It had the most exquisite, satiny feel she could have ever imagined and a small part of her mourned the years she'd lost by not realizing synthetic lube existed and was created by God Himself, because she was still Grace, and heaven forbid she just enjoy a thing totally guilt-free.

Still, she *was* starting to get the hang of it. The earth didn't move this time, either. She'd been right to assume the teen movies had massively oversold the sensation, and it still wasn't completely painless, but there were nice feelings too. Her mind was sort of reeling at the possibilities.

Grace's first college boyfriend had been so annoyed when she couldn't get wet, he insisted on giving her excruciating oral in what she had perceived as punishment. After several failed attempts with her second boyfriend, he had suggested fingering her and then penetrated her with three of them like some kind of exploratory mission in search of water on Mars. When that approach inexplicably didn't work, he said she must be a lesbian, because he'd never had trouble making a girl wet before.

Now Grace was beginning to realize Bryan might have been right about at least one thing—her doctor and those boys were bullshit. She wasn't completely broken. Maybe there was hope for her yet.

After another round, she fell into a deep, uninterrupted sleep.

Chapter Twenty-Eight

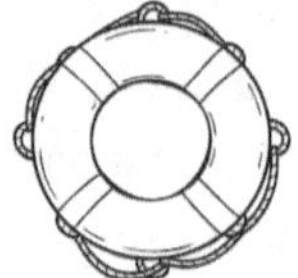

Rather than let the new tub go to waste, Bryan eventually dragged himself out of bed and ran the hottest bath he could stand to soak his wounded pride until long after the water went cold.

When the picketers got too loud with their chanting, he stood up, rivulets streaming down his chest, and shoved the brand-new double-hung window open, yelling, "S-s-say it to my face, if you're going to."

They gawped at his bare chest and the tops of his hips, and then they started protesting again, so he slammed the window shut, drained the tub, and turned on the TV as loud as it would go.

He could drown out the real-time shouts, but he couldn't drown their voices out of his head.

He barely got out of bed the next day, as though all the work and stress and sleepless nights were finally catching up and his body was shutting down. Lùcas came and pounded on the door, but he covered his head with a pillow, drifting in and out of fitful sleep. This wasn't wallowing, it was self-care, he reasoned. He obviously needed the rest.

His cousin finally went away, only to come back later with Eòghann, who yelled through the bedroom window, threatening to break it. Bryan threw his pillow at the curtains and they both left again without making good on the threat.

On the third day, however, Cait proved herself the ultimate traitor, letting his cousins in with yet another spare key, while Bryan sat in his underwear staring into the soggy depths of a bowl of muesli.

"Didn't she like the tub?" Lùcas asked with big grey-green eyes like a kicked puppy.

"No. But that wasn't really the issue in the end," he assured the lad when his face fell.

"What was, then?"

"Me. I said the wrong thing, like always."

Which was fine, honestly, because he'd never wanted to fall for her. The sister of his old friend? Never a good idea. And a tourist, as well? Properly cliché for a reason. Bryan had known better from the moment he saw her on the beach, but somehow she'd wormed her way into his heart the same way she'd wormed her way into his home.

"The place looks grand, Bry," Eòghann said, looking around in breathless wonder.

"Bollocks. Wish I'd never started this mess."

"Why not?" Lùcas asked with that same hang-dog expression.

"Seen the picketers? They'll never accept me—or my distillery, either. Ought to have left well enough alone, left Cait to run her inn," he added with a nod to his sister.

"Bollocks yourself," Cait said. "You think Grandad would've rested easy knowing strangers were trashing his house week in and week out? Every time I dropped off a new one, I was half-afraid he'd come back and haunt me for it. He left the place to you because he knew it would bring you home."

Bryan scoffed and shook his head. He didn't know why

Grandad Mac had left the place to him, but he doubted it was to lure him back to the island.

"I'm not at all sure I should say it, but I can't believe how much nicer you've made this old house. And Grandad would agree."

His cousins nodded, and the knot in Bryan's throat tightened. Praise from Cait was rare and usually couched in insult. He ought to savor it, bottle it up and store it for the open house, when kindness would surely be in short supply, but today he was in no place to hear soft words of affirmation.

"Don't be daft. This house isn't why I came home," he told them.

"Why did you, then?" Lùcas asked.

Bryan glanced over at Eòghann, who tilted his head, waiting patiently for the answer.

"I abandoned you," Bryan told his oldest cousin, his voice cracking at the admission. "You, and everyone, just like Alec abandoned me—abandoned all of us."

"No, you didn't," Eòghann said softly.

"I did. And it's eaten away at me all these years until there was nothing left but raw edges and memories and shame. I wanted to make it up to you, and I didn't know how. I didn't even know how to pick up the phone and wish you happy birthday."

Eòghann frowned at him like he was trying to smile but had forgotten how, and then suddenly he pulled Bryan into a fierce hug, like if he squeezed hard enough, Bryan wouldn't feel guilty anymore. Then Cait closed in, rubbing Bryan's arm hesitantly, and Lùc stood back awkwardly watching, as though all the adults had lost their minds.

Bryan took a shuddering breath. This, right here, was exactly why he'd come home.

"When the opportunity with Jules came up, I realized I had an idea, a good one, and I'd rather do it here among family than anywhere else surrounded by s-strangers. I guess maybe I wanted to prove to the island I'm not just a dumb little kid with a fantastical dream who dates everyone he meets, but a man with a vision for the future. I forgot I'd been gone so long that I'm the s-stranger now."

"You don't have anything to prove," Cait said.

"I absolutely do."

"Pish, no you don't. But so we're clear, mostly you came back because you missed *me*," Eòghann teased.

"Mostly."

"And then you fell in love with a girl," he added gently.

"More fool, me."

"For Christ's sake, Bry, why haven't you said all this to the town?" Cait asked. "Sure and it would get them on your side. I mean, not the part about the girl, that's plain enough for everyone to see after the ceilidh."

"When have they ever listened?" he asked, glancing towards the front of the house where he could still hear the muffled shouts of his picketing neighbors right through the stone walls.

Cait waved them away like they were no more than annoying midges. "This is the first exciting thing they've had happen in a decade."

Instead of irritating him as it would've done at seventeen, her unconcern eased the knot in Bryan's stomach.

"You didn't abandon me," Eòghann said softly. "I never felt you did. You left to become who you were meant to be. I know it, and they will too, if you let them see into this place. Let them see you, no mask, no walls."

Bryan wasn't so sure, but he'd always trusted Eòghann to know what was what—especially when it came to the island.

"Anything left to do here?" Lùcas asked.

"Aye," Bryan told him, because he might as well finish what he'd started.

So Cait elicited a promise he'd come round for a vegetarian meal soon and then left his cousins to help him erect the new rainwater cistern behind some strategically placed shrubbery. Once filled by the next good rain, Bryan could switch over the utility, and the cistern would feed fresh water inside. With the greywater system complete, Grandad's cottage would be fully off the grid.

Job done, Lùc and Eòghann tried to persuade him out to the pub, but he wasn't in a mood for celebrating or socializing.

Instead, he stared down at a fresh document on his tablet, trying once more to form his thoughts into words that could turn picketers into supporters, a speech to welcome his investor and bring the town over to his side all in one go. It really needed to be some Aaron Sorkin–level shit.

He'd have liked to pick Grace's brain. She had such a way with words, and she'd offered to help him on her way out the front door, but… well. What did it matter anyway?

The next time someone knocked, he shouted, "Bugger off," but they just kept on knocking. He really should install a doorbell camera with a rude prerecorded send off.

Finally, he threw open the door, surprised to find Wesley standing there, fist poised to hammer again, and he couldn't help glancing behind and to either side of her in search of her shorter brunette bestie, but Wes had come alone. Even the picketers hadn't yet assembled for the day.

"Forget your specs?" he asked, knowing full well there was no trace of either woman in his guest room, since he'd laid new floors in there the day before.

She shook her head. "Can I come in for a dram?"

"At eight in the morning?"

Wes shrugged. "It's three a.m. where I'm from," she said and sauntered inside, so Bryan finger-combed his hair and went to pour the whisky.

"Is she all right?" he allowed himself to ask calmly while his back was facing his guest.

"She's a mess, actually, but she has been for a long time. That's not on you."

A fresh wave of guilt hit his belly, and he took a fortifying sip of Ardbeg. After all, it was probably five o'clock in Australia.

When he handed a glass to Wes, she lifted it in salute and said, "Slàinte."

"Slàinte mhath," he replied, taking another sip.

"If it helps, she knows she overreacted."

It didn't, really, since they'd parted on friendly-ish terms, a mutual acknowledgment that things were coming to their natural conclusion. Tourists eventually go home—that's their whole allure, and the biggest reason not to get involved.

"Are you really just going to let her go back to Tennessee?" Wes asked.

"As opposed to kidnapping her and keeping her in my cellar?"

Wes grinned over her Glencairn glass.

"Did you convince her to celebrate her birthday?" he asked.

Her smile fell and she shook her head. "I got her a present, but… in light of everything, I didn't feel like I could bully her into my idea of how she should party. Not this year."

An idea tickled in the back of Bryan's head.

"I hate it, you know? *I* am a person who strongly believes in celebrating yourself as often as possible, and you only turn thirty once."

"I think Cait turned thirty two or three times."

Wes didn't pause to laugh at his joke. "She claims to hate birthday parties, and I get it. Some people don't like fun. But the happiest I can remember seeing her was when we tricked her into having a twenty-first."

"I turned thirty alone in a bad karaoke bar," Bryan admitted. It had been grim.

Though he'd mostly known Grace with her nose to the grindstone, it was incongruous to picture her as someone who didn't like fun. She'd resisted going out because of her deadline, but at the ceilidh she'd been lit up by the music and dancing. Why, her first night on Barra, he'd seen her cut loose at karaoke.

"She said she wanted a piñata," he recalled. The tickle in his brain turning into a flood, pushing its way to the surface of his thoughts.

"Oh yeah," Wes grinned.

He glanced at his tablet, which these days he mostly thought of as the library that held a single book by Gracie Rios.

"What?" Wes asked, drawing the word out, reading his face a little too easily.

"Do you know why she cancelled her quinceañera?"

Her brows pinched together, and she frowned. "I didn't know her then. After reading her book, I always assumed she had one. Are you sure?"

Bryan nodded, tears clogging his throat. "There was an incident at school, and she fought with her dad, and… decided she didn't deserve one."

"And she's been punishing herself ever since?" Wes asked, beginning to understand. "That does sound like Gray."

"Maybe it's time we give her the quince she deserves?"

A slow smile spread across Wesley's face. "Well," she said, "She'll either love it or hate it."

"Aye," Bryan agreed. "But we can't do it alone."

Bryan wasn't the kind of person who asked for help easily. It was one thing to implore folk to save the planet by reducing their single-use plastics or planting flowers for the pollinators. But to ask for himself felt like an admission of failure.

As someone who'd grown up under the microscope of a speech impediment, where people held their breaths every time he opened his mouth, bracing for secondhand embarrassment, or else impatiently chivvied him along—he preferred grappling with his own challenges in solitude.

But there was no way he and Wes could plan a double quinceañera on their own in a few short days.

And so, he accepted Cait's invitation to family tea and arrived hat in hand to ask for help from the people least likely to say no.

"What do you need us to do?" his mother asked, dishing out mouthwatering helpings of Parmesan aubergine.

"Any chance the shop could order a piñata in time?"

Her face fell. "Not by Monday, love."

Across the table, Sara bounced excitedly in her chair and Cait shushed her.

"Maybe Teàrlach could pick one up in Glasgow?" Elspeth suggested, but Cait shook her head.

"He's busy all week—Sara will you please sit still?"

"But I have something to say!" the little girl implored.

"Spit it out, then," Auntie Eilidh encouraged her great-great niece, who grinned, suddenly shy.

"Sara?" Cait prompted.

With all eyes on her, Sara took a deep breath and drew herself up straight in her chair. "I know how to make a piñata from papier-mâché. We did them in school!"

"Did you?" Cait asked. "I never saw it."

Sam grinned. "'Cause she beat hers to pieces 'til there was nothing left."

Tossing her brother a withering look, Sara replied, "That's what you're supposed to do."

"Do you think you could make another?" El asked.

Sara nodded, giddy. "Definitely, if you help me."

"Well, that's sorted," Ma said with a nod. "What about food? I've always wanted to try my hand at tamales."

"That'd be grand, Ma," Bryan said, warmth flooding his chest and loosening the eternal tightness inside.

Auntie Eilidh was watching him shrewdly and seemed to

notice his relief. "Don't worry," she said. "This family knows a thing or two about pulling off a grand affair." She winked at Bryan's father, who'd remained unusually quiet so far. "And what about me? What role do I play? You know I love a spectacle," Eilidh added.

Resisting every inclination to chastise his great aunt for lending the girls her old motorboat, while she sat there with a gleam in her eye practically daring him to, Bryan leaned forward and smiled. "Auntie you have the most important job of all. I need you to pull off a miracle, but you've only got a week."

She puffed up just as Sara had done. "Who am I, Jesus?" she scoffed. "I'm a woman, young man. I'll do it in half the time."

Everyone burst out laughing, and as he dug into the plate of cheesy, saucy aubergine, Bryan found an appetite he hadn't known for weeks. It may not be the quinceañera of Grace's dreams, but she certainly wouldn't forget it—or the Hebrides—any time soon. Maybe she'd decide to stay?

He batted that thought away. She had a life back in Tennessee, friends, a job. This was just his way of cementing their friendship, sending her off in style, that was all.

After the meal, Bryan stood in the back garden watching his niece and nephew run around with their dog, when his father approached carrying two glasses and an open bottle of Rionnagach.

"This is the finest dram I've ever tasted, Son," his father said in a gravelly voice. "It's yours?"

Bryan nodded, his own throat too clogged to reply.

Cameron poured them each a drink and held his up in toast. Bryan mirrored his father before wetting his parched throat with a sip.

"Would you like to use the community center for your shindig?"

It was a touching offer, but he'd imagined the party outside on the beach, and he was none too eager to set foot back inside the community center any time soon.

"Thanks, Da. But I was going to hold it out back of Grandad's house."

His father nodded. "You should stop calling it that. It's your place now." He laughed a little sadly. "Always was."

The distance between them was palpable, but his father was trying to bridge it.

"He was always different with you than he was with me. Even when I was young."

Bryan turned in surprise to study his father's face and found it tense with grief and regret.

"If I was hard on you—about the stammer—it's because that's how he was with me. And I outgrew mine. I thought—feared—that you didn't because with you he was always too soft."

Standing there with his father, Bryan's worldview titled sideways, like Uranus, spinning along with an unfamiliar view.

His father'd had a stammer?

"I was so afraid it would stop you living up to your potential, and you always showed so much potential. But I guess we just needed to get out of your way."

Bryan shook his head, eyes watery, unable to speak.

Before turning to go back inside, his father cupped the back of Bryan's neck, the closest they'd come to an embrace in decades.

"Tag, you're it!" Sam shouted, tapping Bryan's leg and darting away shrieking with delight, as Bryan set down his whisky glass and chased after the kids to peals of joyful barks and summer laughter.

Chapter Twenty-Nine

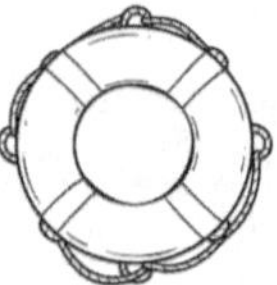

Space and perspective were a pair of double-edged swords. Somehow, after everything, Grace found the ending of her book. It came to her fast and hard, sneaking up like an orgasm, as her fingers flew across the keyboard. Her characters were finally being honest with each other, of all things, and it was somehow exactly the ending she'd been searching for.

When she was finished, she sent it to her agent without stopping to run spellcheck—better to let objective critics have the first pass than to second-guess herself into oblivion and another missed deadline.

After a few minutes, the euphoria wore off and she just felt sad. She'd given her characters the ending she wanted for herself.

Bryan had suggested she write about the love between friends, and so Maya and Blake, who started off as rivals irritating the stew out of each other, had become the best of friends. In the end, their platonic love had developed into something more, and the two teens were planning for futures that would include each other, while Grace and Bryan were preparing to go their separate ways.

In less than a week, she and Wes would climb aboard

Teàrlach's plane having accomplished what they came here for. But in light of what could have been, finishing her novel felt almost hollow.

She couldn't stop wondering how Bryan was holding up. Wes had mentioned running into him and reminded her about the welcome reception for his investor, but she'd conveniently dodged questions about his picketing neighbors. What would the investor do if they arrived to find a hostile crowd surrounding his beautiful home with torches and pitchforks?

To take her mind off the fact that her brother still hadn't texted her back after his game-ending injury, or maybe just to torture herself about her impending departure, she went for a walk down the beach, eventually winding up outside Bryan's backdoor. A faint smokiness from last night's bonfire still tinged the salty sea air, tugging at her heart. Would she ever smell smoke, or even Band-Aids, again without remembering him and longing for his whisky-flavored kiss?

Without stopping to overthink it, Grace made her way up to the patio and tapped hesitantly on the back door. There was no answer, but a sudden urgency to see the finished house came over her. Of course, she could wait until the reception tonight, but Grace wanted a private viewing, where no one could observe her in a state of overwhelm.

She tried the handle that he never seemed to lock and let herself in. The scent of him overpowered any new construction smells—his soap, his cologne, his whisky. It was intoxicating, and tears stung her eyes.

A tea mug still sat on the kitchen counter alongside his ever-present tablet. Grace drew her fingers over the smudges of his fingerprints, as though she could touch his hand, and the screen woke up, showing a document he'd been working on.

As a writer, she knew better than to read it. That would be the utmost invasion of privacy. She absolutely wouldn't do that. But as she turned away, her eye caught a word here and there and a flicker of recognition lit inside her brain.

It was his speech to the town—the one she'd offered to help with—the one she'd told him to write from his heart.

Licking her lips, she pulled the tablet closer. This was merely a professional courtesy, no more an invasion of privacy than him reading her published work, right? He'd been open to help from her once, after all.

And it was a great speech, deeply heartfelt and one thousand percent Bryan. Whispering it out loud to herself, her ears snagged on tricky turns of phrase, on the *B*'s, *P*'s, *S*'s, and glottal stops that might trip him up if he was nervous.

She changed the stylus color to blue and made a few suggestions and tweaks in the margins, little things to make it easier for him to read, without altering the underlying message. At the end she added a quick note.

I hope you don't mind the edit. The words are as perfect as the house—just a few ideas to help it flow.

She took the worry stone out of her pocket and set it beside the tablet. The beautiful rainbow-colored stone had served her well, but this was a big day for Bryan. He might need it more.

I found this stone when I needed it most. If you get nervous, just hold on to it and know that I'm so beyond proud of you.

There was a knock at the front door, and her head shot up guiltily.

She crept to her old bedroom to peek out the window. It wasn't anyone she recognized from town. They were wearing a slick suit with shiny shoes, a rolling briefcase at their side. It had to be his investor, but where the heck was Bryan?

Grace opened the door to the sharply dressed stranger, who smiled broadly and said in a posh Scottish accent, "Don't tell me I've got the wrong house. I'm looking for Bryan MacNeil."

"You've found him," Grace replied. "Err, his house. He's out just now. Please, come in."

"Och, I got an early ferry," they said, shaking short shaggy blond hair out of their eyes. "I did text to let him know. Jules MacRae."

"I'm sure he'll be back soon. Would you like some tea?" Grace asked, thinking quickly. She couldn't mess this up for him.

"Please. Milk, no sugar. Thanks."

"I'm Grace," she said, setting about to make the tea as she'd seen Bryan do, what felt like a million times by now.

"American?"

"Yes. Just visiting. Bryan's been the consummate host."

"Is this the proof of concept?" Jules asked, looking around and holding up their phone to snap pictures.

"It is," Grace said, feeling rather proud of the sunny, cozy cottage.

"It's adorable."

"And completely off-grid. He installed solar panels on the roof. All the electricity in the house is run off the solar cell, and I think there's a cistern to collect rainwater."

While the kettle heated, Grace led Jules through the house, pointing out everything she knew about the work Bryan had done. He'd laid new flooring in the spare bedroom since she and Wes had left and put down a cheerful rag rug. Seeing it all again made her throat catch.

Jules was particularly impressed by the bathroom, and Grace did her best to explain how the greywater reclamation process was supposed work.

"That view," Jules breathed when they entered the living room with their tea and stood before the gorgeous wall of windows staring out at the ocean.

Grace opened the door, and they strolled down to the beach, past the smoky remnants of biochar.

Jules inhaled deeply. "Oh, that's nice. Not peat?"

"No. Bryan will have to explain it, but he's been experimenting with sustainable ways to get the same smokiness without the environmental impact."

"I'd say he's hit on just the thing," the investor murmured. "You're his associate?" The question was casual, and for a moment Grace wondered what they might be to each other besides hopeful business owner and potential investor.

"Tenant," Grace said. "Briefly. I helped a little."

"I'd love to see before and after photos."

"That I can do." She'd seen Bryan taking pictures on the tablet as work progressed.

"I'm impressed. You don't know what time he'll be back?"

"I don't. I'm sorry. I only stopped by for something I left behind," she half lied. "Would you like to see the rest of the island? I could point out some of the spots he mentioned as potential building sites?"

"That'd be grand."

Grace texted Elspeth to pick them up from the pub in the island cab, then led Jules down the beach to avoid the possibility of picketing neighbors.

When El pulled up outside the pub, she gave Grace an assessing look before opening the door to help Jules into the cab for their grand island tour. Thankfully, she didn't say a word about Grace and Bryan, just added local color with stories about the places Grace pointed out as they circumnavigated Barra.

"I have to ask the elephant in the room," Jules said during a lull. "How do the residents feel about the disruption a distillery might bring to such a tranquil place?"

El snort-coughed but didn't comment further.

"Oh, you know," Grace hedged. "It's human nature to fear change, but I think they're coming around to it. They actually seem to thrive on excitement."

She eyed Elspeth, who held her gaze steadily in the rearview mirror, and Jules nodded as though understanding completely.

They stopped at the pier for a long while to let Jules admire the castle as though the rest of Scotland wasn't chock full of them.

"Too bad the distillery can't go there," Jules said. "That would be brilliant."

Grace laughed nervously. "Yeah, too bad."

Finally, Elspeth coughed and said, "I don't want to rush you, but you don't want to be late to your own party."

"Party?" Jules asked, perking up.

"Oh god, the reception," Grace said, checking the time on her phone. There were a dozen missed calls and messages, all variations on a theme.

> Where the hell are you?

> It's almost time for the reception

> Have you fallen off a cliff and died?

> Seriously tho you haven't right?

> Grace?!

> 💀🫠⁉️😭💔

> OMG text me or else!!!!!!!!

> Are you ACTUALLY going to miss Bryan's
> big day?

Grace shoved the phone in her pocket and tried to swallow her butterflies as Elspeth guided them back to the car.

"It's sort of a reverse housewarming, really. For you and the town. Maybe don't tell Bryan I already gave you the tour," she added, wrinkling her nose. She hadn't meant to steal his thunder. She only wanted to help.

She texted Wes a quick apology, explaining about the investor.

Three dots appeared for the longest time, then went away. Finally, Wes messaged back.

> Well thank fuck for that. Your boy was in a tizzy thinking his investor must have also wandered off and fallen down a well. See you in a few.

The short drive back to Bryan's felt interminable, as Grace's butterflies turned into roaring 747s. Hopefully Bryan wouldn't be angry at her for hijacking his investor. Or letting herself in and messing with his speech. When would she learn not to meddle? If she'd wanted to help, she should have chased the picketers away.

Fortunately, they were nowhere to be seen when Elspeth pulled up alongside her grandfather's old house, so thank you for small mercies.

Wes, of all people, met them at the door. "Jules?" she asked. "Thanks so much for coming. Bryan's in the kitchen."

At the sound of his name, Grace's stomach did an embarrassingly large backflip.

"You go in too, El. Have a cold one. People are posting up out back," Wes added magnanimously. Bryan's little sister grinned and traipsed in behind Jules.

But when Grace made to follow them, Wes stopped her, a look of mild panic in her eyes.

"What is it?"

"You're a little underdressed."

"They weren't dressed up," Grace pointed out, but Wes gave her a look. "Okay, Jules was, but El was wearing jeans. *You're* wearing jeans."

"I don't make the rules!"

Grace looked down at her own leggings and hoodie.

"Are you really saying I can't come in because of how I'm dressed?" she asked, noting that while Wesley was wearing jeans and Eòghann's old sweater, she did have on makeup for maybe the second time on this trip.

"Of course not. Come on," Wes said, grabbing Grace's hand and practically dragging her inside, straight to the bathroom.

"Bryan doesn't really seem like the dressy type. Why would he want everyone to get gussied up when he's trying to show the town how down to earth he is?"

"You think you know a person," Wes agreed, shutting the bathroom door behind them.

There, hanging on a hook, was the prettiest dress Grace had ever seen—in real life or her imagination—and she immediately burst into tears.

"Oh shit," Wes said. "Good tears or bad tears?"

Grace couldn't speak. The dress was a deep, inky purple, with gems sprinkled across it like stars in the Milky Way, and a big full skirt like a Cinderella ball gown. It was a quinceañera dress. It was *the* quinceañera dress, exactly as she'd envisioned since the age of eleven, exactly as she'd drawn it a thousand different times, exactly as she'd described it in her first novel.

"How?" she whispered.

"Your man is resourceful. And apparently Auntie Eilidh is a wizard."

Grace reached out to run her fingers over the gorgeous fabric.

"I don't understand," she whispered, though she was starting to.

Wes shrugged. "Happy double quinceañera?" she said hopefully, and Grace started full on sobbing.

"Okay, I can see now that the Stoic Scot might have been right about asking you first instead of springing this on you," she said, rubbing Grace's back.

"I'd have said no," Grace replied, gazing through unstoppable tears at the gorgeous, perfect dress.

"I know. Please don't be mad."

Grace grabbed her friend and wept into her shoulder. "I'm not mad."

"Then get all your tears out so we can start on your makeup."

WHEN SHE FINALLY EMERGED FROM THE BATHROOM DRESSED UP like a Mexican princess, Grace was met with another shock.

"Diego!" she squealed, in a pitch she didn't know she could reach, not quite sure this wasn't all some bizarre back-to-high-school dream. In another moment, she'd be naked and late for a geometry exam.

Her big brother smiled sheepishly, and she threw her arms around him, full on crying once more. It definitely wasn't a dream, he was real and warm and solid.

"God damn it, Bryan, we just did her makeup. You couldn't warn a girl?" Wes yelled.

"What are you doing here?" Grace gasp-laughed at her brother.

"Double quinceañera," Diego said, his voice strained. "I know I'm not Papi, but will you let me present you, Gray?"

More crying. Wes was going to kill her.

"You look so beautiful," Diego whispered, and she shoved him away, then pulled him back for another tight hug. "God, I've missed you, manita."

"Missed you," she agreed. She hadn't let herself realize quite how much she missed him until now.

When she finally stopped crying and caught her breath, Wes tried to retouch her makeup before Diego led her out the living room door to the porch, which was positively covered in white and silver and pearl pink balloons, as well as a large, star-shaped piñata. He led her down to the beach, where the whole town started to cheer.

Bryan emerged from around the side of the house, dressed up all dapper in his kilt and vest, and Grace's knees almost went weak. Both he and Wesley were grinning like anxious idiots, despite the presence of his parents and sisters and cousins. She wanted to jump into his arms, to make sure he knew how much she cared and then demand just how exactly his reception, his moment, had turned into a party for her. Before he got close enough, Eòghann stepped between them and gave her a kiss on the cheek.

"You look amazing," he whispered. "Don't be mad at them."

"I could never," she said.

Next, Bryan's mother squeezed Grace's hands and whispered, "Happy birthday," without any awkwardness over having sold Grace a vibrator just a few days before, and then Great Aunt Eilidh pushed in, grinning wickedly as though she knew all about the vibrator, though maybe it was just because of the gorgeous dress and the rhinestone tiara she placed in Grace's hair.

"Thank you," Grace whispered, trying not to descend into tears a third time.

Taking charge as usual, Cait clapped her hands for attention. "We have tamales and polvorones," she said, glancing to Grace for confirmation of her stilted pronunciation and gesturing towards dozens of powdered sugar cookies. "And my daughter will be devastated if her homemade piñata is still intact by the end of the night, but first—dancing!"

At Cait's cue, Lùcas joined some other boys beside the patio, where they had a few guitars and a drum kit set up, and they began to play "Party" by Bad Bunny, which made Grace laugh.

"You need dancing shoes," Diego said, taking a knee to slip a pair of strappy heels onto her bare feet. Then he offered his hand for a dance.

"How are you here?" she whispered, fighting yet another round of tears.

"MacNeil called. I came."

"Simple as that?"

"Simple as."

"Don't you have a game Wednesday?"

He shrugged. "I'm marked uncertain on the injury report."

"I knew you were favoring your right knee. How bad is it? Why didn't you text me back?"

"I was in the middle of a secret mission. I'll be fine," he said, hugging her close like maybe he needed it just as much as she did. "Will you?"

"I think I accidentally fell in love with your friend," she admitted, and it felt good, and also terrifying, to say it out loud.

"I think he accidentally did too," her big brother whispered. "He's a good dude, but if he hurts you, I'll kill him and dump his body in the ocean."

She laughed at the old threat and rested her head on his shoulder, with a pang of sadness for the distance that had grown between them and the rest of their family, but also with a swelling heart for this gift Bryan had given her, Diego right here in her arms.

Then his cell phone rang.

"Seriously?" Grace teased, as he fumbled for it, a little surprised when he accepted the call instead of turning off the ringer.

But then he held the phone down to her, and there were her parents, one on each side of the screen, all the way from sunny Pensacola and La Vicenta.

"¡Feliz cumpleaños, bebita!"

"Happy birthday, my beautiful girl!"

Grace, of course, started crying again, but her big brother was there with his arms protectively around her. They spoke for a few, all too brief minutes, and when they hung up, Diego squeezed her tight.

"Are we going to dance, or what?" she asked, wiping her eyes and snatching a powdered cookie off the table.

Chapter Thirty

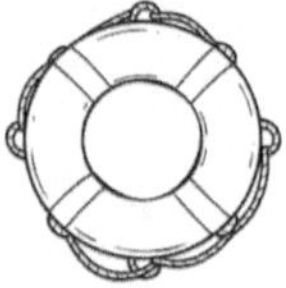

When Grace had first stepped outside with Diego and Wesley, Bryan's heart all but stopped in his chest. Up until that moment, he'd been half-afraid he'd misread the situation, misread her book and all she'd shared with him, as well as all the things she hadn't.

Nervous she might be furious with him for the surprise double quinceañera—for his interference, for asking Diego to fly out—he had taken the risk anyway, to show her what she'd come to mean to him. One look at her in her big brother's arms, resplendent in the dream dress his auntie had turned into reality, and it was all worth it, especially after a glimpse of her face.

Lùc had made sketches of the dress based on descriptions in Grace's book, and Diego had helped with as many details as he could over hurried text messages as he scrambled to make the trip over from LA. That had been worth it, too. In some small way, giving the two of them this moment felt like it made up a little bit for missing Diego's wedding all those years ago.

While she and her brother danced, Bryan busied himself at the dessert table, cutting the cake his sisters had baked to feed the whole town. It hadn't been easy to swallow his pride and ask them for help, but all in all, his family had really come through. Maybe they'd been waiting years for him to ask them to.

Returning home with the decorations only to find his grandfather's worry stone on the counter beside his mess of a speech had felt like a nod of approval from the old man. Bryan shivered, recalling the split second when he thought Grandad's ghost must have rescued the stone from the airport and left it on the counter for him to find.

But no. It was Grace who had found his worry stone, Grace who had saved it just as she saved him, just as she was still trying to help, unaware he'd forgotten—actually *forgotten*—his investor was arriving today of all days. Unaware of what the precious stone meant to him.

She tried to slink up next to him, almost impossible in the massive skirt, and she bumped his shoulder. "Pretty nice party, MacNeil."

He wanted to make some witty reply, but all he could do was grin like an idiot.

"Are you going to dance with me, or do I have to beg?"

Bryan didn't need to be asked twice. He swept her up in his arms and attempted a traditional waltz, though he was pretty sure the music was all wrong for it.

"You looked up these steps online, didn't you?" she teased.

"Guilty."

"Thank you."

"It was Wesley's idea," he demurred.

"It absolutely wasn't."

"No, but she was going to take the heat for me if you hated it."

"I don't hate it. Thank you, truly," she said again, resting her head against his shoulder as they danced.

What god did he have to pray to, to stay just like this forever?

"Jules seems to be having a nice time," she said, and he followed her gaze to see the investor dancing together with Eòghann and Wesley.

"At least they won't have made a completely wasted trip."

Grace pulled back and stared up at him. "Wasted for whom?"

"The town doesn't want me or my distillery. They only agreed to stop picketing 'cause I offered them cake."

"Speak to them. Give them a chance to surprise you."

"I'm not going to be the asshole who makes your day about me."

Grace stopped dancing. "Today was always supposed to be about you. Stop trying to hide your trauma behind mine."

He stared at her. "That's not what I'm doing. Is it?"

"It's a good speech, Bryan. They need to hear it and you deserve the chance to speak it."

He shook his head. "It's grand thanks to your changes, only I haven't had time to memorize it."

"Then read it."

"I can't."

"Of course you can. You read my whole book."

"Not out loud. The stammer… it's easier if I recite."

"They'll know it's from the heart. And if anyone teases you, Diego and I will kill them and dump their bodies in the ocean."

He laughed. "It really doesn't matter," he protested.

"Don't argue with the birthday girl. What do you have to lose?" she asked, stepping away from him and over to Lùc's band to steal the mic. "Excuse me, everyone? May I have your attention please?"

Bryan rolled his eyes and shook his head desperately at her, but she ignored him as his neighbors fell silent around the bonfire, the sky painted in party pinks and golds behind them.

"I know I've only been here a short time," she said. "But in that time, I've really gotten to know the character of this island. You're tough. Hard-working. Extremely close to each other and your history and traditions."

The old-timers murmured their agreement.

"Thank you so much for sharing my traditions with me today. It means the world."

They clapped.

"I'm sure aspects of it were new and strange."

She paused to let them laugh self-consciously.

"But it's been fun, right?"

They cheered in affirmation. How was she so good at this?

"I didn't get to have my quinceañera when I was fifteen because I let fear and anger drive a wedge between myself and the people I loved, and I've regretted it ever since. So thank you, from the bottom of my heart, for sharing this double quinceañera day with me.

"But today wasn't supposed to be about me. It was supposed to be about one of you and his commitment to all of you. It was supposed to be about this gorgeous cottage. I'm sure by now you've all had a chance to see inside. It's a symbol, for so many of you, of the island's past, but the thing is, it could also represent the island's future. So please, because it's my birthday—"

"And double quinceañera!" Wes shouted.

"—and that too, please listen to what Bryan has to say with the same generous spirit you've listened to me. Let him speak, and then decide."

The crowd grew quiet, shifty and uncertain. How was Bryan supposed to follow her?

Cait offered him his tablet, and his hands were so sweaty he almost dropped it, but then Grace pressed the worry stone into his palm, cool and soothing as it always used to be.

"Go on then, lad," Ellis Stewart said.

"Give him a minute," his father commanded before nodding encouragingly Bryan's way.

So he took a breath and read them the speech he'd written, which Grace had so thoughtfully edited.

"When I was young and naive," he began, clearing his throat before it cracked like he was twelve again, "I talked a good talk about making the island green. I distinctly recall a few of you telling me if I took my head out of my arse and looked inland instead of out, it already was green."

A laugh went through the older neighbors, and Ellis shoved his hands deep in his pockets, though he smiled and nodded sheepishly too.

"I was a wee eco-warrior, and you were, rightfully, amused. We may not have seen eye to eye all those years ago, but the one thing we did agree on was our love of this island. All my grand ideas were on account of how much I cared. I wanted to conserve it forever, for my children's children's children."

They were all nodding now, agreeing with the sentiment.

"I'm an island lad through and through, and though I did leave for many years, I took the island with me. I took all of you with me. I learned a trade—I'm good at it. I also learned things about the world. And myself—things I couldn't learn here."

A ripple of dismay at that, but it was the truth.

"I'm an island lad, and though I haven't finished learning, I've come home. My wish—my only wish—is to take what I learned and use it here, as my gift to all of you. It'll mean hard work, but you taught me how to work hard, that the work is its own reward. It'll mean change, but the world out there taught me change doesn't have to be a terrible thing. Good things come too, when you let them."

He took a deep shaky breath.

"As for me, I'll work hard every day to make good change happen, if you'll let me."

Then he breathed out slowly and closed his eyes, gripping his grandfather's stone for dear life. He worried his words weren't polished enough, that he sounded too immature or too earnest to be taken seriously. But he'd gotten through it. And he'd meant every single bit.

No one said anything for a minute, and Bryan tried to think

what he would do if they turned him away. Jules would certainly leave to find some other young eco-minded distiller to invest in.

"I think…"

"Go on, Tom," his Uncle Dàibhidh urged.

"What I think is, a new distillery's a fine idea. You can buy my north pasture to build it on, if you like."

"I agree," Teàrlach jumped in. "We might have to add another flight to keep up with the increased tourism it would bring."

Bryan nodded in thanks to his cousin, who'd spent most of the party catching up with Diego. It warmed his heart to see them reunited again, too.

"Reckon I wouldn't mind sprucing up my cottage a little, the way you've done around here," Old Nellie Coombe conceded. "I wouldn't have believed it if blondie hadn't given me a tour, but you did a real nice job. Your grandad would be proud of you."

Tears sprang to Bryan's eyes.

"All in favor of Bryan's eco-distillery?" Cait called, and everyone shouted, "Aye" except for his next-door neighbor.

"Ellis?" his father prodded.

"Oh, fine, aye—only, can you show me how to install those horrible solar panels so my electric bill won't be so high when the grandkids come to stay?"

Everyone laughed, and Bryan finally released a long-held breath.

Jules approached, carrying one plate piled high with vegetarian tamales and another with cake. "Bryan MacNeil," they said, extending a plate for him to take, freeing up their other hand to shake his. "I looked over the paperwork you sent me. All in all, I'm impressed."

"Are you?"

"These people were protesting with signs outside your house when I arrived this afternoon."

He winced.

"Seems like you've pulled off a minor miracle. Miss Rios tells me you've found a biochar replacement for peat smoke?"

"Tested."

"I'd like to break ground as soon as possible," they said.

"Th-thank you," he murmured, a bit bewildered by the day's turn of events.

"It's been my dream for a long time. You've proven you're more than capable. What are you going to call it?"

"Finnbar," he said.

They grinned and nodded. "Perfect. I'm looking forward to doing business with you."

"Ditto," he said, a little stunned as he watched them walk away.

Chapter Thirty-One

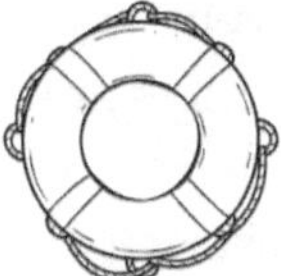

That night, Grace thought Bryan's family would never leave. After Jules had departed and most of the town dispersed, Caitriona, Elspeth, and their mother took over cleaning up from the party, while Great Auntie Eilidh parked herself in the living room with Bryan's father, where she gave a running commentary of everything she liked—and didn't —about the renovation. Her criticisms were mostly hilarious things like *guests would turn lazy, wanting to sit in the sun and read all day*, and *now there was no escaping the view*. Bryan seemed to take it all in stride.

Wes and Eòghann had wandered down the beach together, and Lùcas had gone off with his band. Diego had given Grace the tightest hug ever to make up for all the ones they'd missed, and then he left too, alongside Jules, to catch a flight out with Teàrlach and then back to California. He seemed so sad to be leaving already, but they made plans to meet up in Nashville and Atlanta later in the summer, when his team played out east, and Grace agreed to spend the holidays with him and his family in LA.

She hadn't realized quite how badly she had needed to see her big brother, and she ached watching him leave again so soon. There had been a brother-sized hole in her heart for so long she was almost surprised she hadn't bled to death. And what a joy to watch him turn into a kid again, goofing around with his old pals. The excitement in his eyes when Teàrlach promised to let him ride in the cockpit on their way back to Glasgow…

"Need to get back to your manuscript?" Bryan whispered, resting against the counter, one arm around her as she leaned back against his chest, while they watched his irritating family prove their love to him by overstaying their welcome.

She shook her head. "Turned it in this morning."

"What? Way to bury the lede, Rios. That's amazing," he said, squeezing her tight. "That means—when do you leave?"

"This weekend," she said, turning giddily to face him in time to see his eyes grow dark. "I believe it means I finally have some time to relax," she said, standing on tiptoe to kiss his bristly cheek.

"Get out," he roared, and she jumped back, startled, until she realized he was looking at his family, who were staring back at him with more amusement than surprise.

"Please," he amended ever so politely. "Thank you for everything. I'll come for Sunday tea. Now, would you mind heading home?"

"Of course, love," his mother said, making a sweeping gesture to herd everyone out. "I'll cook a field roast with all the trimmings."

"Need a ride, Grace?" Caitriona asked, just to be a devil.

"No," Bryan answered for her, and Cait snickered.

When they were alone at last, Grace said, "You really know how to clear a room, MacNeil."

"One of my greatest talents," he agreed.

"I can't believe how much you've accomplished here. You must be exhausted. If you want to be alone, I can—" she made to follow his family, but he caught her wrist.

For a moment, her brain tried to make her panic. What if he expected too much? What was the point when she was leaving so soon? What if—

"I haven't given you your gift yet," he murmured.

"Oh, you haven't?" she teased, but he shook his head solemnly and picked up his tablet from the counter behind her.

"Didn't have time to wrap it," he said, handing it over.

Puzzled, Grace opened the folio cover and peered down at the screen which lit up with a beautiful picture of a woman standing on a rocky promontory. She glanced up at him in confusion, and he was holding his breath, so she looked back down at the image in her hands. This time she noticed the fancy lettering: FINNBAR. The name of his distillery. And then: GRACE ON THE ROCKS.

"It's a label," she realized aloud.

His face broke into the biggest smile she'd ever seen. "For my first expression: Grace on the Rocks."

"It's me?"

He laughed and nodded. "Lùc drew it."

"It's gorgeous," she breathed, running her fingers over it as though she could feel the embossed letters through the screen.

He took the tablet back and set it over to the side.

"Five days?" he asked, tilting his head to look into her eyes.

She nodded up at him, having long since kicked off her heels.

"Better make the most of it, then." He lifted her onto the counter, poofy skirt and all, so she didn't have to strain her neck looking up. Stepping between her knees, he kissed her softly but hungrily, as his tongue battled against hers like somehow she had set it free.

He ran his hands up and down her arms, causing wave after wave of goosebumps, stroked her cheek, cupped the back of her head, and all the while he kissed her, trailing fire over every nerve ending. When they finally came up for air, he pressed his forehead to hers and asked, "Is this okay?"

Nodding again, Grace whispered, "Better than okay. I like it that you're checking in." It made her feel so safe, and she needed him to know that. "What's uh… next?" she asked hesitantly.

Bryan peered at her intently, and then he said, "Lady's choice. We could watch a movie? Or make a fire?"

Five different ideas of things they could do flitted through Grace's head one after another, none of them so tame as building a campfire, but she refused to panic. They had all night and five tomorrows. And right now, she had a pretty good idea.

"Is there any champagne left?" she asked before she could chicken out.

Smiling, Bryan reached over her head and into the cabinet for a glass.

She stilled his arm.

"Something that won't shatter on tile."

His eyebrows shot up, intrigued, but he rummaged around until he found an old plastic cup emblazoned with the Celtic football logo and filled it with champagne.

"You owe me a bubble bath," she explained, in case her intention wasn't clear.

"Do you need reading material?" he offered as he led her to the bathroom.

"That would be rude to my companion," she said.

"I didn't want to assume."

"I think you very much wanted to," she teased, skimming her gaze down his front as though she could see a hard-on, and delighting in the flush that tinged his cheeks above his beard.

She leaned against the wall, admiring the way his kilt rose up in the back as he bent to run the water.

"Bubbles?" he asked, glancing over his shoulder and catching her appreciative stare. His eyes heated.

"Absolutely bubbles," she agreed, lifting her cup of champagne courage in mock salute.

After adding a generous amount of bubble bath to the running water, he turned her around to help with the zipper of her beautiful dress, his fingers skimming softly over her skin in a trail of fire.

"Are you certain?" he asked, holding the dress for her to step out of it, as she used his shoulders for balance.

Grace hung the purple masterpiece from a hook on the door and turned back to untuck his shirt from his kilt, finally nodding in answer to his question. "I'm certain," she said softly.

"You'll tell me if you change your mind?"

She practically melted into a puddle right there, but she managed to whisper, "Promise," before sliding into the bath and leaning forward so Bryan could slip in behind her.

For the longest time, they sat back to chest and just held each other in the warm, lilac-scented water. Grace's heart was beating too fast, and she kept having to remind herself to breathe, but the water was relaxing and she wanted this. She felt the panic creep in and threaten her with its old black fog when she realized his erection was digging into her back, but she forced herself to lean forward and take a long swig of champagne. When she leaned back again, he had adjusted himself and her breathing began to level out.

"Thank you for editing my speech," he finally whispered into her hair before planting a kiss on the side of her neck.

"It wasn't presumptuous?" she asked.

"Not even a little. I hadn't thought about using easier words."

"It's normally how you talk, without really thinking about it, I guess."

"Thanks for noticing, then. And for encouraging me."

"I'll never stop encouraging you," she said, tipping her chin down to kiss the arm he'd thrown around her. "Thank you for giving me my quinceañera."

"Double quinceañera. It wasn't… presumptuous?"

"Maybe a little."

"It was all Wesley's idea."

She laughed. "I loved it."

"Completely, one hundred percent my idea."

"I can't believe you got Diego to come."

"It took very little convincing. What was your favorite part?" he asked.

"Your speech, obviously."

"The one part you had a hand in." He tickled her ribs.

"Okay, okay. Your speech and that dress." She glanced to the hook where her childhood dream hung in satin and taffeta reality. "I'm going to need an extra suitcase so I can wear it to all my book signings."

"Would you really?"

"MacNeil, I'm going to volunteer to chaperone prom from now on, just so I can wear that dress at least once a year for the rest of my life."

He snuggled into her neck. "I'm glad you liked it."

"No one ever did anything like that for me before. And my friends have done some pretty incredible, sneaky shit."

"I'd like to meet them—Andy, Beatrix, Jack, Rebecca, and Sadie."

The way he listed them off in alphabetical order… "You read my author's note," she said, trying not to choke on the emotion bubbling out of her like so much champagne, realizing he'd finished her book and kept going, realizing he was saying he didn't want this all to end in five days.

"I would read anything you wrote," he whispered, kissing the place where her neck met her shoulder and sending a shiver down her spine.

"Deal," she agreed, and he held her tighter. "This is a pretty great tub."

"Is it?" he asked absently, kissing down the back of her neck again.

"Really ties the room together."

"You saw the potential of what it could be."

She held up her palm. "I'm getting pruny."

Bryan matched it against his larger hand and then laced his fingers through hers. With her other hand she followed the pattern of his tattoo.

"Wes bought me a vibrator," she said, and he barked out a surprised laugh.

"She's an unusual friend."

"Everyone should be so lucky."

"No argument from me. Any revelations?"

"One or two."

He ran his fingers lazily down her side and towards her hip.

"Does it not bother you?" she asked hesitantly.

When Wes had recommended toys in college, Grace had been tempted, but her boyfriend had thrown the world's largest hissy fit. *Using a vibrator is the same as cheating*, he'd complained, shaming her into changing her mind.

"Not even a little," Bryan assured her. "Maybe one day you can teach me what you learned?" he asked cautiously, and she nodded. "I look forward to it," he murmured.

Grace turned around then, straddling his lap, and for a moment, she outlined his fine lips with her thumb before capturing them with her own, losing herself in the swirl of heat and sensation, kissing until the bathwater turned tepid and they abandoned the tub for his bed.

Once stretched out facing each other in his soft, clean sheets, however, Grace lost some of the bravado she'd found in the tub.

"You are truly breathtaking," he said, and she hid her face shyly in the pillow. "Rios, I mean it." He took her hand away from her face and interlaced their fingers once more. "Breathtaking."

"I don't know what to do now," she admitted.

"Lady's choice," he reminded her, cupping her face in his hands and looking deep into her eyes before kissing her again. "Don't overthink it," he breathed.

"What if I can't?"

"It'll still be fun," he promised. "Our deadlines are over. There's no goals here. Only pleasure."

No braggadocios, *Challenge accepted, baby. I can make you come.* Just pure acceptance of time spent together, joy in the companionship and whatever else they got up to, without an end goal.

"That's a novel concept for an overachiever."

"I believe in you," he whispered, grinning at her with a mischievous twinkle in his eye.

Grace traced the Celtic bee on his forearm once more, back and forth in a soothing sort of way. "You know when we first met, I called you *Mr. Bee* in my head."

He chuckled at that and made a buzzing sound before kissing her earlobe.

"Did you get this because your family took away your *B*?"

He tilted his head in surprise and then rolled onto his back, bending his arm up at the elbow so they could both see the tattoo. "Maybe a little," he said, like it actually surprised him to realize it.

She snuggled closer, still fingering his tattoo, and he took a breath.

"When I was about seven, there was a bumblebee on the playground. Its wing was damaged after a kid gave it a good whack with their workbook. Couldn't fly and they wanted to step on it, but I got it into my lunchbox and took it to Grandad's."

"It didn't sting you?" Grace asked.

"I was the Crocodile Hunter, remember? Anyway, Grandad found me an old cigar box. The hinge was broken, so it wouldn't close, and we filled it with moss and rocks and planted a few fragrant flowers. There was even a little tin can filled with water."

"You had a pet bee." Her heart was officially a melted puddle of warmth. She really could not love him more.

"I did. Called him Brandon."

"Brandon the Bee," she cooed.

"Aye. Took him outside every day for sunshine. Kept his flowers fresh. I think he was happy in his little cigar box home."

"Your first renovation," she said, and he laughed out loud. God, she could get used to the sound of the Stoic Scot laughing.

"Grew rather obsessed with saving the bees after that. Much to the annoyance of the neighbors."

Grace didn't know what to say, so she raised up and kissed his tattoo. Bryan brushed the hair out of her eyes and ran his thumb down her chin, drawing her up to his lips for another kiss, long and sweet.

"Will you touch me?" she finally asked.

"It would be my absolute pleasure," he whispered, leaning over to kiss her as he spidered his fingers softly down her neck and along each breast, making her breath change each time he brushed in an unexpected direction.

He smoothed his hands over her belly, along her bottom, cupping her in a way that caused heat to build within her, and then traced the rim of her hip around to the sensitive inside of her thigh.

He touched her everywhere until she was almost rocking with desire, teasing her until she hesitantly guided his hand between her legs.

"Needy," he whispered, grinning as he tugged at the tight, bath-damp curls for a moment before moving back up to her breasts, determined to make her squirm.

As her need grew, he made more frequent trips down, dipping in with lube and then frustratingly away, until finally he gave her what she wanted, stroking her clit lightly until she bucked hard against his hand in gasping, panting breaths.

Just when she didn't think she could stand another second of friction, he removed his finger and drew her close against him as she curled in and buried her face against his neck.

"Look at me," she whispered.

"Look at you," he replied, and she didn't mind the obvious

grin in his voice as he kissed the top of her head and drew the covers up over them both.

She had achieved the same results alone in her hotel room, but surrendering control and giving herself over to every sensation while Bryan took care of her made it one hundred times more tantalizing and more intense.

"What about you?" she finally asked once she recovered enough to remember this wasn't only about her.

"What about me?" he asked as though he didn't have a care in the world or a rock-hard erection pressed against her belly.

She drew her own fingers down his chest through the soft hair that led directly south and took a firm grasp of his silky length.

He exhaled hard. "Lady's choice," he gasped again.

Grace wasn't sure what her choice would be. She'd given fumbling, exhausting hand jobs and painfully awkward blow jobs out of obligation more than once. In those situations in the past, *lady's choice* would honestly have been to let him ache until his balls turned blue because it was all too difficult to discuss.

"What do you like?" she asked, running her fingers idly up and down. She enjoyed the way it made him gasp and jerk a little, but he caught her wrist, stilling her touch.

"Depends."

"On what?"

"Whether you're going to want to use it later."

"Oh," she said, withdrawing her hand.

"Either is fine. Or neither. I can wait," he assured her, bringing her palm to his lips and then kissing each knuckle.

He scooched back, putting a little space between their bodies, not enough to make her feel cold, just enough to tuck himself away. Then he kissed her cheek, her neck, her lips.

As her mind started to descend into another puddle of desire, she debated with herself. She hadn't planned on *using it*, as he so eloquently put it, but she hadn't planned on *not* using it either. In fact, she very much wanted to eventually, and the longer she waited, the more she built it up in her brain, the harder it would be. No pun intended.

He probably wouldn't feel flattered to know she kept thinking about it like ripping off a bandage, but the thing was, she felt totally safe with him. If she wasn't enjoying it, she knew they could stop—no harm, no foul. So why not try?

"I can literally hear you thinking, Rios," he whispered as he kissed down her neck, trying to draw her out of her head. "Don't talk yourself into anything on my account."

He skimmed a palm over her breast and then traced the underside, making her spasm.

"If we started and I didn't like it?" she whispered, finding and running her thumb over his tip so his whole body convulsed as hers had just done.

"There's no rush," he gasped, leaning up to distract her by circling her nipple with his tongue, and for a minute, she forgot what they'd been talking about.

"But if I wanted to? And then I didn't?" she panted when he finally stopped licking.

"NASA can scrub a launch," he whispered, and she laughed. "If NASA can do it, we can to. At far less expense."

She laughed again. That was new. She'd never laughed in bed before.

"Would it help if you're on top, so you don't feel trapped?" he suggested.

Grace had never thought of trying that before, either, of riding him to her own fulfillment.

"Which lube do you think is best?" she asked.

"Let's see."

She squeezed a little from the bottle he'd used earlier, and he ran it between is fingers.

"We know this one's good."

She giggled and took out the second bottle, giving him a drop on a different finger.

"Too watery. Any more?" he asked, an amused tone to his voice.

So she squirted out the synthetic kind that couldn't be used with the vibrator.

"This one, definitely," he said. "If you're certain."

Grace nodded. "You really don't care if I need help getting wet?" she whispered.

Bryan rubbed down her back and along her bottom. "What's there to be bothered about?" he asked. "Should I mind if you need glasses to read or antihistamines to breathe through your nose? Breathe, by the way," he added, kissing her cheek, and she did then in a sort of gasp.

Bryan rolled onto his back, and she kissed him hard, as he put on a condom. Then she squirted the lube into her palm to prepare him.

"Wait." He caught her arm and lube trickled onto his belly. She looked at him fearfully, and he laughed pushing up on his elbows to kiss her. "I've gone about this all wrong," he babbled. "I ought to have told you already—I love you, Graciela Rios Rivera. No matter if we do this right now, or if we never do it in the traditional way, no matter if you ever orgasm again, no matter if you decide I'm rubbish in bed—"

Grace laughed, because that was ridiculous.

"No matter if you leave in five days. Christ knows I'm no good with words, but you—you're not my puzzle to solve, you've somehow found all my missing, faded, dog-chewed pieces and made them fit together again—made me fit back here again. Gave me back my home. You're everything to me. I love you, and I love being with you. In fancy dresses or wearing flannel on the roof, watching the footy and sunsets, and when you're snarky as all hell. You make me able to see my way clear to becoming the person I always wanted to, and I just thought—"

Grabbing his length with both hands, Grace kissed him to stifle his groan. Her heart was so full if it were a balloon, it would be in danger of bursting. When she raised up to slide onto him, he gasped.

"It… it needed to be sssaid," he finally finished, and she hoped he knew she loved him too.

Because right then, she couldn't say it.

Right then it hurt way too much. She couldn't have said anything if she tried.

The happy tears, already so close to the surface, instantly turned to despair and she fought to hold them in as she breathed through the pain.

Beneath her, Bryan froze. "Rios?" he asked softly, shifting himself to pull out.

"It'll pass," she gasped, trying to stop him. She knew from experience it wouldn't get better, but if she was lucky, she might go a bit numb.

Bryan held still except for one hand rubbing her back while she caught her breath, and after several excruciating minutes she tried to grind on him, to seek her own pleasure, but she bit her lip to stifle a grimace. Despite all his promises that they could stop, she didn't want to be a total cocktease. Not now. She had wanted so desperately for it to work.

He'd seen it, though. He tipped himself to the side and slid out, flaccid. Ironically, the friction of him withdrawing had felt kind of nice.

"It's okay to cry if you need to," he murmured, bending his neck to try and look her in the eye.

"I'm sorry," she whispered, her voice cracking and a tear finally leaking out to trickle down his chest, as she laid there, still straddling him, too embarrassed to dismount.

Bryan kissed her cheek. "What did we say about apologizing?"

"I just don't want you to be disappointed in me."

"I could never be disappointed in you."

"I'm disappointed in me!"

He stroked her hair and said, "Well, I'm not surprised. You're a very tough critic."

That made her sort of laugh-sob. "I just thought—"

He shook his head, unwilling to allow her to feel badly about this. "We have so much time."

She shook hers too, beyond frustrated. "I know but…"

"No goals, remember? We've had a lovely time."

"Well I have, but you…"

"I've been exactly where I wanted to be."

He kissed her again, deeply. Even if he was just being gallant, his words turned her insides to warm butter. But she was still disappointed.

"It's my birthday," she whined.

"It is," he smirked.

"What?" she asked, trying not to pout.

He nodded. "Nature has a way of figuring things out."

"What do you mean?" she asked, flustered and frustrated and he nodded again, towards their lower parts, where she realized she had been grinding against him like a bad puppy.

She was aching with need, and she realized he was growing rigid once more, as his breaths became shallow.

"Really?" she asked, he nodded, running a hand up her side to tease her breast.

"Ride me like that much longer, Rios, and there won't be anything left to ride."

It certainly wasn't traditional, as she ground against him without actually taking him back inside, but he didn't seem to mind as he kissed her ferociously. She lost all sense of time and place, giving herself over to warm, hungry kisses and the heated tingle building, building, building in her core.

Finally, he whispered, "Apologies, my darling, but I'm going to," and then he slipped his hand between them to fondle her clit as she rocked with him until his spine went rigid and he jerked against her. Her climax was only seconds behind his, and then she collapsed on his chest in blindingly sated delight.

"I'm sorry," she whispered again as they lay cuddled close together.

"If you keep apologizing, I may have to—"

"To what?" She sat up, looking down at him feeling vaguely heated by the almost-threat.

He shrugged saucily and kissed her.

"But I am sorry I couldn't…"

"Rios. You came twice for me. I came very hard. We're all winners here tonight."

"I know, but I feel like I let one of us down."

"Well, then one of us had their expectations misaligned."

Oh. When he put it that way… Not *too high*, as though P in V, as Wes liked to call it, was the pinnacle they should be striving for, a height they'd failed to reach. But simply *misaligned.* She liked this new perspective. She liked it very much.

"We can try again, if it's that important to you."

"We do have five days," she agreed, but then melancholy overwhelmed her. "I don't want to go home."

"Don't. Stay here and make whisky with me. Write your next book."

She sighed. "Wouldn't that be the dream?"

He kissed her head and stroked her back. "You don't have to decide now. We have five whole days."

Epilogue

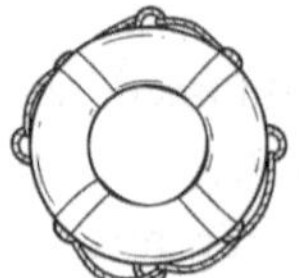

ONE YEAR LATER

Floor-to-ceiling bookshelves were lined with the best and brightest in young adult fiction, or so Bryan had been told, and right in the midst of them, Gracie Rios. The cover of her brand-new sequel was facing out for all the world to see. That was how Bryan knew they were right about the best and brightest.

"Ready?" he whispered, turning to Grace, who looked about as pale as a person could, but she tried to take a deep breath.

"Not even remotely."

He pulled her back against him in a calming embrace, poofy purple dress and all. "You're going to be amazing," he whispered in her ear. "You've already done the hard part."

After Wesley had gone home alone, Grace stayed another month on Barra so they could really get to know each other. They took long walks on the beach and cuddled beside his bonfire until the wee hours watching football or just talking, sharing bits of themselves with each other like buried treasure.

Only this time, she had stayed in his room so Lùcas could finally move into the promised spare.

It had been a long, glorious summer of making plans and pretending they had all the time in the world.

At the end of it, she'd returned to Tennessee, back to her day job, and her friends, and the away-fan bleachers at Diego's games. But Bryan had had plenty to keep him busy for the past year too, building his distillery from the ground up. Thank Christ for video calls, but it was a poor substitute for actually holding her in his arms like this.

After an impromptu trip to visit her in Knoxville, they'd decided to spend another whole summer together, this time in America. She'd taken him to the Grand Canyon, and now they were in La Vicenta, Mexico, where a new release of Ardbeg's Rionnagach was given an award for Best in Class at the whisky festival, along with Best Label for a Lùcas original design featuring the Big Dipper.

"Did you give any input on the new label?" Bryan had been asked this morning during a podcast interview where they were desperate for news about Finnbar.

He had glanced over at Grace and smiled sheepishly. "I had some inspiration, yes."

A podcast in the morning and now this afternoon, Grace was going to speak to a packed bookstore and sign copies of her sophomore novel—the day after her third book had been announced to the press.

What even was their life? Distance and all, he'd never been more content. Or more proud.

"I am so happy to introduce, all the way from Knoxville, Tennessee, Printz Award winner Gracie Rios!" the bookstore owner shouted into a tiny microphone in both English and Spanish. Dozens of teen girls cheered, but Grace's posture went rigid.

"You got this, Rios."

From his pocket, Bryan withdrew the rainbow-colored worry stone—the one they made a point of passing back and forth each time they saw each other based on who needed it most, the one that said they had each other's back without words.

She smiled up at him and kissed his cheek before making her way to the podium to speak, resplendent in the shimmering purple dress and shiny engagement ring.

Part of him still couldn't believe she'd said yes when he knelt along the Southern Rim at sunset, giving himself over to the absolute cliché of falling for his best friend's sister.

Now he stood back in a corner and just watched, basking in her magnificence as the musical cadence of her Spanish washed over him. Diego and their father leaned against the shelf nearby, wearing matching expressions of admiration.

The soccer player looked as exhausted as ever, but he couldn't stop smiling. "My kid sister's really something, isn't she?" he marveled.

"She absolutely is," Bryan agreed. And she was his.

Acknowledgments

Parts of this series have lived in my head for decades, and this was the first romance I planned out before taking a delightful detour into the 18th century. For that, and many reasons, I couldn't be more grateful to those who helped finally make this book a reality.

Always first and foremost, though I usually save you for last: DJ, my own real-life romance hero. Thank you for listening to me ramble about bookish problems and babble about bookish dreams, for catching typos and gross errors of football logic. I couldn't do all this without you.

To my incredible cover designer Jessica Khoury for bringing my vision so spectacularly to life. It is absolute perfection, and I couldn't be happier. I would also be remiss to not thank Emily Lloyd-Jones who told me about Launch Pad Astronomy Workshop, without which I wouldn't have met Jess, and this beautiful cover wouldn't exist!

To my editor, Susan, who goes above and beyond every single time. I feel comfortable not worrying too much about the rules because I know I can trust you to have my back.

To Marisol—thank you so much for your keen feedback and helpful insight. I appreciate it so very much.

To my beta readers, who cheer me on and keep me from throwing the whole dang thing in the bin from time to time: Sarah Blair, Krista Walsh, Jennie Davenport, Angi N. Black, and especially Jessie Parker—this one's for you.

Many, many thanks as well to Isla Parker (no relation) from

the University of Edinburgh's Gaelic and Community Relations Department for helping me name the festival authentically.

To DeAnn, for everything, always. And to the rest of my Writerly crew: Mark Benson, Jennifer Iacopelli, Christian Berkey, Megan Paasch, and Sarah Henning for always being in my corner.

And to every one of you I polled about the series name.

To my parents, family, and friends—and to you, dear readers, for spending your precious time on this adventure with me.

About the Author

Rose Prendeville is a librarian living in Middle Tennessee with her husband, the world's cutest dog, and a garden full of bees, writing stories about found families and flawed people doing their best. The award winning author of *Last Blue Christmas* and the Brides of Chattan historical series is passionate about books with happy endings and their ability to brighten a sometimes dismal world.

If you enjoyed this book, please consider leaving a review at your favorite marketplace.

To stay up-to-date on this series and other news, scan the QR code and sign up for Rose's newsletter or visit:
roseprendeville.com

Books by Rose Prendeville

Last Blue Christmas

The Unknown Birds

Brides of Chattan Series

Mistress Mackintosh and the Shaw Wretch

Lady Len and the Mysterious Mac

Maggie and the Pirate's Son

Tennessee Hebrides Series

Grace on the Rocks

A Faire Affair